PRAISE FOR ROBERT DUGONI'S TRACY CROSSWHITE SERIES

Praise for *In Her Tracks*

"Gripping . . . Fans of police procedurals will hope Tracy has a long career."

—*Publishers Weekly*

"A warmhearted procedural about some ice-cold crimes."

—*Kirkus Reviews*

"Dugoni has produced one of his most shocking twists yet and Tracy, expertly developed over seven previous novels, is almost pared down here, in a refreshing, perspective-changing way."

—Bookreporter

Praise for *A Cold Trail*

"Tracy Crosswhite is one of the best protagonists in the realm of crime fiction today, and there is nothing cold about *A Cold Trail*."

—Associated Press

"Impressive . . . Dugoni weaves a compulsively readable tale of love, loss, and greed. Readers will look forward to the further exploits of his sharp-witted detective."

—*Publishers Weekly* (starred review)

"Crime writing of the absolute highest order, illustrating that Dugoni is every bit the equal of Lisa Gardner and Harlan Coben when it comes to psychological suspense. Call *A Cold Trail* an angst-riddled, contemplative tale, or just call it flat-out great."

—*Providence Journal*

Praise for *A Steep Price*

"A beautiful narrative. What makes *A Steep Price* stand out is the authentic feel of how it feels to work as a police officer in a major city . . . another outstanding novel from one of the best crime writers in the business."

—Associated Press

"A riveting suspense novel . . . A gripping story."

—*Crimespree Magazine*

"Packed with suspense, drama, and raw emotion . . . A fine entry in a solid series."

—*Booklist*

Praise for *Close To Home*

"An immensely—almost compulsively—readable tale . . . A crackerjack mystery."

—*Booklist* (starred review)

"Dugoni's twisted tale is one of conspiracy and culpability . . . richly nuanced and entirely compelling."

—Criminal Element

Praise for *The Trapped Girl*

"Dugoni drills so deep into the troubled relationships among his characters that each new revelation shows them in a disturbing new light . . . an unholy tangle of crimes makes this his best book to date."
—*Kirkus Reviews*

"All of Robert Dugoni's talents are once again firmly on display in *The Trapped Girl*, a blisteringly effective crime thriller . . . structured along classical lines drawn years ago by the likes of Raymond Chandler and Dashiell Hammett. A fiendishly clever tale that colors its pages with crisp shades of postmodern noir."
—*Providence Journal*

"Robert Dugoni, yet again, delivers an excellent read . . . With many twists, turns, and jumps in the road traveled by the detective and her cohorts, this absolutely superb plot becomes more than just a little entertaining. The problem remains the same: Readers must now once again wait impatiently for the next book by Robert Dugoni to arrive."
—*Suspense Magazine*

Praise for *In the Clearing*

"Dugoni's third 'Tracy Crosswhite' novel (after *Her Final Breath*) continues his series's standard of excellence with superb plotting and skillful balancing of the two story lines."
—*Library Journal* (starred review)

"Dugoni has become one of the best crime novelists in the business, and his latest featuring Seattle homicide detective Tracy Crosswhite will only draw more accolades."

—*Romantic Times*, Top Pick

Praise for *Her Final Breath*

"A stunningly suspenseful exercise in terror that hits every note at the perfect pitch."

—*Providence Journal*

"Absorbing . . . Dugoni expertly ratchets up the suspense as Crosswhite becomes a target herself."

—*Seattle Times*

"Another stellar story featuring homicide detective Tracy Crosswhite . . . Crosswhite is a sympathetic, well-drawn protagonist, and her next adventure can't come fast enough."

—*Library Journal* (starred review)

Praise for *My Sister's Grave*

"One of the best books I'll read this year."

—Lisa Gardner, bestselling author of *Touch & Go*

"Dugoni does a superior job of positioning [the plot elements] for maximum impact, especially in a climactic scene set in an abandoned mine during a blizzard."

—*Publishers Weekly*

"Combines the best of a police procedural with a legal thriller, and the end result is outstanding . . . Dugoni continues to deliver emotional and gut-wrenching, character-driven suspense stories that will resonate with any fan of the thriller genre."

—*Library Journal* (starred review)

"What starts out as a sturdy police procedural morphs into a gripping legal thriller . . . Dugoni is a superb storyteller, and his courtroom drama shines . . . This 'Grave' is one to get lost in."

—*Boston Globe*

WHAT
SHE
FOUND

ALSO BY ROBERT DUGONI

The Last Line (a short story)
The World Played Chess
The Extraordinary Life of Sam Hell
The 7th Canon
Damage Control

The Tracy Crosswhite Series

My Sister's Grave
Her Final Breath
In the Clearing
The Trapped Girl
Close to Home
A Steep Price
A Cold Trail
In Her Tracks
The Academy (a short story)
Third Watch (a short story)

The Charles Jenkins Series

The Eighth Sister
The Last Agent
The Silent Sisters

The David Sloane Series

The Jury Master
Wrongful Death
Bodily Harm
Murder One
The Conviction

Nonfiction with Joseph Hilldorfer

The Cyanide Canary

WHAT SHE FOUND

ROBERT DUGONI

THOMAS & MERCER

Text copyright © 2022 by LaMesa Fiction LLC
All rights reserved.

No part of this book may be reproduced, or stored in a retrieval system, or transmitted in any form or by any means, electronic, mechanical, photocopying, recording, or otherwise, without express written permission of the publisher.

Published by Thomas & Mercer, Seattle

www.apub.com

Amazon, the Amazon logo, and Thomas & Mercer are trademarks of Amazon.com, Inc., or its affiliates.

ISBN-13: 9781542008327
ISBN-10: 1542008328

Cover design by Damon Freeman

Printed in the United States of America

For Cristina, Joe, and Catherine. Shining lights during a dark couple of years.

PROLOGUE

February 27, 1996
The Industrial District
Seattle, Washington

Working nights in forbidding areas never bothered Lisa Childress. A reporter for the *Seattle Post-Intelligencer*, Lisa met sources for her investigative articles at all hours of the day and night, and at some questionable locations. The dark didn't frighten her. Nor did haunted houses or horror movies. As a child, she had looked forward to Halloween, with all its creepy costumes and the different ways people tried to spook, surprise, and scare her. They never did. In her teens, she had laughed watching horror movies that caused her friends to run screaming from the room. Being frightened, she concluded early on, was simply a state of mind, just like being cold or being happy. She could control it.

So, it didn't bother her when a source asked to meet at 2:00 a.m. in downtown Seattle's Industrial District. He explained, during their brief telephone conversation, that he had read her most recent news article and had information she might find interesting. Lisa understood why the man would be cautious. The story she pursued, if properly sourced, would blow the top off much of Seattle, and the fallout would be widespread.

She drove south on East Marginal Way, past a cement plant, a glass-recycling center, trucking companies, and businesses that produced raw materials housed in a complex of concrete buildings interconnected by metal bridges. Pipes and stacks spewed smoke and particulates twenty-four hours a day, 365 days of the year. The businesses, if not closed, worked through the night with skeleton crews. Few cars littered their parking lots. The eating establishments that catered to the blue-collar workers would remain dark for several more hours.

Lisa looked through the windshield at clouds crossing a starlit night sky, pushed by a strong, cold breeze. She couldn't help but think the area would make a great location for one of those horror films she'd seen as a teen.

At a stoplight, she unscrewed the cap of her liter of Coca-Cola. The carbonation fizzed. She took a swig that made her sinuses buzz and her throat tingle. Drinking Coke was a habit she'd picked up in college that had followed her to journalism school, and to her job. Coffee upset her stomach, but she needed the caffeine to get through these late-night and early-morning meetings. The Coke helped her to focus—she wasn't sure why—and kept her from crashing. She often worked in rushed spurts, largely because she procrastinated too much. Figured she always would—that thing about zebras not changing their stripes. If she didn't have a deadline hanging over her head like a guillotine blade, she couldn't focus worth a damn. Not that she met them or even tried. She despised deadlines, which was one reason she never told her editors the details of the stories she pursued. If she did, they'd slot her article for a certain run date. She believed investigations had lives of their own, just like stories—a beginning, a middle, and an end. If she rushed the ending, she could miss the real substance. Her editors had given up trying to corral her, so long as she delivered the powerful, hard-hitting news articles that drew local and national attention.

Her husband, Larry, wasn't so understanding, especially now with Anita, their two-year-old, at home. But Larry had known what he was getting into; they'd lived together for almost a year before getting married. Lisa would have been fine without the wedding ring, but they had a little slipup that she discovered when she peed on the stick. Larry said a baby needed a mother and father and one last name. Lisa figured he had a point.

Larry also knew Lisa hadn't been raised in a traditional *Leave It to Beaver* home, where the husband went to work, and the wife primped and had dinner ready. Lisa's mother, Beverly Siegler, was one of Seattle's first female cardiothoracic surgeons—"Don't call me a cardiologist. I work for a living," she used to say. Her father, Archibald Siegler, struggled as a novelist—which he used as an excuse to stay at home and drink like Hemingway.

Larry also knew about Lisa's clutter and lack of organizational skills. He knew her mind shifted from one topic to the next, often without pause and seemingly without reason. Her mother'd had Lisa tested as a child, and the doctors concluded she had autism, which according to her mother meant she was just a shade below brilliant.

The light changed. Lisa turned right on South Fidalgo Street—that was a name she wasn't about to forget. *Fidalgo.* Had to be a person's name. She visualized the Thomas Guide street map.

Continue to the end of the road. Just past a single-story, rectangular, concrete building. Drive through the gap between the corner of the building and the Duwamish Waterway.

The area behind the building was shaped like an isosceles triangle with the Duwamish running along the hypotenuse. Across the water, industrial lights illuminated flat-bottomed cargo ships stacked with colorful containers anchored in the middle of the waterway. Along the shortest side, semitruck cabs had backed up against closed loading bays, their grills smiling at her. Nearby, a car had parked in the shadows cast by the tall grass growing along the waterway. Her source. Lisa shut off her car's headlights. Her source had said he would flash his high beams if it was safe to meet. Again, a bit melodramatic, but when in Rome . . .

She waited.

No high beams.

Maybe she was supposed to flash her car's headlights. She waited just under a minute, then figured it couldn't hurt. She reached and turned the knob on and off.

No response.

She could see the faint outline of someone seated behind the steering wheel and thought again of those ridiculous horror movies—some helpless woman, with an IQ slightly above roadkill, lured to an isolated spot by a deranged killer in a leather mask carrying a chain saw. She usually said something idiotic like "Did I catch you at a bad time?"

And the chain saw fires up so loud, it's visceral.

Rumrum . . . RRRRRRRWWWW!

It was too early in the morning to sit and wait. Lisa reached to the cluttered passenger seat and fumbled beneath papers, notepads, a fleece jacket, and expended fast-food wrappers before finding her microcassette tape recorder. She made sure the battery worked and rewound the tape, then pressed "Record" and slipped the machine into the inside pocket of her jacket. A pen and pad of paper could make a source anxious, no matter how many times Lisa assured she would not reveal the person's identity.

She grabbed her bag, which she used as a briefcase, slipped her car keys inside, and felt a long, cylindrical canister. She knew intuitively what she'd felt, bear spray, and who had put it there, Larry.

Her husband insisted she get pepper spray, but Lisa had not gotten around to it. The bear spray, from their camping supplies, was his not-so-subtle reminder. As her mother would have said, "At least you know he cares."

She pushed open her car door, the dome light illuminating the mess, and stepped out. The early-morning temperature and stiff breeze chilled her. She estimated upper thirties or low forties. The breeze carried a chemical smell from one of the Duwamish plants, or maybe it was just the polluted waterway. The city wrestled with the business owners to clean it up or pay heavy fines.

As she approached the car, the wind gusted, carrying the electric hum of engines at work. She pulled open the passenger door and detected a rank smell she could only describe as the lingering odors of marijuana and a baby's diaper.

The man behind the steering wheel wore a ball cap and a puffy jacket. He did not acknowledge her. He stared out the windshield.

"I'm Lisa Childress," she said.

No response.

"Are you the person who called? Sir?" She reached across the seat and pushed the man's shoulder. He tilted against the driver's-side window, then toppled forward. His head hit the steering wheel before his body listed sideways—like a bag of potatoes shifting weight—and he slumped between the two seats. His hat dislodged, revealing damage to his skull. Blood, the color of chocolate syrup, and bits of brain matter splattered the shoulder of his jacket.

The weeds rustled behind her. Lisa turned. A person emerged but with his face covered beneath a black ski mask. She reached for the bear spray, but not quickly enough. The assailant grabbed her by the throat and shoved her hard against the car. Her head impacted, and a burst of stars momentarily blinded her. His hand squeezed her throat; she could not breathe.

He banged her head a second time. Then a third. Her fingers frantically flicked at the canister's safety cap. The man sensed her movement, but not before Lisa raised the can and depressed the nozzle, spraying him in the eyes. He wailed in pain and released his grip, fingers ripping at the mask. He pulled it free, and for a brief moment Lisa saw him. Then he fled into the darkness.

Dizzy and disoriented, Lisa reached out to brace her arm against the car, missed the frame, and stumbled off-balance. She fell into the weeds, dropping the canister. Dazed, she rose to a knee but, nauseated, she threw up.

Get away.

She struggled to her feet. The building, lights, and night sky weaved and spun.

She stepped, tripped, and felt her body falling forward, weightless, her head striking the pavement.

CHAPTER 1

Present Day
Seattle, Washington

Tracy Crosswhite had no sooner shut her office door than someone knocked. She wanted to tell the person to go away. She wanted a minute to catch her breath. She had just returned to Police Headquarters after notifying another family that their loved one's body had been found buried in Curry Canyon. The prior winter, Tracy had tracked an abducted woman to a cabin in the canyon and discovered a horror show. The property, along with the basement beneath a home in North Seattle, had for decades been the burial ground for two sadistic serial killers. The news was difficult for Tracy to deliver, and harder for the family to hear. Family members expressed relief to finally have closure, but they also reexperienced the pain that had pierced their hearts those many years ago. Each case took an emotional toll on Tracy, who was all too familiar with both the family's grief and the painful healing process they would endure.

She had sought just five minutes of solitude.

Five minutes of peace.

Five minutes of respite.

She didn't have that luxury.

She pulled open the door, surprised to find Chief of Police Marcella Weber on the other side.

"You got a minute?" Weber spoke in a voice that always seemed too deep. In her sixties, Weber was an attractive woman who looked twenty years younger. She'd once credited her youthful appearance and lack of wrinkles to being African American, but it also could have been because she was full-figured. Her pixie haircut made her look youthful, as well. Not that looking young was her goal. She didn't dye her hair, and the strands of gray let people know she had experience under her belt. Though she wore gold stud earrings, her fingers were devoid of jewelry, including a wedding band. She looked at Tracy with eyes the camera loved, but which she could use to burn holes through an officer when necessary. She always wore her police uniform and told those who cared to listen, "I'll always be a cop first."

She considered the disaster Tracy called an office. "Looks like my office some days." Weber laughed. "Would it be better if I came back?"

Black binders, one for each cold case, littered Tracy's desk, the carpeted floor, and the two utilitarian chairs. Stray papers, yellow legal pads, and a coffee mug embossed with "World's Best Mom" teetered atop the binders stacked on her desk. Tracy had either pulled the binders from the shelves or had them retrieved from storage each time Kelly Rosa, King County's forensic medical examiner, confirmed another victim's identity.

The office was a perk that came with being the one detective in the Cold Case Unit, a position Tracy had reluctantly taken when her captain moved her following her return from an extended maternity leave that became a PTSD leave. Prior to the reassignment, Tracy had sat for a decade at a cubicle in the Violent Crimes Section's A Team. While she missed the camaraderie with Kins, Del, and Faz, closing an office door to focus or to take a private call was a luxury. Her goal was to get home and spend more time with Daniella and Dan. That had been one of the benefits her predecessor, Art Nunzio, pitched her—more family time.

Hopefully, but not yet. And definitely not now.

When the chief of police asked if you had a minute, the question was rhetorical.

"Come on in."

"It looks like you just got in." Weber motioned down the hallway. "Do you want to grab a cup of coffee?"

"I'm good. I had a cup on the drive," Tracy said. "Another and I won't be able to sit still."

"I hear you," Weber said.

In all the years Tracy had worked for Chief of Police Sandy Clarridge, he had never come to her cubicle, or any detective's cubicle, as far as Tracy knew. He'd always summoned the officer to his inner sanctum on the eighth floor, which made Weber a breath of fresh air inside Police Headquarters. According to the press release announcing her as chief of police, Weber was born and raised in Seattle to hardworking parents and had excelled in school. Her mother, a court reporter, wanted Weber to become a doctor, but Weber chose to become a Seattle police officer like her father. She had entered the Academy upon graduation from the University of Washington and, after working patrol, excelled in different departments over twenty-five years. The brass quickly saw her political potential as an African American woman with an exceptional record, and groomed her. She served as a lieutenant, captain, assistant chief, deputy chief, and, when Clarridge resigned following the city council's support of protestors seeking to defund the police department, chief of police.

Weber's professional accomplishments were all the more impressive because those inside Police Headquarters understood she and her two siblings had spent much of their adult life helping their mother care for their father, who had intervened in a store robbery and caught a bullet in the back, paralyzing him from the waist down. Upon her divorce, and after her three children moved out of the house, Weber had her parents move in so she could better care for them as they aged.

Tracy moved black binders from one of the two chairs and Weber took a seat.

"Heard it was another busy morning," Weber said.

Tracy stepped over still more binders and settled into her chair. "Unfortunately," she said. On the drive into the office, Tracy had received an unexpected call from Rosa, who had discovered the remains of another victim buried beneath the body they had been exhuming near the cabin in Curry Canyon. "Rosa thinks that's the last one though. The last body. Thank God."

"Thank God." Weber crossed herself with burgundy-colored finger-nails, half an inch long. Tracy's fingernails were a disaster on the level of her office—the product of neglect that would take more time and energy to repair than Tracy presently had.

"That makes seven; doesn't it?" Weber asked, a subtle indication she had paid close attention to the investigation. The seven bodies unearthed in the canyon, and the seven found beneath the home in North Seattle, brought the total number of recovered victims to four-teen. With each solved case came positive publicity the department sorely needed to combat the city council's threats to defund. Weber had used Tracy's success to promote the Seattle Police Department's dogged determination to never give up on any victim, which of course required sufficient funding.

"Honestly, I lost track. But Rosa is providing me what she can in terms of possible DNA evidence, dental impressions, hair samples. If these two women were reported missing and we have a file, we'll ID them both." And Tracy would make the sad drive to deliver the heart-wrenching news to two more families. "I'm very much the bearer of both good and bad news."

Weber shifted gears. "I don't have to tell you this is great work, Tracy, and it comes at a time when we can really use it. So, I come with a proposition."

"What's that?" Tracy asked.

"I'd like to invite several of the families to Police Headquarters for a press conference, with you and Rosa and Rosa's team. I'm hoping you can help us identify those families who would . . ." She paused to choose her words.

"Make the best impression?" Tracy asked, not really comfortable with the publicity. This was not something to celebrate.

"The public needs to see the value in what we do. I'm hoping you can identify those cases that will make an emotional mark. The mayor also thinks it will offset the city council's pandering to protestors who continue to show up at council hearings."

Politics. You had to love it.

"I can ask some families and see if they'd be willing," Tracy said.

"You can tell them it will help other families of missing persons, give them hope that we will someday find their loved ones also, that we will never give up."

"I'll see what I can do," she said.

Weber stood. "Good. You let me know if you want to go back to Violent Crimes and I'll make it happen, but I think you have another career path when you're ready to move on from this office."

"Another career path?"

"You should be running a unit, working your way up the ladder, the way I did."

Tracy immediately dismissed it. "I'm better in the field than behind a desk—no offense intended."

"None taken. But don't be hasty. Think about it."

Tracy's gaze drifted to the shelves of binders. "I do have one request."

"Name it."

"I could use help from time to time with some investigations. I'd like to be able to call in another detective when I need one." It would be an end run around her captain, Johnny Nolasco.

"Consider it done."

"Captain Nolasco won't like it," Tracy said, more to the point.

"I've heard the two of you have a rocky working relationship."

That was an understatement. "It would be better coming from you than me," Tracy said.

"I understand. You got an open door if you need it."

"I appreciate that, Chief."

Tracy walked Weber out and closed the door behind her. She didn't know what to think. On the one hand, Weber could be an ace in the hole—if Tracy needed one. On the other hand, Tracy felt like she needed to take a shower.

Her desk phone rang. Tracy leaned over the clutter to answer it. "Detective Crosswhite."

"Detective, I have a young woman looking for her mother. Says she's been missing almost twenty-five years."

Tracy looked at the binders. Art Nunzio's cautionary voice played in her head, not for the first time. *Just take it one case at a time. I always believe I'm one phone call away from solving another case.*

"Put her through," Tracy said.

CHAPTER 2

An hour later, Tracy studied the pages in a black binder she'd pulled from the vault storage and relished the aromas of fresh-ground coffee and herbal teas. She picked at a blueberry scone and nursed coffee from a mug the size of a bowl, sitting at an upright table in the back corner of the Macrina Bakery on First Avenue in Seattle's SoDo district, an acronym for south of downtown. For meetings outside the office, she often chose the bakery, which was easy to get to and had easy-to-find parking. She loved the smells, especially the fresh-baked bread—a memory from her childhood Saturday mornings when her mother made fresh loaves. She also liked the vibe. The bakery played music, but not so loud you couldn't hear yourself think, or have a conversation—she was becoming her parents—and the interior décor was unpretentious, with an open ceiling revealing the air ducts and sprinkler heads.

Tracy had been prepared to tell the caller what she always told those seeking to find their loved ones. The Cold Case Unit had not forgotten about the missing or deceased person, and if the caller had additional information, Tracy would be happy to receive it. If promising, the information would be followed up, and Tracy would keep the family informed. She tried not to sound rote. She tried to sound sincere. But too often the caller didn't have new information—no fresh leads or evidence. The case had often been picked over from every angle by the investigating detectives, then picked over again when transferred to the cold case detective. But with the publicity from the missing persons she had resolved in North Seattle and Curry Canyon, Tracy received many calls from family members asking to have their loved one's file reopened and reevaluated. She couldn't get to them all.

But something unique and familiar about this morning's caller had struck a chord with Tracy. Anita Childress wasn't looking for a daughter or a sister or an aunt. She sought her mother, missing twenty-four years. That thought was sobering.

Over the phone, Childress told Tracy she had been just two years old when Lisa Childress, an investigative reporter for the *Post-Intelligencer*, now an online newspaper, left home in the middle of the night and never returned. Her body was never found. She had, like Sarah Crosswhite, Tracy's younger sister, simply disappeared.

Tracy looked up from the binder pages when she sensed someone standing at her table. The woman before her was big-boned, and her face struck Tracy as model worthy.

"Detective Crosswhite?" Tracy closed the binder and moved to get up from the bench seat to shake the woman's hand. "Don't get up." Anita Childress extended a hand across the table and introduced herself. She then stepped up into the elevated chair across the table.

"Do you want a cup of coffee or something to eat?" Tracy said.

"I have a tea coming. I ate this morning. Thank you for agreeing to meet with me."

"I was just familiarizing myself with your mother's file. I'm afraid I'm not very far along."

Childress smiled. "It's understandable," she said. "I've been following the story in Curry Canyon and North Seattle—all the bodies they're finding. It's sickening."

"It is," Tracy said.

"It sounds like you've had your hands full, and you've only been in your new post a short time. Congratulations, by the way, on the Medal of Valor. That's your third, isn't it?"

"It is." Tracy smiled, curious. "I don't recall the press release stating it was my third medal though."

"It didn't. And I haven't been stalking you." Childress's smile looked uncomfortable. "But I have done some research. Old habit. Goes with the job."

"What job is that?"

"I'm a reporter for the *Seattle Times*. I cover mostly city government out of the metro desk, but I'm familiar with some of your cases and your successes from past articles."

Tracy put her hand on the binder. "I think I read that your mother was also a reporter. Am I right?"

"For the *Post-Intelligencer*. Back when Seattle was a two-newspaper town."

The waitress called out Childress's tea order, and Childress left her chair to retrieve her bowl. She returned, carefully carrying it. "They don't mess around here; do they?"

"No, they don't," Tracy said.

Childress took a sip and set it down on the saucer. Mint wafted up from the bowl.

"You followed in your mother's footsteps?"

Childress looked away before reengaging Tracy. "I'm not the reporter she was, but . . ." She shrugged. "I figured it would give me access to information that might help me to find her. I know how that must sound—like I'm OCD and I'm chasing ghosts. I'm not. Not OCD anyway. But I *am* chasing a ghost. It's just, well . . ."

"You don't have to explain," Tracy said. She glanced down at the young woman's hand and did not see a wedding ring on her finger.

"Thank you. I know your family lost your sister when she was eighteen," Childress said. "And then you found her remains twenty years later, I believe, in the mountains above Cedar Grove. Several articles documented the story, and the trial of the man accused of killing her. Anyway, hope you'll understand."

Childress *had* done her homework, though no news story explained that Tracy had become a homicide detective for the same reason Childress had become a newspaper reporter—for access to information. Tracy had, for years, investigated her sister's mysterious and sudden disappearance, and the search had become an obsession, one fueled by guilt. Tracy had lived alone in a Seattle studio apartment, forsaking serious relationships so she could return home after work each night and study boxes of materials she had accumulated on her sister's disappearance. She did this until one day she realized what she had become, what her life had become, and she feared she might lose her mind.

"I understand your mother has been missing a very long time," Tracy said. "I'm sorry."

"I haven't heard from the police in several years," Childress said. "I spoke to an Art Nunzio about a year ago, but he said they didn't have any new leads to pursue."

Which meant Nunzio didn't have DNA evidence to process. The decision to reopen an investigation was a simple analysis of effort versus likely outcome. In this case, Nunzio probably deduced the most likely outcome, without DNA evidence, didn't warrant the effort he would have to expend.

"Maybe you can fill me in on some of the details. I'm betting you've spent a lot more time with the facts than I have." Tracy flipped open a notepad.

"Sure." Childress sat up. "My mother disappeared February 27, 1996. My father said she received a telephone call earlier that evening and told him she needed to meet this person, a source for a story she worked on."

"Did this person have a name?"

"It was a confidential source."

"What was the story she was working on?" Tracy asked.

Childress smiled. "That's one of the sixty-four-thousand-dollar questions. I've spoken with my mother's editor at the *P-I* back then, Bill Jorgensen. He didn't know for certain because he said my mother held her stories close to the vest. She often didn't even tell him what she was working on."

"She kept the stories from her editor?"

"My mother . . . what I can piece together . . . Well, she was different."

"How so?"

"She likely had Asperger's, though that word is no longer PC because it was said to be the name of a Nazi who espoused eugenics and murdering people considered low functioning. Now my mother would be considered autistic. My grandmother told me this. She said my mom was often disorganized, forgetful, and had difficulty in social situations, but that she was also brilliant when singularly focused. She heavily sourced her investigative pieces, but she didn't always tell her editors the details of the story she worked on, or when they'd get it. Jorgensen said they gave up trying to set deadlines because she never met them."

Tracy made a note to check the Internet and determine if Lisa Childress's quirks, as Anita had described them, comported with someone with autism and what that meant. "No one had any idea what she was working on?"

"I think I do," Childress said. The young woman reached down and pulled four manila files from her briefcase and stacked them on the table. "These are files I've put together from my mother's notebooks, and from conversations I've had with other reporters and photographers my mother worked with during that time."

"You put these together recently?"

Childress shook her head. "I've been looking into my mother's disappearance for most of my adult life."

Tracy could relate to that as well. "What I meant is, were they part of the cold case detective's file, or the investigating detectives' file?"

"I don't believe so. Not to this extent, no."

"What does that mean?"

"Bill Jorgensen said the police sought my mother's files to determine if my father was lying about my mother leaving to meet a confidential source the night she disappeared."

"I don't imagine that went very far."

Tracy knew the husband was always a suspect in a spouse's disappearance, but subpoenas to newspapers were usually quashed, especially if the subpoena sought the names of confidential newspaper sources. Courts traditionally protected newspapers from being used as a police resource to solve a crime.

"No. It didn't. Eventually the police and the paper reached a compromise—or I should say the lawyers reached a compromise. The paper agreed to provide information about stories my mother was working on, but not give up her notes, if there were any, or her confidential sources. The thing is, the newspaper didn't know my mother's confidential sources or the details of the stories she worked on."

Tracy asked, "Can you get in trouble for turning this information over to me now?"

"I don't see how," Childress said. "It's my investigation. I'm not working it as a reporter for the *Times*. Besides, my mother disappeared almost twenty-five years ago."

"But your position as a reporter provided you with access to confidential information."

Childress shook her head. "Not really. You'll see almost everything in here has been published, or was information provided to me by other reporters and photographers who worked with my mother. It's information the detectives could have had if they had asked the right people the right questions. They didn't. They were fixated on my father. They thought he killed my mother."

That was often the case, Tracy thought but didn't verbalize. "Okay. What do you believe your mother was investigating at that time?"

Childress smiled and put her hand on the top file, which was several inches thick. "First, my mother was pursuing a story involving former mayor Michael Edwards's business dealings while in office."

"Along with just about everyone else," Tracy said. Edwards was notorious for his "pay to play" politics, and a lot of speculation existed that his success in office and his financial wealth stemmed from that philosophy. "But nothing has ever been tied to him," Tracy said, familiar—to a certain extent—with the FBI's and the Justice Department's various efforts to get the former mayor. "Not definitively."

Childress set the manila folder aside and put her hand on the file cover beneath it. "She was also working on a story involving longtime city council member Peter Rivers."

Tracy wasn't familiar with that name. "What about him?"

"Rivers was a staunch proponent of gay rights and backed liberal interests. He had his sights set on the mayor's office, but he never ran and quickly retired from public service. He said he wanted to devote time to his partner and two children."

"But that wasn't true?"

"My mother was working several leads that, while in his twenties, Rivers had picked up and paid young boys to perform sexual acts. There's an indication in my mother's files that at least one of those boys attempted to blackmail Rivers."

Childress set that file aside for the third. "My mother was also investigating a group of police officers, a task force, for allegedly skimming money from drug busts." Again, Tracy figured that story would have been big news, if true.

Childress touched a fourth file, this one not as thick as the first three. "The fourth story she worked was the Route 99 serial killer."

Tracy knew this story, as did most young women who grew up in the Pacific Northwest in the nineties. The serial killer had claimed at least thirteen victims, all young women, some prostitutes. He killed them along State Route 99, also known as the Pacific Highway, then suddenly stopped. "Some people thought it was Ridgway." Childress referred to the notorious Green River Killer. "It wasn't. Ridgway admitted to a lot of killings but not the Route 99 killings. Rumors existed my mother had gone undercover on the Aurora strip to possibly lure out the killer."

"Did you find evidence she did?" Tracy asked, thinking it would have been brave but not smart.

"As much as I would like to unequivocally say no, it does appear from the file that my mother had a confidential source, though there's no indication who that person was."

Tracy looked to the files. "You realize you could be stirring up a hornet's nest."

"It was twenty-five years ago," Childress said.

"True, but if someone was willing to . . ."

"Kill my mother because she figured out one of these files or was about to? You can say it. I've thought the same thing."

"I just don't want to see you possibly get hurt," Tracy said.

Undeterred, Childress said, "Does this mean you're going to look into my mother's disappearance?"

"I wouldn't be here if that wasn't my intent." Tracy tapped her black binder. "I have to ask you some tough questions, Ms. Childress."

"Anita," she said. "And I doubt they're tougher than the questions I've asked myself. Like, could my father have killed my mother and disposed of her body?"

"That would be one."

"The husband is always a suspect, isn't he?"

"He is."

"The detectives looked at my father long and hard. You'll find some evidence in your file, I'm sure, that my mother and father had their disagreements."

"What did they disagree about? Do you know?"

"From what I have pieced together from the police file, and conversations with my grandparents, and with my father, they fought about things married couples always fight about—a lack of money and a lack of time. My father didn't like my mother leaving in the middle of the night to meet sources for her stories without telling him any of the details. On one occasion, the argument apparently got heated and the neighbor in the apartment next door called the police. My father was asked to leave the apartment for the evening and did. There's a report in the file I had pulled from the archives."

"Any indication of physical violence?"

"No, and my father moved back home the next day with my mother's blessing."

"What about the night in question? Did your father have an alibi?"

"Me." Childress smiled, but it waned. "With my mother out at night, my father was my babysitter."

"Did your mother go out at night to meet sources often?"

"Often enough that my father worried about her safety. He told me he had started to put a can of bear spray in her bag because my mother wouldn't get pepper spray."

"Did the police have any other theories about what happened to your mother, that you're aware of?"

Childress leaned away, clearly uncomfortable. "They found my mother's car parked in a garage stall not far from the Greyhound bus station. The detective said they couldn't rule out the possibility that my mother voluntarily got on a bus and left."

Tracy could see the pain in Childress's expression. "What do you think?"

Childress's eyes moistened. She inhaled a deep breath while gazing up at the ceiling and using an index finger to wipe away a tear.

"Take your time," Tracy said.

"My mother had trouble expressing emotions. I would prefer to tell you she loved me and never would have left me, but I can't. Over the years, my grandmother and grandfather assured me my mother loved me, but they also said they didn't think she fully grasped that I was dependent on her for my survival. My father became my caregiver because my mother often became absorbed in one of her stories. There were instances . . ." Another deep breath. "Instances of my mother leaving me at home to chase a source. My father would get home and find me in my crib. I don't really know what to tell you. Other than that, my mother just disappeared. No evidence of foul play. No body. She just disappeared."

Just like Sarah. "Are your mother's parents still alive?"

"My grandmother lives over in Laurelhurst. My grandfather is deceased."

"And your father?"

"My father lives in Medina with his new partner."

"Wife?"

"They aren't married."

"When did he start dating her?"

"Not until after I went to college."

"Did your father have a life insurance policy on your mother?" Tracy asked.

"Not until after I was born," Childress said. "It was a mutual policy."

"Whose idea was it to take out a policy?"

"My father's. He said he worried that if anything happened to him . . . He wanted me taken care of. He didn't think my mother could do it on her own, and he didn't want me to be a financial burden on anyone."

"Did he receive an insurance payment?"

"Not for a long time. The insurance company was waiting for the police to declare my mother dead. My father finally went to court to get a judicial declaration."

Interesting. "Do you know what happened to the money?"

Childress squirmed. "My father gave up his career to stay home and take care of me. We needed the money to live on after my mother disappeared, until he built up his real estate business."

"Is that what he did before he stayed at home? Sold real estate?"

She shook her head, looking more uncomfortable. "He had a start-up company. A tech business. The company failed. He filed for bankruptcy, but the court ruled that about $150,000 of the debt wasn't dischargeable."

He needed money, Tracy thought. "When did he file for bankruptcy?"

"About six months before my mother's disappearance."

Suspicious. No wonder the detectives focused on the husband.

"Something else you should probably know," Childress said. "My mother was pregnant when they got married. My father has told me they always intended to get married, but I came as a surprise, and I was the motivation."

Which was exactly what a good father would tell his daughter, but again, it was a factor that the investigating detectives could not ignore. The couple married because the woman got pregnant. Had the father felt trapped? Obligated? Not long after, the father was in debt, with creditors pursuing him. He had the financial strain of a new baby, a failed business, a wife with autism with whom he was fighting, and he had taken out a life insurance policy on his wife.

"I know how this probably looks," Childress said, as if reading Tracy's thoughts.

"Then you know it doesn't look good," Tracy said.

"But my father didn't take the insurance money and buy himself a fancy car or a boat," Childress said. "He used the money for a down payment on a house in West Seattle, and to get out from under the debt. When he moved to Medina, he gave the house to me."

"Outright, or did you assume the mortgage?"

Another frown. "I assumed the mortgage, but he gave up what equity he had in the house."

"What does he do now?"

"Now? He's retired."

"And his partner?"

"I'm going to just tell you this, so you don't think I'm hiding anything. She comes from money. A lot of money. My father dated her in high school. They were high school sweethearts."

"But they've never married?"

"He hasn't told me this, but I think it's because her parents don't approve."

"Because of the suspicions surrounding your mother's disappearance?"

"Yes."

Tracy left unsaid that giving up what equity her father did have in the house might possibly go a little way toward easing what guilt he also felt for killing his daughter's mother, or toward convincing his partner's family of his innocence.

"Are you and your father close?"

"Very. He was both mother and father to me. I felt bad for him when I got old enough to understand that he was a pariah. He lived a monastic, lonely life until I graduated high school."

"Does he talk about your mother?"

Another headshake. "It was hard for him. What do you tell a little girl when you don't have an answer? Do you tell her that her mother is dead? Do you tell her that her mother just took off one night and never came home? Is that somehow better?" Childress's eyes again watered. This was painful.

"What did your father tell you happened to your mother?"

"He always said my mother loved me, and if she could be with me, she would. He said no one knew what happened to her, but wherever she was, whether she was in heaven looking down on us, or living someplace else, she loved me very much. She always had and she always would."

It was a nice sentiment—enough, maybe, for a young girl to hold on to, for a while at least, until she grew up and wanted her own answers to her own questions about what happened to her mother. Just as Tracy had sought answers about her sister.

"You sound like you love your father very much. Does he know you're pursuing your mother's cold case?"

"He does, but not the extent. He doesn't know I'm meeting with you. I don't believe he killed my mother, Detective. I don't believe him capable."

Tracy had known many people who had said much the same thing about someone they loved, only to be proven wrong. She also knew she'd have to speak to the father and make an assessment for herself.

"And what if, upon reopening your mother's cold case, I find evidence to the contrary? Could you handle that?"

Childress dropped her gaze to the tabletop for a moment, then reengaged Tracy. "I want the truth, Detective. Whatever that may be. Even if finding out what happened to my mother means losing my father."

CHAPTER 3

Tracy hurried up the porch steps, anxious to get home to Dan and Daniella. She stepped inside the front door and dropped her car keys in the bowl atop the pony wall. The sound prompted Roger, her cat, to pounce atop the wall, purring and looking to be fed. She picked him up and petted him as she called out, "Anyone home?"

That set off the home security system—a chorus of deep barks from Rex and Sherlock, the two Rhodesian-mastiffs Tracy inherited when she and Dan married. Roger squirmed free and shot from her arms. A thud, followed by a second thud, came from upstairs. The dogs had been on the bed—against Tracy's rules. Nails clicked on the hardwood floor as the two dogs rushed to the landing at the top of the steps. They looked down at Tracy, tails wagging, but tentative.

"You know you're not supposed to be on the bed," she said. Rex shifted his eyes back to the master bedroom. An admission of guilt. Sherlock, apparently deciding to seek forgiveness, lumbered his 140 pounds down the steps to greet her. "Good boy," she said. "You're in the will. Rex, you get a lump of coal."

Rex whined and trudged back into the bedroom.

The two dogs had taken to Tracy, and she found great comfort in their presence, especially now with a daughter. She thought of Anita Childress, just two years old when her mother had disappeared. What a tragedy, on so many levels, for a young girl to grow up without a mother, compounded by the specter that her father might have been responsible.

Tracy had spent the remainder of the afternoon going through the cold file. Lisa Childress had initially been classified as a missing person before the court declared her dead and the file was transferred to the Homicide Unit. As Anita Childress said, the two detectives didn't appear to venture too far from the theory that the husband was the perpetrator. As far as Tracy could tell, they hadn't looked seriously into any of the four stories Childress said her mother had been working on.

"That you, Mrs. O?" Therese called out, using her abbreviated version of Dan's last name, O'Leary. "We're upstairs on the bed."

Tracy climbed the stairs and entered her bedroom. Therese knelt at the side of the bed, whispering to Daniella, who sat atop the comforter in her diaper and T-shirt, her belly sticking out.

"Who is it?" Therese asked her. "Who's here? Who's here?"

"Mama. Mama." Daniella smiled and held out her arms. Along with "dada" and "dog," or at least what sounded like "dog," the three words composed Daniella's vocabulary.

Tracy kissed and nuzzled her daughter's cheeks, making Daniella giggle. "We were playing with the dogs," Therese said. "They jump on the bed and Daniella tumbles. She laughs uproariously."

Rex glanced up at Tracy as if to say, *I have no idea what she's talking about.* Sherlock would not meet Tracy's gaze and lowered his head to his paws.

"You're teaching them bad habits, Therese. They're not supposed to be on the bed."

"They're protective of Daniella, that's for sure," Therese said, her Irish accent strong. "I'd like to see the bloke who could get past these two. Too bad we can't count on them to be around for when Daniella starts dating."

The dogs would be long gone by that time. The thought made Tracy think again of Anita Childress, as she had for most of the afternoon. She thought of all the moments Anita and her mother should have shared—moments Tracy looked forward to with Daniella: her first period, her first date, first heartbreak, her proms, maybe sports, graduations. Someone had robbed Anita of each memory as much as they had robbed her mother. And no father, no matter how devoted, caring, and loving, could fill that hole. It was simply too deep.

Maybe that was why Anita Childress was willing to potentially sacrifice her relationship with her father. Maybe she'd come to realize the hole in her life could never be filled, so she might as well find out what truly happened. The disappearance might not have been a premeditated act. It could have been an argument that got out of hand, a single blow the husband could not take back.

"Sorry, Mrs. O."

Sherlock lowered his head between his paws. Rex remained upright, unflinching and uncompromising.

"Not your fault," Tracy said. "That was a habit ingrained by Mr. O'Leary before my time. Dan home? I saw his car in the drive."

"Come and gone already," Therese said. "He went for a run."

Tracy checked the time on her Fitbit. "Without me? Or them?" It was standard duty to take the hounds to tire them out and ensure a better night's sleep for all.

"I didn't see much of him. In and out quickly. I think he's in a bad mood. Something at court, if you ask me. You might be able to catch him? Depending on how fast you want to run?" Therese said. "I'm sure these two would track him down."

Better to let Dan run off his anger. "You go on," Tracy said. "I'll take over from here. Has she eaten?"

"Like a little monster. Macaroni and broccoli strewn all over the kitchen. These two were in dog heaven."

"I'll give her a bath, then. You have a class, don't you?"

Therese was a talented painter. "I do," Therese said. "There's hamburger meat in the fridge. I'll make some patties and a salad, and you can take over when Mr. O gets back."

Tracy picked up Daniella and took her into the bathroom, turning on the spigots and testing the temperature with her hand. She'd only fill the tub a few inches. Just enough for Daniella to play and get clean.

Half an hour later, she hoisted a protesting Daniella from the water and wrapped her in a plush towel. The back door closed with a bang, and the two dogs alerted, barked, and thudded downstairs.

"Tracy?" Dan called out.

"Upstairs."

Dan came up the stairs as Tracy carried Daniella from the master bathroom to the bedroom. "Hey," she said. "How come you didn't take the dogs?"

Dan shook his head. "I just needed to get out and run."

"What's going on?"

Dan sat on the edge of the bed. He'd taken his shoes off and left them on the porch to avoid dragging in dirt. He used his shirt to wipe sweat from his brow. Given the dark perspiration rings around his neck and armpits, his run had been ambitious. "You remember that case I was preparing for trial . . . Ted Simmons—the young man who was sexually abused by his foster father?"

Tracy did. Dan had filed a complaint against the state foster-care system. "Did the judge make a bad ruling?"

Dan shook his head. "That I could at least deal with. Two days ago, Simmons called and told me to settle the case. He didn't want to go to trial, didn't want to testify and have his two sons hear what he went through."

"He got cold feet. That's understandable."

"The attorney for the state wouldn't even talk settlement. Arrogant prick knew what my guy was going through. He had used Ted's uncomfortableness to harass him during his deposition and intimated he'd do the same at trial—make public his private humiliation in court." Dan just shook his head as if to say, *It gets worse.* "I called Simmons back and told him we'd take it out of the state's ass at trial. I thought I got him calmed down."

"What happened?" Tracy said, getting a bad feeling.

"He shot himself. His wife found him in their garage."

"Oh no," Tracy said. She could tell Dan was shaken and on the verge of tears.

"I feel so bad for his wife and his kids. He must have been a lot more troubled by what happened to him than he showed." Tears spilled down his cheeks.

"How's the wife doing?"

Dan shook his head. "This will be a scar they all will wear for the rest of their lives."

"I'm sorry," she said. Having lost a father to suicide, she knew Dan was right.

"So . . . ," Dan said with false cheer. "How was your day?"

She reached out and hugged him, Daniella between them. "I met with another family of a victim up in Curry Canyon and gave them the news."

Dan pulled back. "And here I am piling on."

"No. You're not," she said. "It was hard. It always is, but it brought this family some closure, and for that they were grateful and gracious."

"I'm not sure how to bring closure now to Simmons's family."

"That's not your job, Dan. I know that can sound callous, but it's not."

"Doesn't make it any easier."

"I know." She gave him another awkward hug. Then she said, "Why don't you shower? I'll get Daniella dressed and get her down, then make us dinner. We can enjoy a quiet evening."

As Dan left the room, Tracy thought again of Anita Childress and hoped she could bring the young woman some closure, but feared she would only bring her more pain.

CHAPTER 4

The following morning, Tracy pulled into the parking lot of the Glendale Country Club in Bellevue and viewed an expanse of lush, green fairways and manicured greens. White-and-green checked flags marked holes. She walked down steps and found pushcarts and golf carts loaded with golf bags lining the paved asphalt between the pro shop and the locker rooms. A clear, azure sky, not a cloud to be seen, hung overhead, and the temperature hovered between a crisp chill and comfortable.

Moss Gunderson had retired from the Seattle Police Department nearly fifteen years earlier at sixty years of age. He told Tracy on the telephone the prior evening that he had a standing round of golf every Wednesday morning, and that no one and nothing short of his funeral would ever interrupt it. He said he'd played in rain, sleet, hail, even snow—they'd used orange golf balls—and called his foursome "the Mailmen."

Tracy offered to meet Moss after his round, but he said lunch followed the round, when they settled bets and had a few cocktails. He suggested she ride in his golf cart and ask him her questions about Lisa Childress in between his shots. "Either that, or we talk on the phone."

Tracy never opted to speak on the phone if she had the choice. She liked to evaluate a person's facial expressions and body posture as they answered questions, though she didn't think that would be much of an issue with Moss, the lead detective on Childress's disappearance.

Moss gave Tracy directions to the club and told her, "You won't miss me. I glow."

Whatever that meant.

Tracy watched golfers come and go. The clubhouse attendants helped with their clubs, and everyone seemed friendly. Dan had a handicap of eleven strokes at one time, and he'd bought Tracy a set of clubs to interest her. She enjoyed playing, but she didn't have time at present to practice, which made a round of golf a round of frustration. Being at the club this morning and seeing the camaraderie, she thought it would be nice for Dan to have that outlet now.

The glass doors of the golf shop opened and a tall, heavyset man emerged. He definitely glowed in bright-orange pants, a white belt, and a neon-green shirt partially hidden beneath a black windbreaker. Moss Gunderson also wore a black baseball-style cap with the Glendale crest—a *G* with two crossed golf clubs. He carried two sleeves of golf balls and looked like a Norwegian version of Faz or Del. Tracy estimated him to be six foot four and more than 250 pounds.

"You better buy a box if you're playing eighteen holes, Moss," a passing elderly man said. "Six balls won't last you through the first three holes."

"Something you don't worry about with your hundred-yard drives, Stan. Is your husband playing today or are you still hitting from the ladies tees?" Moss laughed and looked at Tracy. "Detective Crosswhite?"

"That would be me," Tracy said.

"Sorry about that."

"No worries. You weren't lying; you do glow."

"I figure if you're going to make a statement, make it loud and bold. Hey, Lou?" Moss called to another man who looked about the same age and was putting clubs on the back of a cart beside another set. "You're riding solo this morning. I'm riding with my girlfriend. Don't tell Frieda."

"What goes on at Glendale stays at Glendale, Moss. Besides, no woman that good looking would spend time with your ugly mug unless she was handcuffed to the cart. No offense to Frieda."

Moss laughed and directed Tracy to the cart with a single set of clubs and colorful clubheads. "This is us." Tracy climbed in the passenger side, Moss hit the pedal, and the cart raced up the hill toward the first tee. The chilled breeze made her glad she'd worn a jacket. Along the way, four people made quips at the retired detective.

"You're well known here," Tracy said.

"I better be. I've been a member twenty-five years, play five days a week, and eat here a couple times a week."

"You must be pretty good."

"I'll let you in on a golfer's secret. Two guys and one woman here can golf. They're in their midtwenties. The rest of us suck. It's just different degrees of suck. My handicap is fourteen. Used to be seven but I got old, and I refuse to tee off from the old-man's tees." He parked the cart alongside the first tee box and turned to her. "Okay, first question and first answer. 'Moss' is a nickname. Apparently, I never sat still, was always on the go, like a rolling stone. Get it?"

"A rolling stone gathers no moss."

"It stuck. Hang on a second. I'm up."

Moss departed the cart and grabbed his driver from the bag. Tracy had been curious about Moss's name, but it certainly wasn't her first question. She deduced Moss liked to tell the story, and she wondered if he had perpetuated the name. Like he said, if you're going to make a statement, make it loud.

Moss stepped to the tee box and placed the ball and tee in the grass. Tracy waited for the customary rituals that often took more time than the actual teeing off, but he simply rifled a shot down the fairway.

"Somebody is getting paid this morning, boys," Moss shouted to his three companions as he picked up his tee.

When he returned to the cart, Tracy said, "Is this speed golf?"

"No sense overthinking it the way these guys will. We got a little time here. You asked about Lisa Childress on the telephone."

Tracy had not spent any more time going through Moss's file after getting Daniella down, sensing Dan needed companionship and comfort. "You recall her?"

"Reporter for the *P-I*. Went missing February 27, 1996. Husband said she left to meet a source in the middle of the night and never came home or showed up at work. We eventually found her locked car in a parking garage with the keys inside, blood on the headrest and steering wheel, and a lot of clutter. Took the standby detectives days to clean it out and get everything inventoried and tested. We found a receipt from a convenience store on Denny Way that confirmed she went out that night around two a.m. She bought a liter of Coke—a bad habit according to the husband and those she worked with. No security camera, and the person working that morning didn't specifically remember Childress coming in, but he did remember her as someone who came in frequently and said she always bought a liter of Coke. Never seen or heard from again."

"You have a good memory."

"And a file. I reviewed it last night." He turned and looked to the tee box. "Hey, Johnson, is that a drive or did you use your putter?"

The man just shook his head and rolled his eyes.

"You kept a file?" Tracy asked. She found it unusual for a detective to keep a file at home.

"Not a complete file, just my report and certain updates. Only case I never solved. It's a pride thing, as I'm sure you can appreciate. I

thought maybe in retirement I'd have time to take a look at it, but truth?
I walked out the door and I never looked back. Not once. Bugged me at
first that I didn't retire with a perfect record, you know? But it was out
of my hands. First time I opened the file again was when the daughter
came to talk to me a few years ago. Second time was when you called
last night. So what's going on? You find a new lead or new witness? Did
the husband confess?"

"No. Nothing like that."

"Why the sudden interest?"

"Daughter asked me to take a fresh look."

"Hell, you must have more than two hundred cold cases."

"Three hundred."

"Three hundred. Seems time would be better spent on cases with
DNA left at the scene . . . with the advances they've recently made."

"That's definitely the trend."

"We ran this down every which way we could and came to the
conclusion that either the husband killed her, or she just took off."

"You were the lead detective?" Tracy asked.

"I worked the case with Keith Ellis. He died a couple years ago.
Shame. Guy retires to spend time with the wife and grandkids, and he
gets a bad cancer. Fought it but couldn't beat it. Okay, we're moving."
Moss hit the pedal, and they sped down the cart path to where his drive
had settled toward the bottom of the sloped fairway. "One minute,
Detective." He got out and, as before, grabbed a club, walked to where
the ball lay, and drove it onto the green. Moss got back in. "So, what
do you want to ask me?"

"Who were your suspects, other than the husband?"

Moss chuckled. "There weren't any, which is why I'm certain it was
the husband. They had financial problems. *He* had financial problems."
Moss repeated what Anita had told Tracy. "New kid, debt, and a wife
who was an odd duck. So what does he do?"

"Convinces her to take out a mutual life insurance policy," Tracy said.

"Bingo. Wife disappears. He gets the money—after he convinces the insurance company that she's dead—pays off his debt, and starts fresh."

"Except he's got a little girl now."

"True."

"No offense, but I don't see many men wanting to raise a daughter alone, without a mother. That's not exactly a fresh start."

"Maybe not. Maybe he had a girlfriend."

"Did he?" Tracy asked, thinking of the high school sweetheart who was now Larry Childress's partner.

"Not that we ever found. Maybe he just wanted the mother out of the picture, or maybe he needed the money and saw no other alternative, or maybe it was a fight that quickly got out of hand. We don't know."

"File didn't indicate any evidence of a fight that got out of hand."

"I'm just saying . . ."

"You said the convenience store checked out, which means Lisa Childress did go out that night?"

"She did. But to get out of the house and away from the husband, or to meet a source? Editor didn't know anything about her meeting a source. What does that leave?"

"Daughter said she didn't always tell the editor what she was doing."

"I recall the editor saying something similar. My point is, we don't know why she went out. Not definitively. The only person who could tell us is gone, and no confidential source ever materialized. So, what's more likely—she met a source in the middle of the night and that source killed her, or she and the husband have a row, and when she takes off to get some fresh air, the husband is home fuming? She comes home. They fight. He kills her. Disposes of her body somewhere and doesn't call us until nearly six p.m. the following evening."

"That long?"

"That long." Moss raised his eyebrows. "Which, as you know, could mean he disposed of the body anywhere and in any number of ways. Didn't I read you had a case about a woman found in a commercial crab pot?"

"I did."

"There you go."

"Did the husband say why he waited so long to report her missing?"

"He said she met sources at all hours of the day and night, and he didn't know anything was wrong until she didn't come home and didn't answer her desk phone. He found her editor's home phone number, and the editor said she had never come in. Hang on. I got to putt."

Moss sped around the back of the first green and got out. He had about a ten-foot putt, lined it up, and drained it. "Tweet-tweet," he said. "Get the birdie juice out, boys." He returned to the cart. "Little celebration we have. A shot of whiskey when someone, usually me, birdies a hole. Would you like one?"

She laughed. "No, thanks. Not while I'm on duty." Not to mention it was eight in the morning. "I assume you went over the car and didn't find anything else of interest besides the receipt and the blood."

"What I recall is we processed the hell out of that car, and it had so much stuff it took a week. We ran the blood type and matched it to her and later matched her DNA."

"Was she bleeding when she went into the convenience store?"

Moss pointed at Tracy. "Thought the same thing. The clerk did not recall anyone coming in that night bleeding."

"Fingerprints?"

"Just hers. All over the car."

"Not the husband's?"

"He said he never drove that car. He had his own car. Nothing to indicate he was in the car."

"So how did her blood get in her car?"

"Not certain. Never figured that out. We got a subpoena for the home but didn't find her blood anywhere, and no evidence of a fight. Nothing. We're moving again." Moss went up a hill to a second tee box, a short par three. As before, he wasted little time, hit the ball high and landed it on the green, then walked back to the cart while his three partners teed off.

"I assume you went through the husband's car?" Tracy said.

"All over it. No blood. Found a set or two of her fingerprints and her hair strands but nothing to indicate he transported a body somewhere."

The report in the file indicated a security guard found Childress's car in a parking structure on Eighth Avenue between Pine and Olive, but not until nearly three weeks after she disappeared.

"Any indication the garage is where she met her source?" Tracy asked.

"Maybe, but then that doesn't explain her blood inside her car."

"They could have talked in her car."

"Nope. Not with the amount of crap in there. Did you pull the photos?"

"I've put in a request."

"You'll see what I mean. We also pulled bank records and found that she'd withdrawn a hundred dollars from the Wells Fargo before going to the convenience store."

It didn't sound like a lot of money, but Tracy imagined a hundred dollars went a lot further back then than it did today.

"What else?" Moss said. "We checked airlines, rental car counters. Didn't find a thing."

"Did they have ATMs in 1996?"

"They did, but ATM cameras didn't come into existence until later that year, so again, no video."

"Any indication of drug or alcohol abuse?"

"Husband said the wife had a glass of wine, and an occasional beer. Never knew his wife to use any drugs, except maybe the caffeine."

"Any idea how the car got to the parking structure if she didn't drive it there?"

"She could have driven there, I suppose, but my two cents? My two cents is the husband put the blood in the car, along with the wife's bag, drove it to the garage wearing gloves, and left it with the keys inside. Probably to hide it, but also maybe to throw us off his scent, make us think his wife took a bus somewhere. The parking structure is just up the hill from the Greyhound station. Again, no security cameras on the streets, in the garage, or at the bus depot back then. So, no way to know for certain."

"Anything else of interest?"

"Not that I can think of, but you'd have to check the evidence log. Like I said, standby detectives went through the car with tweezers."

Tracy specifically thought about the bear spray Anita Childress said her father gave her mother when she went out late at night or early morning. That was unique enough to stand out . . . if the standby detectives found it. "What about close friends?"

"None to speak of."

"None?"

"Husband, parents, editor, and work colleagues all said she was a loner. Colleagues liked her but said she was difficult to get to know, and mostly kept to herself. Rarely socialized with any of them outside the office."

"The daughter said Childress was working on several stories that had the potential to piss off people."

"The argument that she was meeting a confidential source," Moss said. "Like I said, her editors weren't much help. We went to legal and eventually got the subject matter of stories Childress was likely pursuing, but not the names of any sources, confidential or otherwise." Moss shrugged.

"Did you look into the stories?"

"To the extent we could and thought they had legs. I recall one made reference to mayoral corruption—big surprise." Moss laughed. "Mayor Edwards was so crooked he couldn't put on a pair of straight-leg pants, but no one ever caught him—not the FBI or the Justice Department. Another story was allegedly the Route 99 Killer. Her editor thought it unlikely Childress would go undercover, but also said she was a weird duck, so . . ." Moss shrugged. "We never caught the Route 99 Killer, as you know, so we couldn't determine if Childress was one of his victims."

"So, you didn't find anything to support that it could have been someone trying to keep her from writing a story?"

"We pulled the phone records from her home, couldn't get her work calls. My recollection is we accounted for all the calls received and made but one received from a gas station pay phone the evening before she disappeared."

"Someone setting up a meeting for that night?"

"Who knows? Nobody at the gas station recalled seeing anyone making a call, and once again . . ."

"No video back then," Tracy said.

"Let me par this hole."

Moss left the cart. Tracy wasn't sure what to think. It certainly wasn't uncommon for a detective to get a suspect in his or her head and miss other evidence, though it also sounded as if Moss hit legal roadblocks that slowed his investigation.

Moss got back in the cart, and they drove to the third tee, which was elevated high above the fairway. Tracy waited until Moss hit his drive, which hooked to the left and came to rest in the trees. The ball placement didn't seem to faze him, though. When he got back in the cart he said, "Where were we? Oh yeah . . . A newspaper photographer said Childress received a threat from someone under the mayor's thumb. I remember that."

"Anything come of it?"

"Nah. The guy denied it—said he simply told Childress that if she was going to run any kind of investigative piece that put his company in a bad light, he'd like the opportunity to respond."

"What about the neighbors? Anyone confirm they saw or heard a car start up early morning and drive off or maybe return midday?"

"We spoke to the neighbors, but none of them recalled anything like that."

"And nobody saw the husband leave in his car that morning?"

"Somebody did, actually. Saw him leave just before lunch."

"Where did he go?"

"Said he took his daughter to a park."

"You were able to confirm that?"

Moss shrugged. "We found sand in his car."

"Which he could have put in the car to make it look like he went to the park. You process it?"

Moss gave her a condescending grin. "It was sand."

She probably deserved that. "Did any neighbors have any information about the Childresses' relationship?" Tracy asked.

Moss shook his head. "You'll have to check the file notes. I don't recall anything."

They drove down the hill and onto the fairway. Moss hit his second shot from the trees. It landed in a sand trap.

"You losing your concentration, Moss?" one of his foursome called out.

"Yeah, I'm thinking about all the money you're going to owe me."

"I think you're thinking about something, or someone, else."

Moss got back in the cart. "I assume you get that crap all the time. Sorry if it offends."

"It doesn't bother me."

"We never had a female in Homicide when I was there. Not one in twenty-five years."

"I was the first."

"No shit?"

"No shit," Tracy said. "If you were me, Moss, where would you go with this case?"

Moss blew out a blast of air. "I racked my brains for years trying to think of things we could do. Did I tell you my partner and I wanted to send a bulletin to the media and law enforcement, but both the husband and the parents opposed it?"

That definitely seemed odd. "Why would they oppose it?"

"The husband was being hounded by the media. He and his daughter had been ostracized by the community. He said we had made his life intolerable, and he didn't need the story publicized any further at the expense of his daughter."

"And the parents? What was their opposition?"

"They refused to believe Childress would have abandoned her daughter. They were worried, based on the bank withdrawal that night, that she was working undercover, and that the publicity could put her life in danger."

Tracy shook her head, disbelieving.

"Bizarre, huh? After a few weeks, the husband agreed to let us send out a news release but only to law enforcement, not to the media. We got a few hits, pursued those hits, but ultimately, found nothing of interest. As the weeks passed, my partner and I came to the conclusion that unless the husband confessed, or someone arrested for another crime admitted to killing Childress, we were at a dead end. I occasionally worked the case over the years, but when I retired, I had no choice but to send it to cold cases."

"So either the husband killed her, or she took a Greyhound bus and disappeared. But you don't believe she did," Tracy said, summarizing.

"We didn't find any paper trail she did—no credit card receipts, and nobody came forward talking about a woman bleeding at the bus station, which I've got to believe someone would have remembered, though as you probably saw in the file, we didn't find the car until three or four weeks after Childress went missing. But I don't think she just disappeared."

"Why not?"

"Well, it's like you said. I just didn't see a mother up and leaving her child, whatever the reason—bad marriage or not. If she was going to leave, she'd take the kid, wouldn't she?"

Tracy thought of Anita Childress's statement that her father quit his job and stayed home because there had been incidences of her mother leaving her alone to chase a story.

"Normally, one would think that to be the case," Tracy said. But this case seemed to be far from normal.

CHAPTER 5

M oss dropped Tracy off at her car after they came up the fifth fairway. She thanked him for his time, and he provided his cell phone number and told her he would be happy to answer any additional questions.

"I'd like to get this one off the books," he said. "I don't think of it often, but when I do . . . It's like a chore I've never finished. You know what I mean?"

Tracy did.

She left the country club and drove west across the 520 bridge spanning Lake Washington's steel-gray waters. The Seattle skyline popped against a sky streaked with faint cloud trails. She had an interview with Bill Jorgensen, who had been Lisa Childress's city editor at the *Post-Intelligencer* and was now a production editor for the *Times*.

Tracy didn't know what to think of Moss Gunderson. He had certainly lived up to his billing. He definitely glowed. And not just his clothing. Tracy didn't know what type of homicide detective Moss had been. He said he solved every case but Childress, but that didn't necessarily say a lot. Back in his day, according to Del and Faz, detectives couldn't "cherry-pick" their cases, but they could work a sergeant, especially if they were friends, to play favorites. Beyond that, 90 percent of homicides were what Tracy and her colleagues referred to as "grounders"—easy cases to field and to solve. The mysteries were rare. Moss got one. He didn't solve it. He admittedly focused from the start on the husband, as would someone used to fielding grounders. When he couldn't put the evidence together to take a run at the husband, Moss seemed incapable, unwilling, or maybe just too lazy to take the investigation in another direction. Tracy didn't get the impression from her brief review of the file, or from talking to him, despite his bombastic personality, that there had been a lot of outside-the-box thinking.

Maybe it was just Moss's pants that made her think that way. An overstatement. Attention seeking. Neither Faz nor Del would ever wear them. People gravitated to the two of them naturally, like Italians to antipasto. It was the difference between charisma and insecurity. Something behind the gregarious Moss façade shouted *insecure*, but, again, maybe she was just reading too much into the pants or trying to psych herself into believing that she could do what Moss had not. Find Lisa Childress's killer.

Tracy exited the freeway on Stewart Street and maneuvered to Denny Way, where she found street parking, a minor miracle, in an area blocked off to accommodate construction. The *Seattle Times* occupied one of the few remaining industrial-looking, three-story stucco buildings. It wouldn't last much longer, given the high-rise construction going up all around it.

Tracy checked in at a desk on the ground floor to receive clearance, slapped a visitor's badge on her coat lapel, and took an elevator to the third floor. Jorgensen met her when she stepped into the lobby. He had an affable, welcoming face. Balding in a horseshoe pattern, what remained of his brown hair was laced with gray and matched his goatee. He wore jeans and a plaid, short-sleeve shirt.

"Detective Crosswhite," he said.

"Thank you for making time to talk with me," Tracy said.

Jorgensen offered coffee or tea, which Tracy declined. He gestured for her to follow and spoke over his shoulder as they passed by cubicles. She heard the voices of people on the telephone and the clatter of keyboards. "I was surprised to receive your call," Jorgensen said over the din.

"Why is that?"

"Because I've spoken to Anita Childress at some length."

"Recently?"

Jorgensen stepped into a glass-enclosed conference room and shut the door behind Tracy, eliminating the newsroom noise. They moved to cream-colored leather chairs at a conference room table. "Multiple occasions over the years," he said. He pulled out the chair at the head of the table. Tracy sat to his left, with an empty chair between them. "I feel sorry for her, being in a state of limbo like this. I know Anita's motivation." He smiled. "What's Seattle PD's motivation for looking at the file after so many years?"

"I'm working cold cases," Tracy said, matter-of-factly.

"I'm familiar with you and your record, Detective Crosswhite. We covered the Curry Canyon and North Seattle investigations. I'm just curious if anything, in particular, has caused you to reopen this case?"

Jorgensen was a newsman and as such, clearly interested in the news, specifically whether there might be an evolving story about the decades-long disappearance of a Seattle newspaper reporter.

"Nothing specific," she said.

"I was wondering if it could be related to the bodies discovered in Curry Canyon. I thought maybe they found Lisa's body."

"No. Nothing like that."

"I feel like we lost one of our own, you know?"

"I do," Tracy said.

Jorgensen sat back. "So then . . . What can I help you with?"

"I'd like to start by having you tell me about Lisa Childress. What type of reporter was she?"

Jorgensen smiled like the Cheshire cat. "She was a pistol."

"How so?"

"Well . . . how do I put it? Her reporting won the *P-I* three Pulitzers, but she didn't give a crap about awards."

Tracy could relate. "No?"

"Lisa had a nose for a news story and the determination of a bloodhound. She didn't let up until the article went to print."

Tracy detected a hesitancy in Jorgensen's voice. "But . . ."

Jorgensen folded his hands on the table. "But . . . corralling her was next to impossible, and frustrating."

"In what way?"

"In every way." Jorgensen repeated much of what Anita Childress had told Tracy, that her mother hated deadlines and rarely told her editors specifics about what she worked on or her sources.

"Many times, I found myself either scrambling to make space on the front page or trying to fill a last-minute hole. I knew I could count on her for a great story. I just didn't know when I'd get it."

"Her daughter believes she was chasing a lead the night she disappeared."

"I know. And I'll tell you what I told Anita. Because of the nature of this thing—being questioned by the detectives several times all those years ago, and then more recently by Anita, I recall more about this than I otherwise would. You understand what I'm saying?"

"I think so."

"I don't know whether Lisa was meeting a source that night or not. I recall the detective asking me that question. Big guy with an unusual first name."

"Moss Gunderson."

"That's it. I told him what I'm going to tell you. Lisa never told me the names of her confidential sources."

"Just wondering if she could have pissed somebody off enough to kill her."

"I'll leave the speculation to you, Detective."

"Did she tell you what stories she was pursuing before she disappeared?" Tracy asked in a tone meant to convey she didn't completely buy that a reporter would keep the news stories she worked on from her editor.

"I'd get tidbits out of her, Detective. Lisa pursued several investigative stories at a time. I suspect Anita told you about some of the stories she believes Lisa was working on, and I can tell you she knows a heck of a lot more than I ever did."

"What do you recall?"

Again, Jorgensen basically repeated what Anita Childress had told Tracy.

"Anita said she might have been working undercover to try to catch the Route 99 Killer," Tracy said, hoping to get Jorgensen's opinion.

"Lisa was fearless as a reporter, but she never struck me as reckless. I just can't see her taking that path to a story."

"What about the other stories?"

"Hell, we have a file room filled with allegations and innuendo on Mayor Edwards—too much for it to all be bullshit."

"Where there's smoke there's fire?"

"A big fire. But we're a newspaper. We print facts, not innuendo. Something did come up later though, a week or so after Lisa went missing. Her photographer—a guy I assigned to work with her because he was older and had more patience than the younger guys—said that after Lisa had covered a city council meeting Mike Greenhold approached and told her that if she ran a news story about the mayor's business dealings, he'd have something to say about it."

This must have been the threat Moss said Childress received. "Who's Mike Greenhold?"

"Greenhold Construction. His company was doing a lot of projects in Seattle at that time, and he was rumored to be close to Mayor Edwards."

"Do you know what came of it?"

"I gave the police that information and made the photographer available to talk to them."

"Did you ever hear back about it?"

"No. Nothing. I imagine Greenhold denied saying any such thing and it was a he-said-she-said thing, and the 'she' was no longer around."

"What about the other two stories?"

"I recall we had statements from three grown men who told remarkably similar stories about being sexually abused by Peter Rivers when they were under sixteen."

Tracy confirmed that legal consent in Washington at that time was sixteen. Therefore, each allegation, if true, would constitute rape of a child under state law and would have subjected Rivers to possible prison time.

"Were they credible?"

"I'll answer this way. Each similarly described the apartment Rivers rented back then—both its location and the general layout, as well as his certain physical attributes, which only would have been visible if Rivers had his clothes off. But each accuser also had a criminal record for prostitution, drug addiction, robbery, and petty theft." Jorgensen used his fingers to tick off the charges. "And that record got longer as each got older."

"Troubled."

"They didn't exactly project credibility. Two of the men had also known each other as boys at a drug rehabilitation center where Rivers had worked."

"They could have coordinated their stories. And the third?"

"A neighbor who had lived down the street from Rivers."

"So then collectively . . . ?"

"We made the decision to ask Rivers about the three men. He denied the allegations. Said the men were lying. He said if we published the allegations, he would sue us."

"Did you?"

"No, but not because of his threat to sue. We decided that if one or more of Rivers's accusers filed a lawsuit, we would report on the lawsuit. We would not mention other unsubstantiated allegations unless they became part of the suit. If they did, we'd print the allegations in the public record. If not, we wouldn't. We didn't want to unwittingly become part of a political purge, not to mention ruin a man and his family." Jorgensen smiled. "At least not without corroboration."

"But was there some truth then to what Childress had uncovered?"

"Personally? I think there was."

"Which would be very troubling to a man in the public eye thinking about making a run for mayor."

"I'll leave those deductions and insinuations to the police," Jorgensen said.

"Did Childress have your permission to pursue the allegations?"

"Like I said, it was open ended."

"So she did."

"She did."

"And the police skimming drugs and drug money. What came of that?"

"Again, a lot of smoke."

"But no fire."

"Not that I recall."

"Anything about Childress leading up to her disappearance that struck you as different or out of her usual routine?"

"If you talked to Anita, well, then you know Lisa could be quirky."

"Anita mentioned it. When did you last see Lisa Childress?"

"In the office, the day before she disappeared."

"How did she seem to you?"

"From what I recall telling the detectives back then and later telling Anita, something seemed off, but what it was, exactly, I don't know."

"Anything else?" Tracy asked.

"She'd put on weight. Nothing extreme but probably ten pounds. Not surprising, given her diet."

Tracy asked questions for another fifteen minutes but didn't get much more information than she had already received from Anita Childress and Moss Gunderson.

"What do you think happened to her?"

Jorgensen put up his hands. "Not my place to say, Detective."

"No, but you knew her. Was she capable of just disappearing? Walking away?"

Jorgensen looked uncomfortable. "Was she capable? Yeah. I'd say she was capable, but I don't think that's what she did."

"Because she had a daughter."

He shook his head. "Because she had *stories* she was working. I can't see her leaving those stories unfinished. I know how that must sound, but I think it would have driven her crazy to not finish *a story*, let alone to leave several unfinished."

"Was she obsessive?"

"She was about her stories."

"You think it's more likely that something nefarious happened."

"I wish I didn't, but . . ." Jorgensen shrugged. "That would be my conclusion."

CHAPTER 6

As Tracy made her way back to Police Headquarters on Fifth Avenue, she wondered if she had bitten off more than she could chew, if her empathy for Anita Childress had led her to pick a case that couldn't go anywhere. Statistically, when a young woman went missing, the odds were overwhelmingly against finding her alive, and those odds only worsened with the passage of time, especially if Lisa Childress had been sticking her nose in dangerous places.

Tracy found herself at an early crossroads.

She either had to accept, as Moss had accepted, that Larry Childress killed his wife and disposed of her body, in which case she agreed with Moss's assessment that unless Larry Childress confessed and provided details, the investigation had reached a dead end. Or, she had to assume Larry Childress was innocent, and Lisa Childress was killed by someone trying to conceal illegal activity. In which case, Tracy needed to get a much better handle on the four investigations Lisa Childress had been pursuing, somehow determine how far Childress had delved into each story, whom she had spoken with, and whether there had been any threats, other than the one by Greenhold, and whether those threats should have been considered serious.

Maybe Moss hadn't been lazy. Maybe he'd just been practical.

Anita Childress had already done much of the legwork. Tracy just needed time to get up to speed, then devise a course of action.

Inside her office, Tracy put her desk phone on "Do Not Disturb," cleared space by putting the black binders of cases she had solved in a box to be closed and sent back to storage, and pulled out the four manila files Anita Childress had provided. She decided to start with the file that most interested her—Lisa Childress's investigation into police corruption. It was hard to stomach the thought of bad cops on the take, but having once worked in the Narcotics Unit, Tracy knew Washington to be a narcotics distribution point because it bordered Canada, which provided drug dealers with an assortment of ways to smuggle drugs into the state—by car, by boat, by train, or by plane, and those planes could land in remote wilderness locations, including on lakes and rivers.

She'd also read and heard of instances of narcotics agents being corrupted in cities like Los Angeles and Miami, especially in the 1980s, when cocaine distribution escalated sharply. Her narcotics training had included classes on corruption, and she learned of police officers stealing drugs from one dealer and reselling them to another, an act known as "trading licks." In other schemes, police used an undercover cop to make a large drug purchase, busted the deal, then drove to a secluded location and divvied up the take.

Corruption could start innocently. An idealistic young officer, with the best of intentions, graduates from the Academy and sees the world in black and white, right and wrong. Then that officer sees other officers bend the rules, just slightly, to justify a conviction. The bend might be a search that goes a little too far. The officer is told it happens all the time. He wants to be a team player, to be accepted, so he acquiesces. His first mistake. The officer then must fabricate a report to cover up the overaggressive search. Again, no big deal. The case goes to trial, and the officer perjures his testimony to safeguard the false report justifying the search that went too far.

And it works.

The perpetrator is convicted. The officers don't get caught. No harm. No foul.

And each time it becomes a little easier to bend the rules until the officer starts to justify taking the money and reselling the drugs.

Tracy flipped through Childress's notes and came to a copy of a police report that detailed an investigation into two bodies found floating in Lake Union. Nothing in the report indicated drugs or a drug bust. Interesting. Police had responded to a 911 call from the Diamond Marina on Lake Union in November 1995. Tracy read the name of the two responding detectives. Del Castigliano had been the lead detective, and his partner had been Moss Gunderson. Del had to have been a relative newbie on the homicide team in 1995, when he transferred into Seattle from Madison, Wisconsin.

Tracy flipped through the report. The decedents were two men of Mexican heritage estimated to be in their late twenties to early thirties. The two men were subsequently identified by the border patrol as Ayax Florez Navarro and Juvenal Lucio Ibarra, both from Mexico. They had prior convictions for drug smuggling and had been linked to a drug cartel in Oaxaca.

Okay, so the case *was* about drugs. She flipped to the medical examiner's report, which said the two men had drowned. Each had alcohol and cocaine in his system.

Tracy flipped through the rest of the report but did not find any reference to a boat on which the two men had been working, or how they otherwise turned up floating in the water at Lake Union. Del had concluded the two had fallen overboard, from some boat or pier, and drowned, and he closed the file. His conclusion seemed convenient and, at best, sloppy, even for a detective working his first homicide.

Lisa Childress had filed Freedom of Information Act requests to obtain any and all police records, including records from the Harbor Patrol, with information on a boat named the *Egregious*. She was advised that no such responsive documents existed. Tracy figured Childress believed the *Egregious* had been the boat from which Navarro and Ibarra had fallen, a drug-smuggling boat perhaps, but nothing in her file, or in Del's file, supported that deduction.

Tracy turned more pages and came to a xeroxed copy of handwritten notes in what looked like a reporter's six-by-nine-inch notebook. Written at the top of the page and underlined twice were the words "The Last Line."

Tracy struggled to decipher further scribblings and eventually came up with:

Diamond Marina

Egregious/Canadian

HM D. S.

That boat name again. The name of the marina. She had no idea what "The Last Line" or "HM D. S." meant, but she made a note to find out. She shifted her attention and her fingers to her keyboard and typed "Seattle" and "The Last Line" in a search engine, then scrolled through hits for online jewelry, a literary journal, and a book of that name. She gave the search some thought and added "1990s." She scrolled again until she found an article from the *Post-Intelligencer*, though not written by Lisa Childress.

The article detailed how, as the flow of drugs into Puget Sound increased with the surge in cocaine and marijuana use, the State of Washington had put together twenty-four task forces, covering 75 percent of the state. One of those task forces, created by Seattle PD, had been known as "the Last Line." According to the article, except for the task force's sergeant, Rick Tombs, the members were anonymous and wore face coverings during raids to protect their identities. An unnamed source said the Last Line was a reference to the public's last line of defense. Tombs was quoted as saying the task force members ranged in experience from new recruits to SWAT team veterans. Some officers were generational cops and veterans of the Gulf War. Each had been seriously vetted.

> Sergeant Rick Tombs, a fifteen-year veteran narcotics officer, described how undercover narcotics agents could take weeks to set up a buy. When the buy goes down, Last Line officers go in fast and heavily armed. The money seized is locked in a safe at the Public Safety Building until a forfeiture crew can do a specific count. The drugs are registered and locked in the evidence room to be later weighed.

> Tombs said the officers wear masks to conceal their identity. "We don't want anyone to offer a bribe or possibly to threaten that officer and his family."

Tracy finished the article and went back to the other Google hits, pulling up and reading an article written in April 2002 about the Last Line being absorbed into the narcotics division during a reorganization. When done, Tracy looked at notes she'd jotted down while going through the file.

Two dead bodies at a marina.

Both men undocumented.

A boat name but no record of that boat.

A Seattle drug task force.

Tracy set the file aside and stretched her arms over her head. She picked up her "World's Best Mom" coffee mug, but the coffee had gone cold. The afternoon malaise began to cloud her thinking. She could use another cup before she moved on to the next file.

She made her way to the kitchen. Faz and Del leaned against the sink counter, talking. They each had rolled up the cuffs of their long-sleeve shirts and lowered their ties.

"Look what the cat drug in," Faz said. "The überfamous Tracy Crosswhite."

"Bite me, Faz. Just the two of you slouching in here? Where's Kins?"

"That murder up north went to trial. He's sitting next to the prosecutor at counsel table for the next five weeks, and he isn't happy about it," Faz said. "Heard Rosa identified more bodies in that canyon."

"And I heard the chief is genuflecting when she comes down to your office," Del said, putting up his hands and bowing.

"You can bite me too, Del."

"Of course the chief comes to Tracy," Faz said, laughing. "She might justify the entire police budget by herself." He, too, bowed.

"Again, bite me."

"Sleeping over all those dead bodies," Faz said, referring to the house in North Seattle where the forensic medical examiner had found the seven buried bodies. "Man, that's creepy. Gives me the willies just thinking about it."

"That's why they call them psychopaths, Faz. They don't get the willies," Del said.

"How's my goddaughter?" Faz asked, changing subjects.

Tracy took a moment to brag, telling them of Daniella's vocabulary and other tricks. She knew they weren't that interested, but they were always polite. She curbed her enthusiasm and turned the conversation to Faz. "How's Antonio's restaurant doing?" Faz's only son, a chef, had opened an Italian restaurant to rave reviews and heavy foot traffic.

"He's doing well," Faz said. He reached back and knocked on the cabinets. "His take-out business has exploded, especially on the weekends."

"You're looking at the delivery driver." Del threw a thumb in the direction of his partner. "Faz the Uber driver."

"I'm just helping him out nights is all. Might as well, with Vera not home."

"Where's Vera?" Tracy asked.

"She's . . . what do you call it? One of those chefs who does the easy things; you know, boils the ravioli and the noodles, and does all the preparation." Faz dumped the remnants of his coffee into the sink. "Okay, I have now drunk a sufficient amount of coffee that all systems are go and I'm percolating."

Tracy shook her head and called after him as he left the room. "TMI, Faz."

"It's worse when he mentions these things just before lunch," Del said.

"You got a second?" Tracy asked Del.

"A second? With Faz in the can I have way more than a second."

"I spent some time this morning with Moss Gunderson."

"I'm sorry." Del tilted his head left then right as if looking for something.

"What?" Tracy said. "Did I spill?"

"I was just checking to see if you still have both ears."

Tracy laughed. "He is a talker."

"Did he tell you how he got the name Moss?"

"A rolling stone gathers no moss."

"Then he remains true to form." He leaned back against the counter and crossed his arms. "What were you meeting with him about?"

"A cold case. Lisa Childress." Del blinked and his face went blank. He then looked to recover. It was subtle, but Tracy noticed it. "Ring any bells?" she asked.

"No. Should it?"

"Reporter for the *P-I* went missing almost twenty-five years ago. The only case Moss never resolved."

"I remember something about a reporter going missing, but I wasn't working with Moss then."

"No. His partner was Keith Ellis."

"May he rest in peace. What I remember is Moss kept telling everyone the husband killed her, but he couldn't get any traction. I just don't think he wanted an open file on his otherwise perfect record."

"Pretty much sums it up."

"Why are you looking at it? You get some new information?"

"No. Nothing like that. The daughter is grown now and a reporter for the *Seattle Times*. She asked me to take a look at her mother's file."

"Father still alive?"

"He is, and I brought up how she might feel if I determined it was her father."

"What'd she say?"

"She just wants the truth. She's tired of living in limbo."

"But she doesn't have anything new?"

"She pieced together some files that her mother was pursuing back then."

"What kind of files?"

"Investigative stories she was looking into. Your name came up in one of the files." Tracy had been thinking about how best to broach the topic. She didn't want to just say, *man, you did a crappy job.*

"My name?" Del said, though he didn't look or sound surprised. "What file?"

"You and Moss responded to two bodies found floating in the water on Lake Union."

"Vaguely rings a bell."

"You were lead detective."

"I think that was my first year on Homicide."

Tracy thought Del's lack of memory odd. She remembered her first homicide case in detail.

"It wasn't called Violent Crimes back then. Just Homicide. Mexicans, right? Illegals, if I'm recalling the case correctly?"

"You are," she said.

"Moss gave me lead. I thought because he trusted me, but probably more because he was going through a nasty divorce at that time. What about it?"

"You and Moss ever determine how the two men ended up in the lake?"

"Geez, Tracy, that had to be almost twenty-five years ago. I'd have to look at the file, see what it says. Is it important?"

"I don't know. But I pulled the file. It doesn't really say anything except the two men were determined to be undocumented and likely fell from a boat."

"Well, then I guess that's all there was."

"Lisa Childress was working on a story about a boat called 'the *Egregious*.'"

"Yeah?"

"You know of it?"

"No."

"She filed a Freedom of Information Act request but came up empty."

Del made a sour face and shook his head.

"Do you remember who called in the two bodies?" Tracy asked.

"I don't."

"Or who you interviewed?"

"I'm sure witness interviews would be in the file and a lot more accurate than my memory."

"Just wondering if you and Moss might have looked into whether the two bodies were somehow related to a boat smuggling drugs."

"It's a good theory, I suppose. What did Moss have to say?"

"I learned about Childress's file after speaking to him."

"You might want to ask him."

"Yeah. Yeah, I think I will. Just thought since you were here and the lead . . ."

"No problem." Del started from the room.

"Did you ever hear about a narcotics team called 'the Last Line'?"

Del stopped and turned back. "Knew of it. One of many task forces set up in the state in the late eighties. Some were multijurisdictional. SPD's was just narcotics officers. Why?"

"Childress seemed to be looking into it as well. What did you know about them?"

"Not a lot. I think the name was supposed to mean they were the last line of defense between drugs and citizens. But I also heard it had to do with cocaine."

"Cocaine?"

"Yeah, you know, 'the last line.'"

Tracy got it. "You ever hear of any controversies?"

"Like what?"

"I don't know. Seems like Childress thought the marina story and this task force could be related somehow."

"She was an investigative reporter, Tracy. When's the last time you read an investigative story on something positive? Controversy sells. But to answer your question, no. I never heard anything about that unit." Del started from the room, then stopped. After a beat he turned back. "Moss exaggerates," he said. "For the impact."

CHAPTER 7

B ack in her office, Tracy thought about what Del had said, but more about the way he had looked at her when she first mentioned the name Lisa Childress. After a decade working together, she had come to know his expressions, or tells. Faz and Kins had them as well, as did she. Faz said Tracy got a struck-by-lightning look when something clicked. Del had looked and sounded like Tracy had brought up a subject he did not want to talk about, but he also didn't want to tell her that.

Moss exaggerates. For the impact.

She wasn't exactly sure what Del had meant, though she could definitely see the truth in the statement after meeting Moss that morning. His orange pants certainly were for effect, and his grandiose personality also might have been. Did he tell stories to match his personality and clothing? To be the life of the party? He was the life of the foursome.

At her desk, Tracy thought of the double entendre. The Last Line. A line of defense or a line of cocaine? Like Moss's colorful outfit, the name could have been camouflage, to hide the truth about the task force.

Tracy opened the file on Councilman Peter Rivers and quickly went through the three statements of the men who alleged Rivers abused them in their teens. As Bill Jorgensen had told her that morning, the stories were remarkably similar, and it would have been difficult to conclude all three men were lying were it not for their arrest records, which cast shadows over their allegations, the kind of shadows a good lawyer could use to make an accuser look like an opportunistic thief.

There was smoke, certainly, and maybe even some burning embers, but had that fire ever flamed? Had Childress found another accuser, someone to throw gasoline on the embers and make it all explode? If so, had Childress pushed too far and forced a man under siege into a corner he had to fight his way out of to protect himself and his family?

She set the Peter Rivers file aside and opened the thinnest of Childress's four files, a manila folder she expected to be the Route 99 serial killer file, but the tab read "Angel of Death." The moniker gave her pause because she'd never heard it. Tracy had an intentionally sheltered childhood. Her parents had moved before her birth from Seattle to Cedar Grove, a tiny town in the North Cascades, but Tracy might as well have been raised on the moon. What news reached Cedar Grove arrived slowly and sparingly. Most was irrelevant to the small town. The residents didn't discuss it. Her parents took her and her sister into Seattle once a year during the Christmas holidays for a fancy dinner and whatever holiday play was being performed at the 5th Avenue Theatre. Cedar Grove residents, however, made sure their young women knew of the Route 99 serial killer and his victims, even before Cedar Grove resident Heather Johansen disappeared in 1993, six months before Tracy's sister, Sarah, had also disappeared. Paranoia and hysteria set in, but neither disappearance was related to the Route 99 Killer.

Having once been head of the Cowboy serial killer task force, Tracy had a hunch about the name "Angel of Death," and she opened the file, finding newspaper clippings. Beneath the articles she found notes on the same spiral notebook paper written in what she now recognized to be Lisa Childress's handwriting. The notes looked to be of media briefings held by the task force charged with finding the killer. The task force lead was none other than her current captain and nemesis: Johnny Nolasco. To protect the public, but also to generate potential leads, the task force provided broad details on the nature of the killings, on the victims, as well as an FBI profiler's description of what the killer might look like—his race, size, and possible background.

On the final page, Tracy found five names—Childress had drawn a line through three of the five names. Beneath those names, she had drawn what appeared to be two question marks facing one another. Beneath the question marks she had scribbled three more lines.

ʕ?

Angel's Wings

Carved. Left Shoulder

Angel of Death

The question marks did look like angel's wings. Tracy flipped again to the beginning of the file and reread the *Post-Intelligencer* articles, as well as Childress's notes of press briefings, but none of it mentioned the symbol, nor the moniker "Angel of Death." She was not sure if the notes represented that the killer had a tattoo or something more nefarious. She looked again at the word "Carved" and felt a chill. She read the articles but did not find an instance that indicated the task force had disseminated the name to the general public or to the media. Task forces were paranoid about the release of information to ensure the police arrested the right person and not a copycat killer. To get information that had not been released to the general public or, from what Tracy could decipher, to the media, Childress either had a source within the task force, a source with intimate knowledge of its workings, or possibly someone inside the medical examiner's office. Tracy clicked the keyboard and entered SPD's cold case files, pulling up the Route 99 serial killer file. The investigation had never been closed, but when the killer went dormant, and remained dormant, the task force had disbanded, and the victims' files became cold cases. The task force concluded the killer had either died or possibly been picked up and incarcerated for a different crime and would spend the rest of his days in prison.

Maybe, but that kind of speculation didn't sit well with Tracy. Just like the families of the victims in Curry Canyon, the thirteen families of the Route 99 victims had lived for decades without closure. She'd mark the file and keep it at the top of her stack.

She considered the names of the members of the task force and recognized two besides Nolasco. Moss Gunderson and Vic Fazzio. Tracy pulled up three of the victims' files on her computer and found their autopsies. As Tracy suspected, in each of the three cases, the medical examiner had noted, and photographed, the angel's wings just above each woman's left shoulder blade.

Tracy flipped again to the last page and considered the five names Childress had scribbled. Were these suspect names? If so, Tracy had a hunch as to why Childress had crossed out three of the five names. The task force, or Childress, had likely eliminated the three as the killer.

At her computer she typed the three men's names into four federal databases: the National Crime Information Center—NCIC; the Combined DNA Index System—CODIS; the Integrated Automated Fingerprint Identification System—IAFIS; and the Violent Crime Apprehension Program—ViCAP.

Within minutes, she had confirmed two of the three men had spent time incarcerated in Washington state prisons. She didn't bother to read their profiles. She checked the dates of their incarcerations and compared those dates to those of the most recent Route 99 killings. Both men had been incarcerated at the time of the thirteenth victim's killing—one had also been incarcerated when the eleventh and twelfth victims were killed. Neither could have been the Route 99 Killer.

She searched for the third name and found a copy of a Georgia state driver's license with an address in Pierce County, Georgia. The license had been obtained shortly before the dates of the twelfth and thirteenth killings, making it unlikely the man had been the Route 99 Killer.

Could Childress have tried to lure one of the two remaining suspects to a meeting? Jorgensen had described Childress as an odd duck, but not reckless. Could she have believed bear spray would protect her? Tracy ran the two remaining names through the same federal databases. She did not receive a hit for Dwight McDonnel, meaning he had never been arrested for a crime, but didn't rule him out as the killer. The second man, Levi Bishop, had been incarcerated in Washington State for domestic abuse, a felony, not long after the thirteenth victim was killed. He spent six years at the Monroe Correctional Complex, received parole in 1999, and, after probation, moved to Idaho. Tracy would check the National Crime Information Center but doubted the Angel of Death Task Force would have remained disbanded if Idaho suddenly had a rash of killings of young women with their left shoulders carved with angel's wings.

She ran the name Dwight Thomas McDonnel through a general Google database but did not get a hit. She'd also run McDonnel's name through other databases to try to find out where he had lived the past thirty years, then determine if there had been any unsolved abductions or murders of young women in those areas.

Tracy set the file aside and was about to reach for the final file on Mayor Edwards when she noted the time in the lower right corner of her computer screen. It neared the end of the day and she wanted to get home at a reasonable hour. With one more thing on her to-do list, she picked up the phone and called an extension she knew well.

Faz answered on the second ring. "Violent Crimes. You bag 'em, we tag 'em."

"Funny," she said.

"To what do I owe this unexpected pleasure?"

"You got a minute?"

Faz didn't immediately answer, and Tracy mentally pictured him checking his wristwatch.

"I could spare a few. Wouldn't mind getting out of here a little early though. What are you thinking?"

"High Bar?"

Another pause. Faz's prime factors in his choice of bars and restaurants were walking distance and price. The High Bar was one thousand feet atop the Columbia Center, the building kitty-corner to Police Headquarters. Tracy and Dan were members; Dan used the bar to schmooze clients, which he could write off. Tracy got the membership benefit by virtue of the wedding ring. "I'm buying," she said.

"I'm drinking. I'll be by in a minute."

CHAPTER 8

On the walk from Police Headquarters to the Columbia Center, Tracy and Faz caught up on things at home and recent cases, including Kinsington Rowe's marathon in a King County courtroom. She missed this aspect of working on the A Team, the camaraderie she had with the other three members, and the chance to talk about things other than work. They rode one of the multiple elevator banks to reach the High Bar atop the seventy-six-story black monolith. The view and weather remained heavenly; the sky free of all but a few cirrus clouds hovering over the Emerald City. Veteran Seattleites never questioned good weather. They just enjoyed it. The rain would return soon enough.

Tracy and Faz sat at a table on the west side of the tower and looked down on Elliott Bay's sparkling water and the wakes created by crossing ferries and speedboats. On the horizon lingered an orange haze, which had never existed when Tracy first moved back to Seattle some twenty years ago. Hopefully, the next wind would blow it out to sea.

Faz ordered a Manhattan and munched on cashews from a bowl. Tracy ordered a cosmopolitan.

After more small talk, Faz said, "So, again, to what do I owe this great pleasure, or did you just miss my company?"

"I miss your company," Tracy said. Faz was like a big brother. He teased her, but he cared for her. "And I miss Del and Kins as well."

"Don't you get lonely working those files on your own? It would drive me bonkers. I got to talk to people, reason things out."

"I do sometimes," she said. "But for now, Cold Cases has its advantages, mainly that I get home at a decent hour to spend family time."

Faz pointed at her. "That's important. Don't give that up. I see Antonio and I can't believe he's a grown man. It goes by quick."

"Any new wedding plans?" They'd called off the wedding for now and were waiting until they could actually celebrate.

"Not that he's telling me or his mother. And trust me, Vera could get a Cold War spy to sing. She's chomping at the bit to become a nonna. Me, not so much."

"Why not?"

"Gonna make me feel older than I already feel, being a grandfather. I'll settle for godfather for now."

The cocktail waitress brought their drinks and more cashews. They declined food or menus.

"*Salute.*" Faz raised his glass.

Tracy returned the gesture. "*Salute.*" The cosmopolitan was strong with a touch of bitters. "I need to ask you about something."

Faz grabbed another handful of cashews. "Shoot."

"I'm working a cold case, Lisa Childress."

"The newspaper reporter."

"You got a good memory."

"Not that good. Del mentioned you were working it."

"When?"

"Yesterday or today. Said the daughter got ahold of you."

"How'd that come up?"

"Just shooting the shit. Maybe he said you asked him about Moss Gunderson."

"I did. What was your impression of Moss?"

"A blowhard."

"You worked with him on the Angel of Death Task Force."

Faz paused his chewing midcashew. "Angel of Death?"

"The Route 99 Killer."

"I know what you meant. I was wondering how you know the name 'Angel of Death.' We kept that within the task force."

It confirmed what Tracy had reasoned. The task force didn't release the information. "Childress had the name in her notes."

"I'm not following, Tracy. How the hell would a reporter know that?"

"That's what I'm wondering." She told Faz about the investigative files Childress had been working at the time she disappeared. "It seems she had a source."

"It does," Faz agreed.

"Any idea who might have been her source?"

"Wasn't me. I was a young pup back then, just doing what I was told and trying not to get in any trouble."

"Anyone you can think of?"

"I don't even remember all the task force team members, Tracy. Moss liked to run his mouth, as you already know, but I don't see him leaking task force information. What is he going to get out of it?"

"Maybe he just wanted to look like the center of attention, a big shot with all the answers."

Faz made a face and shook his head. "Seems like a stretch."

"Why the pause?"

"Moss changed when he got divorced."

"What do you mean?"

"His wife left him for a younger man with a lot of money. He became bitter and not a lot of fun to be around. It's understandable."

"When was this?"

"When he and Del worked together. Then he found himself a young wife, evened the score, I suppose, and went back to being the obnoxious Moss we all knew."

"What about Nolasco?" Tracy said. "He likes the limelight, especially if it increases his chances of getting in a reporter's pants." She was thinking specifically of Maria Vanpelt, the Channel 8 reporter with whom Nolasco had a relationship, though well after the Angel of Death Task Force.

"Possible, and I can see what he might get out of the relationship, but would he have been that reckless?"

"How'd he become the task force lead?" Tracy asked.

"He caught the first couple of killings and pieced them together," Faz said. "You know how it is, 'No solved crime goes unpunished,'" he said, repeating another Faz mantra. He ate another cashew, then he added, "Del said you were also asking about the Last Line."

Again, Tracy wondered why Del would bring up the subject with Faz. "Childress was investigating the possibility they were skimming money from drug busts."

"How'd it come up?"

"I don't know for certain, but I found her notes in a file about two bodies floating in Lake Union. Moss and Del handled it. Del was lead. He seemed reticent to talk much about it."

Faz sipped his drink. Tracy got the impression he was buying time. Stalling. "What is it, Faz? I can tell you're holding back."

"No. Not really. It's just that a lot of smoke surrounded the Last Line. They had a lot of success. Too much, some people might say."

"Someone was tipping them?"

"Maybe."

"That might just be good police work."

"Might have been," Faz said, but he didn't sound like he believed it.

"I found notes to indicate that maybe Lisa Childress had a source, like the Angel of Death case."

"Like I said, Tracy. There were rumors. I didn't know anything definitively."

"Del never said anything about it?"

"You should talk to him."

"He didn't seem to want to talk." When Faz didn't respond, Tracy said, "Any idea why the Last Line was disbanded?"

"I think narcotics expanded and took over."

"Nothing came of the rumors?"

"Why? Something else come up?"

"No. Just curious."

Faz peered as if looking through her. "Listen, I know you're doing your job, but you be careful what stones you turn over, Tracy. You got a husband and a little girl now to take care of and watch over."

"What's that mean, Faz?"

He took a sip of his drink and set it down. "The Last Line . . . *if* they were doing those things . . . then they were also prepared to protect themselves from getting caught and going to jail. You know what I'm saying?"

"Is that based on anything specific, Faz?"

He popped a few more cashews. Then he said, "Just thirty years of studying human nature. The strongest biological urge may be to procreate, but it's not far ahead of man's innate compulsion to protect himself."

CHAPTER 9

Tracy left the High Bar thinking of all the embers burning around Moss Gunderson and wondering how they had not individually or collectively conflagrated. Moss had been the investigating detective on the Lisa Childress case, which was never resolved; a member of the Route 99 serial killer task force, never solved; and Del's partner on the investigation into two drownings at the Diamond Marina, which seemed perfunctorily solved. Why? Why was Childress investigating drownings? The logical conclusion was the drownings had something to do with drugs and the Last Line.

But how, exactly?

Tracy arrived home to the pungent smell of garlic, onions, spicy Italian sausage, and tomatoes. Dan's pasta sauce simmered on the stove top, and the recipe called for enough garlic to ward off at least three vampires. Daniella sat in her high chair, struggling to pick up an assortment of Cheerios and peas and guide them into her mouth. Judging by the number she had discarded on the floor, two things were apparent. She was failing more than succeeding, and Rex and Sherlock were locked in the backyard. The pediatrician told Tracy that letting Daniella feed herself was good for developing her dexterity.

Daniella smiled and kicked her legs and arms when Tracy entered the kitchen. "Mama." She held out her hands, peas squashed between her chubby fingers.

"How's my little angel?" Tracy said.

"Your little angel was tossing food over the side of her chair to Rex and Sherlock," Dan said. "And getting a big kick out of herself doing it."

Tracy kissed Daniella's cheeks, and her baby smiled and kicked harder. "Figured that was why the two hounds weren't in here."

"Rex and Sherlock acted like they hit the jackpot on the dollar slot machines in Vegas," Dan said. "She laughed uproariously, as Therese likes to say."

Tracy grabbed paper towels and ran them under the faucet, then cleaned up Daniella. "You're home early," she said.

"I didn't really work today. Just a few hours in the home office."

She threw the paper towels into the garbage, lifted Daniella from the chair, then kissed Dan. "Everything okay?"

"Still feeling numb from Ted Simmons's suicide," he said.

"You all right?"

Dan sighed. "I will be. Just . . ."

He shook his head. Tracy waited. Daniella pressed her hands to Tracy's cheeks, and Tracy pretended to eat her fingers.

"I just wonder if I could have handled things differently," Dan said. "Maybe I shouldn't have pushed him to go forward. Maybe if I had spent more time listening to his concerns . . ." Dan shook his head. "I got wrapped up in beating that little shit at the city attorney's office, and I can't help but think I missed signs that might have saved Ted."

Tracy knew regret was much harder to live with than failure. Regret caused you to second-guess what you hadn't done. "That's an awful burden to put on your shoulders, Dan."

"I know."

"Take it from someone who spent years wondering if she could have saved her father. People who commit suicide, especially men, have their minds made up, and there's little anyone can say or do to dissuade them."

Dan looked to the pot of boiling water and changed the subject. "I thought we could have my famous pasta—"

"Infamous," Tracy said, trying to get him to smile.

"Open a good bottle of wine to go with it, get Daniella down early, and watch a movie."

"Whew," she whispered and ran a hand dramatically across her forehead. "For a minute I thought you were going to end that sentence with *and make love*."

"That's not a bad option either."

"Unfortunately, Little Miss Dog Feeder needs her bath, and after we both eat your infamous sauce, we won't be able to stand being in the same room together."

"Garlic's a little overpowering?"

"Like a stake through the heart of Count Dracula."

"Well, we still have option A."

"I'll get Daniella a bath and open the door for the hounds to clean up her mess," Tracy said. She got a whiff of Daniella and lifted her up to smell her diaper. "Speaking of odors . . ."

—

Forty minutes later, Daniella was in her crib, and Tracy cleaned up what remained of the sauce on her plate with a piece of garlic bread. "Nothing like garlic and garlic," she said.

Dan refilled her wineglass. "How was your day?"

"You want to get more depressed?" Tracy asked.

Dan smiled. "Helps me to change the subject."

"Okay." Tracy set her plate aside, picked up her glass, and sipped her wine, a Barolo from the Piedmont region of Italy and generally considered the finest of Italian reds. Dan had talked of putting a wine cellar in the basement, and he had been trying different wines to stock. She told him about Anita Childress and about what Tracy had learned about Anita's missing mother. "It was originally considered a missing person case, not a homicide."

"And how are you considering it?"

"Homicide. I don't have any doubt she's dead."

"Has anyone considered otherwise?"

"It's statistics, Dan. Unless a missing woman is found within forty-eight hours, the odds of her being alive are greatly diminished. After twenty-five years . . ."

"What if it was neither of those?"

"Neither of what was neither of those?"

"That was a mouthful. Maybe we should cut off the wine." He moved the bottle to the side. "I meant, what if Childress wasn't abducted. Then maybe she isn't dead."

"The odds strongly favor that she is dead."

"But odds are only created if a probability exists that there is an alternative."

"Speaking of cutting someone off . . . Did you open a bottle of wine before I got home, Dan O'Leary? The probability she is alive is extremely low."

"If she was abducted. What if she just walked away?"

"And left her child? Her daughter? I've considered it, but I'm having a hard time believing it."

"It would increase her odds of getting away with it, then, wouldn't it?"

"How?"

"Because people would think just as you're thinking—that a mother would never leave a daughter."

Tracy considered Dan's reasoning—circular, for certain, but tough to refute. "Maybe. But the evidence strongly indicates Larry Childress killed her."

"Maybe you're right. I'm just saying her walking away is another possibility to consider. Doesn't sound like anyone ever looked at it seriously."

Tracy knew that it was a possibility, particularly if Childress's autism affected the way she related to being a mother. She didn't know much about autism, but she wondered if perhaps Lisa Childress thought her daughter would be just fine without her, as Anita had intimated happened when her mother pursued a story. Still, she didn't think it likely.

"It's a possibility, but not a probability."

"So then why are you concerning yourself with her investigative files if you think the husband killed her?"

Tracy knew why. "Honestly, because I don't want to tell a woman who lost a mother that she's also going to lose a father. I don't think she fully understands the ramifications of what that might mean."

"You're protecting her."

"I don't want to give her the false hope that her mother might be alive. I thought maybe if I could find enough evidence to indicate it could have been someone other than her father, that would at least be something she could take solace in."

"Everyone who buys a lottery ticket has false hope, Tracy, even the person who actually wins. People figure, *What can it hurt to buy the ticket and entertain that false hope?*"

"Again, maybe I've had a glass too much, but not following . . ."

"What can it hurt Anita Childress if you run it up the flagpole that maybe her mother took off?"

"Once again, Dan O'Leary, you are the eternal optimist, but I get your point."

"Maybe I am. I'd rather be the guy actually holding that winning lottery ticket, but . . . even I'm not that eternal of an optimist."

CHAPTER 10

The day had dawned with early-morning sprinkles, and Tracy returned to the Macrina Bakery. Anita Childress came in dressed in jeans, tennis shoes, and a green-and-black Gore-Tex jacket. She looked like a young girl. She wasn't, of course, but Tracy already felt protective of her, for what Anita had been through. Tracy sat in the same booth at the back, and Childress climbed onto the chair across from her with an expression of concern and curiosity.

"Sorry I'm a few minutes late. Had to take care of something at work," Childress said.

"No problem."

"You spoke to Bill Jorgensen," Childress said.

"I did."

"Does this mean you're pursuing my mother's files?"

Tracy got to the reason for calling and asking for this meeting. "Last night my husband said something that made me realize perhaps I wasn't pursuing your mother's case as fully as I should."

"What did he say?"

"He asked me what if your mother wasn't abducted. What if she just walked away?" Tracy studied Childress for a reaction. The young woman nodded knowingly and gave a small shrug. "I know you've considered that possibility," Tracy said.

"Many times," Childress said. "As I said, I even asked my grandmother about it, but she's defensive."

"How would you feel if that is what happened?"

"I guess I'd be overjoyed to learn she was alive, but emotionally conflicted because it would mean she left me. I don't really know how I might react."

"You've been proceeding, then, under the assumption that your mother is not alive."

"I know the odds are not good, and I've reconciled myself to what might await me, but I don't think it can be worse than living in limbo. It's like you start out each day in one place, live your day, and think you're moving forward; then I suddenly think about her and I realize I'm right back at the same spot that I started."

Groundhog Day. Tracy thought of the Bill Murray movie with Andie MacDowell. Most people considered the movie a comedy—a man reliving Groundhog Day in the same small town over and over. Tracy saw it as a sad commentary on her life for many years. It wasn't until she determined what had happened to her sister, Sarah, as hard as that had been, that she could move forward with her life.

"I'm tired of it," Childress said. "I'm tired of the speculation, and I grew tired of the innuendo and the whispers. I'm tired for myself, and I'm tired for my father. As I told you before, I just want to know the truth."

"I understand," Tracy said.

"I'd hoped you would," Childress said.

"Here's what I'd like to do. I'd like to continue exploring the files you gave me. In that respect, I'd like to speak with your father. I'd also like to use social media and determine if anyone recalls seeing your mom in 1996 or thereafter, maybe even recently. You have pictures of her from that time period, I assume."

"Yes, but how are you—"

"I'm also going to need pictures of your maternal grandparents when they were between fifty and sixty years old. I have a forensic artist lined up, a woman we use to age abducted children. I've asked if she could do a composite sketch of what your mother would most likely look like now."

"I can get those photographs over to you this afternoon. What else do you need?" Childress said.

"I'd like pictures of you and your parents before your mother disappeared. I was told by the detective who handled your mother's investigation that your father didn't want publicity. Putting it out in social media might upset him."

"What are you going to do, exactly?"

"A number of Facebook pages are devoted to finding missing persons nationwide. I'm going to access those sites and post her pictures there."

"There's something like 600,000 people a year who go missing in the United States," Childress said, sounding skeptical.

Tracy had already considered this and come up with what she hoped would be a likely solution. "I'm also going to prepare a page dedicated only to your mom. I'm not going to make it a police page. I'm going to make it a personal page, written in first person from your mother's perspective. I'm going to re-create what happened those last few hours as best we know, and I'm going to ask if anyone recalls seeing her then or possibly now. I'll have a dedicated tip line set up for callers. We're going to get the cranks, the nuts, and the evil, but we might also get a nugget of useful information."

Childress wiped tears from the corners of her eyes.

"Here's the more difficult thing to consider, Anita. I can do this with your permission. You're an adult."

"My father won't stand in my way," Childress said, anticipating what Tracy was about to say. "My father will talk to you . . . Not for himself, but for me. I've already told him I've spoken to you and that you might want to speak to him."

"Okay," Tracy said. "I'd like to do that as soon as possible."

Childress pulled out her phone. "No time like the present. I think we both appreciate that more than most."

CHAPTER 11

A nita Childress emailed Tracy photographs of her mother, father, and herself from the time period just before her mother's disappearance, as well as photographs of her maternal grandparents at roughly sixty years of age. Tracy got the information over to Katie Pryor in the Missing Persons Unit, who arranged for the forensic sketch artist to draw what Childress most likely looked like at various ages in her life, including at present. Tracy then went to work writing a first-person social media account from Lisa Childress's point of view. She started with the facts that she knew: Childress's employment as a reporter, what she had done the day before she disappeared, the time that she left the house early the following morning, her purchasing a liter of Coca-Cola at the all-night convenience store on Capitol Hill, and where the detectives subsequently found her car. She added that Childress might have taken a Greyhound bus.

Tracy wanted the account to have an emotional appeal and added that Childress had a two-year-old daughter whom she hadn't seen in twenty-four years. She posted a picture of Childress holding Anita. She also mentioned what others who knew Childress described as her quirks—scattered focus, drinking Coke by the liter, social awkward-ness, and lack of organization—in case someone knew anyone with those same quirks. She sent the material over to Anita Childress for her approval and professional editing. While she waited, she called Billy Williams in the Violent Crimes Section. Williams had been Tracy's sergeant and had been promoted to lieutenant. She asked if he could spare someone to set up and track a tip line several times a day and make follow-up calls to weed out the cranks, the people who had also lost a loved one and wanted Tracy's help, the mistaken, the wannabe detectives, and those poor souls who were lonely and just wanted to talk.

Williams said he'd make it happen.

When completed, Tracy made the more difficult call, to Larry Childress. Childress was cordial but cool on the phone. His daughter had indeed spoken to him, and while he might have told Anita that he approved of what she was doing, his tone with Tracy indicated he was not happy about it. That could be because he had something to hide, or he simply did not want to be dragged through the muddy past again. Tracy said she had no intention of using Larry Childress's name or of going to the press, but if that appeased him, he gave no such indication. Tracy even offered to meet him at a coffee shop, but he declined and asked that Tracy come to his house in Medina that afternoon, when his partner would be away at a book club.

Tracy jumped in the car and drove east across the 520 bridge. She was familiar with the exclusive and wealthy Medina enclave on the shores of Lake Washington. Of the roughly three thousand residents, several were billionaires or multimillionaires—Microsoft, Google, Amazon, and other industry executives who won the tech lottery. In 2009, the residents had paid to have cameras installed at intersections along roads entering the city. The cameras captured the license plate number of every car that drove the streets, and a security system auto-matically notified local police if the plate number existed in a database of criminal offenders. Since installation of the cameras, Medina had not had so much as a break-in, car theft, or theft of mail or delivered packages.

Tracy drove up to an intercom in a river-rock stone pillar and identified herself. The wrought-iron gates pulled apart, and she drove her Subaru up to what was, for Medina anyway, a modest home, but with a substantial and well-manicured yard, including fruit trees. She parked beside a new BMW on a cobblestone drive and stepped out, noticing a camera atop the garage peak. She estimated the two-story home to be three to four thousand square feet on maybe half an acre, which meant a price tag of at least $5 million. Location. Location. Location.

The front door was beneath an arbor of sweet-scented flowering silver lace. Larry Childress opened the door before Tracy could knock. He looked like his photographs, thinning gray hair on a narrow face with a prominent nose and thick, black glasses. Childress considered Tracy with an expression she would best describe as reticent. After introductions, Tracy said, "Silver lace. It's beautiful. Wonderful aroma."

Childress, maybe an inch taller than Tracy, tilted his head as if just noticing the vine but otherwise didn't respond. He led Tracy into a home tastefully decorated but certainly not ornate. From the front entrance Tracy looked across a sunken living room to plate-glass panels providing a view of lush, green lawn edged with flower beds that sloped gently to a rock bulkhead. A glistening red-and-white speedboat sat raised on a lift above the water. The pier extended into a Lake Washington cove of blue-green water, choppy from a light wind. She could see the backyards of homes with their private piers and boats on the other side.

Tracy reevaluated her pricing estimate. The property was likely to fetch $7 to $8 million.

"Are you the gardener?" Tracy asked.

Childress glanced at the backyard as if seeing it for the first time. "Can I get you something to drink?"

"No, thank you."

He gestured to one of two red leather chairs and took a seat on a white couch across a glass coffee table. "I'm answering your questions because my daughter asked me to," he said, voice deep and guttural.

"I imagine you answered a lot of questions over the years."

"Too many," he said. "And I'm well aware that the husband is always the primary suspect in the case of a missing spouse."

"Where did you learn that?" Tracy asked.

"The investigating detectives made that quite clear."

"Keith Ellis?"

"No. Moss Gunderson. That's a name you don't easily forget."

"I would think not," Tracy said. "I told your daughter I'm looking at your wife's case in three ways, and yes, one way is that you had something to do with her disappearance."

"And the other two ways?"

"That her disappearance was caused by something she learned from one of the investigative stories she pursued, or she simply walked away."

"That's two more possibilities than the first detectives entertained. Thank you." His sarcasm was not well hidden.

"Why do you say that? Was it something in particular?"

"They didn't do much to get Lisa's files. I told them she was an investigative reporter and that she'd had a meeting very early that morning with a confidential source. At least that's what she told me. I could tell they didn't believe me. Even when they found the receipt and confirmed she had gone into a convenience store at two in the morning to purchase a liter of Coke, they never seemed to consider that she was killed by someone she met that evening."

"Did you push them?"

Childress smirked. "I encouraged the newspaper to cooperate with the detectives. I made several calls to Lisa's desk editor, but he claimed she told him little about the stories she pursued and even less about her sources. I think Anita has gotten further than anyone."

"Who was the editor you spoke with?"

"Bill Jorgensen."

Tracy changed subjects. "Did you know or suspect any of her sources?"

"No."

"Did Lisa get calls at home that concerned you?"

"She never talked to me about the calls so, no."

"Do you think your wife could have walked away?"

Childress took a moment and Tracy watched his chest rise and fall. "I'd like to think not, for Anita's sake."

"But?"

"But Lisa was different," Childress said. "I don't know how much Anita told you."

"I'd like to hear what you thought."

For the next several minutes, Childress largely repeated what Anita had told Tracy about her mother. "She could also retain incredible amounts of information—almost ninety percent of what she'd read, sometimes verbatim. But that ability came at an expense. She filtered out information like having a daughter she needed to care for."

"Anita said you stayed at home to care for her."

"That's right."

"What about work?"

"What about it?"

"How did you work while staying home to care for a toddler?"

Childress paused. He'd been down this line of questioning before. "I wasn't working at the time. I was between jobs."

"What did you do, before you stayed at home?"

Childress told her of his dot-com business that went bankrupt.

"You had debt?"

"Are you asking or telling me?"

"I read in the file that $150,000 was not dischargeable in bankruptcy."

"Then you know. Some debt I also chose to honor—investments from family and friends."

"Did you pay off that debt?"

"Eventually."

"How?"

"I sold real estate, but back then I couldn't very well get a real estate business off the ground and care for a baby girl. I was also worried about Anita—if anything happened to me, that Lisa wouldn't be able to handle things on her own. So I took out an insurance policy."

"Not long before your wife disappeared."

Childress glared at her. "Are we back to option one, Detective?"

"It's a fact I have to consider."

"I thought it prudent given how unreliable Lisa was turning out to be. I worried about who would care for Anita if something happened to me. I wanted my wife and my in-laws to know I'd planned for Anita's care."

"But the insurance company didn't immediately pay. How did you take care of Anita?"

"The best I could. I had my in-laws care for Anita when necessary, or I took Anita to day care when I had to show a home."

"You didn't want the detectives to go to the media with the story of your wife being missing. Why not?"

"Anita," Childress said.

"Can you explain?"

Childress dropped his head, showing his frustration. When he spoke, his voice had a bite to it. "She was a little girl who lost her mother and lived under the stigma that her father was somehow responsible. Yes, she was a child, but she would grow up and realize we were not wanted in many social circles. I should say, I wasn't. I didn't want it broadcast to the world any more than the media already had. I thought it would only make Anita's life more difficult."

Concern for his daughter, a good answer, but Tracy wasn't convinced, given that Anita had been too young to perceive being a social outcast. Then again, Tracy knew it would break her heart if Daniella were ever viewed that way. She decided to push Childress. "What did you use the insurance money for?"

Childress shifted his eyes before reengaging Tracy. "To care for my daughter."

"And to purchase a home."

"In West Seattle," he quickly added. "To get a change of scenery and a fresh start. I wanted to get Anita into a more stable environment. I wanted to give her a home with a yard. A new school. We got a dog."

"You didn't remarry."

"No."

"Why not?"

"Anita had lost her mother. I didn't want her to feel like she was losing her father as well. I wanted to give her a good home. I didn't want to introduce a stepmother into the picture until Anita was old enough to understand. I waited until after Anita graduated high school and went to the U."

"Your current partner was your high school sweetheart?"

"That's right."

"May I ask why you've never married?"

"Annabelle comes from old Seattle money. Her father made his fortune owning real estate—residential and commercial—and he invested wisely."

"The old-fashioned way." Tracy smiled. Childress did not.

"He watched his daughter lose half of everything he gave her when she divorced. He didn't want to watch it happen a second time."

"Her father opposes your marriage."

"Yes."

"Does his opposition have anything to do with Lisa going missing?"

"I'm sure it does."

"And as the years have passed, has his attitude toward you changed?"

"He and his wife don't think I'm going to murder their daughter and try to take her money . . . if that's what you're getting at." He paused. "You'd have to ask him."

"Do you still sell real estate?"

"No."

"When did you stop?"

"When I moved here."

"That doesn't exactly seem prudent, given your partner's parents' concerns and suspicions."

"Actually, they were thrilled. You know . . . the less I was out there in the public eye, the better." More sarcasm.

"I see."

"No. You don't see." A small fire stoked in Childress's eyes, and the tone of his voice changed again, harsher, challenging. This was the person Tracy had been trying to provoke—to determine if Childress was capable of losing his temper and killing his wife.

"The two other detectives didn't see either. You say you see. You pretend to sympathize, but until you've been through what I've been through . . . Until you catch people staring at you in the grocery store, when you're out to dinner, when parents walk away from you at soccer games, when your daughter is not invited to classmates' birthdays and homes, you don't see, and you never will."

"It must have been painful."

"Because I knew it hurt my daughter. Do you have children, Detective?"

It sounded like a challenge. Tracy met it. "A daughter, sixteen months."

Tracy's answer surprised Childress. Had he been standing, she would have said her answer rocked him onto his heels.

"Then maybe you do know. I'm sorry."

"No apology necessary," she said.

As if reading her mind, Childress said, "I did not kill my wife, Detective. I don't know how I can say it more plainly. I loved her. I worried about her."

"Tell me about the night she disappeared."

Childress sighed as if the memory required great effort, but Tracy had seen the response enough to know it was born from frustration and aggravation at having to answer the same questions too many times.

"She didn't ever reveal the names of her sources to me, which, when she left late at night, could be infuriating."

"You thought she could be having an affair?"

"Lisa?" he said, nearly chuckling. "No. But I didn't especially like the idea of my wife being out at two a.m., alone, meeting people who had sensitive information that could embarrass or wreck careers. I worried about her safety."

"Did Lisa ever express concern for her safety?"

"Never. My wife wasn't afraid of anything. It was the reason she never bought pepper spray, though I repeatedly asked her to do so. Her safety didn't even enter her thinking. I finally got to the point where I would put a canister of bear spray in her bag before she went out. Something big enough that she couldn't miss—big enough for her to find easily and use if she needed it."

"You have no idea who she met that night?"

"None."

"No idea where she went?"

"No."

"Does either the name Dwight McDonnel or Levi Bishop mean anything to you?"

"Not to me. Are they somehow involved in this?"

"What about Rick Tombs?" Tracy asked, referring to the sergeant of the Last Line drug task force.

Childress shook his head.

"Delmo Castigliano?"

Another headshake.

"A police unit called 'the Last Line.'"

"No."

Tracy switched subjects. She didn't need Larry Childress's permission to run social media, not with Anita's permission, but again, she wanted to gauge his reaction. "I'd like to use social media to see if it generates any leads about what happened to your wife, where she might be, if she's still alive."

"Are you asking my permission or telling me you're going to do it?"

Childress was smart. "Anita is an adult," Tracy said.

"Then you have your answer. Anita is old enough to know the consequences of her actions . . . whatever those consequences might be."

"And you?"

Another smirk. "I understand very well what those consequences might be, Detective, and have for many years."

CHAPTER 12

Tracy left the Medina home thinking about what Larry Childress had said, how he understood well the consequences of his daughter pushing the investigation into her mother's disappearance. Did he mean he had already lived those consequences? Or did he mean he knew what might be revealed and the consequences of that revelation?

Since it was afternoon, and Tracy was already on the east side of Lake Washington, she saw no reason to drive downtown only to then drive home. She had Childress's investigative files in her car and could work a few hours at home.

When she arrived, Therese's car was not in the circular drive. Therese often took Daniella out. Tracy and Dan had purchased passes to the zoo, the Pacific Science Center, the aquarium, and just about everything else. Therese also took Tracy's place in the Redmond Library reading circle for moms and a PEPS group for parents and their young children. But on beautiful days like today, Therese yearned for the outdoors and often took Daniella in her stroller on walks or to the playground, or on hikes in a backpack. Rex and Sherlock had gone with Dan that morning into the office, which was dog friendly.

"Looks like it's just you and me, Roger," she said when the cat jumped onto the pony wall's marble top and purred needfully, then jumped down and rubbed up against her legs. It might have been affection, but it was also a desire to be fed at any time after two in the afternoon.

"Dinner isn't for a couple of hours, Roger, though you're welcome to join me in the office."

He mewed and did not sound happy.

When Dan and Tracy remodeled their Redmond bungalow, they had put in an airy office with large picture windows, a sliding glass door, and skylights. Dan used the office more than Tracy did, but she loved to slip in to read or catnap in the cushy, brown leather chair beneath a Pendleton blanket. Not this day.

She grabbed a cup of chamomile tea, asked Alexa to play a Jack Johnson set, then settled in at the desk. She pulled up her desktop computer at Police Headquarters using an encrypted remote connection and checked her emails. Not seeing what she searched for, she emailed Katie Pryor, asking if the forensic artist had completed the age-progression photographs of Lisa Childress. While waiting for Pryor's reply, Tracy pulled up an email from Billy Williams, who confirmed that a dedicated tip line had been established, and he had assigned a detective to monitor incoming calls. Tracy would call the detective after she got off the phone.

Pryor replied by email and attached two pictures of an aging Lisa Childress. Tracy considered the pictures, which were skillfully drawn, and looked remarkably similar to Childress's mother. She then opened and reviewed Anita Childress's suggested edits to the Facebook material Tracy had prepared, made the indicated changes, and called SPD's Public Affairs Office, which told Tracy she had a green light, and that a dedicated tip line would be attached to the social media page the minute it went live, probably early the following morning.

That task completed, Tracy pulled out the fourth of Lisa Childress's investigative files, this one on Mayor Michael Edwards's business dealings. Edwards had been incredibly popular, especially with business owners. Those businesses provided jobs, salaries, and other capital that translated into residential and retail growth in downtown Seattle and the Puget Sound.

To get it done, however, Edwards had what became known as his "juice clientele"—lawyers, lobbyists, campaign donors, and political players who had influence with the mayor and his political team that doled out hundreds of millions of dollars in building contracts, land deals, and favorable regulatory rulings. Bribes and payouts were suspected, never directly tied to the mayor. A former lawyer, Edwards understood the rules of evidence and the term "chain of custody." He rarely used the phone, never used email, and had so many intermediaries that no link in the chain could be tied back to him.

The dynamic had sparked several public corruption investigations by the FBI and US Attorney's Office but no convictions.

Tracy flipped the page and found articles and handwritten notes on an airport expansion project undertaken by Greenhold Construction the year Lisa Childress disappeared. Bingo. Beneath the articles she found three xeroxed contracts, bids by different building contractors, each worth hundreds of millions of dollars. Of the three contracts, Greenhold was not the lowest bidder, but Greenhold was the chosen bidder.

Taken in context with the threat supposedly made by Greenhold against Lisa Childress, the pricing certainly could not be ignored. Tracy made a note to determine if Greenhold remained alive and, if so, to speak to him.

She now had a number of different directions she could go, which generally boded well for an investigation, but she didn't feel buoyed. She felt the way Moss Gunderson and Keith Ellis must have felt, like she was reaching dead ends. Certain things were out of her control—whether someone recognized the photographs she had posted, or some new piece of information proved Larry Childress killed his wife.

And Tracy didn't like not being in control.

CHAPTER 13

The following morning, Tracy left her house and drove west across the lake, but rather than drive into downtown Seattle, she proceeded north on I-5 and drove around Lake Union, crossing the Fremont Bridge above the Fremont Cut to Westlake Avenue. She followed her GPS to a Shell gas station from which, in 1996, a call had been placed to Lisa Childress's home phone. The gas station remained, but the pay phone was no longer present. Of more interest was the phone's former location, less than two-tenths of a mile from the Diamond Marina, where the bodies of the two crewmen had been found three months before Childress disappeared.

From the gas station, Tracy drove to the marina, a complex of three two-story, brown stucco buildings. Wrought-iron gates spanned the gaps between the buildings, and posted signs attached to the bars indicated passage to the marina was limited to boat owners and guests. Marina signage appeared above the entrance to the building in the center and the building on the left, advertising moorage rate specials. Tracy would start there. She climbed the building's wooden stairs and pulled open a red door. At the front counter she flashed her police credentials and told a young man she'd like to speak to the owner, manager, or whoever was in charge. The young man left the counter and moments later returned with another man, who identified himself as the marina manager.

Tracy asked for a moment of the man's time. He looked apprehensive but led Tracy to his office on the second floor. Windows provided Tracy with an eastern view of Lake Union beneath an overcast morning sky that turned the water slate gray. Boats of all types, shapes, and sizes were moored at slips and beneath a wooden, barn-style boathouse. Across the lake were still more boats, along with industrial-style buildings, and Gas Works Park's green lawn.

The manager introduced himself as Pete Welsh. "What is it I can help you with, Detective?"

"How long have you been here?"

"About six years."

"I'm looking into a cold case that took place well before your time, November 1995 and 1996, but I have some general marina-type questions I'm hoping you can help with."

Welsh seemed to relax. "I can try."

Tracy pulled out a xeroxed copy of Lisa Childress's handwritten notes mentioning the Diamond Marina. "Specifically, I'm hoping you can help decipher these notes from a reporter."

Welsh slipped on a pair of reading glasses that dangled from a Croakie around his neck. He took the sheet of paper from Lisa Childress's file and studied it, then looked up at Tracy.

"The name 'Diamond Marina' obviously refers to this marina," Tracy said. "And I'm fairly certain the word 'Egregious' is the name of a boat. I'm uncertain what the word 'Canadian' beside it means, but I'm assuming it was a Canadian vessel?"

"You said these were a reporter's notes?" Welsh asked.

"That's correct."

"Not a harbormaster's?"

"Why do you ask?"

"I'm assuming that's what HM/D. S. means. With D. S. being the harbormaster's initials."

"What's a harbormaster?"

"How technical do you want me to get?"

Tracy smiled. "I'll let you know when you're losing me."

"A harbormaster is responsible for enforcing the regulations of a particular harbor or port, as well as for the security of the harbor."

"That sounds official. How about unofficial?"

"They can be more like glorified parking attendants. They collect moorage fees, tell boats where to moor, which slip, and provide the marina rules."

"How long can a person rent a slip?"

"Some rent monthly, some six months. Some only want a night's moorage on their way east to Lake Washington or west to the locks leading to Elliott Bay and Puget Sound, maybe all the way out into the Pacific Ocean, or the Inside Passage north into Canada."

"So the word 'Canadian' next to *Egregious* could mean the ship was headed to Canada?"

"It could," Welsh said. "It might also mean it was a Canadian ship, registered in Canada. We get those as well."

"How would I know that, whether it was a ship registered in Canada?"

Welsh turned to his computer and started tapping the keyboard. "You'd go to Transport Canada." He turned his screen so Tracy could read it. "That's the Canadian agency responsible for the registration of vessels. It provides title to boats, the way the DMV provides title to cars. Do you know the type of boat?"

"No."

"That makes it more difficult, since more than one boat can have the same name, and the case is so old the boat could have sold."

"And changed names?"

"Possible but doubtful. There's a lot of superstition regarding changing the name of a boat."

"I'm assuming the Canadian registrar would have a paper trail of some kind if the boat changed owners?"

"They could, but again, not every boat has to be registered. They have regulations and exemptions that set that all out and, again, there can be more than one boat with that name."

"How might I find the boat, if it did come down from Canada and it was registered?"

Welsh gave her question some thought. "First, you're not likely talking about a speedboat, especially not in November. Probably not a sailboat either."

"Why not?"

"The wind can howl through the Inside Passage, and the waters can get rough," he said, referring to the passage that boats took from Seattle northwest along Canada's coast to Skagway, Alaska, to avoid the Pacific Ocean. "Especially that time of year. The boat would have to be big enough to handle the waves and the currents and to store enough gas to get from one marina to the next. I'd look for a commercial boat—a crab or salmon boat, something seventy to seventy-five feet or more."

"When a ship goes though the Ballard Locks, is there a paper trail documenting it?" she said, referring to the locks ships passed through to get from the saltwater Pacific Ocean to the freshwater Lake Union and Lake Washington. "Does someone at the locks document each boat coming and going?"

"Not to my knowledge, not now, anyway. I don't know about back then specifically, but if they don't keep a record now, it seems unlikely they did in either 1995 or 1996—but I don't know for certain; I'm just surmising. Think of the locks like a stop sign before people pass through east or west."

"Who would I ask at the Ballard Locks?"

"Ask the lockmaster. That's the person who raises and lowers the water to allow boats to pass."

"What about when a boat arrives here at the marina and wants to moor? Do you keep records?"

Welsh made a face. "We have computer records now, certainly, for tax reasons. Back then? I don't know for certain but again, for tax purposes, I would think that was standard procedure." He paused.

"But?" Tracy asked.

"But I can also tell you that boats looking for moorage for only a night often pay in cash, and there's no guarantee the harbormaster would have recorded each boat if it didn't plan to stay more than a night. You like to believe people are honest, but money does funny things."

Tracy knew this too well. She pointed to the initials on the note beneath "Diamond Marina."

"Would you have records here that indicate who was the harbormaster at that time?"

"Not here. I can call the marina owner's office and ask the accountant to go through her records, if she has them from that long ago, and see if she can come up with a name starting with those initials."

"I'd appreciate it," Tracy said. "I'd also appreciate it if she could find any moorage records for the *Egregious* for a particular day and night."

Welsh had a pen in hand and was taking notes. "Again, I can try. What days?"

The two bodies had floated up to the marina the morning of November 20, 1995. "Say for November 18 and 19, 1995." She gave it additional thought. "Actually, if the accountant has records, I'd be interested in any dates in 1995 that the *Egregious* moored here at the marina."

Welsh made a face. "I can't, for the life of me, think of a reason the marina would have kept records going back that far—the IRS only requires five years—but I can find out. *If* the records exist, that could take some man-hours to go through them."

"I'll take what I can get. Let me ask you this: Are you aware of any boat currently in the marina that was here back then?"

Welsh shook his head. "I'd have to ask around, Detective, see if anyone knows more than I do. Can I ask what this is about?"

"November 20, 1995, two bodies were found floating in the water at the marina. Two men drowned. I'm trying to determine how they might have ended up in Lake Union. Any ideas?"

Welsh again gave this some thought. "They could have fallen overboard. That would seem to be the most likely. But if they could swim . . . the lake isn't that big, but people do drown here. You said it was November?"

"Yes."

"Water can get down to thirty-seven, thirty-five degrees in the winter. It doesn't take long for someone to drown when the water is that cold, especially if they can't swim. Even if they can, if the wind is howling and creating waves . . . hypothermia only takes about fifteen minutes. Or if the men were impaired in any way . . . I'd check the weather records for back then."

Tracy removed a business card from her briefcase and handed it across the desk to Welsh. "I'm most interested in finding D. S. If your accountant can find records of the *Egregious* mooring back in 1995, those would also be helpful."

Welsh placed the card on the desk. "I'll call her right now."

Tracy left the marina and drove to the Ballard Locks, which were close. She met the lockmaster, Kevin Lohman, who told her the locks were the busiest in the United States with more than 645,000 boats passing through each year and as many as 250 each day. With so many boats, there was no time to document each boat's passing.

Another dead end.

—

After leaving the locks, Tracy called Mike Greenhold, who she had determined was alive and living on Mercer Island.

Tracy made the decision not to surprise Greenhold at his home. After twenty-four years, she figured he'd be surprised enough just to answer questions about Lisa Childress, and he sounded that way on the phone. She also made the decision not to lie to him. She told him she was looking into the Childress cold case.

Greenhold paused several seconds before responding with the common refrain. "Has something come up?"

"No," Tracy said. "Nothing specific." Though each time a person asked her that question, she wondered what the person might be hiding.

"I've answered questions before, Detective. I'm sure those answers were recorded somewhere in the file."

"They are," Tracy said, though Moss's summary had been minimal and not helpful. "Can we talk?"

"I'm retired," Greenhold said. "And I've talked about it enough already. Too many times, in fact. I really don't have anything more to say. Besides, I'm watching my grandkids this week, and that's precious time for me and my wife."

Tracy tried but failed to convince Greenhold, and with no real means to compel him to speak to her, or to bring him into Police Headquarters, it was, at least at present, another dead end.

Tracy disconnected the call and immediately received another. No caller ID displayed, and she didn't recognize the number.

"Detective Crosswhite?"

"Speaking."

"This is Pete Welsh at the Diamond Marina." Tracy hadn't expected to hear from Welsh this soon. "We're still looking for those records, but I think I found out who D. S. was, and a little more information about that boat, the *Egregious*."

"Let me pull over so I can write," she said.

"Actually, are you around tomorrow? I have someone I think you're going to want to speak with."

Tracy's pulse quickened with anticipation, but at the same time she thought, *Saturday. Family time.*

"What time tomorrow?" she asked.

CHAPTER 14

Saturday morning, Tracy met Pete Welsh in the lobby of his office building. The weekend had dawned gloriously, and Tracy regretted agreeing to the meeting. She would much rather have remained home with Dan and Daniella. Dan tried to make the situation better by telling Tracy he would take Daniella on a walk at Marymoor Park, but it only made her FOMO—an acronym he fondly used that meant Fear of Missing Out—worse.

"We'll catch up to you at home in the afternoon," Dan said.

Which was fine, except Daniella took her naps in the afternoon. Tracy was back to seeing her little one in a crib.

"Thanks for coming back," Welsh said, greeting her.

Welsh had given her some information the prior afternoon. Dennis Hopper Junior had lived on a houseboat at the marina off and on since 1990. "He says he knew D. S.—David Slocum—well. Slocum was the marina's harbormaster back then."

"I'm anxious to speak to Mr. Hopper," she said.

Welsh described Hopper as a bit of a character and said he had frequently rented out the houseboat when he left to pursue work as a roustabout and roughneck on oil rigs in the Gulf of Mexico, as a greenhorn on Alaskan fishing boats, a cook working a small cruise ship between Florida and the Cayman Islands, and other interesting jobs. Welsh said Hopper had once told him he'd even been employed flying hot-air balloons.

Welsh led Tracy from his office and headed to the piers with more than 250 houseboats. "Hopper also served as the harbormaster for a short time, as I understand it, but the marina couldn't really count on him. He picked up and took off without much notice and never knew how long he'd be away."

They emerged in bright sunshine with the same glorious view Welsh had from his second-story marina manager's window. Boaters pushed what looked like blue plastic wheelbarrows filled with boating equipment, coolers, and toys down the piers to their slips. Some greeted Welsh by name. Welsh punched in a code on a second gate across one of the finger piers. The gate had sharp arrow tips extending off the sides and the top to prevent someone from reaching or stepping around it.

Some of the houseboats were elaborate and beautifully maintained. Hopper's was best described as eclectic. Beside a yellow front door that faced the lake was a garage-style roll-up door. The second story was stacked over the first and looked to have been added on. Welsh rang the bell, which elicited a voice from above.

"That you, Pete?"

Welsh looked at Tracy and smiled. They stepped back from the door and looked up at a wiry-thin, shirtless man with a silver ponytail leaning over the second story. His skin was the color of a weathered, well-oiled baseball mitt. "How are you this morning, Dennis?" Welsh said.

"I'm good. Just soaking up some vitamin D. Got the plants out this morning and decided if it was good for the plants, it was good for me."

"The legal plants, right?"

"Of course," Hopper said. He looked to Tracy. "You must be the detective."

"I am," Tracy said.

"Pete didn't say you were good looking." Hopper chuckled. "He's married, by the way. But I am flying solo."

Tracy smiled. "My solo days are long gone. I'm married."

"Happily?" Hopper asked, still smiling.

"Very. With a little girl, two dogs, and a cat."

"You're a Norman Rockwell painting. Can't blame a guy for asking."

"I don't."

"Come on up. Door is unlocked."

"I'll leave you to it," Welsh said. "By the way, the accountant grumbled, but she's looking for records. You might not need them though. Dennis is like a repository when it comes to the happenings around here and at the marina. Don't ask him about any of his other jobs if you're looking to get home before next week."

"Got it," Tracy said. She pushed in the door. The interior was surprisingly well decorated and also eclectic. Somehow it all worked. A chandelier of hubcaps dangled from the ceiling over a dining room table with legs carved to represent African animals. The room held the sweet aroma of marijuana. Directly before her was a spiral staircase. Tracy climbed it and emerged on a deck with two blue-and-white beach chairs that looked to have seen better days. Hopper gave Tracy a tour of his plants and flowers growing in pots all around the deck—roses, bamboo palms, a lemon and an orange tree, an avocado plant, and various perennials.

"Impressive." Tracy had tried to grow a lemon tree, without success, and had been told not to even bother with an avocado plant. "You have a green thumb," she said.

"The real foliage is inside beneath grow lights, but I figured it probably best a police detective didn't see that aspect of my operation."

Tracy laughed. "I know nothing."

"It's just survival. The stuff they sell in those stores is crap, and way overpriced. I always felt like, Why pay for something you can grow yourself?"

"Makes sense," Tracy said.

"Do you smoke?"

"I don't," she said. "I envy your ability to grow a lemon and an orange tree though. I've tried and failed."

"Tough up here in Puget Sound with all the cloudy weather. Having the grow lamps helps. What did the woman do when a lemon tree fell on her cat?"

"I don't know. What did she do?"

"Nothing. Just stood there with a sour puss." Hopper beamed and Tracy laughed. "Can I get you anything to drink?" he asked. "I got some cold beer in the fridge."

"I'm fine." Tracy looked out at the view of boats moored and on the lake. "It's nice up here."

"I love it," Hopper said, spreading his arms. "This is my nirvana."

"Pete Welsh says you've been a resident at the marina a long time."

"Moved onto the boat in 1990 after the wife threw me out. Turned out to be the best day of my life. Rented for six months, then bought the boat with the divorce settlement and have been here ever since, when I wasn't working anyway. I often thought of moving, but the water always called me home."

"Looks like you put on an addition."

"I added on this deck for my grow operation, and that room to accommodate a nephew who came to live with me for a few years. He didn't have the best home life."

"How's he now?"

"Working in LA for one of those movie studios. He builds out many of the sets you see in movies. Built one for a movie starring Dennis Hopper, which I think was preordained since my parents named me Dennis after watching the movie *Easy Rider*. Might be why I never stay long in one place."

"I understand you were here in 1995 and knew the harbormaster."

"You'll have to be more specific about the month, but generally yeah, and I knew David. He lived a couple piers over and we had some things in common. We traded snippets of our various plants and tried to graft them to grow the best pot in the Pacific Northwest."

"How'd that work out?"

"We liked to think we achieved it, but we were high, so what did we know."

Again, Tracy smiled. "And do you recall a boat named the *Egregious*?"

"A purse seine fishing boat out of Vancouver, BC. Remember it well."

"I don't know boats," Tracy said. "What kind of boat is that?"

"Seventy- or seventy-five-foot long, sky blue with white masts, commercial fishing boat. But that was just a front. The *Egregious* was running drugs, I can tell you that."

That caught Tracy's attention. "Yeah? How do you know it was running drugs?"

Hopper laughed like she was naïve. "Well, for one I tried to sign on, more than once. I worked fishing boats in Alaska and figured this would be a hell of a lot closer to home, but the captain turned me down flat every time. Said he didn't need the help even though I never saw a crew when he came into the marina. Never saw no fish neither. Second, the *Egregious* only came down to the marina once a month, and it stayed for just the one night. Used to pull up to the dock after dark, meaning after the management went home."

"So he could have had crew who you just never saw?" Tracy asked.

"Could have. The captain's name was . . . Hold on; I'm having a senior moment. It was Jack something. Had to do with fire . . . It will come to me. Anyway, he'd pull in after dark, find David, and pay the daily moorage, always in cash."

Cash likely meant under the table. "Did David keep a record of the cash payments?"

Another smile. "You might find a few just to keep things on the up-and-up." Hopper snapped his fingers. "Jack Flynt—that was the captain's name. Told you it would come to me. I ain't dead yet. I'm good with names. I can remember the name of every kid in my grammar school. I relate them to things. Like Flynt to fire."

"You said I might find some records just to keep things on the up-and-up."

"Not you. I mean, I assume you're on the up-and-up. David didn't record every visit. You know what I mean?"

"Tell me."

"Flynt paid cash, came in after management left, and was gone before they arrived next morning. It was a cool way to make some good cash money, and no one was ever the wiser."

"You know this for certain?"

"You hang around docks long enough, you start to figure things out."

"This Captain Jack Flynt was buying David Slocum's silence?"

"Not like David was part of the drug operation Flynt was running. Nothing like that. I'm just saying it was a way for David to make a little extra money. We can all use help in that department."

"But you thought this boat was running drugs?"

"I thought it." Hopper smiled. "Then I knew it when David told me the police raided the boat and busted Captain Jack."

There it was. "Were you here when that happened?"

"No." Hopper shook his head and stretched out his legs. "I was in the Gulf of Mexico on an oil rig. Missed all the excitement. David told me when I got back."

"What did he say?"

"They raided the *Egregious*. Came running down the pier with guns and face masks."

"Face masks?"

"That's what David said."

"Did they identify themselves?"

"If they did, David didn't hear it and didn't know." In her mind, Tracy saw Lisa Childress's handwritten note. *The Last Line*. "David thought it was DEA or FBI. He had his own little grow operation to worry about. Thought they came for him. Scared the shit out of him. When he realized they hadn't, he wasn't going to stick his prominent nose where it didn't belong, and neither was I."

"What did David say when you talked to him?"

"He said they came in fast and heavily armed. Put Captain Jack in handcuffs and hauled him and the boat away. David, being the harbormaster, had to get involved. He told me he fabricated a payment in the logbook that said the *Egregious* paid cash, so he wouldn't lose his job. He couldn't very well backdate all the records, because if he did, then the monthly income wouldn't add up and the marina manager would know David was dipping into the company inkwell."

"Did David have any way to quantify the amount of drugs Captain Jack had on board?"

"Their cash value?"

"Yeah."

"No idea, but I can tell you that if Captain Jack was running cocaine, he could put an amount worth millions in briefcases. If he was running marijuana, that takes up more room, but he had a lot of room in the hull of the *Egregious*."

"Best guess," Tracy said.

"Best guess . . ." Hopper looked up at the sky and looked as if he was calculating and running numbers. "To run a load down from Vancouver it had to be something sizable. They weren't going to make that trip for a few thousand or even a million. I'd guess you're looking at ten to twenty million dollars. Maybe more."

That was a big score, but Tracy wondered if Hopper was exaggerating for effect.

"How big a crew is needed to run a boat that big?"

"Not many. I'd say it was Captain Jack and the two Mexican crewmen."

The comment again caught Tracy's attention. "There were two Mexican men on board the boat?"

"Can't say for sure since I wasn't here, but David said two men floated up to the marina two days later and it was just too big a coincidence not to be from the *Egregious*. I remember he said they didn't fall from the heavens."

"Maybe it was a different boat."

"And maybe pigs can fly, but I doubt it."

"David call it in?"

"Had to."

That was the case Moss Gunderson and Del worked. "The police show up?"

"David said they did. Twice in fact. He said a cop asked him a lot of questions about the *Egregious*, how often it came, and what kind of records David kept. He thought for sure he'd get busted, that the police would seek the records."

"You said the police came twice?"

"That's what he said."

"Do you remember the names of the officers who came?"

Hopper chuckled. "I got a good memory for the minutiae, Detective Tracy, but not that good. Not from twenty-five years ago. Just remember he said police came to talk to him."

"The name Moss Gunderson mean anything to you?"

"Nope."

"What about Del Castigliano?"

"Nothing."

"Do you know if David Slocum told the police about the raid on the *Egregious*?"

"He told me he did, but it was a bit dicey, mind you."

"Because David was taking cash under the table."

"That and the bunch of marijuana plants on his houseboat," Hopper said, voice rising with a chuckle. "If the marina manager found out, David would be fired. I remember he said he just asked, kind of casual like . . . 'What happened to the raid on the *Egregious*?'"

"Did David tell you what the police said when he asked them about the raid?"

"I don't recall specifically. I think he said they said something about that being the Narcotics Unit's business, and they didn't know anything about it. After that, David figured it best to just shut up and let it go."

"You said David said the police came twice."

Hopper snapped his fingers. "Oh yeah. This is where it gets weird. David said a detective came a second time and seemed surprised when the subject of the raid on the *Egregious* came up."

"Surprised how?"

"I guess like he didn't know anything about it. I don't really know anything more since I wasn't there."

"You ever see the *Egregious* again, after that night it got raided?"

"Never did. Figured they impounded it and Captain Jack did time."

"You're sure that was two nights before they found the two bodies?"

"David said so. I mean technically it was a morning since it was after midnight, but I believe he got it right."

"Why's that?"

"Because we don't get a lot of excitement around here, Detective Tracy. You tend to remember the nights when more than the crickets are chirping. When you get two incidents like that in a row . . . Hell, that's like national news around here."

"How might I find the *Egregious*? You think it's still around?"

"It wasn't that old in 1995, maybe five years, and those boats tend to stick around forever."

"How would I find it?"

"If it was me, and I was you, I'd check with your impound, call the US customs service and see if the boat was forfeited and sold. Likely it was. Then just follow the bills of sale."

"You said the boat came from Vancouver, BC, though."

"Yeah, that's right. You could look it up, find out the authority that registers the boats in Canada, and probably find the hailing port."

"What's a hailing port?"

"Where the boat was moored up there. The marina it was kept at."

"When's the last time you spoke to David Slocum?"

"The last time? About a week before he died."

"He's dead?" Tracy asked, feeling the air quickly leave her sails.

"Figured that was why you were asking me all these questions. Yeah. David shot himself."

More red flags. "Where?"

"In his car."

"Here at the marina?"

"No. Someplace in Seattle."

"Do you know why?"

"No idea."

"Did he give you any indication he was depressed or suicidal?"

"Nothing I could put a finger on, but like I said, I was in and out back then."

"How long after the raid and the two bodies being found did this happen?"

"Not long. I'd say three to four months, but don't quote me on that, Detective Tracy. I'm an old man who smokes a lot of pot, so my brain isn't what it was."

"Did David strike you as the type of person who might kill himself?"

"What 'type' of person is that?" Hopper asked. "I don't think we really know 'cause I don't think there's a type."

"Your memory has been very good, Dennis. I'm grateful for the information."

Hopper spread his arms. "Anytime. And let me reiterate, if you're ever looking for something a little more adventurous, you're always welcome here."

Tracy smiled. "My two dogs each weigh 140 pounds, Dennis. They're liable to sink your boat."

CHAPTER 15

Tracy kept her word and drove home to spend the rest of the weekend with Dan and Daniella. Physically present anyway. She had a thousand questions swirling through her head, foremost being, What had happened to the *Egregious*? And to David Slocum? And what did Del know about it? She'd try to find out Monday morning, but that didn't mean she could turn off the spigot and keep the questions at bay. Dan commented that Tracy seemed distracted and asked if she wanted to talk about it. She told him it was work related and no, she didn't want to take away from precious family time. There was no point. Lisa Childress had been missing twenty-four years. Waiting thirty-six hours before delving back into the case wasn't going to jeopardize anything.

Monday morning, which dawned gray and bleak with the promise of showers, Tracy hit the ground running. She reached her desk at Police Headquarters and pulled from storage the file on the two men who had drowned on November 20, 1995. She read the contents thoroughly, but the file made no mention of a raid on the Diamond Marina either November 18 or 19. Seemed Moss and Del would have logically asked

about the raid to determine if it could have been related to the two
drowned men.

She called the US Customs and Border Protection for the Port
of Seattle, the DEA, and the FBI, and provided the information and
asked for records. She called Bennett Lee, the public information officer with whom she had a close working relationship, and asked if he
had any stored files on such a raid. A drug bust that big—if Hopper's
estimates were accurate, especially by a task force designed for just that
purpose—would have been big news back then. Hell, it would be big
news now. Half an hour after Tracy placed the call, Lee called back. He
had found nothing.

Customs and Border Protection called back late in the day. They,
too, had no records for the dates provided or for the name of the boat.
The DEA and FBI had the same response.

Tracy checked the SPD evidence room's archived files. Back then
they didn't have computers to keep track of evidence admitted and
released, which made it easier for evidence to get lost. The detective at
the evidence room bitched about the extra work and claimed he was
busier than a one-armed paperhanger, but he, too, called Tracy back.
No drugs or drug money had been checked into the evidence room the
nights of the eighteenth or nineteenth or the morning of November 20.

Tracy ran the *Egregious* and Hopper's description of the boat through
the Washington Department of Licensing as well as the Washington
Department of Fish and Wildlife. There were multiple ships with the
same name, but none was a seventy-five-foot purse seine fishing boat.

She called the Canadian Register of Vessels and asked that they
search for legal title to the fishing trawler. An hour later they emailed
her a hit, with photographs. The commercial fishing boat had been
commissioned in 1985. They found a record of the boat subsequently
being sold to a Jack Flynt, who registered it in September 1989. The
records indicated Flynt owned the boat until it was seized in American
waters on March 10, 2002, roughly ten miles west of Cape Alava, just

south of the entrance to the Strait of Juan de Fuca. The boat contained 3,300 pounds of cocaine and marijuana with a street value of more than $30 million.

Hopper had not been exaggerating.

Tracy called the Coast Guard Investigative Service, asked if the agency had existed back in 1995 or 2002, and if so, if it had any records related to the purse seine fishing trawler, in particular its impoundment. The Coast Guard emailed her records that matched the information she had learned from the Canadian Register of Vessels. The *Egregious* had been seized on March 10, 2002.

Hopper had been correct that the ship had been used to transport drugs, but could he have been off on his dates? Could he have remembered something that happened in March 2002 instead of November 1995? Could he have related the drowning of Navarro and Ibarra to the seizure of the boat? He was, after all, a self-proclaimed aging hippie who had smoked a lot of pot. She dismissed the thought almost immediately. Hopper's recollection of the date Slocum told him the two men floated up to the dock had been accurate, and it seemed highly unlikely David Slocum would have had the opportunity, let alone any reason to question Moss or Del about the raid, had they not come to the marina in response to the two drowned men. As Hopper had said, you didn't forget things like that, especially when they happened so close together.

So what happened to the *Egregious* and its drugs in November 1995? And why hadn't Del put the information of the raid in his file?

Tracy ran the name Jack Flynt through several databases but did not find any records that charges had ever been filed against Flynt in the United States. Further digging at the customs department revealed the 2002 seizure case had been handed off to Canadian law enforcement, since Jack Flynt was a Canadian citizen and the *Egregious* a Canadian vessel. The boat had been dry-docked in Port Angeles while the US customs service completed a forfeiture process.

Tracy called Staff Sergeant Tyner Gillies, who ran the drug unit of the RCMP in Surrey, British Columbia. She had assisted Gillies on a prior case in Washington that involved a Canadian citizen, and she eliminated a number of legal hoops Gillies would have otherwise had to jump through. She hoped Gillies could do the same. She asked Gillies to run the name Jack Flynt through their system and let her know if anything turned up.

An hour later, Gillies called her back and advised that Flynt had pled guilty to smuggling cocaine and marijuana into the United States in March 2002, received a twelve-year sentence, served just five years, and had been paroled. At the time of his parole in 2007, he lived in Vancouver, British Columbia. Five years seemed like an incredibly short time to have been incarcerated, given the quantity of drugs confiscated and the length of the sentence imposed, but maybe the Canadian system was more forgiving. Gillies told her Flynt had been pinched more recently and was currently imprisoned at the Mission Institution outside of Mission, British Columbia, an hour from Surrey.

Tracy explained her situation and asked Gillies if he could make arrangements for her to speak with Flynt in prison. He said he'd see what he could do.

When she disconnected the call, her instinct was to turn around and speak to Del—an old habit. Del used to have the desk directly behind her in the four-detective bull pen that made up the Violent Crimes Section's A Team. She wanted to ask Del about Navarro and Ibarra, and whether Slocum had questioned him and Moss about a raid. She wanted to know if either Del or Moss had looked into the veracity of Slocum's statement. It didn't appear either had. But she recalled Del's seeming lack of memory about the case, though it had been his first homicide, and the way his face had changed when she mentioned Lisa Childress. She did not yet have any hard evidence a raid had occurred. What she had was the hearsay recollection of what David Slocum had allegedly said to an aging, pot-smoking vagabond, and as much as she liked Dennis Hopper, that was not likely to get her far.

She decided to find something more concrete before she went to Del. In the interim, she tried to dismiss the notion that Del had been involved in illegal activity, but that thought was tempered by the knowledge that twenty-five years ago, Del had been new to homicide and to SPD. Could he have unwittingly stumbled onto something, then found himself in no-man's-land? Did Del learn about the raid but was told to keep his mouth shut, then saw no way out of the situation except to continue his silence and hope for the best, knowing that speaking out would likely ruin his career or possibly get him killed?

She went to the computer, pulled up a search engine, and typed in the name David Slocum. It generated 329,000 hits. She refined her search by adding "Seattle" and "Washington State." After some additional filters, and some starts and stops, she found a 1996 obituary for a David Allen Slocum, age forty-two. Details were provided for a funeral and celebration of Slocum's life. A summary of his work history included a four-year stint as a civilian harbormaster at a marina in Seattle. There were no details of the cause of death. His mother and father, a brother, and a sister were identified as his surviving family.

Tracy exited the article and scrolled further down the links. She found a short *Seattle Times* news story. David Allen Slocum, forty-two, had been found dead from a single gunshot to the head. He had been seated in his car behind a building in Seattle's Industrial District on February 27, 1996.

Tracy felt her pulse quicken. She reread the date.

She didn't have to look at the Lisa Childress file to confirm the date of Slocum's death matched the date Lisa Childress had disappeared. No way this was a coincidence.

She recalled Dennis Hopper saying Slocum had died roughly three to four months following the two bodies washing up to the marina—further evidence nothing was wrong with Hopper's memory.

Tracy opened the SPD database of closed cases and found the David Slocum file. She called the Evidence Unit and asked them to pull any evidence sheets and photos, assuming they had not been purged, then left her desk and went to the vault to get the file.

An hour later, she sat at her desk reviewing the file contents. The Evidence Unit also had provided the evidence logs and photos. She went through the police incident report and the death investigation checklist. February 27, 1996, Seattle Police Department officers had responded to a call from a supervisor at a plastics company in Seattle's Industrial District. The supervisor reported a black Ford parked at the rear of the building near the loading bays. The car was impeding the company's semitrucks, but that wasn't the primary reason for the call. The reason for the call was the man in the driver's seat slumped sideways, his head below the passenger seat, the passenger door open.

Officers arriving at the scene immediately determined the driver to be deceased and noted a handgun on the floorboard of the passenger compartment. They called the Homicide Unit. Detectives Keith Ellis and Moss Gunderson were dispatched as the two standby detectives to process the scene.

There were those names again. She felt another tingling sensation in her stomach.

At present, a violent crime investigation was given to the detective team next up. She wondered if Moss had lobbied to get the Slocum case. He certainly had the seniority to do so.

She went through the witness statements of the plastics company supervisor and the semitruck driver who arrived just after 5:00 a.m. and noticed the car. She viewed a series of gruesome photographs of the car interior and of David Slocum, shot once in the left temple. After the photographs, she found the medical examiner's report documenting the time of death, based upon rigor mortis and body temperature, to be approximately four to five hours, or roughly two or three in the morning. Other than the single gunshot wound to the left temple, the medical examiner's autopsy failed to reveal any other wounds, bruises, cuts, or scrapes to indicate a struggle.

Tracy worked her way through the file. A ballistics test indicated the gun had been recently fired and, from the extent of the burned flesh at the wound to the temple, embedded powder grains, and human tissue blowback in and on the gun barrel, the weapon was confirmed to be the weapon used in the shooting.

Detectives dislodged a bullet from the passenger-side door, but the damage was too severe for the ballistics team to confirm the bullet had been fired by the found gun, though that seemed to be a foregone conclusion. Fingerprint experts found the victim's fingerprints on the gun grip.

Tracy went through the evidence log inventorying the car's interior, including the glove compartment. It did not list a suicide note. A subsequent search of Slocum's houseboat also failed to turn up a suicide note, but it did turn up marijuana plants. Again, the information caused Tracy to pause. She considered the telephone call made to Lisa Childress the day before Childress had disappeared. It had come from the Shell station just a block from the Diamond Marina, David Slocum's home.

She wondered if Childress's notes were a record of that call.

She went back to the file. Slocum's phone records had been reviewed and each phone number investigated and determined to be unrelated to his death. Interviews of persons living at the houseboat community and who worked at the marina, including Dennis Hopper, did not turn up any indication Slocum had been depressed or otherwise suicidal. He was not known to own a handgun.

Tracy looked for but did not find any further investigation to explain how Slocum came to possess the 9 mm weapon. The serial number required to be engraved on the handgun by the Gun Control Act of 1968 was not documented anywhere in the file, nor had Ellis requested that the Bureau of Alcohol, Tobacco and Firearms (ATF)

National Tracing Center determine the gun's origins. No documents explained how David Slocum had come to possess it.

Tracy closed the hard file and reviewed the evidence log of items found outside and around Slocum's car—cigarette butts, aluminum cans, a tennis ball, pieces of ripped and torn paper, and other items. She quickly scanned the list, still considering the date of Slocum's death, the Shell station phone call, and thinking it all too big a coincidence to not be related to Lisa Childress's disappearance.

An item on the list caused Tracy to sit upright and her blood to pulse.

She went again to the crime scene photographs accompanying the list of items and found photographs to document where each item had been located in relationship to the car.

> 8.1-ounce, 8-inch tall, red can of
> counter-assault bear spray in a cloth sleeve.

The standby detectives found the can in the weeds between the paved parking area and the Duwamish Waterway. Nearby they had found a dislodged black safety cap they subsequently determined to fit the can. Unlike the other items photo documented, the can appeared relatively new. The detectives indicated the can was nearly full but had been sprayed, based upon chemicals identified in the nozzle screw and the spray swirl piece.

Keith Ellis, the investigation's lead detective, did not relate the can of bear spray to the suicide. Tracy found nothing to document whether the can had been checked for fingerprints. She stood and went to the box of materials the Evidence Unit had pulled for her. As she suspected, the can was not in it. It had been purged.

At best, it had been poor police work by Ellis. At worst, it had been a deliberate attempt to ignore evidence and possibly misdirect an investigation—to quickly classify the death as a suicide and close the file without further inquiry. Nothing in the file indicated Moss Gunderson ever mentioned Slocum had been the harbormaster he had interviewed at the Diamond Marina in the drowning deaths of Navarro and Ibarra, that Slocum had died the same day Lisa Childress had disappeared, or that Larry Childress had given his wife a can of bear spray to protect herself. If Slocum had mentioned to Moss the raid on the *Egregious*, as Hopper relayed to Tracy, it raised further questions about Slocum's death—questions that should have been red flags billowing in front of Moss's face.

He'd missed or deliberately ignored them.

If Slocum did not tell Moss of the raid, then Moss could argue that Tracy was working with hindsight, with information Ellis and Moss did not possess at the time of their investigation. But, at the very least, Moss should have identified the can of bear spray to be an item not typically found in the weeds behind a plastics company, and mandated that further investigation take place. If Moss had done so, it was inconceivable he would not have linked the found can to Larry Childress's statement that he had given such a can to his wife. Moss then could not have ignored the fact that the telephone call to Lisa Childress had come from a gas station pay phone just down the street from the Diamond Marina, where David Slocum had lived on a houseboat.

Moss Gunderson, the golfer in the bright clothing, seemed to be doing his best to camouflage what had happened. Why? Tracy suspected it had to do with the raid never reported, and she wondered if Del could also somehow be implicated, and if so, just how deeply.

Tracy checked her watch and quickly called the detective monitoring the Lisa Childress tip line. The detective told Tracy the tip line had received 150 tips since the site went live, all but a handful from cranks, the lonely, and junior wannabe detectives. She was following them up and would pass along any she deemed worthy. Tracy thanked her and hung up.

On her computer, Tracy put together a timeline of the events and the people she wanted to speak with.

> November 18, 1995, unconfirmed. Unknown unit conducts a raid on the *Egregious* fishing trawler at the Diamond Marina in Lake Union. RCMP attempting to arrange interview with ship captain Jack Flynt.
>
> November 20, 1995. Moss Gunderson and Delmo Castigliano respond to call from Diamond Marina of two dead bodies floating in Lake Union.
>
> November 20, 1995. Harbormaster David Slocum tells detectives Moss Gunderson and Delmo Castigliano about raid on the *Egregious* two nights previous. Unconfirmed.
>
> No record of a raid, of any forfeiture of drugs, or of the fishing trawler found through inquiry to normal channels.
>
> February 26, 1996. 7:37 p.m. Call made from pay phone at Shell gas station near the Diamond Marina to Lisa Childress's home phone number.
>
> February 27, 1996. 2:00 a.m. Lisa Childress leaves her home to meet with confidential source. Husband says he placed bear spray in her bag.
>
> February 27, 1996. 2:17 a.m. Lisa Childress stops at convenience store and buys liter of Coke. Never seen again. Moss Gunderson and Keith Ellis later investigate.
>
> February 27, 1996. 5:17 a.m. Supervisor at plastics company calls police about dead body in a car in Seattle's Industrial District. Body is identified as David Slocum, harbormaster, Diamond Marina. Investigating detectives are Moss Gunderson and

Keith Ellis. Does not appear they tried to determine where the gun came from or how it came to be in Slocum's car.

February 27, 1996. Detectives processing the Slocum crime scene find can of bear spray, without top, in reeds by car containing body of David Slocum. Detectives inspect can and conclude it had been recently sprayed. No fingerprints.

March 10, 2002. The *Egregious* is seized roughly 10 miles west of Cape Alava, just south of the entrance to the Strait of Juan de Fuca, by the United States Coast Guard. The boat contained nearly 3,300 pounds of cocaine and marijuana with a street value of more than $30 million. Captain Jack Flynt pleads guilty and is sentenced to 12 years in a Canadian prison but only serves five.

Tracy picked up the phone and called Tyner Gillies, the Canadian staff sergeant she'd spoken with earlier in the day. "Don't have anything for you yet, Detective," Gillies said.

"Was hoping to ask another favor?"

"Shoot."

"I'd like to know the name of the attorney who defended Jack Flynt in the drug-smuggling actions and whether he might also still be around."

"I'll call you back as soon as I have anything for you," Gillies said.

CHAPTER 16

Tracy spent the next few days speaking with forensic anthropologist Kelly Rosa and contacting and speaking with the families of the final victims found in Curry Canyon. At Chief Weber's request, she had asked several families if they would attend a news conference to bring closure to the matter. All agreed. Then she tried to think of what she might say at that conference.

In between, she ran down leads that the detective screening the Lisa Childress tip line deemed worthy of pursuit. The leads, unfortunately, had led to either dead ends or cases of mistaken identity, neither of which came as a surprise. After reading the evidence log identifying the can of bear spray along the Duwamish Waterway where David Slocum had supposedly shot himself, Tracy was even more convinced Lisa Childress was dead.

Tracy had called Larry Childress—who did not sound happy to hear from her—then sent him a picture of the can, and asked if it was the bear spray he'd put in his wife's bag. He couldn't say for certain, not definitively, but he said it looked to be about the size of the can he recalled. "It wasn't small, and that was on purpose."

He asked Tracy where she had found it. She told him she could not yet say but hoped to provide him and Anita with an update soon.

"It would at least confirm I was concerned about my wife's well-being, wouldn't it?" Larry Childress had asked.

It could, but that might have been deliberate, to make the detectives believe Larry loved and cared for his wife. The latter, she didn't say. What was more important was why Moss Gunderson and Keith Ellis had not tied the can to Lisa Childress's disappearance. If, in fact, Slocum had witnessed a raid that had never been investigated, it further thickened the plot. Tracy's father had liked to say, *a lug nut has more sense*, and she thought the phrase equally appropriate here with respect to Moss Gunderson certainly, and maybe Keith Ellis. So much so that she no longer believed she had an advantage because she was looking at both cases with hindsight and had Anita Childress's investigative files. Tracy was operating under the assumption that Moss and Ellis had covered up a piece of evidence that tied both cases together—and that the unreported raid on the *Egregious* might be the knot in that rope.

Late in the afternoon, Tyner Gillies, the RCMP staff sergeant in Surrey, called Tracy back.

"I've located the attorney who defended Jack Flynt when his boat was seized seven months ago. The same attorney who got him the plea deal when he got busted in 2002 negotiated the terms of his most recent plea. That's not unusual. Drug dealers tend to have money to afford a good lawyer, and when they find one, they keep him or her on speed dial. I've arranged a gate pass from the warden for you to speak to them at the same time. When would you like to come up?"

"Why am I speaking to Flynt and his attorney at the same time?"

"Flynt wouldn't speak to you without his attorney present."

"Did he say why not?"

"No. Just said no lawyer, no conversation."

"Does that strike you as odd?"

"How so?"

"Flynt pled and served his time for the 2002 bust, and the statute of limitations here in the United States would prevent us from bringing any other charges. I also imagine his attorney doesn't perform pro bono work."

"He doesn't."

"You know him?"

"We've dealt with Kell J. Gordon over the years. He does a lot of criminal defense, a lot of drug cases. He likes to get cases thrown out on technicalities, which doesn't endear him. My best guess is Flynt talked to Gordon, and Gordon saw a chance to make a buck. What do you want me to tell him?"

"Tell him I'll be there."

Gillies finalized arrangements for Thursday at the Mission Institution, and they agreed to meet at RCMP headquarters in Surrey. He reminded her to leave her gun at the Blaine, Washington, police department before crossing the border.

—

The drive north Thursday morning took just over two hours through Skagit Valley farmland rimmed to the east by low, rolling hills and, in the distance, the nearly eleven-thousand-foot, snow-covered Mount Baker peak and the North Cascades. A low mist hung over fallow fields, so thick it almost obscured the intermittent barns and farmhouses. Tracy had always enjoyed driving. It gave her time to think, time she didn't get in her office or at home. She went over the timeline she had created and wondered if David Slocum had gone to Lisa Childress, an investigative reporter, and told her about the raid on the *Egregious*. But even as she considered this possibility, it didn't make sense, not if Slocum was growing and selling weed on his houseboat. That would have been like a gnat asking that the bug zapper be turned on.

She also wondered why Jack Flynt would not speak to her without his attorney present. Flynt might be concerned about getting pinched for other drug smuggling, as Gillies had suggested, but Tracy didn't think so. She thought it had something to do with the raid that had never been reported, and the reduction of Flynt's twelve-year prison sentence to just five years. That significant a reduction was not likely due to good behavior; Flynt would have needed to either have been a saint who performed bona fide miracles or received a presidential pardon. Tracy suspected Flynt's reduced sentence had been part of his plea deal, that the US Attorney's Office and Canadian authorities hashed out something in exchange for information Flynt could provide, perhaps information on his drug ring or other dealers and smugglers. That seemed more likely given that Flynt had, apparently, remained in the drug-smuggling business after his release from prison. Could Flynt have become an informant? Was his current one-year sentence as a low-security prisoner to protect him—to convince others he was not a government rat? Tracy knew the Hells Angels actively smuggled drugs into the United States from Canada. If Flynt was associated with them, those were not the type of people to piss off.

Tracy had no difficulties crossing the border at Blaine and met Gillies at the RCMP detachment on Fifty-Seventh Avenue just off the British Columbia Highway in Surrey. Gillies was an attractive man with a youthful face and easy smile. Well-built, he had the broad shoulders and beefy arms of a weightlifter. He shaved his head but for a tuft of hair. Gillies and Tracy stepped into a Ford Interceptor Utility vehicle from the RCMP fleets.

Gillies told her he had arranged to be present at the federal penitentiary in case Tracy encountered any problems gaining admittance. "I speak Canadian," Gillies said.

"You ever tied Jack Flynt to a Hells Angels organization up here?" Tracy asked.

"Nothing like that in his file, though given the size of the load he was smuggling when he got pinched in 2002, one would suspect he is connected to a sizable organization."

"What do you know about the plea deal?"

Gillies shook his head. "Not much except it came together quickly. He pled guilty and served his time."

"Have you seen the terms?"

"The US Attorney and Canadian authorities have a confidentiality agreement in the file but not the terms of the agreement."

"You think those terms included Flynt becoming a government informant when he got out?"

Gillies gave it some thought. "It could be why no terms were provided. They'd want to protect him."

"I'm wondering if that's why he was prosecuted again and given such a seemingly light sentence—to protect him, make him look legit."

"Possibly," Gillies said. "That would require cooperation between the US and Canadian authorities, and that would be well above my pay grade."

"Mine too. Just wondering if we're on a wild-goose chase here."

"We'll know soon enough."

The drive took just over an hour. It was another twenty minutes to pass through various gates, secure Gillies's firearm and other possessions in lockers, obtain guest passes, and step through metal detectors. During this process Gillies advised that the federal institution had a capacity of just under six hundred inmates, most living in medium and minimum security. That included convicted murderers and others who had committed violent offenses, but who were deemed not to be high-security risks. Once inside multiple locked doors, the facility hummed with the cacophony of voices and other noises at an irritating decibel. Tracy knew prisoners often said the most difficult thing to get used to wasn't being locked behind bars or doors, but learning to deal with the constant noise, the lack of any peace or privacy.

The guard led Gillies and Tracy to a glass-enclosed room with tables and plastic chairs placed in a horseshoe pattern. At the front of the room stood an easel with a flip chart and colored pens.

"Looks like a classroom," Tracy said.

"It is," the guard said. "Couple weeks ago, the writer Jack Whyte taught a class on writing. That one usually attracts a crowd." The guard checked his watch. "Flynt and his attorney were meeting, but I'm told they're on their way over."

Minutes later, a reed-thin Jack Flynt entered the room in a blue long-sleeve shirt and pants. According to his record, Flynt was sixty-eight. It took Tracy a minute to place who he looked like. He reminded her a lot of the thin and scruffy actor who had played Toot-Toot in the movie *The Green Mile*. The attorney, Kell Gordon, accompanied Flynt. Gordon was heavyset and wore a dark-brown suit, yellow button-down dress shirt, and paisley tie. Gordon looked like a sweater—a term her colleagues bestowed upon attorneys who perspired profusely in a courtroom.

The four of them pulled out chairs. Gordon immediately attempted to establish himself as the alpha dog. "I want to be sure that you both agree my client will not answer any questions seeking information on any drug smuggling he may or may not have performed after 2002."

Gillies had pegged Gordon's concern on the head, and Gordon had, in essence, confirmed that his client had continued to engage in drug smuggling, which fit with Tracy's suspicion that he had become a government informant.

"I don't have a problem with that," Tracy said.

Gordon looked to Gillies. "Detective?"

"I'm just here to translate for Detective Crosswhite," Gillies said.

"I'll take that as a yes," Gordon said.

Tracy set a file on the table. "In 1995, what was the name of the boat you captained?"

"The *Egregious*," Flynt said in a voice that was higher pitched than Tracy anticipated.

"What type of boat was the *Egregious*?"

"Seventy-five-foot fishing trawler."

"A purse seine fishing trawler?"

"Yep."

"Prior to March 2002, did you make runs from Vancouver to Lake Union in the *Egregious*?"

"I did, yeah."

"Did you on occasion dock the *Egregious* at the Diamond Marina in Lake Union?"

"I did on occasion," Flynt said. He looked to have settled in.

"Do you recall the name of the harbormaster?"

Flynt looked to the ceiling and strained, then shook his head. "No."

"Does the name David Slocum ring a bell?"

"Was he the harbormaster?"

"About five foot eight with a ponytail?" Tracy said.

"Yeah. He'd be the guy."

"Did you pay David Slocum cash for the slip?"

Gordon sat forward. "I'm going to object, Detective. What relevance is that?"

"I'm just asking how he paid, trying to establish I'm in the correct universe." Tracy had spoken to enough inmates and suspects with their counsel present to know when an attorney was just demonstrating to his client that he was earning his pay.

Gordon nodded to Flynt. "I always paid cash," Flynt said.

"Do you recall how much you paid?"

Flynt chuckled and shook his head. "That was a long time ago."

"Did you pay Slocum more than the asking rate for the slip?"

Gordon shook his head. "Again, Detective. What is the point of the question? There's nothing illegal with paying more than the going rate."

"I agree," Tracy said. "There isn't."

Gordon acted perturbed but waved to Flynt. "Go ahead."

"Yes."

"Did you know that David Slocum was not recording your moorage in the Diamond Marina's books?" Tracy didn't know for sure but suspected this based on what Dennis Hopper told her.

"No," Flynt said.

"Before 2002, did you run drugs in the *Egregious*, and on occasion moor overnight at the Diamond Marina?"

"I'm not going to let him answer that," Gordon said.

"I'm asking him about before 2002, for which the six-year statute of limitations to bring any drug-related action has long since expired."

Gordon gave her comment a moment of thought. "Go ahead," he said to Flynt.

"Before 2002 I did use the *Egregious* to run drugs, and I did on occasion moor overnight at the Diamond Marina."

Each answer added credibility to Dennis Hopper's hearsay statement that Slocum told him the *Egregious* had been raided. Tracy didn't want to go there yet. "Did you have a crew?"

"Usually."

"How big a crew? How many?"

"Usually, just me and one or two others. It didn't take more than that to run the boat."

"Were these regular crew members or did they change?"

"They changed."

"Was a crew member placed on board the ship to keep an eye on the product for whoever supplied it?"

"Yeah. That happened."

"Two Mexican men?"

"Again, usually."

"Were you ever raided at the marina in Lake Union?"

"Don't answer that," Gordon said.

"Before 2002, while you moored the *Egregious* at the Diamond Marina, were you ever raided?"

"He's not going to answer that."

Tracy got a hunch and played it. "Per the terms of the confidential plea agreement?"

"Per the terms of the confidential plea agreement," Gordon confirmed.

A light flickered. The plea agreement had not been reached to get Flynt to reveal information, but to conceal it. Tracy opened her file and removed a multipage document stapled in the corner. She acted as if she were reading it, flipped over a sheet, and continued reading. In her peripheral vision she could see Gordon shifting in his chair.

"Per the terms of this agreement entered following the seizure of the *Egregious* by US customs and the Coast Guard in March 2002, you agreed not to mention a raid that took place on your boat on November 18, 1995, and in exchange for that agreement, your sentence on felony drug trafficking was reduced from twelve years to five years. Is that correct?"

"He's not going to discuss the terms of that agreement," Gordon said. "The written document is the best source of that information anyway."

"How much product was on the *Egregious* the night it was boarded?"

"Don't answer," Gordon said.

"What was the street value of that product?"

"Again, don't answer."

"Where was the *Egregious* taken to offload that product the night it was raided?"

"Shilshole—"

"Don't answer that question."

Tracy wanted to get back to questions Flynt would answer. "You were the captain of the *Egregious* from roughly 1989 until it was seized March 10, 2002, correct?"

Flynt looked to Gordon, who again nodded. "That's correct," Flynt said.

"Prior to 2002 your boat was never impounded by United States or Canadian authorities, correct?"

Another nod from Gordon.

"Correct," Flynt said.

"You didn't see the faces of the officers who raided your boat on November 18, 1995, because they wore face coverings; did they not?"

"Don't answer that," Gordon said.

Tracy got another hunch and, again, she played it. "The night of November 18, 1995, your crew was thrown overboard by the men who raided your boat so they could not support your story to your employers that the boat had been raided, though the authorities did not detain you, and the *Egregious* was not impounded; isn't that true?"

"Don't answer that," Gordon said.

"They wore masks," Flynt said. Gordon grabbed Flynt's forearm. Flynt pulled his arm away. "So, I couldn't identify them even if I had wanted to."

"Jack. Do not answer the question," Gordon said.

Flynt stared at Tracy, but his eyes softened. Then he grinned. "She's not interested in me, Kell. I'm just a cog in the wheel she's trying to spin. Isn't that right? You're not interested in the drug deals at all, are you?"

"Jack," Gordon said.

"No. I'm not," Tracy said. "I'm a cold case detective. I'm trying to find out who killed David Slocum, the harbormaster at the marina the night the *Egregious* was raided."

"Jack, as your attorney I advise you that you are breaching provisions of the confidentiality agreement and if you do so . . ."

"I know, Kell. I may have to serve the rest of my suspended sentence. But I'm not about to tell the authorities." He looked at Tracy. "And you aren't either, are you?"

"No, I'm not," Tracy said.

"I'm just here to translate," Gillies said.

Flynt turned to his lawyer. "So that would leave just you, Kell."

Gordon shook his head.

"Then we're good," Flynt said. He looked at Tracy and she read the expression on his face. After all these years, Flynt finally had a chance to even a score, one he had been forced into keeping secret by a confidentiality agreement he'd signed in exchange for a shorter sentence.

"Off the record," Flynt said.

"Jack," Gordon pleaded.

"Sure." Tracy set her pen on her notepad.

"Jack, I cannot protect you if you violate the confidentiality agreement . . ."

"I told you. She doesn't care about the confidentiality agreement, and she isn't here to pinch me for what happened in 1995 or 2002. And I'm not going to say a word to anyone else but her." He stared at Tracy. "You just want to know if I know who raided the *Egregious* that night."

"Do you know?"

"I wish I did, Detective. But like you said, they wore masks. They weren't in uniforms, and I saw no markings on their clothing to let me know who they worked for. But I can tell you they weren't another drug ring or a bunch of punks. They were military or police."

"How do you know that?"

"One, because they went to the trouble of making sure I couldn't identify them by their clothes. Two, it was a well-oiled hit-and-run. They came in fast and heavily armed, and we departed the marina just as fast. And three, something I overheard."

"What did you hear?"

"One of the men turned to the guy who was in charge and called him 'sergeant' before he caught himself."

"What happened to your crew?"

"They thought they were going to kill us and dump our bodies someplace where the tide would take us out to sea. They panicked and jumped overboard."

"Did the men who raided the ship make any effort to rescue them?" Tracy asked.

"None," Flynt said. "Maybe they assumed they could swim. I remember one of the guys who raided the ship saying something like they couldn't say anything anyway, and they'd be happy to just go back to Mexico."

"Where did they take the boat?" Tracy asked.

"Back through the locks to the Shilshole Marina. They had vans waiting and offloaded the drugs in minutes."

Flynt told her the cocaine was wrapped in plastic bricks that weighed one kilogram or roughly 2.2 pounds. "The bricks were then wrapped in paper with a dragon logo."

"How much is a kilogram of cocaine worth?"

"In 1995, upwards of $75,000. But the street value was somewhere between $160,000 to $240,000."

"How many kilograms were you transporting?"

"Fifty."

"How much was that worth, total?"

"Street value? Roughly eight to twelve million dollars."

"The men who raided your boat let you go?"

"Why wouldn't they?" Flynt asked. "I was like the two crew members. Who was I going to tell? Plus, without the crew, I had my own problems. I had to answer to my bosses in Vancouver alone, and they were prepared to kill me."

"What did you do? How did you convince them you were telling the truth?"

"I didn't," he said. "The harbormaster did." Flynt proceeded to tell them what David Slocum had told his bosses. "They came down a few nights after the raid and the harbormaster told them what happened.

He told them about the raid, that they took me and the boat—that I hadn't made it up."

"The harbormaster saved your life," Tracy said.

"I guess he did," Flynt said. "Wish I could have saved his. Wish I knew who killed him. There's no statute of limitations on murder, is there?"

"No. There isn't."

Flynt's face shifted again to that faint smile, like he knew something no one else did. "You strike me as the kind of officer not about to let this go, confidentiality agreements be damned."

"I am," Tracy said.

"Then maybe God exists."

Tracy made a face, not following. "I'm sorry?"

"'When justice is done, it brings joy to the righteous but terror to the evildoers.' Proverbs 21:15."

———

Tracy and Gillies retrieved their possessions and left the prison. On the walk to their vehicle, Gillies said, "That was one hell of a performance."

"I got lucky," Tracy said.

"Bullshit. You knew exactly what you were doing. Just took you a little time to determine which button to push. Who knew a drug dealer was a man with a conscience?"

Tracy smiled. "Not to mention an unquenched thirst for justice."

"Not to mention."

"Problem is, he won't say a word on the record about it. He doesn't want to spend another seven years in prison for breaching his agreement. I have a dead man, a prisoner who won't talk on the record, and a hippie who only heard after the fact."

"I was about to say, from where I sit, you know what happened, but you don't have any credible evidence to prove it."

"I don't, but that's never stopped me before."

Gillies pulled open his door and slid behind the wheel. "I'd sure like to stay involved in this one, Detective. This has got all the earmarks of a brouhaha, as my father liked to say. And I've been in one or two in my day. Keeps this job interesting."

"You look like you've finished a few brouhahas."

Gillies smiled but didn't respond. He didn't have to.

"Make sure Flynt stays safe," Tracy said. "No one knows I came up here. I'm a unit of one. And I've been playing this one close to the vest."

"What do you usually do in a situation like this?"

"I usually charge forward, like a bull in a china shop, until one of my horns sticks in something solid."

Gillies grinned. "Sounds like you're partial to brouhahas also."

"I've been in my share," Tracy said.

CHAPTER 17

Tracy used the drive home that afternoon to go through what she now knew and what it might mean. Dennis Hopper's memory had not been muddled by too much pot. The *Egregious* had moored at the Diamond Marina November 18, 1995. Unfortunately, no written record would confirm it. Captain Jack Flynt had indeed paid cash. Hopper's recollection that David Slocum had told him of a raid on the *Egregious* occurring two nights prior to the men floating up to the dock was also accurate, but not admissible evidence. Hopper hadn't been there the night of the raid. And anything Slocum told him was hearsay. The fact that Slocum was dead and could not testify might constitute an exception under the law, but how far would Tracy get with the word of a marijuana chain-smoker without documentary evidence or testimony to support him? Jack Flynt would not talk on the record, and Tracy couldn't blame him. Flynt's testimony might not do much good anyway; a good attorney would also decimate a twice-convicted drug smuggler.

The next question to explore was, Who raided the boat?

The Last Line, the task force Lisa Childress had been investigating, was the most likely. Flynt said one of the men who had come that night slipped and used the term "sergeant" to address the person who appeared in charge. The articles in the files Anita Childress had put together mentioned a Sergeant Rick Tombs. And Tombs had said in the article that the members of the task force covered their faces to protect their identities—ostensibly from the drug rings they busted, but more likely to protect their illegal activities. The Last Line was disbanded April 2002, shortly after Flynt's arrest and plea deal. If Flynt initiated that deal, the timing made sense. Authorities, unaware of Slocum's death or the deaths of the two crewmen, might have decided to cut Flynt a deal for his silence since they couldn't get him or the Last Line on a drug charge for 1995 anyway. Instead, they disbanded the Last Line rather than highlight what would have been an embarrassment of the highest order without any recourse to prosecute the drug charges, since the six-year state and federal statutes of limitation would have also run out.

Deals like that only got made with the blessing of high-level authority.

Beyond all that was the seeming connection between David Slocum's death and Lisa Childress's disappearance. What Tracy couldn't rationalize was why Slocum would have turned to Childress. According to Dennis Hopper, Slocum had his own secrets to hide. Why get involved? Why reach out to Childress?

Maybe Slocum hadn't reached out to Childress. Maybe Childress had reached out to Slocum, not realizing the extent of the danger to which she had exposed them both.

—

Friday morning, Tracy arrived early to Police Headquarters, grabbed a cup of coffee, turned on her computer, and waited for her messages to load. Like all the detectives, she kept two email accounts, a personal account and her police account. Similarly, she used two cell phones. Her work computer loaded only work-related emails. She expected to spend at least part of her day following up on leads that had come in over the dedicated tip line. After her emails had loaded, Tracy scrolled through the various senders. Most were internal emails from names she recognized. She found an email from the tip line detective, who advised that she'd culled the phone calls and passed on half a dozen for Tracy to further consider. Below that email was a message from an address Tracy didn't recognize.

No-reply@guerrillamail.com

She was about to delete it, thinking it junk mail or a potential virus that would cause her computer to implode, but the department had a server that weeded out such email and protected against viruses. In theory anyway. Tracy clicked on the email.

Re: David Slocum Autopsy

Tracy's stomach fluttered. Goose bumps ran along her arms, like being home alone on a dark night with the drapes open and feeling as though someone was watching her. She read the email.

- Gunshot residue minimal on David Slocum's right hand. None on left hand.
- Slocum left-handed.
- Bullet entry left temple.
- Bullet trajectory angled slightly downward.
- Slocum did not own a gun.
- No suicide note.

Tracy hit "Reply" and typed, "Who is this?"

Moments later she received an expected reply indicating no such address.

She printed out the email, afraid it might disappear, or self-destruct like in the old *Mission: Impossible* television shows. She studied what had been typed. As interesting as she found the contents, she was even more interested in the sender. She forwarded the email to the tech department asking that they identify anything and everything about the email including from where it had been sent.

She went back to the six bullet points. Slocum being left-handed made it far more probable he would have shot himself in the left temple, but also that residue would have been found on Slocum's left hand, not his right. Tracy closed her eyes and thought of the gruesome photographs of David Slocum seated in the driver's seat, his left temple exposed to the window. If someone had shot him, the killer would have been standing, and the angle of the bullet would have been downward. The gun had been found on the passenger-side floorboard, which seemed near impossible if Slocum had shot himself with his left hand. The gun, absent some gymnastics, would have more likely been found near the driver's seat.

Whoever sent the email intended to communicate something Tracy already suspected but could not yet prove. David Slocum did not kill himself. She was about to forward the email to Kelly Rosa and ask her to quietly go through the autopsy report and provide Tracy with her assessment, but she didn't want that request on the police server. She'd send Rosa an email from her private account.

About to log off her computer, she stopped when an email from Chief Weber popped up atop her list. A moment later Tracy's desk phone rang. Caller ID indicated the call was from Chief Weber.

"You got my email?" Weber asked.

"Just opening it now."

"You're prepared for the press conference at ten o'clock this morning to discuss the final bodies found in Curry Canyon and bring closure of this matter?"

Tracy had completely forgotten about the press conference. She lied. "I'm prepared," she said, though she'd spent less than ten minutes thinking about what she might say.

"This matter can be closed; can it not?"

"Rosa has confirmed that no other bodies have been found or show up on ground imaging."

Tracy snuck a peek at the clock in the right corner of her computer screen. The press conference was in just thirty minutes. She swore under her breath.

"I want you to go over the number of victims in general but also specifically, if asked. There will be family members of the two latest victims present, as well as family of the other victims, and I want to present a unified front that we have brought closure to these families." More public grandstanding, Tracy knew, but necessary. "Rosa will be present to answer any questions related to medical and forensic issues and specifically to advise that no more bodies are buried up there, that we aren't abandoning the site. We worked it, and we're confident we have not left a body up there."

"Understood," Tracy said.

"Good. What are you working on?"

About to answer, Tracy caught herself. Maybe Childress had the right idea not to tell her bosses the details of what she worked on. "I'm cleaning up the files from Curry Canyon. Then I'll start evaluating files with the greatest chance for a resolution."

"You might want to come up with something more concrete. I'm going to emphasize that we are moving expeditiously to close as many cold cases as advances in science allow, and that is now your responsibility. I'd like to give the press something concrete."

"I'll take a look at some of the files Nunzio had at the top of his list."

"I'll see you in the conference room at nine forty-five."

That left Tracy fifteen minutes. This would be like cramming for a final.

She hung up and pulled up the cheat sheet she had created for each of the victims buried under the home in North Seattle or in Curry Canyon, including the names of their family members. For the next ten minutes she studied the material. The information came back to her quickly, but not quickly enough. She was out of time. She decided to bring the sheet with her in case she needed it. She set it aside and picked up Nunzio's summary of his most promising files for resolution—those with available DNA. She looked at the clock on her computer screen. No time. She'd read it on the way.

She stepped from her office with both cheat sheets and hurried down the hall, studying Nunzio's list.

—

Tracy waited in the conference room adjacent to the pressroom. Chief Weber, Kelly Rosa, and several members of the forensic team were already present. Weber wanted a strong presence. Tracy stepped to the side to talk softly to Rosa while they waited. "I got an autopsy I'd like you to quietly consider. I need your assessment."

"What about it in particular?"

"Cause of death."

"Sure, send it over."

"I'd like to keep this off the server. Can I send it to a personal account?" Rosa gave Tracy an inquisitive look, but she provided her personal email address.

At ten o'clock sharp, Bennett Lee, who ran the Press Information Office, pushed open the conference room door. "They're ready for you."

"How big a crowd?" Chief Weber asked.

"Packed house." Lee looked at Tracy when he made the comment, not Weber. He'd privately told Tracy that she had become the department's best press draw. Tracy didn't consider the notoriety a positive. Nunzio had neglected to tell her that when you worked as a unit of one and had success, anonymity was not in the cards.

Chief Weber stepped to the podium in front of television cameras, reporters, and photographers. Tracy and the others filed in behind her, with the Seattle Police Department logo on the wall as a backdrop. Weber was all business as she moved through her reports on the findings in Curry Canyon, commended her detectives and her forensic team, expressed her condolences to the families, and reiterated the importance of bringing them closure. She told the assembled that the Seattle Police Department would never give up on a case, no matter how old, that the department would always remember they worked for the people of the state of Washington and would take that responsibility seriously. To that end, she introduced Tracy as "one of Seattle's most decorated violent crime detectives," now devoted to resolving Seattle's backlog of cold cases.

Tracy had attended enough press briefings to know the trick was to say as little as possible while looking completely transparent. She provided those assembled with details about the final two victims, reiterated that she had notified the two families personally, noted their presence in the room, and said she gained her commitment from the strength and the faith shown by every one of the families of the victims. She concluded that the forensic team was satisfied no more bodies were buried in the canyon, and the file could be closed.

"I'll turn the podium over to forensic anthropologist—"

Several reporters spoke up, but one voice resonated above the din. To Tracy, the nasal twang still grated like nails on a chalkboard. "Is it true that after your success in Curry Canyon, you are looking into the disappearance of Seattle investigative reporter Lisa Childress?"

Maria Vanpelt's question hit Tracy like a gut punch, and that feeling that she was being watched again washed over her. Vanpelt, the onetime girlfriend of Violent Crimes Section captain Johnny Nolasco, had been sidelined by Channel 8 when she improperly exposed the wrong man in a serial killer investigation on national television. Vanpelt blamed Tracy for the error, but the two hadn't liked one another before that incident.

Tracy recovered quickly. "We don't discuss active investigations."

"So that investigation is again active?" Vanpelt said. "Is there a new development warranting the reactivation of a twenty-five-year-old disappearance?"

"Again, I can neither confirm nor deny that I am working any particular case."

"The investigation of Childress's disappearance focused on the husband, Larry Childress. Do you have new developments tying Larry Childress to his wife's disappearance?"

"I won't discuss any case, open or closed, until it is resolved. Does anyone have any questions regarding Curry Canyon?"

Other reporters jumped in on topic. Tracy answered several questions, then turned the conference over to Kelly Rosa. She stepped to the back of the room, fuming.

Fifteen minutes later, when the conference ended, Tracy adjourned to the adjacent conference room. Weber dismissed the others but asked Tracy to remain. "I'd like a word."

Weber dropped her public persona. "When I spoke to you earlier this morning you told me you were closing out the Curry Canyon matter and would decide other cases to pursue. Have you started another investigation?"

"It's preliminary. The reporter's daughter recently contacted me and asked me to take another look."

"That's a big case given the victim. Is there some new development warranting another look? New DNA evidence?"

"No. Nothing like that," Tracy said. She almost brought up the can of bear spray found at the David Slocum crime scene, but given what had just transpired in the pressroom, and the mysterious email, she decided again to keep everything close to the vest. Someone had fed Vanpelt information, and that could only be a handful of people, not that Tracy considered Chief Weber one of them.

"How far have you gotten?"

"Not far. As I said, I just pulled the file."

"And dumped speculation back in the husband's lap without any new evidence to justify doing so. You heard Vanpelt. They will go after him."

"I made his daughter aware of that possibility when I first spoke to her."

"I want you to concentrate on cases with DNA evidence. We owe it to the loved ones of those victims to resolve cases that have a scientific possibility of resolution. Unless you have some new evidence justifying reopening the Lisa Childress file and dragging the family through her disappearance again, shut it down and prioritize your cases, as Nunzio did. Am I making myself clear?"

"You are," Tracy said.

Weber seemed to gather herself. "Good work today. I hope to do another of these press conferences soon. They're important for the public and the city council to hear, and they're important to our bottom line."

Tracy returned to her office and heard her desk phone ringing. She checked and confirmed it was an outside line. The receptionist advised the caller was Anita Childress. Tracy took the call.

"Anita?"

"What's going on, Detective?"

"You saw the press conference?"

"What press conference?"

"What are you talking about?" Tracy asked.

"I just got off the phone with my father. Camera crews are parked outside the gate to their house in Medina, and he is receiving calls about you specifically reopening my mother's cold case. He said it was like reliving a nightmare. Are you telling me you held a press conference?"

"No. The conference was about a completely unrelated case, but a television reporter asked about your mother's case."

"How did she find out about it?"

"I don't know, Anita. I'm sorry. I had nothing to do with this."

"I thought we would have a resolution before this went public. I thought it would exonerate my father."

Now was not the time to remind Childress that Tracy had warned her that reopening the case might impact her father. She also decided against telling Childress that Weber had just ordered her to shut down the investigation unless she found some new evidence.

"I'm not sure I can drag my father through this again," Childress said, sounding emotional. "It's not fair to him."

"Again, Anita, I'm sorry. I can try to find out how this happened."

"I'm going to have to rethink this," Childress said. "I'm going to need the weekend to decide whether I want to go forward."

"Does your father need any help?"

"No. The Medina police are out there, and he said their presence is just making it worse. He's going to leave home for a few days and go to their house on Whidbey Island. I'll call you Monday."

Tracy exhaled a long sigh. She couldn't help but think that someone had leaked the information on purpose to complicate the pursuit. She couldn't help but think it also meant she was on the right path, and that path was scaring some people—enough to try to intimidate her and Anita Childress.

And that just made Tracy all the more determined to pursue the case.

Chief Weber told her to shut down the file unless she had new evidence. That gave Tracy the weekend. She looked at her computer and pulled up the leads the detective had culled for her from the tip line.

CHAPTER 18

Tracy organized the half dozen most promising leads. She made phone calls, reaching five of the six people, and asked them a series of questions to determine how much they knew about Lisa Childress, her disappearance, and what new information they thought they possessed. Two of the five seemed worth further investigation. As she considered the information and debated how she might use it, her desk phone rang. Another outside caller.

"Detective Crosswhite, I'm returning your call about a tip I left regarding a picture of a woman on Facebook."

"Yes. You must be—"

"Olga Holley."

"Thanks for calling me back. I'd like to hear what you know, Ms. Holley."

"Well, just what I said on the message. The woman in the photograph, the younger photograph, looks an awful lot like a young woman who once did my bookkeeping."

"Your bookkeeping?" That did not seem likely.

"Yes. Back in 1996 and '97 when my husband and I lived in Escondido."

"Where is Escondido?" Tracy asked.

"Southern California. About thirty-five minutes north of San Diego. She had a different name—the woman had a different name than the Facebook post, but she sure looked like the woman in that picture. My husband thought so as well. We used the tax firm for several years while we lived there."

"What was the woman's name?"

"I actually looked," Holley said. "That's how much the woman resembles the woman on Facebook. I don't have the returns anymore, but I found a letter. Her name was Melissa Childs."

Melissa Childs. *Huh,* Tracy thought.

Holley provided Tracy the name of the tax company. "She met with us to go over our documents for the accountant who filed our returns."

"Did she sign anything?"

"I don't think so. The accountant would have signed our returns and, as I said, we didn't keep them this long. I was surprised I found the letter."

"Anything about her that you remember? Anything specific?"

"Nice lady. Quiet. Didn't say a lot. Not unfriendly but reserved. Maybe that's the word."

"Uncomfortable?"

"Yeah. I guess you could say that."

"Socially awkward?"

"I wouldn't go that far. That's kind of cruel."

"Do you happen to have the number of that accountant?"

"Let me look."

A few moments later the woman returned with the telephone number. "No idea if it is still any good."

Tracy thanked her and hung up. The chances of Lisa Childress being the bookkeeper seemed remote, but the name certainly raised flags. Melissa Childs sounded a lot like Lisa Childress, as did the woman's description of Melissa Childs.

Tracy called the number. It was still in service. She introduced herself and the reason for her call and asked, "Who am I speaking with?"

"Chris. Chris Taylor."

"Chris, how long has the company been in business?"

"I bought it from my father in 2004. He started the branch in about 1975, I believe."

"Is your father still around?"

"No. Dad passed in 2010."

"I'm sorry."

"Thanks, but he was eighty-four and lived a good life. What can I help you with?"

Tracy explained she was looking for someone and asked if he had records that would show the company employed a Melissa Childs.

"She a fugitive?" Taylor asked.

"No, nothing like that."

"If she worked here, it would have been before my time. Is it important?"

Tracy rolled her eyes. *No. I just like calling up random tax companies and shooting the crap.* "It is, Chris. Very important."

"It's just that we're in the middle of tax season, and I'm up to my eyeballs with the April fifteenth deadline looming."

Tracy hadn't considered that. Mentally, she chastised herself. "I have a young woman who hasn't seen her mother for twenty-four years. I have my doubts your Melissa Childs is the same woman I'm looking for, but I'm obligated to pursue this." Tracy wasn't, of course, but she thought it sounded good.

"Okay. Let me get a pen and you can tell me what you need."

Tracy asked for a driver's license or a Social Security number, and a last known address and telephone number. She also asked for a middle name or middle initial, and any photographs, if they had any, which she doubted.

"Photographs aren't likely, unless it's a driver's license. I'll put somebody on this and call you back as soon as I know something. Detective?"

"Yes?"

"Don't take this the wrong way, but I'm going to call back this number and make sure you are who you say you are."

"I think that's an intelligent thing to do."

"Hate to give out the information to some crazy . . . You get my drift. If this is the woman, she has a right to some privacy. Am I right?"

"You're right. Call back to the main line and ask your questions."

"All right. I'll be talking to you."

"Hopefully soon, Chris."

"Quick as I can."

Tracy hung up the phone and killed time going through Nunzio's cheat sheet. She focused on three cold cases that had solid DNA evidence. As technology progressed, scientists could now create DNA "fingerprints" from much smaller DNA samples, just a drop of blood. And next-generation sequencing allowed scientists to analyze and differentiate between mixtures of DNA samples, as might occur when DNA is collected from a rape victim. Detectives could get results much more quickly and at a lower cost, which definitely helped the department's bottom line and allowed the lab to whittle down its significant backlog of cases. The use of familial DNA had also greatly expanded the pool of potential perpetrators to be analyzed, though some ancestry sites did not allow access to their DNA databases, believing the use of their sites to locate a criminal to be an invasion of privacy.

Tracy asked that the three most promising cases be pulled from storage. She'd review them and have them sent to Oz, Mike Melton, the wizard over at the Washington State Patrol Crime Lab. She might be able to keep Chief Weber at bay long enough to find new evidence in the Lisa Childress investigation to justify going forward. If Anita Childress didn't back out.

While she waited for the files to be pulled, Tracy searched the Internet for articles on drug busts in the 1990s, the Last Line, and police corruption in Seattle. She found several articles covering press conferences at which Sergeant Rick Tombs stood at the podium in the PSB, or Public Safety Building. In one photograph, Mayor Michael Edwards stood beside him to announce the arrest of twenty-two suspected drug dealers across the city. Tombs was thick limbed, with a crew cut and intense eyes. He stood and gazed at the camera. A silver badge rested prominently on his thick chest.

"We did our jobs," Tombs was quoted as saying. "And we will continue to do our jobs for the people of Seattle and this state. I hope this sends a message to the drug dealers out there that they do not want to do business in Seattle. We will find you and we will arrest you."

Tracy sifted through more articles detailing the arrests and pleas of all but one of the dealers. Henderson Jones, one of the twenty-two arrested in the sting, had been exonerated when the district attorney dropped the charges on the eve of trial. Jones, twenty-nine, had refused to plead or to take a plea, claiming he was innocent, that the charge had been fabricated, and he had been out of state visiting a brother at the time of the alleged drug deal that implicated him. Jones had documentation to confirm he had not been present—receipts from gas purchases and restaurants near his brother's home hundreds of miles away. Police claimed he had fabricated the receipts, that someone other than Jones had obtained them for Jones to use as an alibi.

Tracy checked the story byline. Lisa Childress. She felt her heartbeat quicken.

"I haven't sold drugs in years and the police know it," Jones had said. "I've been working on a construction crew, bringing in a regular check, getting taxes taken out of my money, making something of myself for my family. And then the police fabricate this BS charge."

Jones, of Rainier Valley, said that since his arrest and yearlong pre-trial hearings, he had been fired from his job and unable to secure employment. "People see the arrest and, you know, they don't want the liability of hiring a drug dealer."

Jones said the Last Line's motivation to go after him went back a long way, when he had run drugs in Rainier Valley. "I did things back then I'm not proud of, and people obviously haven't forgotten. But I've been clean since my son was born. I want my children to have a more stable home."

As the articles printed, the machine humming and clicking, Tracy called the King County Prosecuting Attorney's Office and asked to speak to Rick Cerrabone. Cerrabone was a senior prosecuting attorney in the Most Dangerous Offender Project, MDOP for short, and had been at the prosecuting attorney's office for more than two decades.

"Cerrabone."

"You sound busy," she said, not bothering to identify herself. She and Cerrabone had worked many cases together.

"I'm always busy. What's up?"

"I'm hoping someone could pull a file for me."

"I heard you're no longer working active investigations. You just got a big fancy award; didn't you?"

"This is for a cold case."

"You got the case number?"

"Wouldn't be bothering you if I did. I got a name and a date. The prosecuting attorney dismissed the case. I'd like to find out why."

"Give me the name. Not going to get to it today. Probably have the paralegal pull it Monday."

"Monday works." Tracy provided the name, Henderson Jones, and the date of his arrest.

"How's life outside the shithole?" Cerrabone asked.

"Bright and shiny. You?"

"Not complaining. Planning a family trip to Europe this summer. If I don't die before the plane takes off. I'll have someone call you Monday."

Tracy signed off. Someone knocked on her door and Tracy called out for the person to enter. A young man wheeled in three boxes stacked on a handcart—the three cases she'd asked to be pulled from storage. She'd deliver them to Melton over at Park 90/5 and ask him to work his magic, then head home early.

The desk phone rang. "Typical," Tracy said, answering it.

"Detective Crosswhite. This is Chris Taylor from Escondido. I found that employment file for Melissa Childs. I'm going to scan it. I'll need an email to send it to."

Tracy looked at the time, but that wasn't the reason she provided Taylor with her personal email address. The thought of Maria Vanpelt getting ahold of the information remained fresh.

"How long before you send it?"

"After I close up today at seven; if that's okay."

Tracy knew Taylor was under the gun with the April fifteenth tax deadline closing fast. "That's perfect. Thanks for your assistance."

"Hope it helps that woman find her mother. Can't imagine what that would be like. I still miss my dad and we lost him twelve years ago."

Tracy knew what it was like. It was like waking every morning with a dull ache in your heart.

She disconnected. She had one last thing she needed to check. She called Personnel and asked for the last known address and phone number for Sergeant Rick Tombs. Officers provided the information upon retirement to receive their pension checks. It was also not uncommon for a detective taking over a case file to call a retired detective with questions. She heard the woman in Personnel typing on the keyboard.

"Got an address and phone number," she said. "But the file also indicates the individual is deceased."

CHAPTER 19

After dropping off the files at Park 90/5 and sending Mike Melton an email explaining what she needed, Tracy received the email she had requested from Personnel. The fact that Sergeant Rick Tombs was dead only increased her interest. Tombs retired to an address in Scottsdale, Arizona, and left a cell phone number with a 480 area code, which Tracy presumed was also for Scottsdale. Tracy looked up the address on a search engine. The house was located in Desert Highlands, a golfing community. Curious, she used the search engine to look up other homes in that community and didn't find one under $2.5 million, and that didn't include the likely cost of a golfing membership and the monthly dues. Tombs certainly seemed to have done all right for himself in retirement. She typed in the name Rick Tombs and Scottsdale, Arizona, in a search engine, and one of the first hits was an obituary. Tombs had passed away almost five years ago. His cause of death was not provided.

So he definitely wasn't doing so well.

Tracy arrived home at just after 5:00 p.m. She was anxious to see Daniella. She opened the front door and called out, which elicited the expected Rex and Sherlock alarm bells. Nails clicked on the tile like hail patter on a metal roof. The two dogs came around the kitchen corner so fast they slid sideways, Rex into Sherlock and both dogs taking out the throw rug and crashing into the back of the couch, a tangle of legs and paws, before they righted to greet Tracy.

Tracy kept telling herself it was unconditional love, and she could not put a price tag on that, but she was glad Dan had talked her into tile floors in the entry and kitchen. The hardwood wouldn't have lasted a week under that kind of pounding.

"Where are you two coming from?" Tracy said to her greeters. She set her briefcase on a kitchen chair and scratched each dog and patted both backsides as she worked her way to the rear of the house. "Dan?"

"Outside."

Tracy stepped onto their wood porch. Dan looked to be in the midst of a massive project. Four sturdy beams, ten feet tall, delineated the corners of the porch, and what looked like a thousand other parts—crossbeams and nuts and bolts—lay on the patio or remained in the open cardboard box. Therese gave a wave from the swing set in the corner of the yard in between pushing Daniella seated in a basket. "Do I dare ask?" Tracy said to Dan.

"It's a gazebo," Dan said matter-of-factly. "At least the start of it."

Tracy looked again to the four standing beams.

"It will cover the deck, and the roof is two tiers with space between the tiers to allow smoke to escape from a firepit or a barbecue." Dan held one hand six inches above the other.

"Did we talk about this?" Tracy asked.

"We talked about an outdoor living space we can use year-round, and Costco was having a sale. We saved six hundred dollars."

Tracy stepped along the porch and eyed all the pieces. "And how much did we spend to save six hundred dollars?"

"Twelve hundred dollars."

"Twelve hundred dollars and you have to assemble it yourself? That will take until next summer."

"When we'll use it the most."

"I didn't mean this summer. I meant the following summer."

"Oh, ye of little faith," Dan said. He picked up a thick booklet.

"Look at that instruction manual. It looks like the Gideon Bible. What page are you on?"

"Eight."

"Out of how many? Two hundred?"

"This would go a lot faster if I had more help and less skepticism."

"No doubt. Where are you going to find it?" Tracy walked past him to Therese and Daniella.

"Who's here?" Therese repeated to Daniella. "Who's here, Daniella? Mama. Mama."

"Mama," Daniella said, kicking her arms and legs.

Tracy bent and kissed her. "What are you doing? Are you swinging?" Tracy lifted Daniella from the basket and hugged her.

"I'm worried about Mr. O," Therese said under her breath. "He didn't go into work again today, and when he came home this afternoon, half that box was sticking out the back of his car. I thought it was going to flip over."

Tracy, too, worried that Dan was depressed over his client's suicide, and though he reasoned aloud it had not been his fault, reasoning and believing were not the same thing, Tracy knew. "Well, that project will keep him busy for a few days. Maybe take his mind off things."

"You two should take a break and go away for the night. I'll take care of Daniella for you."

It was not a bad idea. They could go to Cedar Grove Saturday morning and do nothing for the weekend but hike the mountains and relax by the fire at night reading books and sipping wine. But Tracy hated to leave Daniella, and Dan did as well. She spent too few waking hours with her daughter during the week; she tried to put aside everything but Daniella on weekends. If she and Dan could get away, they would bring Daniella with them.

She took out her cell phone and checked the weather in the North Cascades, but the weekend forecast was for rain with sleet and high winds. So much for that idea. Maybe they could get out and golf. Tracy carried Daniella back to the porch where Dan read the manual. "You get it all figured out?"

"I think Mandarin would be easier to follow."

"It's getting late. Call Tim and see if he has time to help you tomorrow or Sunday." Tim Berg was a retired Boeing engineer who could fix just about any problem. Tracy had initially met his wife through her parenting group, and the four had become fast friends. "I can invite Brenda over and we'll take the girls to the park and cook dinner when you're done."

"Done? You said I wouldn't be done until next summer."

"Yes, but that was before I thought of Tim."

Dan frowned. "Funny."

"I'll bring you a beer and we can enjoy what daylight we have left. What do you want for dinner?"

Neither felt up to cooking so they ordered Thai food, then drank beer on the back porch, killing time before Dan left to pick up the order. Tracy fed Daniella in her high chair. In between spoonfuls of yams, Tracy's phone pinged. A new email from a CTaylor.

Tracy opened the email, which included four attachments. Tracy opened the first attachment, a copy of Melissa Childs's California driver's license. She used her fingers to increase the size of the photograph. When she did, the photo nearly took her breath away.

"Oh my God," she said.

If it wasn't Lisa Childress, it was an uncanny likeness.

Tracy quickly opened the other documents. One was a Social Security card. Tracy would have to compare the number with the card in Lisa Childress's cold case file and compare the handwritten signatures.

Daniella squawked. Tracy held the spoon with a scoop of yams inches from the poor girl's mouth. "I'm sorry, baby," she said. She fed her, wiped the corners of her mouth, and fed her another spoonful. Then she went back to the driver's license. The address was in Escondido, California. Melissa Childs's date of birth was June 1, 1967. Tracy recalled Lisa Childress's date of birth to have been in January 1965. But something about that photograph nagged at Tracy.

Daniella let out another yelp. Tracy shook her thoughts and lowered her phone. Daniella stared at her. "Sorry about that. Did you want Mommy's attention? Are you all done?" She scooped the remaining yams and fed Daniella, then she wet paper towels and cleaned off her daughter's hands and mouth. She was about to lift Daniella from the high chair when she heard Dan's SUV pull up to the front of the house, again triggering the dog sirens. Startled, Daniella cried. Tracy lifted her from the chair and consoled her as the dogs shot out of the room, their nails again clicking on the tile just before they slid.

Tracy didn't immediately bombard Dan with the email she had received and the picture of Melissa Childs. After they ate, she got Daniella to bed, and she and Dan eased into the hot tub, setting a bottle of Syrah and the baby monitor on a table within reach.

"Boy, have our lives changed," Dan said. "We now pair a Syrah with a baby monitor."

Tracy laughed. She didn't bring up the topic of the suicide, figuring Dan needed the break. They talked instead about the outdoor project and Dan's motivation.

"I guess I just needed a mental break," he said, raising the subject himself.

"A mental break? Einstein couldn't build that thing."

Dan laughed. "Tim will be a big help. He'll probably reengineer the entire gazebo and make it better. How was work?"

She recognized the change in topics. "You want to hear something unbelievable?"

"Good news or bad news?"

"I don't know yet, but I may have found Lisa Childress."

"The reporter who went missing?" he asked, sounding skeptical.

"I think so." She told Dan about the tip, then grabbed her phone from the deck and held it above the frothing water. "Take a look at this." She showed him the picture of Lisa Childress and the driver's license photo of Melissa Childs.

"Holy shit," Dan said. "Sure looks like her."

"Then I'm not imagining it?"

"What are you going to do?"

"Try to make contact."

"What about Chief Weber?"

"She wants me to pursue cases with evidence that can bring a resolution. I'd say this qualifies. I'll take a sick day or a personal day and take a flight down to Escondido Monday."

"Have you spoken with the daughter or the husband?"

"No. And I don't intend to—not until I know for sure it's her and find out whether she wants to be put in contact with her daughter." Tracy could think of no worse anguish than to tell Anita Childress she had found her mother alive, only to then have to tell her it had been a mistake or, worse, that Childs did not want to meet her.

"That raises another issue; doesn't it?" Dan said.

"If it's her, she left her daughter, her husband, and her parents and let them think she was dead."

Dan shook his head. "How does somebody do that to people they love?"

"I don't know," Tracy said.

A person could voluntarily disappear. Nothing illegal about it; if that was in fact what Childs had done. Women in abusive situations often fled, sometimes with the help of agencies who found them places to live and provided them with new identities with the hope that their abusive significant others never found them again.

"Have you spoken to the daughter since the press conference?"

"Only the one phone call."

"What will you do if she doesn't want to go forward?"

"I'll still fly down. I've come this far. I'm going to finish it."

"I don't blame you, Tracy, but are you going to be able to sit on this, if it is Childress and she tells you not to say anything to her daughter?"

"I'm going to have to."

"But can you? That's a heck of a burden to carry."

"I'll take it one step at a time. You want to watch a movie and go to bed early?"

"Yeah, that sounds good," Dan said softly.

"Don't sound so enthusiastic."

He smiled. "It's going to take a little while."

"I know," Tracy said.

"Thanks for understanding and, most importantly . . ."

"What?" Tracy asked, concerned.

"Thanks for calling Tim, because I was about to throw the whole thing out."

She splashed water at him.

⸺

While Dan showered, Tracy went back to the email from Chris Taylor and took her phone down to the home office where she had Lisa Childress's file in her briefcase. She turned on the desk lamp, pulled the file out, and looked at the Washington State driver's license. It had been issued in 1990, likely Childress's second license, if she got her first at sixteen.

She looked at the California driver's license that Chris Taylor had sent. It was issued June 15, 1996, not long after Lisa Childress had disappeared. She opened the third document and found an employment application. Melissa Childs's middle initial was A. She applied for part-time work at H&R Block. Under the section asking for education, Childs had put *Palomar College—Escondido Center*, with a start date of *6/96*. She did not provide an end date. She had drawn a slash line through the box asking for degrees earned. Under Major/Subject she wrote: *bookkeeping/firefighting*. An interesting combination. Under Special Skills, Childs wrote: *Fast learner*. She did not provide any prior work experience.

It was almost as if Melissa Childs had fallen from the sky that June 1996. Everything flowed from that date. Tracy wondered. Could it be possible? Could Childress have done as Dan had speculated? Could she have just walked away from a daughter, started fresh?

Tracy thought of Daniella and didn't think it possible.

It also didn't explain the can of bear spray—or David Slocum.

CHAPTER 20

Monday morning, Tracy called Police Headquarters and told the Personnel Department she didn't feel well and was taking a sick day. It was a white lie, and it didn't hurt anyone but herself. She'd use one of her sick days.

She'd have the house to herself. Therese took Daniella to a day-care session that was supposed to introduce Daniella to other children and teach her things like sharing. Tracy thought it dubious, but it was a chance for both Therese and Daniella to get out of the house and for both to be with children and adults the same age. Dan had gone into his office that morning. He seemed better. The weekend project had proven to be therapeutic. Tim and Dan spent all day Saturday and Sunday constructing the structure—it had been that complicated, but they got it put together and the four of them ate beneath it Sunday night.

Tracy shut the door to her home office and requested that Alexa play a classical station. She found the phone number to the Escondido police station and asked to speak to someone in the Missing Persons Unit. She was told a missing person would be handled by the Investigations Bureau. After several starts and stops, a lieutenant in the

Special Investigation Division picked up, and Tracy explained who she was and the purpose for her call.

"Can you give me the name and date of birth again of the missing person?" he asked.

Tracy did. "What would you like us to do, Detective?" he asked in a less than enthusiastic tone, likely concluding that after twenty-four years, Tracy was conducting a wild-goose chase and he would be coming home with an empty sack.

"I'd like to find out if she's still living at the address I provided, or if she's even still in Escondido. I ran her through what databases I could up here and came up empty."

"You said you're trying to determine if she's a person who went missing twenty-four years ago?"

"That's correct."

"And you said she worked as a bookkeeper and maybe as a firefighter?"

"That appears to be what she was studying at the local college there."

"Did you call the fire department? Maybe she worked for them."

He was passing the buck, but at least the pass seemed to be in the right direction. "Do you have a number?"

"The fire department administrative office is here in this building. That would be your best bet, rather than calling each fire department in town." Tracy didn't know the number of departments in town, but after witnessing the Southern California summer wildfires on the news the last few years, she knew there were never enough firefighters. The lieutenant provided the number and told Tracy to call back if she struck out and he'd try to track down a current address through the California DMV and property rolls.

Tracy thanked him. Minutes later, she was working her way through the Escondido Fire Department's administrative offices.

"What year was that?" a woman asked.

"Had to be 1996 or thereafter."

"Hang on." The woman put Tracy on hold again. Several minutes later, another voice came on the phone, a man. Tracy expected him to also pass the buck.

"This is Fire Chief Mark Davis. How can I help you?"

Tracy hadn't expected the chief, and she wondered what would warrant her talking to the top brass. She provided an abbreviated story, expecting to get kicked back to the police department. When she finished, she heard only silence. "Hello? Chief Davis?"

"Yeah, I'm here." He sounded like he had a lilt in his voice, almost like when someone said, *You're kidding, right?* Tracy couldn't blame the man.

"I thought we got cut off," she said.

"No. No we didn't. It's just . . . well, Detective, there have been some folks waiting twenty-four years for this call."

———

Late that afternoon, Tracy stepped off a plane at San Diego International Airport into sunshine, palm trees, and a warm breeze that brought the smell of the Pacific Ocean. Just outside the airport terminal, a silver-haired man about Tracy's height waited for her in navy-blue pants and a light-blue, short-sleeve shirt with the Escondido Fire Department emblem on his shoulder. Chief Mark Davis greeted Tracy with a warm but hesitant smile. He looked like a fireman, a cliché for sure, but he was lean, muscled, and seemingly in excellent shape. He also had a bronze San Diego glow—someone who spent time outdoors.

"Sorry," he said. "I must look like the village idiot, grinning this way, but this is about as strange a situation as I have ever been a part of."

"Me too," Tracy said. "I really didn't expect to find Lisa Childress alive—if it's Lisa Childress."

"Well, I'll let the police chief fill you in on those details and you can decide."

"You've spoken to her? She wants to meet with me?" Tracy had asked Davis to determine if Melissa Childs wished to speak to her.

"She does. She definitely does." Davis flashed that same bright smile that seemed as permanent as his Southern California tan. "She's nervous. 'Confused' might be a better word. But like the rest of us, she's also intrigued. I'll fill you in on what I know on the drive back to Escondido. It's just over an hour. We'll hit some traffic at this time of day, but hopefully not too bad."

Davis led Tracy to the passenger side of a fire-engine-red truck, the door emblazoned with the Escondido Fire Department emblem above the words "Fire Chief" in gold block letters.

The interior of the truck had the smell of fresh leather and the vanilla-scented deodorizer tree hanging from the rearview mirror. The radio was tuned to a newscast. Davis shut it off.

After pleasantries and a little groundwork to set the scene, Davis said, "Melissa came to the fire department from Palomar College. A good many of us studied fire sciences there. She also studied bookkeeping. She got a part-time job at the H&R Block in town—back then there was only one or two—and she volunteered at the fire department. She's smart. Picks up things quick. It wasn't a real surprise when her part-time bookkeeping work became full-time, and she scaled back her volunteer hours at the fire department to weekends. Everybody in town pretty much knew about her circumstances, showing up at the shopping mall and not remembering who she was, but in time she settled in and just became part of the community."

"How did you know her?"

"I was a newbie at the fire department when she started volunteering. I can't remember who came first, but she volunteered at several of the station houses."

"What did you know about her, outside of work?"

"Not a lot. She didn't really talk about herself much, and I respected her privacy. Most people did."

"What was she like?"

"When she started?" Davis kept smiling, and Tracy realized the smile was his demeanor. She knew people like Davis, who seemed eternally happy, and she wished, at times, she could emulate them. "She was like a lost soul. Quiet. Polite. Deferential. A little different," Davis said. He looked to be struggling with words.

"What do you mean 'a little different'?"

"She's a bit awkward," he finally said. It fit the Lisa Childress Anita had described to Tracy. "She keeps to herself—but she's friendly when you engage her," he was quick to add. "She's a hard worker. We enjoyed having her around the firehouses."

"She doesn't work for the fire department anymore?"

"No. Not for some time now. Her employer at H&R Block encouraged her to go back to school and become a CPA. She's had an accounting office in Escondido for years. A lot of people use her because she's whip smart. Saved me a lot of money on taxes more than once."

"She's still a CPA then?"

"Still has a practice in town."

"Married?"

"No. No kids either. Not that I'm aware of, anyway. I shouldn't say this. It isn't exactly kind, but we used to wonder if maybe she was an alien who dropped from the sky, you know? Like Jeff Bridges in that movie . . . Back before *True Grit* and he started playing every role like he was Rooster Cogburn."

"*Starman*," Tracy said. She and Dan had stumbled on the movie one evening and found it cute, a tearjerker.

"That's the one. Melissa has no history. No past. She was just here one day. The police even checked with authorities in Ireland. Never found out a single thing about her."

"Ireland?" Tracy asked, surprised. "Why Ireland?"

Davis looked across the car and for the first time lost the smile. He gave her an inquisitive look. "She's Irish."

"Are you sure?"

"The person you're looking for isn't?"

"Maybe ancestrally, but Lisa Childress was born and raised in the Pacific Northwest."

Davis shook his head. "I'm sorry, Detective. I hope this hasn't been a wild-goose chase. The Melissa Childs I know has an Irish accent. It's not as thick as it was when she first showed up, but you can't miss it, even after twenty-five years."

—

Less than an hour later, Davis pulled off the interstate and drove through a quaint valley ringed by rocky hills of scrub brush. Palm trees lined the streets, their leaves rustling gently in the warm breeze. The buildings, and what homes Tracy could see, like most in Southern California this close to the Mexican border, had a heavy Spanish architectural influence, stucco with tile roofs.

"Beautiful town," Tracy said.

"You should have seen it thirty years ago. It's sprawling now, comparatively. Entire towns have sprung up all around us."

Davis pulled into a parking lot off the Centre City Parkway, a main thoroughfare, and parked in a spot bearing his name and position as fire chief. They approached a cream-and-salmon-colored stone building. It looked more like a symphony hall with two-story columns atop steps framing a glass entrance. Davis explained that the building housed both the Escondido Police Department, which consisted of roughly 170 sworn officers, and the fire department's administrative offices.

"It looks brand new." Tracy slipped on sunglasses, a rare need in Seattle in April.

"It's a decade old now, but we like it," Davis said.

Davis escorted Tracy through security to elevators that led to a second-floor receptionist. She put them in a conference room, offered them coffee or tea, which they both declined, and told them Police Chief Rafael Beltrán would be with them momentarily. As Davis poured two glasses of water, Tracy walked to the conference room windows and looked out at a city park. More palm trees stretched above other foliage. Behind the greenery, the rattlesnake-colored hills and the tile roofs reflected the glow of the afternoon sun.

Beltrán entered the conference room with general greetings and shut the door behind him. Unlike Davis, he wasn't smiling. He looked skeptical, as if reserving judgment. Tracy didn't blame him. Beltrán had a barrel chest, thick limbs, and short gray hair. On the drive from the airport, Davis told Tracy Beltrán had, as a young man, played major league baseball in Mexico before immigrating to the United States, where he'd become a police officer and a scratch golfer.

Davis made introductions and Beltrán invited them to take seats at the table. "I thought I'd give us a few moments to chat before Melissa arrives," Beltrán said, and Tracy heard a trace of his Spanish accent. "You can imagine this is a call we never thought we'd receive."

"Detective Crosswhite is confused, Rafa," Davis said. "The person she's looking for grew up in the Northwest and definitely did not have an Irish accent."

Beltrán looked from Davis to Tracy.

"Everything else seems to fit the timeline when Lisa Childress went missing, and the photograph is spot on," Tracy said. "If it isn't her, it's her doppelganger."

"I take it you've brought photographs of Lisa Childress," Beltrán said.

Tracy removed the file from her briefcase and set the photographs on the tabletop along with the forensic artist's drawings of what Childress would likely look like at fifty-five years of age.

Beltrán picked up the photographs and Davis moved behind him. The two men studied them. Davis smiled. "Sure looks like Melissa," he said.

"If it isn't her, it's like you said. It's her twin," Beltrán said.

"Perhaps you can tell me what you know about Childs, how she came to Escondido," Tracy said.

"I wasn't here back then, but I know the story, and I pulled her file while I was waiting," Beltrán said. "Twenty-four years ago, I believe it was February or March, a security guard at the local mall found a woman wandering around as the stores were closing. He said she looked confused, and he offered assistance. The woman said she was lost. He asked her name, and she said she didn't know. He asked for ID, and she said she didn't have any."

Seattle police had found Lisa Childress's bag with her wallet and all her identification in her car.

"All she had was a copy of a book, and if you've read the classics, you'll think this really odd. I sure did. She had a copy of *The Count of Monte Cristo*."

Tracy did indeed know the story of Edmond Dantès, falsely accused of treason by his erstwhile but envious friend and sentenced to prison. While in solitary confinement, Dantès communicated with the prisoner in the cell next door and learned of an immense, hidden treasure. A daring escape, a fortune found, and Dantès returned as the count of Monte Cristo to exact revenge on all those who betrayed him.

"She also had a car key, a torn Greyhound bus receipt, and cash."

Tracy thought of the garage just a few blocks from the Greyhound bus terminal in Seattle and the fact that Childress had withdrawn a hundred dollars from her account that evening.

"The guard and Childs tried every car in the parking lot, but the key didn't fit," Beltrán said. "He eventually brought her to the police station, which was at a different location back then, and the police ultimately took her to Palomar Medical Center, which had a behavioral center. She stayed there while they tried to determine who she was and where she'd come from. I'm not sure where the switch was missed, like I said, I wasn't here then, but the police never got a hit."

"Do you know to whom they sent her photograph?"

"My understanding is the police agencies in California, as well as to the FBI and Interpol because Childs spoke with an Irish accent."

"But not outside of California?"

"I don't believe so. No."

"Did she speak Gaelic?"

"I don't know the answer to that question. According to what I read in the file, they did say the accent was thick. Nobody said it wasn't legitimate. The file also indicates the police searched flights from Ireland to Southern California for a woman flying alone and between the ages of twenty and thirty-five, but they never found a match."

"How long was she in the hospital?"

"Just about four months. The doctors decided they'd done all they could to help her."

"What do you mean? Was she physically hurt?"

"She had a head wound when they found her, but she couldn't tell them how she got it. But that's not what I meant. Seems the doctors concluded Childs had amnesia. They said her memories might or might not come back."

"The doctors diagnosed her with amnesia?"

"That was their diagnosis." Beltrán shrugged. "After four months trying to restore her memory, they helped her restart a life. She obtained a new driver's license and a Social Security card, and she was given a place to live in a home until she got on her feet."

"Eventually she went to school at Palomar," Davis interjected. "She was bright. There was nothing cognitively wrong with her."

"So then she knows she has amnesia?"

Beltrán shook his head. "You'll have to ask her, or somebody at the hospital."

"It all just seems too coincidental, including the name, to not be her," Tracy said. The name sounded like something a person in hiding might use. It was similar to her real name and could be easily remembered. Lisa Childress. Melissa Childs. "She has a middle initial of A. Do you know what it stands for?" Childress's middle name was Janet.

Beltrán and Davis both shook their heads.

The conference phone in the center of the table rang. Beltrán answered it, thanked the caller, and disconnected. He looked at Tracy. "You can ask her. She's here. I'll go get her."

CHAPTER 21

The woman Beltrán escorted into the conference room looked tentative, confused, and uncomfortable, which was certainly understandable. Tracy thought again of Anita Childress's description of her mother as being autistic, and she wondered if that explained this woman's demeanor, or if it was the demeanor of someone hiding for decades who had just been caught. Whatever the answer, Tracy was still coming to grips with the realization that Lisa Childress was alive. She hadn't truly expected this person to be Childress, even on the drive from the airport. When Davis mentioned the Irish accent, Tracy had resigned herself to the likelihood that she had found the wrong person. Even now, seeing Childress in the flesh, a part of Tracy still doubted it. The woman looked like the photographs taken decades ago, and even more like the forensic artist's sketch drawing, but that isn't what convinced Tracy. What convinced Tracy was Melissa Childs looked very much like Anita Childress—thick boned with dark hair; round, youthful features; and dark, inquisitive eyes that found Mark Davis, a familiar face, first.

"Hi, Mark," she said, voice quiet and unsure.

"Hello, Melissa. How have you been?"

"I've been all right. In a bit of a shock at the moment." Her accent reminded Tracy very much of Therese's accent, which Tracy had become familiar with. She listened intently to see if Childs might break character and say a word that didn't sound quite right.

"I think it's a shock for all of us," Davis said.

Childs looked to Tracy from across the conference room table. "Are you the detective from Seattle, then?"

"I am," Tracy said, offering a soft smile.

"Well then . . . I guess we should get down to it."

They pulled out chairs and sat at the table. Childs repeated what Beltrán and Davis had already told Tracy, but Tracy let the woman talk, tried not to interrupt, and just listened to her story. She wanted Childs to relax. Childs told Tracy it was like she had awakened in the Escondido shopping mall from a deep sleep. She had no idea how she got there or who she was. Nothing she possessed, not the novel *The Count of Monte Cristo* or the bus ticket, had any context to her. She couldn't recall being on a bus, and the fragment of the ticket she had only provided the destination, not the starting point.

"Sometime later, I don't know when, I recalled a woman brought me to the mall, but not too clearly."

"You must have been terrified," Tracy said, still evaluating Childs, looking for any inconsistencies in her accent or her story details.

"I was for sure. It was as if I'd been dropped from space and landed here." Tracy glanced at Davis, who smiled at Childs. "I was like a book that you open and find all the pages blank. I couldn't remember a thing. Not one."

Childs discussed the security guard at the mall and eventually how she ended up at the hospital. "That was tough. The confusion gave way to a deep depression. I looked at all the people around me—the nurses and the doctors and the people who came to visit other patients—and I could rationally think to myself that I should remember a mother and a father, at least. I wasn't hatched, you know. I was born and raised just like all those other people. I knew, intuitively, I had to come from somewhere. I just had to." Childs paused. A tear ran down her cheek.

Davis grabbed a tissue box from the back of the room and slid it down the table. Childs thanked him and pulled a few tissues, blowing her nose. Davis poured her a glass of water and set it on a coaster.

"It's just such a lost feeling to not know who I am, or how I fit in this world. I had no choice but to forge ahead . . . stiff upper lip and all. But from where I was forging . . . I didn't have a center post to ground me. I didn't have any concept of my past. Was I married? Did I have children? I didn't know if I had an education, and if so, in what subjects. I watched television in the hospital, and I'd lost everything historical as well. I didn't know the people—not the actors or the news anchors. I didn't know the news. I didn't recognize anything happening in the world, or its meaning." She dabbed at more tears. "This call came like a jolt of electricity. It shocked me. Is it true? Do you know who I am? Can you tell me?"

Tracy had come armed with photographs of Lisa Childress's family . . . her mother and her father, her husband Larry, and of course Anita. She'd also come with news articles of Lisa Childress's disappearance, and articles that Lisa had worked on during her final days at the *Seattle Post-Intelligencer*. But how much should she tell a woman who didn't seem to remember any of it? How much pain would that cause Melissa Childs, and hadn't she suffered enough? Could Tracy somehow be that jolt of electricity that shocked the woman's brain or heart beyond repair? *Slowly,* she said to herself. *Start slowly and see how she handles the information provided.*

"I can . . . some of it. The better question, Melissa, is how much do you want to know and how fast do you want to know it? I guess what I'm asking is how much do you think you can handle, after all these years?"

Childs seemed to consider the question. Her gaze moved from Tracy to the tabletop and back again. "You have to understand . . .

I have no concept of who I am . . . So I have no concept of what my dreams, my aspirations, or my goals were. I didn't even understand the holidays. I'd never had a Halloween or a Christmas. I'd never carved a pumpkin and I didn't know who Santa Claus was. I'd never been to Mass . . . didn't know what it was or if I was religious. That first Thanksgiving I had my first bite of roast turkey." She shook her head. "I can remember one of those first nights in the hospital, looking out the window and seeing all those lights in the sky, and I had no idea what they were. I saw the moon, but I had no idea what I was looking at. If I could make it through those days, I can make it through whatever you tell me. I don't think I can be any more terrified than I was then. I think you should just start, Detective, and I'll let you know when it becomes too much."

Tracy opened her file and took out the pictures of Childress at various ages. The photographs included a driver's license. Tracy also provided the copy of the Social Security card bearing Childress's name and her signature. She slid them across the table one at a time. "Your maiden name is Lisa Janet Siegler," she said. "You were born January 18, 1965."

"Did you say '1965'?" Childs looked up at Tracy, but she appeared to be doing math in her head. "I'm fifty-five then? Not fifty-three?" She looked to Davis. "How do you like that, Mark? I've lost two years just sitting here at the table."

Davis offered a wistful smile.

Tracy slid over two photographs of Childress's parents as they looked in 1995. "That's your mom, Beverly Siegler."

Childs picked up the photograph and considered it. Tracy had expected perhaps a tear or two, but Childs viewed the photograph as if viewing someone else's photo album, polite but not invested. "That's my mum?"

"Yes," Tracy said handing her a more current picture.

Childs considered the second photograph. "I look like her, don't I? Around the eyes I mean. Is she alive, my mum?"

"She is. She's in her eighties now. She was one of the first female cardiac surgeons in the United States."

Childs's eyes widened and she gave a hint of a smile. "Was she really?"

"She was," Tracy said, but Childs didn't ask anything further. She studied the picture as if viewing a stranger. Tracy handed Childs a picture of her father. "This is your father, Archibald Siegler."

Childs considered it. "What did he do?"

"He wrote novels."

"Really? Anything I would have read?"

"I don't know," Tracy said. She felt a depression settling in, wondering if she was somehow setting up Anita and Beverly for more pain. She would bring home a woman who didn't know them as her mother or as her daughter. They would just be people.

"I didn't inherit much of his genes, then. I can't write a lick. I'm much better with numbers."

"Actually, I'll get to that in a minute."

Tracy pointed to a more recent photo of Childress's father. "This was your father later in life. He's passed away, I'm afraid."

"Do you know what from?" Childress asked, again seemingly without any emotional attachment.

"I don't," Tracy said. She thought of those many nights she had spent in her one-bedroom apartment, poring over her sister Sarah's file after their father had taken his life and her mother had become a recluse in Cedar Grove, thinking perhaps that finding Sarah might help Tracy to find the young woman she had once been and provide a sense of belonging. She had no one to love, no real family, not the one she had known. She had only her job and her obsession. She simply survived, until she met and fell in love with Dan, and Daniella was born. She wondered if Childs had survived because she didn't know what she had missed, and Tracy wondered how she would react when that curtain raised, and she realized she was both a daughter and a mother.

"But you had more in common with him than you think," Tracy said.

"Did I, now?"

Tracy handed Childs the articles from the *Seattle Post-Intelligencer*. The woman took them tentatively. Tracy detected no reaction when Childs scanned the headlines or the byline, no expression of recollection. She looked over the articles, then back to Tracy. "Lisa Childress? Is this me?"

"You were a reporter for this paper."

"Get out." Her voice rose.

"An investigative reporter. A very good one." Tracy watched Childs for any kind of reaction, anything that might give away . . . something. Might reveal that Childs knew more than she was letting on. But if she was, Tracy didn't detect it.

Again, Childs looked to Davis. "Never thought I could write a grocery list, let alone a news story."

"You learn something new every day," Davis said.

"You certainly do."

Tracy pulled out the photographs of Larry Childress in 1995 and at present. She slid them across the table. Again, Childs gave no indication she recognized the man. "That," Tracy said, "is your husband."

Childs dropped her gaze to the photographs. "I figured I was married when you said my mum and dad's name was Siegler. How long were we married?"

"About three years," Tracy said. "You changed your name to Lisa Childress."

"What did he do?"

"He was in technology for a bit, then real estate. He sold homes. But mostly . . ." Tracy reached into the file and took out pictures of Anita Childress as a two-year-old and as an adult. "He stayed home and watched your daughter."

Tracy watched Childs closely. Unlike the prior photographs, she did not reach for the pictures of her daughter. They remained on the table-top. Childs brought a hand to her mouth and Tracy noticed a tremor.

"Are you okay, Melissa?" Beltrán asked.

She nodded but did not verbally respond.

Davis slid the glass of water closer. "Do you want some water?"

"Yes, please," she said softly. She took a sip and set down the glass. "Thank you." Tracy waited, quiet. Childs picked up the photograph of Anita as a two-year-old. After a minute she said to the photograph, "I've seen her."

Tracy and Davis exchanged a glance. "When?" Tracy asked.

Childs's gaze shifted to the tabletop. "When I closed my eyes those many years ago, I would see this child. I had no idea who she was. I thought maybe it was me as a little girl, but I saw her . . . and I felt her." She raised her gaze to Tracy. "I felt a bond. You know what I mean; I can tell you know what I mean. You have a child."

"A little girl."

"How old?"

"Just about half a year younger than your daughter in that picture."

"You know what I mean when I say, I felt her."

"I think I do." Tracy's mother used to say the strongest natural bond is the bond between a mother and her child. Humanity would not exist without it.

"She's the reason for my name," Childs said.

"What do you mean?" Tracy asked.

"I didn't know my name." She gave a small shrug. "I had to invent one just like I had to invent myself. I had to come up with a name, an identity to get my driver's license and Social Security card. Where do you start?" She gave another shrug. "Then I remembered this little girl from my dreams. My little child, I thought. Somehow. That's how I decided. Melissa Childs. My little child."

Tracy thought Childs chose the name because it so closely related to her real name, but nothing in the woman's voice or her demeanor indicated she was lying. After a moment, Tracy asked, "And the *A*? Your middle initial. What's it for?" She thought Childs would say *Anita*.

But Childs raised her gaze from the photographs and said, "Anonymous. Melissa Anonymous Childs."

CHAPTER 22

As the light faded outside the conference room windows and the hillside light softened from a fiery red and yellow to muted grays, Tracy concluded the meeting with Melissa Childs, maybe after imparting too much information. "I'm going to leave you with your thoughts."

"Are you staying in town?" Childs asked.

"No. No, I'm going back home on a flight tonight."

"To see your daughter."

Tracy almost said, *I don't like to be away from her,* but caught herself. "I'm going to leave those materials with you to look at. You can decide what you would like to do. It's a lot to think about. I want to caution you that this could be painful, and you shouldn't make this decision lightly, whatever you decide to do."

"I think I've caused enough pain," Childs said. "I can only imagine what my mother and daughter went through."

Tracy noted that Childs had not mentioned her husband. "You should know that your husband was suspected of having something to do with your disappearance."

"Why?"

"The husband is always a suspect. The press and . . . the police can be merciless in this regard. Even though your husband wasn't officially charged or prosecuted, many condemned him as guilty. It was not an easy time for him, and that suspicion became difficult for your daughter as she got older and could understand."

"That sounds like a reason to come back. So people know I'm all right."

"Your husband has moved on. He has a new family. My finding you could reopen old wounds."

"And for my daughter, Anita?"

"Anita is the one who asked me to find you, but she's vacillating now, seeing the pain that reliving your disappearance has caused her father. Don't get me wrong. Your daughter and your mother will be elated to know you're alive and well, but outside factors also need to be considered."

"Like the media," she said.

"Like the media. This won't remain hidden. You were a reporter, after all. You're newsworthy. Your coming back will be news, and you won't be able to hide forever, no matter how hard you try."

"Might be best to just tear off the Band-Aid then."

"I don't know. Maybe a media consultant could guide you. But I will keep this as quiet as I possibly can. You should also know that before Lisa Childress disappeared, she was working on some sensitive stories. They're the kind of stories that could injure some people, and I have uncovered some evidence that your disappearance might not have been completely accidental."

"I don't understand?"

"When the security guard found you, did you have any blood on your body or your clothing?"

Childs looked like she was slipping back a million years, though her gaze never left Tracy. "How did you know?"

"They found blood, your blood, in the car you drove."

"That was why I sought the guard's help. I had blood on my jacket and my shirt, but I didn't know how it got there."

"Do you know where the blood came from?"

"The back of my head, I assumed. I had a welt and a cut. It's why they thought I had fallen and struck my head. They thought that was maybe the reason I couldn't recall anything."

"Would you mind if I obtained a copy of your medical records from the time you were admitted until the time you were discharged?"

"We have them," Beltrán said.

"Sure," Childs said. "By all means. Take a copy."

"We'll make you one," Beltrán said.

"Are you saying that I was in danger . . . because of the stories I wrote?"

"And the stories you were investigating. I'm trying to find out more."

Childs seemed to give this thought. After a moment she said, "But those stories were twenty-five years ago, thereabouts. I mean, they couldn't hurt anyone now, could they? I couldn't be in danger now, could I?"

"I can't say that you're not, Melissa, not with any certainty. That's why I'm obligated to tell you."

"I can't even remember the stories."

"I know that," Tracy said. "But it's possible people won't believe you have amnesia."

"What would they think? That I just walked away?"

"It's possible."

She sighed and sat quiet for a moment. "Does my daughter have a family?"

"No."

Childs looked again at the tabletop strewn with photographs of relatives she didn't know.

"Think about it," Tracy said. "Nothing has to be done tonight."

"Is there a number to call after I've made my decision?"

Tracy handed Childs a card with her personal cell phone number. "It's your decision." Tracy thanked Rafael Beltrán and left the conference room with Davis, who would take her back to the San Diego airport.

"Has to be the strangest thing you've ever dealt with," Davis said, still smiling.

"It's certainly up there," Tracy said, though she seemed to be a magnet for the bizarre. "I hope it turns out well, for her and for her daughter."

"You and me both," Davis said. "It's hard for me to imagine. I've been married to the same woman for more than thirty years, and I have three great kids and two grandchildren. I sit in my backyard and watch them swim in the pool, and I think, man, life doesn't get any better than this. But I know a lot of people out there not as fortunate, people for whom a redo, or a start over, would have some real appeal." He paused, then asked, "Do you think she's telling the truth?"

"You've known her almost twenty-five years; what do you think?"

Davis laughed. "I know I couldn't fake an Irish accent for twenty minutes, let alone twenty-some years. So, yeah, I think she's telling the truth."

"So do I."

"You think she could be in some danger?"

"I think it's a possibility," Tracy said, "which is why, if she decides to go forward, I'm going to push the amnesia story as much as I can, and we'll make sure she has security, at least for a while."

"And maybe people will believe she really can't remember?"

"Maybe," Tracy said, though she knew human nature and, like her, most would be inclined not to believe.

After Davis dropped her at the airport and Tracy weaved through the precheck screening and reached her gate, she had time to kill. She found a place to grab a bite to eat and to have a drink. She needed one. She took out her cell phone and called Dan.

"It's her. It's Lisa Childress."

"No kidding." She could hear the chuckle in his voice. "What did she say? Why did she leave?" They were questions for which most people would want answers.

"She doesn't know." Tracy told Dan an abbreviated version of the story.

"You believe her?"

"I do, but mostly because the people who've known her all these years believe her. I listened to her closely; I knew what words to listen for from living with Therese all this time. She never broke her accent. Never has, according to the people who've known her."

"How did she get an accent?"

"No idea. I'm getting her medical records to see if it's mentioned." Tracy told Dan that Childs looked at the photographs of her mother and father as if she was looking for the first time at photographs pulled from someone else's photo album, but not when she saw Anita Childress's photo.

"That's the thing that convinced me she was being truthful. If she was faking this whole thing, she would have faked not knowing her daughter also, wouldn't she?"

"Seems likely."

Tracy explained to Dan what Childs had said. "Do you remember when I was pregnant, and I had those vivid dreams?"

"I thought that was from the bizarre cravings you were having and what you were eating."

"I dreamed of Daniella. I told you I dreamed of a little girl, but more than dreaming about her, I felt an attachment to her."

"So what now?"

"That's up to her. I told her when she'd made a decision, I'd help her, whatever she decided."

"Did you tell her you might be giving someone another bite at the apple, that someone might have tried to kill her twenty-five years ago?"

"Not in so many words, but yes, I warned her about the investigations she was working."

Dan offered to pick up Tracy at SeaTac, but she was landing late and told him she'd catch an Uber and see him at home. She disconnected and took a sip of her Tito's vodka with cranberry before she opened her emails and listened to voice mails she'd neglected all day. Anita Childress had left a message and asked Tracy to call. With some trepidation, Tracy did.

"Detective Crosswhite. Thanks for calling me back."

"Not a problem."

"I wanted to apologize about my call the other day. I was just upset because of what my father was going through."

"There's no need to apologize, Anita. I know how difficult this must be."

"You were right though. You did warn me. I just didn't want to hear it. My father and I talked, and he said the decision was mine to make, that he could handle whatever I chose to do." Tracy had the sense that Anita was going to back out; her father's pain would be too great. "I want to know," she said. Tracy let out a held breath. "I want you to move forward."

The question now, however, was whether Melissa Childs wanted to move forward. She'd spent more than two decades in Escondido. She'd established a residence, started a business, found a life. No doubt she felt comfortable there. Escondido had become her home. Would she risk all she had established to meet people she did not know and had no history on which to build? Would she upend the safe, secure life she had forged for herself for uncertainty? Had she just left a husband behind, Tracy didn't think Childs would do it.

But it wasn't just a husband.

It was also a mother. And a daughter—physical bonds that tugged at Childs's subconscious, that even her amnesia had not completely severed.

CHAPTER 23

Back in Seattle, Tracy spent the next morning going through Melissa Childs's medical records. The pages documented how Childs had arrived at the Palomar Medical Center's behavioral center, and each day of the four months she had spent there. The doctor in charge of her treatment, William Wexell, a neurologist, initially opined that Childs's amnesia was the result of the head wound she'd suffered and that her memory would come back to her in time. As the weeks passed and that didn't happen, Wexell grew increasingly more interested. Tracy assumed Childs was the lab mouse who didn't react to the stimuli like all the other mice, which made her unique and worthy of study. Wexell tried a number of different techniques to jar her memory, including medications, each without success. His interest grew and eventually peaked, then seemed to decline, marked by some frustration, and finally ended with resignation.

Childs was not going to get better.

She was not going to recover her memory.

His treatment pivoted to helping her start a new life. In June, the hospital facilitated her securing a California driver's license and a Social

Security card and learning how to drive again. The hospital rehabilitation center gave her several tests to determine her interests and her proficiencies. Childs had a gift for numbers and expressed an interest in working in a compatible field. She enrolled at Palomar, and a nurse at the hospital knew the owner of the H&R Block in town and secured a bookkeeping position on a trial basis. Childs worked part-time while she went to school. She checked in with Wexell every two weeks, then once a month. Each meeting she reported no change in her memory, but a growing satisfaction with the new life she was creating.

As her sessions progressed, Wexell asked Childs if there were any people in her life outside of work colleagues, whether she'd started dating, had any feelings for anyone. She didn't. Wexell told her it would be healthy for her to consider dating, as well as finding a hobby that might expose her to members of the opposite sex. Childs chose volunteer firefighting.

She spoke about the young girl in her dreams, but never much beyond a feeling that she knew the little girl and felt an emotional attachment to her. Wexell explored this and concluded the girl was likely Childs in her youth, a memory that had not been completely erased.

After a year, Childs declined further treatment. She didn't see the point of continuing. With her permission, Wexell wrote an article, referring to Childs as Patient X, that appeared in the *New England Journal of Medicine* to some acclaim. He presented her case study a dozen or so times throughout the country.

Unfortunately, Wexell had passed away and would not be a resource for Tracy. She switched gears and called the University of Washington's Memory and Brain Wellness Center, which specialized in Alzheimer's and dementia research. They directed her to Dr. Kavya Laghari, a memory and amnesia specialist. Over the phone, Tracy provided Laghari with a *Reader's Digest* version of the events surrounding Lisa Childress. Laghari, soft spoken, with an Indian accent, sounded skeptical but asked Tracy to send over Childs's medical records to review, and then they could set up a mutually convenient time to speak.

Upon hanging up the phone, Tracy received a call from Kelly Rosa on her personal cell phone. "I looked at the medical examiner's report for David Slocum," Rosa said.

Tracy had almost forgotten she'd asked Rosa to review the report. "And . . ."

"It's not clear cut."

"Tell me why not."

"Slocum was left-handed, but a lot of left-handed people are not left-hand dominant. So that doesn't mean a lot. Besides, if he was left-hand dominant, then the wound to the left temple makes sense."

"And the angle of the bullet and lack of GSR residue on his left hand?"

"In the vast majority of suicides with a pistol, the bullet angle is tilted slightly up. However, in this instance, Slocum was in his car. He didn't have a lot of room. He could have shifted in his seat to move away from the door and window and make room for the gun, in which case the trajectory of the bullet would have been at a downward angle. You with me?"

"I'm with you," Tracy said.

"And if he was leaning, it could also explain why he was found slumped so far to the right, as well as why the gun also fell in that direction."

"What about the lack of GSR?"

"Inconclusive. The medical examiner noted gunshot residue on Slocum's temple and the left side of his clothing, which is to be expected. Gunshot residue can travel over three to five feet. However, recent studies have found that even in known suicides, GSR is positive on the hand in only fifty percent of the cases."

"That low?"

"That low. Gunpowder residue is the consistency of flour and typically only stays on the hands four to six hours. Slocum was found at five a.m., with a time of death estimated to have been between two and three in the morning. His hands were not bagged by the medical examiner at the scene. Therefore, it is possible that, even if GSR had been initially present on his left hand, it could have worn off."

"You're telling me the entire medical examiner's report is inconclusive."

"If I was called to testify, that's what I would be compelled to conclude."

"I appreciate you taking a look."

"Not a problem. How's that baby of yours?"

"Growing like a weed."

"Tell me about it. I have one still in college and a second about to graduate high school. Stay healthy. Be safe."

"You too."

Tracy hung up the phone and let out a breath. She was about to call Melton and nudge him on the DNA cases she'd sent over to keep Chief Weber happy when her computer pinged. She hadn't checked her emails that morning. She had made a commitment many years ago that she would resist the Pavlovian reflex to look to the computer screen or pick up the phone with every buzz, chirp, ping, or chime.

She decided she would review her emails, then visit Melton. He'd know Tracy was nudging him, but she'd bribe him. She scanned the emails, and her gaze fixated on one in particular midway down the list.

Noreply@guerillamail.com

"You weren't much help, whoever you are," Tracy said. She opened the email.

Follow the money trail like a rolling stone.

Tracy looked at the last two words. "A rolling stone gathers no moss," she said.

Moss Gunderson.

She thought of the marina, of the raid that clearly happened, but for which she found no record. The raid on a boat with a substantial amount of cocaine, according to its captain. The money. Was the anonymous emailer telling her that Moss was paid off?

She was tempted to call Del and have a sit-down, but she decided it best to do so with something solid. If Tracy went to Del with what she currently had, and insinuated some guilt, she could ruin a friendship. She thought again of calling Moss and asking him more specific questions, then gauge how he reacted, but given what she'd witnessed at the golf course, he'd likely be adept at deflecting her questions.

The golf course.

She recalled standing outside the clubhouse with the pushcarts and golf carts. Moss had seemingly known everyone. *I've been a member twenty-five years, play five days a week, and eat here a couple times a week.*

There it was. Twenty-five years. She could easily find out a detective's salary in the early nineties, but she had no idea what a country club membership might cost. She looked up Glendale online, found a number for the clubhouse, called and asked to speak to the general manager. Minutes later she had her answer. A golf membership at that time was $43,000, with monthly dues of roughly $220, not to mention miscellaneous costs like new clubs, clothing, lessons, and food and beverages. It wasn't a fortune, but it was a considerable chunk of change, especially on a police officer's salary that long ago. The average salary of a Seattle police officer, at present, was roughly $60,000 a year; it was nowhere near that amount in the nineties. Tracy's educated guess was a policeman's starting base salary back then was likely between $25,000 and $30,000, not including overtime compensation. Even as a detective, Moss likely wasn't making $50,000 in base salary.

A thought struck her while talking to the general manager. "I wonder if you could tell me when Keith Ellis became a member?" she asked, referring to Moss's partner.

The general manager asked her to hold. Fingers typing on the keyboard came through the receiver. "Looks like Keith Ellis joined January 1996."

Tracy thanked him and hung up. She looked again at the email open on her computer.

Follow the money.

It was possible Moss had inherited money. It was also possible his wife came from money or that *she* had inherited money, but Del had told Tracy that Moss was in the midst of a nasty divorce in 1995, which made that scenario highly unlikely, and made it improbable he had disposable income to spend on a golf membership at a country club. Moss's file indicated he also had five children. Twenty-five years ago, those children would have likely been in grade school, maybe early high school. Moss would have been in that period of life all parents go through—when their children could cost them an arm and a leg in school tuition, extracurricular sports and activities, food bills and clothing. And besides all of that, what was the probability that Keith Ellis had also inherited money, or that both he and Moss had invested wisely? Low. Very low.

Moss had come into some money. Ellis also.

But they hadn't inherited it and they hadn't earned it.

They'd stolen it.

At noon, Tracy drove to the clinic at the University of Washington Medical Center. Along the way she crossed the Montlake Cut, where the Washington rowing team dominated, and viewed the football stadium, which rose out of the ground like a huge W and provided spectators with a spectacular view of Lake Washington.

Dr. Laghari, who said she was eager to meet when she called Tracy back, greeted Tracy in the clinic lobby and led her to her office, which had a view of Portage Bay. Dr. Laghari had a soft physical presence that matched the tone of her voice. Laghari's hand felt as small as a child's and so delicate Tracy feared she might break it when they shook hands. A silk throw rug, expensive from the looks of the intricate weave, covered much of her office floor. The colors picked up the pale blue of the office walls, as well as the red in an abstract painting of bejeweled elephant heads. Dr. Laghari wore a white lab coat over black slacks and a white blouse. She offered Tracy a seat on a couch in her office and sat in a chair to the side.

"The case you sent over is fascinating," Laghari said with the hint of a smile. "One doesn't get such cases very often."

"But can such a case occur, in your experience?"

"It is not common, but they most assuredly can occur."

"Anything that you read in the file that gave you pause or made you think perhaps that the woman could have faked the scenario?"

"No. Nothing. But no two cases are alike, and I would require interviewing Ms. Childs and running tests before I could be certain."

"I understand," Tracy said, satisfied some medical explanation existed for what had happened to Lisa Childress. "Maybe you can give me a crash course on amnesia and what you think likely happened in this instance."

"Of course. Let me walk you through it."

"Just go easy on me," Tracy said, drawing a smile from the doctor.

"Memory is information stored in the form of facilitated synaptic tracts in the brain. Each time certain sensory signals pass through a specific sequence of synapses, they imprint."

"I'm with you . . . I think," Tracy said.

"Memory is imprinted on the brain the way that songs were once imprinted on vinyl albums, so the song, or in our case the memory, can be played over and over again, if the person chooses to do so."

"And like a vinyl album, is it also true that as the memory gets older, the recollection of the past event is not as clear as that first time the person experiences it?"

"Not a bad analogy, Detective. I may use it." Another smile. "Amnesia is defined as a temporary or permanent state of decreased memory. Depending on the cause of the damage, amnesia may result in partial or complete memory loss."

"And what can cause it?"

"A number of things. Physical injury to an area of the brain, substance abuse, psychological trauma." Laghari pointed to a cabinet on a wall in her office. "If I may?"

"Please," Tracy said.

Laghari opened both sides of the cabinet, revealing a whiteboard and dry-erase pens. On the left panel she wrote *anterograde amnesia*. On the right panel she wrote *retrograde amnesia*.

"The hippocampus is present in the medial temporal lobe of the brain and is involved in the formation of long-term memory. It has been found that the removal of the hippocampus in some patients results in the patient's inability to store new information. This is referred to as 'anterograde amnesia.' The person can recall memories stored in the brain prior to injury but cannot store memories after the injury. This does not appear to be the type of amnesia your individual suffered, at least not based on her medical records."

Laghari stepped to the right side of the board. "The second type of amnesia is known as 'retrograde amnesia.' In this type of amnesia, the patient is unable to recall memories stored in the brain prior to the damage, but she can form and recall memories of events occurring after the damage."

"You keep saying 'damage.' Do you mean a physical injury?"

"A physical injury can be head trauma but also such things as cere-brovascular accidents, or a stroke."

"And it can result in complete memory loss?" Tracy asked.

"That depends on the extent and degree of the injury to the brain, or the severity of the psychological trauma. The degree and the length of memory loss can both be impacted. It may last hours, days, and in this instance, years."

"If someone were struck in the head, that could cause the type of amnesia she is experiencing?"

"Absolutely. We've seen patients who have suffered car accidents, a fall from some height, been hit in the head with a metal rod, and suf-fered head trauma during a fight. Any head trauma that breaks the skull and meninges can cause serious brain injury and result in anterograde or retrograde amnesia."

"And you said psychological trauma can also cause this?"

"By psychological trauma I mean traumatic events that are so dis-tressful the mind prefers to forget them, instead of dealing with the stress caused."

"Like giving birth," Tracy said, smiling.

"I swore after my first child I'd never have a second," Laghari agreed. "I have three."

"I understand amnesia can cause a person to forget his or her past, but can it also cause her to forget who she is?" Tracy asked.

"It can. This is referred to as a fugue state. It is rare. It is even less common to last twenty-five years."

"So, if this patient's amnesia is legit, we're looking most likely at a physical injury?"

"Most likely, yes, but not necessarily and not exclusively. Some people can also have a vulnerable brain."

"What does that mean?"

"Maybe the person doesn't have coping mechanisms and so, in a psychological crisis, the person just shuts down and essentially runs away and forgets."

"What if the person is autistic? Would that impact the coping mechanism?"

"I don't know of any clinical studies, but autism can be associated with difficulty making personal relationships, so I suppose it's possible that such a person could be more vulnerable to an amnesiac episode."

"Can the memories come back? Is there any treatment to bring them back?"

"Memories can come back, certainly. A person can forget what they were doing on a particular day, but if the memory is jogged, they can recall those events. But a person with retrograde amnesia usually can't access the memory even if it is jogged. You take them back to their home, or their high school, and the experience is interesting, but it's like they're learning someone else's life, not recalling their own."

Tracy had that very thought when she presented Melissa Childs with the photographs of her past, that Childs was viewing someone else's life.

"But this person, if she was intelligent, could she learn new things and remember them?" Tracy asked.

"No two cases of amnesia are the same but yes, generally, retrograde amnesia results in loss of declarative memory."

"Which is what?"

"Declarative memory is memory related to facts such as how to spell a word, and episodes such as the events of a person's daily life. Non-declarative memory is memories associated with skills and learning. It is acquired by practice, not by recollection."

"Meaning a person could be taught to learn new things."

"Yes."

"And if a person was brilliant before their injury and picked up things quickly, they might still be able to do that after suffering retrograde amnesia?"

"The short answer is yes, though I'd like to ask her a number of questions and run my own tests."

"Have you ever heard of a patient who suffered a physical injury that resulted in them speaking with an accent?"

This seemed to get the doctor's attention. "Have I? No."

"Is it possible?"

"You're talking about acquired savant syndrome. That is, a person suffers a brain injury and acquires new skills or an ability they didn't previously possess. Clinical studies exist of patients who couldn't remember their name for longer than a minute but who could play concerts on the piano flawlessly. One clinical study discussed a young man who had never picked up the guitar, but after a traumatic brain injury, he played the instrument beautifully. Another study detailed how an injured child could sculpt lifelike sculptures without any training. Others become mathematical geniuses. So . . . Could it happen?" Laghari shrugged. "Anything is possible, Detective."

CHAPTER 24

Tracy left Dr. Laghari's office with a better sense of what had happened to Lisa Childress and, more importantly, that such things could occur. She was contemplating what to do, mentally juggling the number of different things she had going at the moment, when Rick Cerrabone called her cell phone. Work had a way of finding her. She didn't have to look for it.

"You asked me to pull a file on Henderson Jones," Cerrabone said.

"I thought you were preparing for trial and going to have your paralegal call me back."

"My trial went away. Defendant took the plea."

"Small miracle. Did he or his lawyer find religion?"

"Lawyer said his client was taking the plea against his advice . . . blah, blah, blah. They're all tough guys when the fight is over. The good lawyers don't need to expend all that hot air; they've paid their dues."

"So then what are you doing in the office? You should have at least taken a long weekend."

"You know the drill. I'm trying to dig out from under the pile I let smolder while I prepared for a trial that is not going to happen."

Cerrabone did not sound happy. He sounded like he was already thinking of what kind of revenge he could exact on the defense lawyer. The Seattle legal community was bigger than it had been when Cerrabone started, but the adage "What goes around comes around" remained true.

"I appreciate the call back," Tracy said, thinking about her smoldering piles.

"Henderson Jones was charged with possession with intent to distribute, among other things. He was one of about two dozen charged but the only one to not accept a plea. He claimed the police framed him and he'd been a good citizen for years before his arrest."

"How much evidence did the prosecutor have?"

"Not much. The file is thin. They had a police officer's statement that an informant would testify that Jones was regularly dealing in Rainier Valley."

"That's it?" Tracy asked, incredulous.

"That's it. Like I said, 'thin.' Jones's attorney provided gas and restaurant receipts as evidence Jones was in Los Angeles visiting a brother."

"Legit?"

"Doesn't appear the prosecutor followed up. There's a *Post-Intelligencer* article in the file, though, that indicates a reporter did follow up and confirmed some of the receipts were legit. Anything else?"

Tracy assumed it was the article written by Lisa Childress but asked Cerrabone to read the byline.

She heard the pages rustle. "Lisa Childress."

"Did the prosecutor's file have an address and phone number for Jones or his attorney?"

"Both," Cerrabone said, and he waited for Tracy to get out a pen and a pad of paper before he gave her the information. "That was a long time ago though."

"Yes, it was." Tracy thanked Cerrabone and disconnected. She called the attorney's work phone number, but a recording told her the number was no longer in service. She called the last known number for Henderson Jones, but it, too, was no longer in service. She called Police Headquarters and asked Faz to run Henderson Jones's name through the DMV and provide her with an address. A long, pregnant pause followed. "Faz?"

"Yeah, I'm here. The name was muffled. Say it again."

"Henderson Jones."

"What are you working on?" Faz asked.

The question caught Tracy off guard. "Just trying to track down a relative of one of the victims." She didn't like lying to Faz, but she didn't want to get into a protracted discussion, nor did she want to put Faz in a difficult position. Faz and Del were like peanut butter and jelly, and good partners never lied to one another. The relationship depended upon trust. Partners spent eight hours of every day with each other and picked up on each other's tells.

"Here he is," Faz said. "You have a pen?"

"Fire away."

Faz provided her a Seattle address. "Do me another favor," Tracy asked.

"At your beck and call," Faz said.

"Run his name and tell me the last time he was charged and convicted?"

Faz's thick fingers again stumbled over the keyboard. A minute later he said, "The last time? The last time would have been August 1989. Possession with intent to distribute."

Tracy thanked him and hung up. In the newspaper article discussing Jones's refusal to enter a plea to drug charges, Childress quoted Jones as saying he had not dealt drugs since the birth of his son. Either he'd been telling the truth, or he just hadn't been caught, which seemed unlikely since he was on the Narcotics Unit's radar and they'd be looking for him to slip up. That meant Jones likely told Childress the truth, that the charges levied against him by the task force had been fabricated.

The smoldering pile was starting to catch fire.

Tracy followed Google Maps into Rainier Valley, a once mostly African American neighborhood, though with housing in high demand in one of the nation's fastest growing cities, the neighborhood had gentrified and home prices soared to nearly three-quarters of a million dollars on average and higher near Lake Washington's shore. She parked at the curb in front of a one-story, redbrick home with a well-maintained yard. A wooden wheelchair ramp and railing extended from the front door to the cement walk that split the lawn down the center. She got out of her pool car to the unwelcome stares of five young men seated in lawn chairs next to the address she hoped still belonged to Henderson Jones. In Tracy's experience, people living in these neighborhoods had a police radar, and they could pick her out as a cop no matter how she dressed. Over the years, she'd had people tell her they recognized the pool cars, but also the way cops walked, or the cocksure manner in which they stood, and, in some cases, their "holier than thou attitude."

As Tracy drew nearer to the home with the ramp, she caught sight of one of the men approaching in her peripheral vision.

"Can I help you?" He stopped several feet away, his head tilted, and he held an expression that could best be described as *Whatever you're selling, we aren't buying.*

"Do you know if Henderson Jones lives here?"

"Depends on who's asking, and why?" A gold chain with a crucifix dangled around his neck.

"Do you know Mr. Jones?"

"Again, depends on who's asking and why."

"Fair enough. I'm a Seattle police detective and would like to ask Mr. Jones about an incident that occurred in the 1990s."

"The 1990s? Man, why don't you people leave him alone. That was a long time ago, and he isn't that guy anymore."

"That's what I want to talk to him about. I want to talk about the charges that were dismissed."

"Why?"

"I'd prefer to tell Mr. Jones."

"Well, I'm his son, and you're not going to see him unless you tell me."

"Okay. I'm working a cold case, and I think Mr. Jones might have information about the narcotics task force that arrested him that could help me."

The son studied her.

"Can I speak to him? I would have called, but the number on file is disconnected."

"There is no number anymore, not a landline anyway. Just an unnecessary expense. Everyone has a cell phone now. But that isn't why you're here, because the number was disconnected, is it?"

Tracy smiled to defuse the situation. "Easier to disconnect a call than to slam a door in someone's face."

The young man smirked. "But not nearly as satisfying." He stepped past Tracy and mumbled, "Wait here." He walked up the ramp to the front door and disappeared inside the house. The other men in the yard watched Tracy with defiant expressions. Tracy busied herself reviewing her emails and felt the warmth of the sun on her face despite the chilled reception.

Minutes later, the young man opened the door and gave Tracy a soft whistle to get her attention. He waved her forward. She walked up the ramp and stepped inside.

Henderson Jones sat in a wheelchair on hardwood floors. He looked like an older and heavier version of the man in the newspaper article. Such pictures always made Tracy melancholy because they documented the aging process. Almost everyone's hair grayed, and they put on weight. Their skin sagged and wrinkled. You could fight it with diet and exercise, but it was like those smoldering piles Cerrabone referred to—you never caught up and you never got ahead.

"You're a detective?" Jones said.

"That's right," Tracy said.

"What division?"

"Cold Cases."

He gave her a curious look. "My son said you wanted to talk to me about the time the police tried to frame me."

"I do."

"Why would a cold case detective want to ask me questions about something that happened that long ago?"

"I'm working a cold case about a woman who went missing, a reporter who was looking into the task force that tried to frame you." Tracy said the word with intention. She wanted Jones to know she didn't believe the charges against him.

"How do you know the police framed me?"

"You would have pled if they hadn't—if they had any evidence to support the charges. The penalties make the risk of going to trial too high."

"You talk like you know what you're talking about."

"I spent some time working narcotics. I also looked you up. You haven't had an arrest since 1989."

"Maybe I'm just stubborn."

"Or you had something to be stubborn about." She looked to the young man in the room, who appeared about the right age, and recalled Childress quoting Jones as saying he gave up dealing when his son was born.

"You said this reporter went missing?" Jones asked.

"She did."

"Doesn't surprise me. The things they were doing."

"Will you tell me?"

"Not sure what I can remember. That was a long time ago."

Tracy had a hunch Jones knew more than he was intimating. "Just what you remember," she said.

Jones studied her for a moment, then motioned for Tracy to take a seat on a brown corduroy couch in a room that was neat but sparingly furnished, likely to maintain open spaces for Jones's wheelchair. Recently refurbished hardwood floors led to tile in the small entryway, and a doorway presumably led into a kitchen. No carpet or throw rugs to impede the wheels of his chair. Tracy detected the smell of lemon, a cleaning product. His son sat on the other end of the couch, looking distrustful. Jones wheeled to a recliner with a collapsible walker beside it. On a small table beside it rested the remote control to a flat-screen television, the newspaper, an open magazine, and a basket with several prescription bottles. A University of Washington Yeti tumbler was set beside the basket. Jones didn't get up from his wheelchair.

"I don't have a mark on my record in more than thirty years because I haven't dealt drugs or broken the law in thirty years," Jones reiterated when Tracy settled onto the couch. "I gave up that stuff when my first boy, Marshawn, was born. You've met Deiondre." He motioned to the young man now seated on the couch. "Got a daughter too, Lachelle. I couldn't be much of a father if I was in prison. Can't be much of a role model either. I didn't want my life for my kids. I knew that the moment Marshawn popped out. My wife didn't either. She told me to give it up or give her up. I gave up selling to raise my kids. I'm proud of them. All three are college graduates. Lachelle is a lawyer in California. Marshawn works for Boeing, and Deiondre is in computer technology at Microsoft and comes over every Tuesday afternoon to look in on me and clean the house. All the kids look after me."

Deiondre kept his gaze on the hardwood floor while his father spoke.

"You have a lot of reasons to be proud," Tracy said.

"I certainly do. And I thank the Lord for my blessings every day."

"Tell me about the task force that falsely accused you."

Jones smirked. "That was a long time ago, Detective. Water under the bridge now."

"Maybe for you. I'm just trying to solve a cold case."

Jones frowned. "They were a bunch of cowboys. Mostly white. They came out with big promises to stop the flow of drugs into Seattle. That's what they said, anyway. Stopping the flow of drugs into Seattle is like sticking your finger in one leaky hole after another. Pretty soon you run out of fingers. What they said and what they eventually did were two different stories."

"What did they do?"

"What I heard is they got a taste for the money, some of them at least. More money than they would ever see being a cop. I know first-hand all that money can be intoxicating. It can get to be too much. But I think some were dirty from the start."

"Do you know which of the members of the task force were dirty?"

"Not specifically, no. What I know is that they would wait outside bars where dealers transacted business. Someone was tipping them. Found out later it was the bar owners—a couple in particular who were in on the take."

"You have the names of the bars?"

"I'm sure I could remember some of them with a little time, but most don't exist anymore. Developers are putting in apartments and condos and strip malls."

"What did this task force do, specifically?"

"They'd wait outside the bars, then pull the dealers over under a false pretense—speeding, running a red light. They'd go through their clothes and cars, and take whatever they found. Guys sometimes carried three to five thousand dollars."

"You know this firsthand?"

"Nah. Just what I heard. What I heard was the police would have them sign two documents. One wouldn't identify the drugs or the money. The other would. They told them they'd let them go with a traffic ticket but if they made any trouble, they'd file the second document and come back and arrest them."

"But they took the drugs and the money."

"Absolutely. Said the dealers forfeited both, and they would put it in the lockup and use it as evidence if they made trouble. That was bullshit."

"How do you know?"

Jones made a face like Tracy was just naïve. "Because word travels fast around here, especially when word is about the police. I was out of the business then, but I still knew people involved."

"What were you told the police would do with the drugs and the money they took?"

"I was told was they'd take the drugs and sell it back to another dealer at a discounted rate and make *more* money. Also heard they kept some to plant when they brought false charges against anyone who got out of line."

"How long did this go on?"

Jones shook his head. "Don't know. What I do know is the dealers learned the bar owners were on the payroll and stopped using the bars to make transactions. That's when they had that big drug bust and arrested a couple dozen, including me. The mayor and that top cop got up in front of the cameras and microphones and announced how they were shutting down the drug dealers in Seattle. Except I was no longer in the business. That was after I had got out, and I'd taken the wife and kids to LA to visit with my brother and his family. I could prove it too. Just had to get the credit card receipts."

"If you were out of the business, how were you supporting your family?" Tracy asked, not completely believing Jones had left the business cold turkey. As he'd said, the money was alluring.

"I was working legit jobs on a construction crew. All that went away when they arrested me though. I lost my job. But I wasn't going to jail and leave my wife to raise my kids. I knew where they'd end up, and that wasn't going to happen to them."

"You fought the charges."

"Wasn't much of a fight. They kept telling my attorney they had all this evidence, but every time he asked to see it, they didn't have any. This went on for about a year. My attorney talked to the others who'd been arrested, and they told him what had been going on, what that task force had been doing. My attorney made this clear to the prosecutor."

An attorney would be a better witness, if Tracy got that far, than a supposedly reformed drug dealer. Maybe. "Do you have a current contact for Tommy Ford?"

Jones shook his head. "Tommy is dead. Cancer ate him up."

"But he told you this?"

"He told me." Jones paused before adding, "But I heard about much of it on my own, and I know it was true."

"How do you know it was true?"

"Because after Tommy went to the prosecuting attorney, police cars and unmarked cars started driving past my house. One time an officer made a gun with his hand, pointed it at me, and pulled the trigger. My wife and kids were playing in the yard. They wanted me to know they could get to me, a warning to keep my mouth shut, that they could get to the people I loved. That was when I came close to pleading. What was the point of fighting to protect my kids if I was putting a target on their backs?"

"Did you make a report of any of these drive-by incidents?"

"To who?" Jones looked and sounded defiant.

"Why didn't you plead?"

"My wife. She told me if I pled, the police would never leave me alone. She told me we would get through it. The prosecutor finally got around to looking at my case, admitted the police had nothing, and let me go. He was disgusted, according to my attorney. He didn't say it, but my attorney said he could tell. He dismissed the case. Took me another six months before I could get my job back."

Tracy figured Jones likely had his ear to the ground after the task force tried to charge him. "Did you hear about other schemes this task force was running . . . other than the false stops outside the bars?"

"Yeah, I heard things, but as I said, I was out of the business by then so I don't know what was true and what was just bullshit talk."

"What did you hear?"

"I heard about raids on drug houses where the drugs went out the back door and back to the street. I heard about drugs going missing from the lockup and charges having to be dismissed."

Tracy knew from experience that, in a system in which thousands of pieces of evidence are stored, things could get lost, unintentionally or deliberately, especially before the implementation of computers. She knew of cases in which the prosecuting attorney showed up in court without the drugs needed to prosecute a drug case and would have to dismiss the charges. In the 1980s, corruption was also well documented in narcotics units in Los Angeles and Miami. She'd read that the system was most vulnerable when a case ended and the judge issued an order for the drugs to be incinerated, because the drugs did not need to be seen again. If the senior police officer decided to slip the drugs, or a portion thereof, out the back door, no one would know it. The justice system depended on integrity and officers policing other officers, but Tracy knew cops didn't always trust the confidentiality of reporting systems, which deterred officers from whistle-blowing.

"What else did you hear?" Tracy asked.

"Nothing specific."

"You ever hear about them stopping boats bringing in drugs?" Tracy asked.

"Not specifically, but it wouldn't surprise me. I knew guys who used to get their drugs from a coffin manufacturer who shipped the drugs inside the coffins. It all makes sense."

"What does?"

"Think about it. If the police take a big score before it gets distributed, it's more money for them and less risk. What's the dealer gonna do about it?"

Just like Jack Flynt. Flynt had been too busy trying to figure out how to prove to his ringleaders that he hadn't ripped them off, that they shouldn't kill him.

Jones was right. A bust of a boat or a plane would be big money, tens of millions of dollars. She wondered if it had been just the Last Line that Lisa Childress's investigative reporting could have impacted. She wondered if those benefiting could have included high-level politicians, like Edwards. She thought again of Jack Flynt, of how he had his sentence significantly reduced, and how the story never saw the light of day. Was that because the wrongdoing implicated many in positions of power, or was it because the Last Line's final score was the $20 to $30 million taken off the *Egregious* in November 1995, and when Flynt finally brought that to law enforcement's attention, the statute of limitations prevented anyone from being prosecuted? Why embarrass the entire city without any recourse?

"Other than what you heard, were you aware of any evidence . . . hard evidence that this occurred?"

Jones shook his head. "Just what people were saying, but more than half of those people are dead by now."

"Did you hear anything about why the drug task force broke up? Why it dissolved?"

"Nah. I don't know nothing about that. Did hear there was an investigation, might have had something to do with that."

"What did you hear?"

"Should have said I assumed it because I had two detectives come here asking me the same questions you're asking, but then they didn't do anything."

"When was this? Recently?"

"No. Not long after they tried to frame me."

Tracy thought this had to be Moss Gunderson and Keith Ellis.

Jones continued. "I told them just like I told you. Never heard another word about it."

"How many times did you talk to these detectives?"

"Just the one time."

"Do you remember them?"

Jones frowned. "Not their names. But, hell, they were like bookends on a bookshelf. Two big Italian guys. Looked like those guys you see in the movies. Came in a coat and tie and looking official."

Del and Faz.

"You told them what you told me?"

"Yep. Didn't do nothing about it though. Nothing I ever saw or heard about."

Tracy now knew the reason for Faz's pregnant pause.

"I told them to show me they meant business. I told them to go after the task force and I might have more information for them about who was tipping the task force about the drugs here in the valley. They never came back."

"You know who was tipping the task force?" Tracy asked.

Jones paused. He glanced at his son, who had his head tilted toward his father, looking impassive. Then Jones redirected his gaze to Tracy. "I'll make you the same deal I made with them. You show me that you mean business, that you're gonna do something this time. Show me, and I might have a name for you."

CHAPTER 25

Tracy left Henderson Jones's home no longer certain about anything. His son walked her outside and closed the door behind them.

"You know what it takes to raise three kids in the environment that surrounded us and have us all come out clean? Don't buy drugs. Don't sell drugs. Don't use them," Deiondre said.

"He sounds like a remarkable father."

"He raised us after my mother died unexpectedly at forty-two. He had help from my grandparents, but the responsibility fell to him and he did it. And he didn't go back to dealing drugs to do it either. He worked multiple jobs, sometimes getting just four hours of sleep a night so he could give my brother and sister and me a better life. But he did it. And what did he get for it?" Deiondre raised his eyebrows as if waiting for an answer. He wasn't. "Nothing. He stood tall when everybody else rolled over. I know my father, and I know you coming around here asking him questions is making him stand tall again, hoping that the rich and powerful get their due, and I don't have the heart to tell him it isn't going to happen. Is it, Detective?"

Tracy couldn't immediately answer.

"That's what I thought. Think about it. A young kid gets pinched for having a couple ounces of pot and fifty dollars on him. The rich and powerful, they get away with stealing millions of dollars and nobody does anything. They sweep it under the rug, so the city doesn't get embarrassed on a national stage."

"I think you're right," Tracy said. "I think that's exactly what happened. But some people did get hurt, and that's my priority at the moment, finding the people responsible and trying to bring them to justice."

"Yeah? Well, see if maybe you can spread that justice around a little bit."

"Can I ask what happened to your father, why he's in the wheelchair?"

"Diabetes. He's got neuropathy bad in his feet, but he keeps on trucking every day. That's my dad."

Deiondre walked across the lawn to friends, who continued to give Tracy the stink eye. She didn't blame them. Each was likely to get a big laugh when Deiondre told them why she had come to visit his father. They'd laugh because they'd experienced it too much, a justice system that too often meted out judgment based on color and race.

Tracy got back in the car and drove from Rainier Valley. What Henderson Jones had told her tested so many of her basic precepts of being a Violent Crimes detective, precepts she had learned from both Faz and Del. Now it appeared Del had withheld information on the raid of a drug boat that had led to the deaths of two crewmen and the theft of potentially millions of dollars in drug money, not to mention putting those drugs back out on the streets of Seattle. Faz also must have known about it. That was the only rational explanation for why he came with Del to talk with Henderson Jones. Faz was not Del's partner back then. Not yet, anyway.

The unreported raid on the *Egregious* had also, not so inadvertently, led to the death of David Slocum and, for all intents and purposes, the death of Lisa Childress. She wasn't six feet under, but Tracy could only imagine what it must have been like to wake up one day and not know who you are and not recognize any of the people in your life. Maybe it was just being a mother and thinking of the pain it would cause her to not know Daniella. Tracy's maternal grandmother had Alzheimer's, and for the last years of her life, she didn't know anyone, not even her daughter or her grandchildren. The disease had stripped her of all the people she had once loved and all the memories she had once shared.

Tracy thought it to be the cruelest of all the diseases, and she prayed she was not genetically disposed to suffer the same fate.

As she got back on the I-5 freeway, she wondered what had happened, what had gone wrong. Del had been a new homicide detective when he worked with Moss Gunderson. Faz, too, had come up the ranks about the same time. Had they been sucked in by the money? Or had they just gone along to get along, then found themselves in too deep to get out? Had that been the reason they talked with Henderson Jones, had they been trying to claw their way out of a situation only to find the walls were sandstone and the more they clawed, the more the walls crumbled, leaving them without a perch on which to stand?

Had Del and Faz been complicit in the death of David Slocum? Tracy couldn't bring herself to believe it possible. Had Slocum been prepared to tell Lisa Childress about the raid at the marina and the drowning of the two men because Del and Moss had ignored him? That certainly seemed to be the reason for Slocum's death. Tracy didn't believe for an instant that he committed suicide. But if members of the Last Line killed Slocum, why hadn't they also taken out Childress at the same time? The presence of the bear spray seemed to make it a near certainty Childress had been at the site. Had she arrived after the murder? Had the shock and the horror been too much for her and led to one of those psychological injuries of which Dr. Laghari spoke?

Maybe, but that didn't explain the head injury Childress presented with at the mall in Escondido. Had she struck her head or had the blow been inflicted? If so, why had they let her live, a reporter who could, potentially, take down everyone? Had they decided that, without Slocum, Childress had no corroboration? Had they decided they couldn't kill an investigative reporter? Or were they just waiting for a more opportune time, and Slocum's death was meant to be an explicit message to Childress that they could get to her sources and they could get to her?

Tracy's cell phone rang. She accepted the call.

"Detective Crosswhite?" Tracy recognized Melissa Childs's voice.

"Yes, Melissa."

"I've given what we talked about a lot of thought, and I want to thank you for being so considerate, for letting this be my decision."

"Of course," Tracy said. "The decision remains yours."

"Well . . . As I said, I've thought about it and I don't really see the advantage for me to go back to being Lisa Childress. I've made a life for myself here in Escondido, a good life. It's not great but it's a life in which I can function."

"I understand," Tracy said. In her mind she could see Deiondre Jones shaking his head and smirking at her. It would be just like last time.

"But it's not just me, is it?" Childs said.

"What's that?"

"I said, 'It's not just me.' I have to think about the other people this impacts; don't I? I have a mother who hasn't seen her daughter for twenty-five years. I can only imagine the pain she's suffered, thinking I'd died but not really knowing. And my daughter. She grew up without a mother. In a sense what happened to me, not being able to remember them, was a blessing. I imagine their memories must have been very painful."

Tracy recalled her mother saying something similar about her grandmother, that her grandmother was lucky because at least she didn't know what she wasn't remembering. The disease was much harder on those who could recall what her grandmother had been like, and all the good moments they had shared.

"What would you like me to do?" Tracy asked.

"I'd like to meet them—my mother and my daughter. I suppose my husband also. I think I owe it to them."

"When would you like to do that?"

"Well, I guess now is as good a time as any."

"Then I'll make it happen," Tracy said. "And I'll do my best to keep it quiet, so you can have some peace."

CHAPTER 26

As Tracy took the exit and drove to return the pool car in the garage on Sixth Avenue, her work cell phone buzzed. Caller ID indicated Police Headquarters but did not provide a name, which meant it wasn't Faz, Del, or Kins. No name usually meant the brass. The only brass she now dealt with was Chief Weber. The only reason Tracy could think of why Weber would call would be for an update on the cold cases Tracy was pursuing, but even that seemed to be overkill. No. It *was* overkill.

In all of Tracy's years working Violent Crimes, Chief Clarridge had only asked her about one case, the serial killer they called "the Cowboy." Clarridge only stepped to the podium if the case was high profile, or if the case resolution made the department look good, like Tracy finding the bodies buried by the serial killers in North Seattle and Curry Canyon.

Regardless of the reason for the call, Tracy let it go to voice mail, then checked her messages. Chief Weber told Tracy to call her and left a number. Not just yet.

She backtracked to Park 90/5. She'd pay Oz, Mike Melton, a visit and see if he'd worked his magic to pull DNA from the cold cases she'd sent over. If he had, Tracy would seek to match that DNA with a person in their system. Then she'd talk to Chief Weber and tell her the progress she'd made on three cases.

She stopped at Salumi and ordered a hot sopressata-and-provolone sandwich and a Leonetta's meatball sandwich to go. Yeah, she was bribing Melton, again. Both were his favorites. But as her mom had said, the quickest way to a man's heart was his stomach.

—

Having worked in a number of different CSI divisions as she made her way up to Violent Crimes, Tracy knew the Park 90/5 complex well. She surprised Melton, who tapped the keys on his keyboard with his head angled to read thru his bifocal glasses. He jumped when Tracy blurted out, "You cut your hair."

She couldn't help it. Melton's other nickname had been "Grizzly" because he had the wild mane and matching beard that resembled the actor in *Grizzly Adams*. Melton's hair no longer touched the collar of his shirt and showed more gray. Tracy couldn't ever remember seeing Melton's ears, which seemed too small for his head, or his neck—he'd also trimmed his beard, which lessened the effect of the two fangs of gray and made his head look smaller.

"Good thing you're a detective," Melton said. "Nothing gets by you."

"You look younger."

"You're a poor liar. The gray makes me look older. Do I look any thinner?"

Tracy played it safe. "I hadn't noticed."

Melton made a face. "I was hoping for thinner. The family's been after me to lose some weight."

"You're not heavy."

"I'm big-boned," he said. "With too much on those bones. My cholesterol is high. So's my blood pressure. I told my doctor it comes with the job. Pesky detectives. Doctor is talking about medication. Getting old ain't for sissies."

"Well, as a friend of mine likes to say, the alternative to getting old is worse, so count your blessings."

"Every day." He shifted his attention to the bag. "Smells like something one might use to jump the line and get her cases put ahead of the other detectives pushing me."

"Would it work?"

"Depends on the bribe."

"Salumi."

"Not on the diet."

Tracy's shoulders sagged. "Hot sopressata or meatball?"

Melton held out his hand. "I won't tell if you don't."

"I don't want to contribute to your delinquency."

"Sopressata," he said, motioning with his hand for Tracy to hand it over. "I'll eat a salad for dinner. I'm beginning to feel like a damn rabbit."

Tracy handed Melton the hot sopressata sandwich and sat in the chair across his desk. They opened the wraps and dug in. Melton took a bite and made a face like he'd died and gone to heaven. "My God, I've missed food."

They caught up on private lives and talked shop. Tracy told Melton about Dan's home project.

"Maybe it's a midlife crisis," he said.

"Trying to get his mind off a tough case," she said. "Lost a client to suicide."

She told Melton all of Daniella's latest tricks and abilities, though she knew Melton had seen it all before. He had six daughters. Five were married. The youngest, Patricia, was working in Brazil.

"She's gay," Melton said in between bites of his sandwich. "She called us in the middle of the night to let her mother and me know. Woke me from a sound sleep. I thought someone had died. I was relieved."

"How did Linda take it?"

"She told Patricia we'd known for years and to call her back at a reasonable hour. I asked Linda why, if she knew, she'd never shared this news with me. She said it was Patricia's decision when to tell us."

"You didn't know?"

"Suspected. Didn't know."

"You good with it?"

"Absolutely. My aspirations for her are no different than for my other five daughters. I hope she pursues what she's passionate about, finds someone to share that passion who makes her happy, and together they can be a family."

The pleasantries aside, they got down to the reason for Tracy's visit. Melton told her he had extracted DNA samples from two of the three cases she had sent over and was continuing work on the third, which was more problematic, but with the improvements in DNA processing, he remained confident they'd get a sample.

"Thanks, Mike. I needed this."

"You sound like you're back working under Nolasco. Who do you have to answer to? Aren't you a team of one?"

"Chief Weber has taken an interest."

"In cold cases?" He made a face like he didn't believe it. "Seems she should have enough on her plate."

"Annual battle with city council for funding is coming up. I think she's worried the cases in Curry Canyon are losing their bloom. This might be the most important council meeting SPD has ever had."

"They won't defund," Melton said. "They'll talk a good game about things like sending social workers into domestic disputes, but not one of those social workers is going in without an officer, and as soon as everyone realizes that downtown Seattle is now a graveyard, the way it was in the 1980s, and homicides and gun violence are up, the pendulum will swing back the other direction. It always does. Money talks, and tourism is going to take a huge hit."

"Anyway," Tracy said, wrapping up half her sandwich. "The three cases should be enough to appease her."

"Something else bothering you? You don't seem your normal self. No engaging me in battle with your gift of repartee?"

Melton could read people, likely because being a dad to so many children gave him a sixth sense.

"I'm working another case and it's becoming more and more clear that some bad things happened at a very high level of the department, and possibly the government. I just found out two people I know and respect might have been involved."

"And you're worried that pursuing the case might jeopardize their careers?"

"I don't have all the facts, but it definitely looks to be headed down that road."

"What are you going to do?"

"I'm not sure yet."

Melton lifted the paper in which his sandwich had come and carefully tilted it toward the garbage can so as not to have crumbs cascading on his keyboard. Then he wadded the paper and dropped it in the pail. "Here's the thing I've come to learn about my job. You can decide if you can relate or not."

"Okay."

"I get requests from people like you to run this test and that test, to analyze this and that, compare this thing with that thing. What I decide will impact someone's life, maybe even an entire family. It might send a father or a mother to prison. It may cost them their jobs. Any number of things. But the consequences aren't because I did my job. In very rare circumstances do I become vindictive. Most of the time I'm just doing what I get paid to do. The consequences are because of the actions a person chose to take, whatever that person's reason or justification. The consequences lie with them. Not me. You know who told me that?"

"Who?"

"Cerrabone."

"Rick?"

"After he got a conviction, then sought and obtained a death sentence. It would be a hard thing to stomach if you couldn't separate the outcome from the job. You just do your job, Tracy, and the chips will fall where they fall. You get me?"

Tracy did.

She left Park 90/5 and before driving back to Police Headquarters, she checked her emails. The tech department provided her with what information they could find on the guerilla email account. It had come from a server in the Fremont neighborhood in Seattle. Tracy couldn't think of anyone she knew in Fremont.

On the drive, she returned Chief Weber's call and reached voice mail. She told Weber the truth, a truncated version of the truth, but the truth nonetheless. She summarized her meeting with Melton and said she would take all appropriate steps and keep Weber informed. She figured that should be enough to keep the chief happy.

She had another stop to make, and she hoped the person would be more than glad to see her.

CHAPTER 27

Tracy entered the *Seattle Times* building, obtained her pass, and rode the elevator to the third floor. When she stepped off, Anita Childress waited. She looked tentative, like a child with an upset stomach. "I secured a conference room," she said.

Childress didn't make small talk as they walked to the same conference room in which Tracy and Bill Jorgensen had met. She believed Tracy to be the bearer of painful news—not unexpected, but also not welcome. Telling the families of victims what they already suspected never made it any easier on the family or on Tracy. While the family might have resigned themselves to the thought that their loved one was dead, they'd not fully accepted it. They couldn't. That tiny flame of hope, no matter how small, flickered, and it provided just enough light for them to believe that maybe . . . just maybe, their situation would be different from all the others they had read and heard about. Tracy had always thought hope to be cruel, a tease that filled people with positive emotions, without any real basis.

She also knew firsthand how cruel hope could be when that flame was extinguished.

But that was for another day.

Inside the conference room, Childress shut the door. Tracy didn't think the poor woman would make it the few steps to the table, but she didn't want to give her the news until Childress sat. She'd been to enough homes and delivered enough shocking news to know that people could faint.

She looked across the table at Childress and said simply, "Your mother is alive."

Childress put a hand to her mouth, eyes pooling with tears.

Tracy watched her closely to make sure the young woman didn't start hyperventilating. "Are you okay?"

Tears flowed down Childress's cheeks, rivulets she made no attempt to deflect.

"She's in Southern California, a town called Escondido about forty miles from the Mexican border."

Childress shook her head. "I don't understand. Why?"

"She has amnesia, Anita. She doesn't remember anything about her life as Lisa Childress."

Childress lowered her hand. She grabbed tissue from a box on the counter behind the table and dried her eyes and blew her nose. After a minute, she said, "Amnesia?" as if trying to understand the word.

"I obtained her medical records and had them reviewed by a specialist here at the University of Washington. What happened to her is rare, but it does occur."

Childress shook her head. "I don't understand. How does something like this happen?"

The important news imparted, Tracy went back and filled in the blanks.

"She doesn't remember anything?" Childress asked, still disbelieving.

"That's not entirely accurate. When I showed her your pictures as a little girl, she said she had seen you in her dreams. She didn't know who you were, but she felt a connection to you, a bond. She doesn't remember her mother or father, or your father. But she remembered you."

"How did you find her?"

"A tip from the Facebook page I created," Tracy said, explaining.

"She's a bookkeeper?"

Tracy smiled. "She's apparently a genius when it comes to numbers and couldn't fathom that she'd once been a reporter."

Childress pushed back her chair, paced a few steps behind the table, and let out a burst of air. Then another. She wrapped her arms across her body, then looked at Tracy with a wistful smile, as if embarrassed. "I don't know what to say. I wasn't expecting this."

"None of us were, Anita. She'd like to meet you, and your father, and her mother."

"She said that?" Childress asked.

"She did, but I want to caution you not to get too hopeful. It's highly unlikely she's going to see you and suddenly recall any of you. It could be very hard on you. On all of you."

"When?" Childress said. Tracy could see, despite her admonition, that the young woman was already envisioning the unlikely. It couldn't be helped. Tracy just hoped the reunion wasn't painful.

"Thursday. She's never been on an airplane, at least not that she remembers. A friend is going to take her to the San Diego airport and walk her onto the plane." Tracy had arranged for Mark Davis to do this and he had gladly agreed. "I'll make arrangements to be at the gate when she arrives in Seattle."

"I want to be there," Childress said.

"I'd advise against that. She's likely going to be on sensory overload. Give her time to get used to her surroundings. I'll drive her around a bit, let her get oriented before I bring her to meet you." She gave Anita Childress time to process what she'd been told. Then Tracy said, "You need to talk to your grandmother and to your father. Those aren't conversations to have over the phone."

Childress sat, as if from the weight of the responsibility. "No, they're not," she said. "It's good news but . . . it's not."

"It's good news, Anita," Tracy assured her. She'd delivered and received tragic news. "Your mother is alive. That is usually not the case after this long. This is one of those rare occasions."

"I don't know how my father is going to react to this . . . after all he's been through. He's moved on. He . . . I just don't know."

Melton's advice remained fresh. "That's not up to you," she said. "That's up to him. You need to decide where you'd like to see her. Where would you and your family like to meet?"

Another burst of air. "I assume my grandmother's house would be best. My mother grew up there. My father and I can meet you both there."

"Okay. I'll need that address."

Childress smiled for the first time and it looked genuine. "What's she like?"

Tracy smiled. "Well, she's different."

Childress laughed. "I know that."

"That's not what I meant. I didn't notice any of the autism traits you described. The people who've known her in Escondido used the same words you and others who knew her used to describe her—they said she was quiet, kept mostly to herself, and had some quirks, but . . . I'm not sure if her amnesia somehow impacted those traits. That's a better question for the doctors."

"What did you mean, then, by different?"

"It's, uh . . ." Tracy fumbled for the right words, then decided it wasn't for her to filter. "She has an Irish accent."

"An Irish accent?" Childress asked, looking more confused.

"Yes. And it's legitimate, from what I can tell anyway, and what others who've known her have told me."

"How does that happen?"

"I don't know. The doctor I spoke with couldn't say for certain. She did mention something called 'acquired savant syndrome.' Case studies exist documenting people suffering amnesia but suddenly being able to play an instrument they've never played, perform complex mathematical equations, and, in your mother's situation, speak with an accent."

"This is all so unbelievable. It's a lot to digest."

"It's why I want to give you and your family time."

"Did she ever marry? Does she have another family?"

"No. From what I've been told she's lived a quiet life. When the hospital discharged her, she went back to school and became a CPA and a firefighter."

Childress let out an *are you kidding me* laugh. "A firefighter?"

"Apparently her doctor told her she should try to meet people."

"You mentioned a head injury. Was she in a car accident? Did she fall?"

"I don't know yet," Tracy said, and she wasn't lying. She didn't know. Not with any certainty. She changed the subject. "I want to keep this quiet. Your mother does also."

"My mother." Childress said the words and smiled.

"Anita. Did you hear me? Your mother wishes to keep this quiet."

Three knocks on the conference room door startled both women. Bill Jorgensen, who had been Lisa's editor, entered. He looked as if he was trying to read their facial expressions. His gaze darted between them, uncertain whether to express his condolences, no doubt a deduction he had made from seeing Anita Childress in tears.

"She's alive," Childress said to Jorgensen.

Jorgensen's eyes widened. He looked to Tracy. "You're shitting me?"

Tracy shook her head.

"She's alive? Lisa Childress is alive? Where the hell has she been for the past twenty-five years?"

"Escondido," Childress said, smiling.

"Mexico?"

"Southern California."

"She just walked away? She just left?"

Tracy shook her head, but this was no longer her story to tell. She still recalled Jorgensen's expression when they first met, how he had clearly been a newspaperman, and his first instinct was to hunt for the story. And this was a hell of a story.

"She has amnesia," Childress said.

"Amnesia? Is it real?"

Unfortunately, it was a question Tracy knew many would ask, and that's what worried her. "According to her doctors," Tracy said.

Jorgensen looked to Childress. "It would make a hell of a story, Anita. You could write it first person. Open with an embedded narrative. Maybe start with when you started your search."

"I can't make that decision right now," Childress said. "I'm too overwhelmed."

"It's news." Jorgensen gave a small shrug. He looked to Tracy. "It's news, Detective. Big news. Even if she doesn't want to talk, you can't hide something like this. People are going to want to know how this happened."

"I don't disagree with you, but it's not my story to tell, and I won't confirm or deny anything until Lisa and Anita have a chance to decide what they want to do."

"How did it happen?"

"The doctors don't know."

"She was hospitalized, then?"

Again, Tracy could see the wheels turning in Jorgensen's mind. He'd have someone calling every hospital in Southern California.

"Does she know who she is?" he asked. "Did she recall her name?"

"No," Tracy said, not elaborating any further. She turned to Anita Childress. "I'm going to go. You have my phone number. Let's talk later." Tracy turned to leave.

"Detective," Childress said. Tracy turned back as the young woman approached. Childress paused, then she reached out and hugged Tracy, and Tracy wondered if the young woman had ever experienced that kind of hug, certainly not from her mother.

———

Tracy returned home to Dan and Daniella. Outside the picture windows a light rain fell, and Dan had lit a fire in the fireplace insert. Tracy told Dan and Therese all about her meetings.

"An Irish accent," Therese said. "Do you know where from?"

Tracy didn't. "I'm not sure it matters."

"You Americans think we all sound the same, but the accent varies from place to place."

"I didn't mean that," Tracy said. "I meant she's definitely not Irish." She explained what the doctors had hypothesized.

"When's the reunion?"

"Thursday. I'm hoping Jorgensen will at least hold off until then."

"He's waited twenty-five years," Therese said. "He can't wait a few more days?"

"He was definitely more interested in the story."

"Well, she was one of their own," Dan said.

"It made me realize the family's not going to be able to keep this quiet, no matter how they handle it. The story is going to get out, and I'm not sure how Melissa Childs will handle it. She's lived an isolated life until now, and suddenly she's going to be front-page news and on every television in America."

"Eventually it will die down," Dan said. "The news always moves on to the next story."

"That's not what I'm worried about. I'm worried that whoever did this, whoever killed David Slocum and possibly injured Lisa Childress, will react the way Jorgensen first reacted. They won't believe she has amnesia."

"You think she could be in some danger?"

"I think it's a possibility, unless I get ahead of this. I need to go out again tonight," she said to Dan. "I need to talk to someone, and I can't do it at the office."

CHAPTER 28

"Tracy," Vera Fazzio said when she pulled open the door to their two-story Craftsman home in Green Lake. "Vic didn't tell me you were coming over."

"I didn't get the chance to tell him," Tracy said. "This is sort of spontaneous."

"Well, come on in out of the rain," Vera said, smiling. "Vic's in the back watching television."

Tracy walked to the tiled fireplace and considered the pictures on the mantel of Faz and Vera and their son, Antonio, at various points in their lives. It made her think again of all that Anita and Lisa Childress had missed out on.

"Tracy?" Faz entered the room looking confused and concerned. "What's wrong? What's going on? You all right?"

Tracy smiled so he wouldn't worry. "Yes, Faz, I'm fine. I'm sorry to show up unannounced."

"Don't be silly," he and Vera said at the same time.

"You're family, Tracy. You're always welcome here. You know that." Faz and Vera were Daniella's godparents. During her years working

Homicide, Tracy had leaned on Faz too many times to count, but the self-proclaimed big goombah was always there for her no matter the time of day or night.

"Can we talk for a minute?" she said to Faz.

"Sure. Sure. Come sit down." Faz offered her one of two comfortable chairs near the fireplace. "Let me take your jacket." Tracy handed it to him. Faz hung it on an unused brass hook with other coats just inside the front door. Tracy had eaten some of the best dinners of her life at Faz and Vera's. They'd celebrated various occasions and holidays together, and she'd always found the small Craftsman to be homey, something out of a Norman Rockwell painting with crown molding, multipaned windows and doors, dark hardwood floors with throw rugs, heavy red curtains, and the old-style easy chairs.

"Can I get you anything, Tracy?" Vera said. "A cup of coffee or tea?"

"No, I'm fine, Vera. Really, I don't want either of you to worry. Dan and Daniella are fine. This is work related, and I promise I'll try not to take up too much of your family time."

"I'll be in the back," Vera said. "Stay as long as you like."

Faz sat in the red leather chair across from Tracy and leaned forward, forearms on his knees. He looked concerned despite her assurances. "What's going on? What did you want to talk about?"

"I think you know, Faz."

"What's that?" His neck and cheeks splotched red.

"I think you know why I'm here."

"Tracy, I don't know . . ."

"You're the guerilla emailer."

Faz eyed her, but he didn't deny it.

"I had the tech department trace the IP address to Fremont. I don't know anyone who lives in Fremont. I've been racking my brain. Then I remembered the night we all went to Antonio's new restaurant to try out his menu items before the grand opening. Me and Dan. You and Vera and Del and Celia. Fazzio's. In Fremont."

Faz sighed. "I'm just trying to help out a friend, Tracy."

"What did Del get himself into, Faz?"

"It wasn't his fault, what happened."

"Tell me."

"As a detective or as a friend?"

"That's not fair, Faz."

"I know. But sometimes we got to choose."

"Is that what you did?"

"Del and I were both relatively new on the homicide team. I'd come up through the different divisions in Seattle so I'd kicked the tires for a few years, but Del transferred in from Wisconsin. He was fresh off the boat."

"And he got assigned to Moss Gunderson to show him the ropes."

"That's right. It was just being in the wrong place at the wrong time."

"The two crewmen whose bodies floated up at the marina?"

Faz nodded, then said, "But listen, Tracy, I'm not going to shoot off my mouth. If Del wants to talk about this, that's up to him."

"I'm hoping that I can help him, Faz."

"How? This is deep."

"Lisa Childress is alive."

"What?" Faz said. "The newspaper reporter? Has to be twenty-five years since she went missing."

"It has been."

"What's she got to say?"

"Not much. She can't remember a damn thing that happened to her, but she's alive. And I got a hunch when that news breaks it's going to make a lot of people uncomfortable. I need help."

"She's alive," Faz said, not sounding convinced. "Sweet Jesus."

Tracy told him the story of how she'd found Lisa Childress. "Why'd you email me, Faz?"

"Del's been carrying this burden on his shoulders for twenty-five years, Tracy. He feels responsible for what happened to David Slocum, and what he thought happened to Lisa Childress. He's not."

"Then why does he feel responsible?"

Faz made a face like it hurt each time he spoke. He shook his head and put up his hands. "I don't think this is my place to tell you this, Tracy. I think it should be Del."

"Will he talk to me?"

"I don't know. But if I was him, I'd want to get this off my chest. He just hasn't had the right opportunity."

"Can you call him? Talk to him?"

"Yeah. Yeah, I'll help you both. But let's not talk here. I don't want Vera to hear and think any less of Del. What happened wasn't his fault, and he could not have prevented it."

"Where do you want to talk?"

Faz checked his watch. "I know a quiet place. A restaurant doing a killer take-out business and all the privacy we could ever want."

Maybe, Tracy thought, but it didn't quell the butterflies congregating in her stomach. She thought of Del as an uncle and a colleague who had guided her career and stood up for her when she was the only female homicide detective in the Violent Crimes Section. She hoped she didn't have to do anything that could jeopardize his career—and their friendship.

———

Fazzio's was located at a busy intersection on Fremont Avenue in the heart of the Fremont neighborhood. Antonio had worked hard to give the restaurant an old-world feel. A black awning extended over the door and sidewalk, the word "Fazzio's" facing the street. Menus adorned a lighted stand beside an ornate, cast-iron bench. Inside, the maître d' greeted Faz warmly. Soft lighting descended from the copper-tiled ceiling and subtly lit the hardwood floors and brick walls. Copper pots and pans hung on hooks from the wall. The windows were curtained. To Tracy it felt like eating in Vera's dining room, which was how Antonio had been raised. The tables were full, and waiters in formal white dress shirts and black slacks covered by long black aprons tied at the waist scurried from one table to the next, delivering baskets of bread and olive oil and plates of hot food and refreshing wineglasses.

Antonio met his father just inside the door and they exchanged kisses on each cheek. The young man Tracy had first met as a boy was as tall as his father and looked the way Tracy imagined Faz had looked playing power forward on his high school basketball team, tall and lean. "I got the room set up for you in back, Pop," Antonio said.

"You don't worry about us," Faz said. "You take care of your customers."

"It's no worry, Pop."

"Del here?" Faz asked.

"Just arrived. I put three glasses back there with a nice Syrah, and I have some calamari and bruschetta on the way."

"You didn't have to do that, Antonio," Tracy said.

"You come to my restaurant and not eat? My mother would disown me." He smiled. "Okay, Pop, I got to get back to it. You need anything you just ask, okay?"

"You're doing good, huh?" Faz asked.

"We're killing it, Pop. Serving Mom's gnocchi and sausage with peppers tonight. I'll put some aside for you to take home." Antonio winked. "I'll check in with you later."

Faz led Tracy down a narrow brick hall past the kitchen. The aromas of pasta sauce, garlic and capers, and fish flooded her senses. The hallway ended at a curtained room at the back of the restaurant, a heavy red drape pulled across the entrance. Tracy and Dan had celebrated with Faz and Del in this room, but this would not be a celebration.

Faz pulled back the curtain, and he and Tracy stepped in. A dark oak table and eight chairs, three per side and one at each end, dominated the room. Del stood at the head of the table dressed in slacks and a collared shirt, his sleeves rolled up. On the wall hung his black leather car coat and porkpie hat. Del sipped a glass of wine. He looked nervous. Tracy had never seen Del nervous in all her years working Violent Crimes. She had always thought him unflappable.

They exchanged greetings in soft voices. Del took Faz's and Tracy's coats and hung them on hooks. Light Italian opera music filtered into the room from ceiling speakers.

"Thanks for seeing us," Tracy said.

"Hey, let's not be formal like that, okay?" Del said. "We've known each other, what? Ten or twelve years?"

"Sure, no problem," Faz said. "Right, Tracy? No problem."

"No problem," Tracy said.

"And don't do that either," Del said.

"What?" Faz said.

"Don't intercede, okay? I'm a big boy. I can handle myself."

Faz raised both hands in surrender. "The floor is yours, my friend." He poured Tracy a glass of Syrah, then filled his own glass and acted like a disinterested consigliere.

"I knew when you came to me asking about Lisa Childress that it was just a matter of time before we had this conversation. Anyone else . . ." He waved with one hand. "I would have said *no way*. But you . . . You're like a dog with a bone, Tracy. You don't give up. Where'd they find her body?"

"She's alive, Del," Tracy said.

Del looked from Tracy to Faz. Faz raised a hand. "Don't look at me. You told me to keep quiet."

"She's alive?" Del asked Tracy. "Lisa Childress is alive?"

Tracy told him everything she'd told Faz—the tip that came from the tip line on Facebook and her trip to Escondido.

"Amnesia?" Del said. "Do you believe her?"

"I had my doubts," Tracy said. "Until I heard her speak. She speaks with an Irish accent. Has since the day they found her. No way somebody can pull that off for twenty-five years. I figure if she wasn't faking the accent, seemed unlikely she faked the amnesia."

"She doesn't remember anything?" Del said, more of a statement than a question.

Tracy shook her head. "Not a thing. Tell me what happened, Del. Tell me about the marina and Moss Gunderson."

Del sipped his wine and turned sideways to cross his legs. "I'm embarrassed, Tracy."

"Just start, Del."

He set the glass on the table. "I was new here in Seattle. Back then they put us with an experienced detective to teach us the ropes. I got Moss, and I got an earful every day, but I learned to cut through his bullshit, and to listen to the important stuff. Moss was old-school. He made it clear from the start that if we were going to be partners, we had to have each other's backs. He said he'd watch mine as best he could and help me to stay out of trouble. The guy was charismatic," Del said. "He was straight from central casting. We couldn't walk into the Public Safety Building without a dozen guys calling out his name and giving him a hard time. Around town he knew everyone, and everyone knew him."

Having witnessed much the same thing at the country club, Tracy understood what Del had experienced. It had to have been intoxicating for a detective new to Homicide to be the partner of someone seemingly so well respected.

"I'm not on the job more than a week or two and we get called out in the early morning. Two bodies found floating in Lake Union. We get there and meet the harbormaster, David Slocum. Moss starts asking questions about the two men. Slocum said he hadn't seen them before. Moss, I could tell he wasn't that interested. It was blistering cold and windy that morning. He wants to get moving. He tells me to go down to the dock and get a look at the bodies, then talk to the guy who found them and anyone else who saw anything. I'm there for, I don't know, a couple of hours. Nobody knows nothing about these two guys. Moss decides the two guys probably fell off a boat and the current brought them into the marina."

Del took another sip of his wine. A waiter pulled back the red curtain and stepped into the room carrying the calamari and the bruschetta. The smell of butter, lemon, and garlic filled the room. The waiter set the plates on the table beside small appetizer plates and forks and rolled napkins. "How you doing, Mr. Fazzio?"

"Doing good, Ricky. Doing fine. How's your old man?"

"Back's bothering him. Needs to lose weight. Can I get you another bottle of the Syrah?"

"No. Nothing else. We're good. You go do your job."

The waiter left. No one touched the food. Del continued. "Moss says he wants me to handle the case, take the lead. I thought, terrific. Give me a chance to show my chops to the captain and others in Homicide. Moss even tells me to run everything through him so he can make sure I don't make any mistakes. I was grateful to the guy." Del shook his head. "Moss sends over his report on his conversation with Slocum. Nothing in that report says anything about a raid.

"I started asking around all the other marinas if anybody recognizes the two guys. Nobody does. A couple of weeks pass, and Funk sends over the toxicology report. The two guys had narcotics and alcohol in their systems. Okay, I think, so maybe they were fishing and fell in. The logical starting point is the marina, right? That's where they found the bodies."

Faz put a bruschetta and pieces of calamari on a plate and handed it to Del, then handed a second plate to Tracy. "I'm good, Faz. I ate at home."

"You can't come to Fazzio's and not eat. It's an insult to the chef . . . and his father."

Tracy took the plate. Del took a bite of the bruschetta and made a face like he'd fallen in love. "This is better than Vera's, but you tell her I said anything, and I'll deny it."

They all laughed. Nerves. Del sipped his wine and leaned forearms on the table. "I finally go back to the marina to see if the harbormaster has a thought or has heard something more, and the guy, David Slocum, he says to me, 'What did you ever find out about the raid?'

"I must have looked like a deer in headlights because Slocum, he says, 'I told your partner.'

"'Told him what?' I say. He says, 'I told him about the raid on the fishing boat two nights before the bodies floated up to the dock. Half a dozen guys.' Well, by now I realize I can either look stupid or try to bluff. So, I bluff. I look stupid enough on my own." Del gave a half-hearted smile. "I say, 'Yeah, he wants me to get a little more detail about that,' and Slocum proceeds to tell me that two nights before the two men floated up to the dock, these guys raided the marina and impounded the boat for running drugs. I just let him talk 'cause this is all new to me. He said they took the boat from the marina and that's the last he's ever seen of it.

"I'm asking myself why my partner did not tell me this, since it might have made my life a lot easier figuring out the identities of the two men. I smell something rotten. I get back to the office to find Moss, but I run into Faz and we go to lunch. Eventually I get around to the information I acquired and Moss not sharing it with me. I tell him Slocum said the guys who made the raid wore face masks, and Faz tells me to talk to Rick Tombs in narcotics."

"He ran the Last Line," Faz said.

"Tombs tells me two cartels are fighting over distribution in the Pacific Northwest and he'll ask around. More bullshit, though I don't know this. I get back to my desk and Moss drops a report on it. Says the Border Patrol ID'd the two men and he was right. He said they're illegals and part of a cartel. Moss tells me to send the file to him and he'll wrap it in a bow and send it over to the DEA, that our investigation is done.

"Now I know something is up. On my own I track the boat to Vancouver, Canada, but I can't find anything to indicate the boat was ever impounded, that it was raided for drugs, or that any drugs or cash were ever put in the evidence room. I checked the Coast Guard here and in Canada, Border Patrol, customs officials. No one ever heard of it.

"But I'm a rookie," Del said. "I'm trying to walk in the dark; you know? I'm not sure what to do. Am I going to go running off and accuse a decorated narcotics unit of something illegal? What proof do I have?"

Tracy couldn't imagine what Del went through. He must have felt like he was on an island, alone.

"I dig up articles on the Last Line and read them in my apartment. It confirms everything I've been told about the group being small and anonymous, except for Tombs. There's another article in the *Post-Intelligencer* about this drug bust of some two dozen dealers in Seattle by the Last Line and how all these dealers were pleading out, all except this one guy."

"Henderson Jones," Tracy said.

"Jones said he had hard evidence to prove he was somewhere down in LA, so I decide to talk to Mr. Jones, but who do I take with me?" Del said. "Can't take my partner, and I ain't going into Rainier Valley to speak to a supposed drug dealer—alone." Del looks across the table. "So I chose the other Italian; you know? I'd heard the area was once known as Garlic Gulch because of all the Italians who migrated there. Figured we might fit in."

Del and Faz both chuckled. "Like two trees in Greenland," Faz said.

"This guy, Henderson Jones, he doesn't want to talk to us."

"No, he does not," Faz said in between bites of his calamari.

"He was mad," Del said.

"Spitting mad," Faz interjected. "Said he had an attorney, and he was going to sue the city for false arrest."

Del continued. "So I say to the guy, 'Listen. We just want to hear what happened, okay? You tell us what happened.'" Del told Tracy basically the same story Henderson Jones had told her.

Then he said, "Well, now I'm screwed. And worse, I screwed Faz now too."

"No question there," Faz said.

"What are two rookies on Homicide going to do, become rats? What proof did we have?"

"None," Faz said. He took a sip of wine to wash down the calamari. "You think SPD is an old-boys club now, Tracy? You remember what it was like when you started?"

"Remember? How many times did I have to hear the joke that I was 'Dickless Tracy'?"

"Yeah, well, multiply that by five or ten, and you'll understand what we were dealing with back then," Del said. "And Moss was the hub in the wagon wheel around which all the other detectives rotated. We go after Moss and we kiss our careers good-bye, even if we win, and we wouldn't have, because Moss had leverage over me. He'd created a fake file."

"Vera and I had just bought a house and wanted kids," Faz said.

"You let it go," Tracy said. "I understand. I'm not judging you." She didn't want to judge Del, but inside she wondered if she would have done the same thing, if peer pressure and the fear of being ostracized would have compelled her to act as Del had acted. She hoped not.

"Faz let it go," Del said. "I didn't. I confronted Moss about the raid, in the police parking lot. At first, he denied it, says he's got no idea what I'm talking about. I tell him I talked to the harbormaster. He says the harbormaster is mistaken. Then he says, 'But if he wasn't, you were there, too, and heard it; didn't you?' I say, 'What are you talking about? You had me go talk to the people at the dock.' He says, 'That's not what the police report says.' I said, 'I wrote the report. It doesn't say anything of the kind.' 'No, it doesn't,' he said. 'But the report I got, the one I took home, says I put down what Slocum said about the raid and you were there. Now why wouldn't you, the lead detective, put that in your final report to the captain?' That's when I realized the son of a bitch has me by the balls. If he goes down, he's taking me down with him."

"What happened to him? I understood he was a good detective."

"He got divorced," Faz said. "Wife left him for a wealthy, younger man. And he got bitter. And maybe he needed the money. He did a good job covering it all up, but it ate at him, big-time."

"Yeah, well, this was eating at me. Every day I was thinking of what I might do. I'm thinking of a way to maybe get in touch with the *P-I* reporter who did the Henderson Jones story. I'm thinking maybe an anonymous tip to put her in touch with Slocum and let her run with it, get the story out into the public domain. I figured she'd call me as the lead detective, and I could have corroborated what Slocum told her about the dead bodies and about learning of the raid from David. From there I could take my chances, but at least, once it's in the public domain, it can't be ignored. I figure maybe the Justice Department gets involved, and I'd have a layer of insulation. Anyone tries to kill me, it only confirms the story she's running in the paper. I'm debating my options when I hear about a suicide in the Industrial District. Then I hear about a reporter going missing. I put the two together and realize it's the harbormaster and Childress. I break out in a cold sweat because I smell something bad, Tracy. But now, what can I do? The autopsy says Slocum was a suicide, and there is enough evidence to indicate the husband killed Childress. I've lost the one witness who can talk about the raid. I didn't have anything but my word, and Moss still had the file implicating me." Del sputtered, looked away, and took a couple of short breaths.

Tracy dropped her head. Her emotions overtook her. She took her cue from Faz and remained silent. After a beat, Del gathered himself.

"Sorry."

"You just take your time, Del," Faz said. "We ain't in no rush here."

"Don't beat yourself up, Del. I've run down many of the same sources you did and I'm stuck too," Tracy said. "I spoke to the captain of the *Egregious*, Jack Flynt. He's in prison in Canada."

"What did he have to say?" Del asked.

"Basically what Slocum told you. When Flynt got busted in 2002, he told the feds he wants to make a deal and has information to trade. Problem is the statute of limitations to prosecute the guys on the Last Line for the drug charges has already run."

For a moment, Del didn't say a word. He shut his eyes, and Tracy could see the muscles of his jaw undulating as he struggled to get his emotions under control. When he spoke, it was in a shaky voice. "There's no excuse for what I did. If I had said something, maybe what happened to Slocum and Childress might not have happened. I should have gone to somebody in the FBI or the DEA and told them what was happening."

"You didn't have any hard evidence to prove anything, Del," Faz said.

"And you didn't kill David Slocum or Lisa Childress. Don't take the blame for what this group did. They killed Slocum and they killed the two crewmen. They ran drugs and they framed people, including you."

Del took a moment to compose himself. Then he said, "Do you know what happened to Childress? Did she run?"

Tracy told Del and Faz what she had been able to piece together and deduce from there. She told them about the bear spray found at the site that Larry Childress confirmed he put in her bag before she went to meet her source.

"Why didn't they kill her, then?"

"I don't know. The top was not on the bear spray can. The detectives found it a few feet away, and the can had been recently discharged."

"You ever got a whiff of that stuff?" Faz asked.

Tracy shook her head.

"If she sprayed someone in the face, they didn't have a choice but to let her go. It's incapacitating to a bear; imagine what it does to a human.

Their eyes would have been on fire and they would have struggled to breathe."

"Any idea how she ended up in Escondido?" Del asked.

"Again, I'm speculating based on what I know." She told them about Childress's car in the garage near the Greyhound bus terminal and her blood found in the driver's seat. Her blood. And then Childress turning up in Escondido with a Greyhound bus ticket. "Best I can piece together, Childress took a beating before she was able to use the bear spray. Somehow she gets on a bus headed south, and when she wakes up, she has no idea who she is or how she got there."

"And now she's coming home?" Del said.

"I'm worried, Del. I'm worried people might do her harm to protect themselves. I might just be bringing Childress home for a big reunion that could get her killed."

CHAPTER 29

Wednesday afternoon, Tracy made arrangements with Alaska Airlines to meet Melissa Childs at the gate when she stepped off the plane in Seattle the next day. She and Anita Childress spoke, and Tracy told her she would bring her mother by Beverly Siegler's home in Laurelhurst at roughly five o'clock. She again cautioned Childress about media attention. Anita agreed it was best to keep the story quiet, at least until her mother was acclimated and could decide how she wanted to go forward.

Mark Davis called Tracy just before eleven Thursday morning and told her that Childs had boarded her flight, eliminating one worry. Tracy would not have been surprised if Childs had backed out at the last minute, too overwhelmed to get on the plane.

"The package has been delivered," Davis said, and Tracy could hear the smile in his voice.

"How does she seem to you?" Tracy asked.

"Nervous. But determined."

As she waited at the gate at SeaTac Airport, Tracy again went over the places she'd take Childs. She had called and consulted Dr. Laghari about ways to potentially trigger Childs's memory. Laghari said it was not likely, but she didn't rule it out either.

"As I said, no two cases are alike. If Childs truly has amnesia, it's doubtful taking her places will cause her to remember things, especially if you showed her photographs of her family and she didn't recall them. But, you also said that she removed herself from this environment completely."

"She moved to Escondido."

"She changed her context, so she never confronted people and locations from her past. Her memories. If you place her in that context, well, don't get your hopes up, but who knows? No one can say for sure, but I caution you, Detective. If the memory was unpleasant, it could have a deleterious effect on the woman."

"Deleterious how?"

"The best that I can relate it, like soldiers who come home from war with PTSD. Their memories remain dormant for years until something triggers them and those horrible moments come rushing back. Imagine the distress that could cause a person."

Tracy decided she'd drive Childs downtown to the apartment building where she and Larry lived and had first raised Anita. She'd also take Childs to the waterfront building where Childress had once worked as a reporter. The *Post-Intelligencer* had not been printed in years. It had become an online newspaper with a dramatically reduced staff, but the iconic eagle sitting atop a thirty-foot neon globe with the words "It's in the P-I" remained and had become a Seattle landmark.

If Childs showed no reaction to those two sites, Tracy would take her to the Duwamish Waterway, to where David Slocum's body had been found, along with the can of bear spray.

Just after two in the afternoon, the airport announced the arrival of the Alaska Airlines flight from San Diego. Tracy waited by the door as passengers exited. Childs came down the jet bridge dressed in jeans and a long blue coat with a hood. The coat looked new. She rolled a suitcase behind her and gave Tracy a nervous smile.

"How was your flight?" Tracy asked.

"Nerve racking," Childs said.

"Do you have other luggage?" Childs shook her head. "We have a few hours, Melissa. I thought I'd take you around the city. Show you some places."

"Okay," Childs said, sounding hesitant.

—

Tracy paid her parking tab and pulled onto the airport expressway, taking ramps to 518 and then to I-5 north. The sky was clear and the weather had warmed. For once, Tracy cursed her luck. She had hoped for overcast skies and rain, something Childs might have better recalled from her years growing up and living in Seattle.

"You doing okay?" Tracy asked. Childs had not said more than a few words since getting off the airplane.

"Is it always this busy?" Childs asked, eyeing the cars around them.

"Usually it's busier," Tracy said.

"I would think that would be hard to get used to," Childs said.

"Do you drive?" Tracy asked.

"Not a lot and not very far," Childs said. "But people encouraged me to study to get my license, so I did, then I had to learn to drive."

Fifteen minutes on I-5 and Tracy pointed through the windshield at downtown Seattle. "There it is," she said.

Childs just stared. "I used to live here?"

"You did," Tracy said.

Childs gave a nervous laugh and shook her head. Tracy took the exit and drove through downtown, pointing out the different areas of the city, then turned and proceeded along the waterfront. "There used to be a freeway running overhead that blocked much of the view of the buildings along the waterfront."

"It's beautiful," Childs said. "So open."

"The owners of those buildings made a killing," Tracy said.

"What is that?" Childs pointed.

"That's the Space Needle. It was built for the 1962 World's Fair." Tracy watched Childs for a reaction but got none.

"It's futuristic," Childs said, sounding subdued.

Tracy drove along Western Avenue and slowed when the *Post-Intelligencer* globe came into view. She looked to Childs, but the woman showed no reaction, not even a question.

"You used to work in that building."

"Which building?" Childs said.

"The one with the globe."

"That's where I was a reporter?"

"That's where," Tracy said.

"It's hard to imagine. I can hardly write a grocery list."

"You were a good reporter."

Childs smiled, but otherwise didn't respond.

Tracy backtracked through Seattle to the Industrial District. She watched Childs closely as they neared what had been a plastics company when Slocum had been killed. The concrete warehouse was now empty. Tracy drove around the corner of the building. Grass peeked up through cracks in the asphalt pavement, and the weeds and grass between the Duwamish Waterway and the parking area were waist high.

Childs's demeanor seemed to change. It was subtle, but she seemed less interested and more concerned. "Why have we stopped?" she asked.

"Do you recognize this place, Melissa?"

Childs gazed out the windshield, then turned to Tracy. "Should I?"

"I believe this is the last place you went—the night you disappeared."

For a solid minute Childs didn't move. Tracy waited. Childs surprised her and removed her seat belt. She pushed open the passenger door and stepped out, walking toward the small patch of grass between the building and the waterway. Tracy followed, but not too closely. Childs looked to the empty loading bays.

"I do know this place," she said.

Tracy's heart pounded. "What do you recall?"

"It's like the little girl in my dreams. I can feel it."

"Take your time."

"It was dark. Night."

"Do you know why you were here?"

A breeze rippled the water and blew the weeds and tall grass. Childs looked to the grass, then to the pavement. She then looked at Tracy. "No."

"Do you remember anything else?"

"Light," she said. "I remember a bright light." She turned and looked across the waterway at the anchored ships with the colorful boxes. "From over there."

Tracy gave her more time, but Childs didn't add anything. She walked back toward the car.

"Are you ready to meet your family?" Tracy asked.

Childs looked over her shoulder, back to the paved area between the loading bays and the grass. Then she looked at Tracy. "What? I'm sorry."

"Are you ready to meet your family? It's time."

"I don't know," Childs said. "I guess I'll find out."

Tracy's cell phone rang. Anita Childress. Probably wondering where her mother was and if she'd had a change of heart.

Tracy answered. "We're on our way."

"There's a problem," Childress said. "And I'm not sure how my mother is going to react, given what you've said about her."

Back in the car, Childs again became quiet.

"There's a problem," Tracy said.

Childs's forehead furrowed. "A problem?"

"That was . . ." Tracy almost said *your daughter*. "Anita. Somehow your arrival leaked to the media. There are news vans and reporters just down the block from your mother's home."

Childs looked terrified. "I thought this was going to be a private meeting."

"So did I," Tracy said. "I don't know what's going on. I don't know what happened. What do you want to do?" Tracy had the feeling Childs was going to tell her to take her back to the airport. "I can call Anita and arrange a different meeting place."

Childs took a deep breath. After several long seconds she said, "No. They'd likely find us. My mother and daughter have waited long enough. Let's get through it."

"Let me make a call," Tracy said. "I can at least get police out there to push the reporters back."

Twenty minutes later, Tracy took the Forty-Fifth Street exit and continued through the University District, then wound her way through Laurelhurst, one of the most expensive Seattle neighborhoods. The homes on the water now cost in the multimillions, and those around them not much less. Beverly Siegler lived on a horseshoe-shaped street a block above the water. Tracy watched Childs for any reaction, any sense that she recalled her childhood. Childs looked impassive, as if seeing the area for the first time and not understanding its significance.

Tracy made a turn, proceeded down a narrow street, came around a bend in the road, and saw multiple news vans, antennae extended from the roofs. A crowd of reporters stood behind several uniformed officers. The officers had put sawhorses across the road fifty feet from Dr. Beverly Siegler's driveway.

Tracy lowered her window, showed the officer her badge, and explained who she had in the car. The officer stepped back and motioned to another officer at the driveway to move cones so Tracy could park. She pulled the car behind an eight-foot laurel bush privacy hedge. She removed Childs's luggage from the back seat as Childs exited. Anita opened the front door, and she and a woman Tracy assumed to be Beverly Siegler stepped out, both crying. Siegler was a distinguished-looking woman with snow-white hair cut short and deep-blue eyes. Larry Childress, who appeared more curious than emotional, came out the door behind them.

At the front porch, Tracy remained back, giving the family space. The three women stared at one another, each uncertain what to do or to say. Anita spoke first.

"Mom. I'm your daughter, Anita." She gestured. "This is your mother, Beverly."

Childs showed no defining emotion. She looked like a robot try-ing to process the information. Anita stepped to the side and gestured behind her. "This is Larry. My father. Your husband."

Again, Childs did not react. She directed her gaze back to Anita. "I dreamed of you," she said. "I dreamed of a little girl. I didn't know who she was. I didn't know your name." She looked to Beverly. "I'm sorry," she said. "You must have been so worried. All of you."

"Come in," Beverly said, fighting back more tears. "We have a lot of catching up to do."

After the family went inside, Tracy walked to the street and spoke to the uniformed officers. Reporters shouted questions from behind the barrier. She ignored them. "This was supposed to be done quietly," she said. "Do you have any sense what happened?"

The officers shook their heads.

Tracy looked down the block at the distinctive logo for Channel 8 on the side of a van. Maria Vanpelt stood beside it, no doubt shooting a segment to air on the six o'clock news. Vanpelt's van had prime real estate up front, and Tracy wondered if that was because the meeting had been leaked to her, and by whom?

She went back to her car and called Del. She asked him to check around and try to determine how the leak had happened. While they talked, her phone buzzed. Caller ID indicated it was Bennett Lee from the Public Affairs Office. She told Del she'd call him back and took Lee's call.

"Tracy, I'm getting calls from reporters asking for you and asking if it's true that you located a *Seattle Post-Intelligencer* reporter who went missing twenty-four years ago."

"I just reunited the family, Bennett. It was supposed to be a private reunion. Do you know what happened, how the information leaked?"

"I don't, but we need to make a statement to the press. This is taking on a life of its own."

"Tell them the family has asked for privacy, and you don't know if they're going to make a public statement or not."

"Chief Weber wants *you* to make a statement."

"I'm not going to do that without the family's permission. They're entitled to their privacy. If the family wants to make a statement, that's up to them."

"When will you know?"

"I can't say."

"Help me out here, Tracy."

Tracy liked Lee. He was often walking a tightrope trying to disseminate information and maintain the confidentiality of investigations. "Let me talk to the family." Tracy disconnected and walked back to the front door. She knocked gently. Larry Childress answered. "I need to speak to Anita."

"She's with her mother," Childress said. "It's going to have to wait."

"I need to know if she wants to make a statement to the media or wants me to make one for her?"

Childress paused for a moment and Tracy sensed a strange vibe. Who would have incentive to tell the media? Certainly not Anita Childress or her grandmother. Larry Childress had been vilified in the press twenty-four years ago, and more recently when the news first went public. He had told Tracy the looming uncertainty had been the reason he and his high school sweetheart had never wed, that her father had opposed their union. He had an incentive to make the story public, to exonerate himself.

"Did you notify the press, Mr. Childress? Was this your doing?"

Childress's face colored red. He stepped over the threshold and closed the door behind him. "Do you blame me?"

Tracy shook her head. "You couldn't have waited?"

"How dare you. How dare you judge me after everything I've been through, the accusations and insinuations. You all started this when you blamed me."

"I'm not judging—"

"I've waited twenty-four years for this moment, Detective," he said, his tone angry.

"For Lisa to come home, or for you to be vindicated?" Tracy had the distinct impression it was the latter.

"I've lived under a cloud of suspicion every day for decades. Do you have any idea what that is like? My daughter and I suffered immensely because of what the police put me through. You have no idea. None. You have no right to judge me."

He was right. Tracy did not know what he had been through, not in detail, and she had no basis to judge him. But he also had no idea what he might have unleashed by going public with the information. Tracy had no idea what Childress had told the newspapers. If he'd told them where Lisa had lived for the past twenty-four years or her new name. He might very well have put his former wife's life in danger.

"We need to make a statement that your wife has amnesia and doesn't remember anything about what happened."

"We'll make a statement when we are ready, and we will say what we choose to say. You're free to say whatever you want." With that, Childress stepped back inside the house and shut the door.

CHAPTER 30

Tracy returned to Police Headquarters around 6:00 p.m. and was summoned to Chief Weber's office. Weber had a flat-screen television tuned to a news station, and she stood watching live coverage of the story of Lisa Childress's return to Seattle, and the circumstances surrounding it. The story had already gone viral.

Since the staff had left for the day, Tracy knocked on Weber's door and stepped in. Weber did not look happy to see her.

"What I want to know is how this reunion happened. The news stations indicate you were involved in making it happen."

"I told you that I was asked by Anita Childress—" Tracy started before Weber interrupted her.

"And I thought I told you to focus your attention on cases that had the potential to be resolved."

"This case was resolved," Tracy said. "Childress was considered a missing person presumed deceased. Now she isn't."

"This was not a case with DNA evidence nor was it a case likely to be resolved when you chose to pursue it against my specific directive."

"You said to pursue cases that had a likelihood of being resolved. I received a tip after we spoke that Lisa Childress was alive, and I pursued that tip. Not every cold case has DNA evidence that we can follow, Chief. Some are going to require police effort, talking to witnesses—and I did that."

"What I need are numbers to justify our budget."

"And I gave you one. A case that is getting positive feedback."

"We have a city council that would like nothing better than to defund this department."

Tracy couldn't rationalize Chief Weber's reaction. "This is a positive case, Chief. It's a win. It's receiving more local and national attention than the bodies discovered in Curry Canyon. I don't understand what the problem is."

"What the problem is?" Chief Weber pointed a remote at the television in her office and hit "Fast Forward." Until that moment, Tracy didn't know she had been watching a recording.

Weber stopped the recording when Larry Childress appeared on the screen, alone, facing a dozen reporters in the driveway of Beverly Siegler's home. Tracy had a bad feeling about what was to come.

Chief Weber hit "Play" and Tracy listened to Childress speaking to reporters from notecards. He told them his ex-wife was alive and had been living in Escondido, California, for the past twenty-four years. He then chastised the media and said he'd been vindicated after being vilified. He cast blame on the Seattle Police Department, who he said had rushed to judgment and failed to follow other leads that might have resolved this case much earlier. He said police incompetence had led to the loss of his wife and his daughter's mother, and they had both paid for it with a quarter century of their lives.

"It didn't have to be this way," Childress said, looking very much like the grieving husband. "We all suffered because the police department refused to consider any other possibilities, even when I called those possibilities to their attention. They were lazy," he added, a bite in his tone. "And their laziness cost all of us dearly. So do not paint this as positive police work. This case, the disappearance of my wife, is an illustration of what happens when police officers *don't* do their jobs. When they pick the low-hanging fruit and hang on to it even without evidence to justify doing so."

Tracy felt sick to her stomach.

When asked about his wife's claim of amnesia, Childress's answer was vague, intimating that he didn't understand the circumstances well enough to comment.

Weber hit "Pause." "The other stations are broadcasting the same message."

"He's wrong, Chief. Larry Childress refused to let the department send out a news release to other police stations and the media. He hand-cuffed their efforts to protect himself. He's protecting himself now."

"And do you want to get up in front of cameras and say that?"

Tracy knew the question to be rhetorical and bit her tongue.

"His statements will be national news. You still think pursuing this case helped us?"

"It isn't about helping us," Tracy said. "It was about helping a daughter and a mother find some closure. When I took cold cases I was told that I would have latitude which cases I pursued."

"Not by me," Weber said. "I understand you called in sick on Monday."

The statement caught Tracy out of the blue. "That's right."

"Tell me you did not fly to Escondido and speak to the chief of police with Lisa Childress or Melissa Childs, or whatever her name is?"

Again, the question sounded rhetorical. "I took a sick day. I didn't use police resources."

"You deliberately went behind my back."

In a way, Tracy had, and she could understand why Chief Weber was not happy about it, but she wished Weber could see the flip side, that despite Larry Childress's negativity and hostility, this was a rare success, a woman missing twenty-four years found alive. This was a moment to be celebrated, if she spun it correctly. "I have three active files with DNA that Mike Melton is processing. Just as you asked," Tracy said. "And this . . . this is a positive outcome. We can get a statement to Bennett Lee highlighting how rare these circumstances are."

"Is that how you see it?"

"I had an open file. I had a lead. I pursued that lead, and I achieved a positive result for the family and for this department."

"The husband—"

"Is a bitter, angry, little man," Tracy said, feeling herself getting defensive. "Are we going to let him and people like him dictate how we do our jobs?"

Weber paused. "No. I will dictate how *you* do your job." She moved back to her desk. "Why did you take a sick day?"

"To not use police resources."

"Don't bullshit me. You took a sick day to do an end run around a direct order I gave you to set this case aside and pursue cases with DNA evidence that had a reasonable chance of success."

"I did pursue cases with DNA evidence, and Mike Melton told me he will have DNA available in all three cases shortly. I had a strong lead after you and I spoke that Lisa Childress was alive, and I pursued that lead."

"Bennett Lee says the phones are ringing off the hook. The media would like a statement about this case."

"I spoke to Bennett and told him the family has asked for privacy, and I'm going to honor that request."

"Apparently not." Weber gestured to the television. Then she picked up a sheet of paper from her desk and handed it to Tracy. "I asked Lee to put together a statement that will cast you and this department in the best light possible given the circumstances."

Tracy read the statement, which gave details on Melissa Childs's life in Escondido and her allegation that she had suffered from amnesia.

The intimation was that Lisa Childress had simply walked away from her responsibilities to start a new life, thereby absolving the police department.

"You want me to sign this?"

"No. I want you to make a statement to the media in time for the ten o'clock news."

"I told Lisa Childress and her daughter that I would respect their privacy. I also told them that I would not reveal her life in Escondido. And this statement is not accurate. She did not walk away."

"That cat has been let out of the bag."

"Not by me."

"But because of your actions."

That was no doubt true. But Tracy would not go back on her word. Honoring her word was more important than pleasing her chief, though it certainly would not be without consequences. It might not be the smartest decision Tracy ever made, but it was the honorable one. "I won't read this statement without the family's permission. It's a violation of the promise I made to them, and it gives in to the husband. Why draw more attention to him and the situation? Why not just let this be for a bit?"

"I'm giving you a direct order, Detective Crosswhite."

Tracy held her breath. She knew where this was headed. "Then I'm going to have to respectfully refuse that order."

"Then you're suspended pending an internal investigation by a unit sergeant. I'd suggest you get in contact with the union. You'll need legal defense."

As Tracy started for the office door, Chief Weber said, "I'm disappointed, Detective Crosswhite."

Tracy stopped and turned back. "Not nearly as disappointed as I am."

CHAPTER 31

Tracy cleared her desk of her personal effects, and though she believed she had done the right thing, it had not been without some regret and some anger. When she arrived at home, Dan was in the backyard sitting beneath the pergola. He had put up a flat-screen television and heaters, a suggestion by Tim, who helped him run electrical wiring and installed the outlets. It was pleasant beneath the shade.

"Hey," Dan said. "I wanted to surprise you. Comcast just extended the cables out here and apparently just in time. Your name is all over the local and national media with the story of Lisa Childress's return to Seattle."

"It's big news. Just not for the police department."

"What are you talking about?"

"Chief Weber just suspended me."

"What? Why?"

"I refused a direct order to read a prepared statement."

"That doesn't make any sense."

"It does, actually. She gave me an order to not pursue the case and to focus on cases with DNA evidence. I didn't advise her of the lead I received about Lisa Childress maybe being alive in Escondido."

"So what? This is positive publicity."

"You haven't seen the news."

"I've seen some of it."

"Then you haven't seen the part where the husband rips the Seattle Police Department for rushing to judgment twenty-five years ago, thereby causing him and his child to be scorned and ostracized for decades."

"He didn't. Why would he do that?"

"Because it's true, and he's bitter and angry. That's exactly what Moss Gunderson and Keith Ellis did. They made him the only suspect to divert any investigation into Lisa Childress pursuing a story on the Last Line and going that morning to meet with her source, the harbormaster, David Slocum. But I don't have solid evidence to prove that, and I don't want anyone outside of Del and Faz, whom I trust, to know."

"Why exactly were you suspended?" Dan said, quickly shifting into his lawyer tone.

"She believes I went around her direct order not to pursue the case and because I refused to break my word to Anita Childress and Melissa Childs that I wouldn't make a statement or respond to media questions without their blessing. The latter is true. The former I can dispute. She told me to pursue cases with evidence that might lead to a resolution. I received a solid tip. It wasn't DNA, but it was solid and it led to a resolution."

"Weber wants you to be the department's sacrificial lamb."

"Maybe."

"Why not read the statement? The family clearly has gone public." Dan pointed to the television.

"That was her argument, but she's wrong. That was just an angry little man seeking his revenge. I'm certain it wasn't Anita's or Melissa's decision, and Lisa didn't walk away, not deliberately. I want no part of it."

"Call them up. Ask them—"

"Do you know what it took for Melissa to return to Seattle? She's never traveled. She's spent all that time in Escondido because it was safe. Now she arrives to news trucks and reporters? I'm not going to put her through more of that, Dan. The brass can take matters up with Larry Childress as they see fit."

"You need to get ahold of the union. Tell them what transpired, that you pursued a case with a solid lead. Get legal counsel."

"I don't know, Dan. This job has become politicized with everything going on now. You can't do or say anything without the far left or the far right attacking. I feel damned if I do and damned if I don't. Maybe it's time I retired. A lot of my colleagues have already come to that conclusion. I'll stay home and raise Daniella and think of what I might do next. I can always teach. If there's one thing this case has taught me, it's life is precious and the people in it even more precious. I'm sacrificing my time with Daniella for what?"

"So that people like Anita Childress can reunite with her mother, Tracy," Dan said softly. "So all those families of all those victims in North Seattle and Curry Canyon can find some form of closure." His words hit home. "Screw Weber. You do good work. You do damn good work. You never let Nolasco take that away from you. Why are you going to let her take it away?"

"I'm tired of the fight," she said, but she knew she was only feeling sorry for herself.

"Where's the person who told me I couldn't blame myself for what happened to Ted Simmons, who said that I did my job and I did it well?"

"Don't throw that in my face, Dan."

"You threw it in mine . . . And it worked, Tracy. We can't always control the outcomes, but we can control what we do. You didn't do anything wrong. You did your job. Weber is the one failing to see the forest for the trees. She could spin this into a positive news story."

Dan sounded like Mike Melton. He made sense. Tracy calmed. "Maybe. But I'm not going to read that statement, and I'm not going to answer the media's questions just to get my job back."

"I'm not telling you to read the statement. I'm telling you to fight for what you've worked so hard to achieve. Fight for yourself as hard as you fight for all those victims you help. If you lose, then go down swinging and get in a few licks."

Tracy couldn't match Dan's level of combativeness, at least not at the moment. She was tired of the fighting—with Nolasco and now with Weber. Seemed as though no matter how successful she was, there was always another obstacle in her path. Her personal cell phone rang. She checked caller ID. Del Castigliano.

"Saved by the bell," Dan said.

Tracy answered her phone and put Del on the speaker. "Is the rumor going around true?" Del asked.

"Depends on the rumor," Tracy said.

"I heard Weber suspended you pending an internal investigation for insubordination and refusing multiple direct orders."

"That would be true."

"Is this related to Lisa Childress?" Del asked.

"It doesn't matter, Del."

"It does to me. Is this related to Lisa Childress?"

"Weber told me to back off my Lisa Childress investigation—"

"Why?"

"She wanted me to focus on cold cases that had DNA evidence and the best chance of resolution and paint the department in the best possible light."

"What the hell does she call this?"

"Watch the news. The husband didn't do us any favors. And Weber's got her eye on the city council. She's trying to combat the defund-the-police movement with numbers."

"She can't suspend you for getting a positive result," Del said.

"Watch the news," she said again. "It's not so positive at the moment. Larry Childress went public and ripped the police department, saying their rush to blame him led to the loss of his wife and Anita's mother. Weber does not see this as positive. She wanted me to fall on the department sword, and I'm not going to do it."

"Seems like the husband already thrust the sword into our collective guts." Del sighed. "Weber's making an example of you."

"A part of me deserves it, Del," Tracy said.

Del didn't say anything for a moment. Then he said, "You got time for a meeting tonight?"

"What type of meeting?"

"Me, you, and Faz."

"I don't know, Del. I want to spend time with Dan and Daniella."

"She'll be there, Del," Dan said into the phone. "Count on it."

Del disconnected the call before Tracy had time to argue.

Tracy sighed and looked across the firepit at Dan, who was unsuccessfully trying to hide a smile. "What are you smiling about?"

"He wants you to fight the suspension."

"Maybe you should go to the meeting," Tracy said. "You seem to have all of this worked out already."

"No," Dan said. "But I know you. You'll hem and haw for a bit, but in the end, you'll go because you hate to lose—at anything."

"That's not true."

Dan's smile broadened.

"It's not true," Tracy reiterated.

"You're doing it now."

"Doing what?"

"Trying to win this argument."

Tracy shook her head. "I'm going to go change. It would do us both a world of good if when I came back, you had poured me a glass of one of those red wines you're trying out." Tracy went inside and marched upstairs. She spent time with Daniella, then asked Therese if she could feed her.

"Not a problem, Mrs. O."

After Therese and Daniella left the bedroom, Tracy sat on the ottoman at the foot of the bed and took off her boots. She set them on the floor and looked to Rex and Sherlock, both attentive, staring at her.

"You two waiting for an answer also?" The dogs' eyebrows danced, and Tracy reached out and hugged them both. "You're loyal; aren't you?"

"Rex, Sherlock. Dinner," Dan yelled from downstairs. The two dogs nearly trampled each other getting out of the room. "But loyalty is no match for dog food and gravy," she said.

She went into the bathroom and washed her face, rubbing a gentle soap on her skin that was supposed to prevent wrinkles—fat chance—then washed it away with lukewarm water and patted her face with a soft towel. She wondered how Melissa Childs and Anita were doing with the crowd outside Beverly Siegler's home. She wondered if either knew about Larry Childress's statement to the press. She wondered if Childs wished she had remained in Escondido, living in her safe and protected environment. It made Tracy think of Childs's decision to return to Seattle, then to run the gauntlet of reporters. She wasn't doing it for herself. She was doing it for the daughter and the mother who loved her and who had grieved, thinking she was dead.

It was a selfless act.

Tracy thought of Dan's statement and chuckled at the irony. He was right. She wouldn't just walk away, not without a fight. She owed it to the victims not to just give up. She hadn't quit when Captain Johnny Nolasco made her life difficult, and she wouldn't now. Dan was wrong about one thing though. Her motivation wasn't driven by winning or losing. It was driven by doing the right thing.

It was about the fight.

Though winning was always better than losing.

And she intended to win.

CHAPTER 32

Tracy stepped into Fazzio's restaurant and Antonio, talking to a table of customers, excused himself and immediately came over. Faz had told Tracy that Antonio, at his mother's suggestion, came out from the kitchen each night to thank each guest for choosing to dine at Fazzio's, and to ensure their meal was up to the standards he set for himself. Antonio told the maître d' he'd take care of Tracy.

"Pops is in the back with Del, Tracy. Can I get you anything?"

"What are they drinking?" Tracy asked.

"Red wine," Antonio said.

"Then just a glass," Tracy said. She had quickly eaten some leftover Thai food, but the smells coming from Antonio's kitchen made her mouth water.

"I'll take you," he said.

"Don't be silly. You got paying customers and I know my way. Take care of them."

Antonio stepped between tables and returned to the kitchen. Tracy took the same narrow hall to the curtained room. When she stepped in, Del and Faz were huddled at the end of the table, leaning forward in their chairs, talking.

"Don't let me interrupt," she said.

Both men stood.

"You're standing for me now? Sit down. I might confuse you two for polite."

"Del was just filling me in on what happened," Faz said. "You're going to fight it, right?"

"I'm going to do better than fight it. I'm going to find justice for Lisa Childress, David Slocum, and the two crewmen whose bodies floated up in Lake Union."

Faz held out his hand to Del, who reached into his pocket and gave him twenty dollars. Faz smiled. "I told Del you wouldn't take this shit."

Tracy laughed. "What about you, Del? What I want to do could cause you some problems."

"I'm tired of taking punches. When I was boxing in the Golden Gloves, my old man trained me, and he used to tell me, 'Take the fight to your opponent, Del. That way, even if you get beat, at least you got in your licks, and that feels a hell of a lot better than just covering up and absorbing punches.'"

Tracy pulled out a chair. "Pour me a glass. We have work to do."

—

The following day, Tracy met Rick Cerrabone for an early lunch. Cerrabone had free time after the plea deal, but not a lot. He usually packed a sandwich and ate at his desk, working through lunch so he could get home at a reasonable hour. It helped free him from his chains when Tracy mentioned she'd treat him to Little Neon Taco on Boren Avenue, one of Cerrabone's favorite restaurants.

That was one reason Tracy chose it. The restaurant was also far enough away from the courthouse and the police department that it was unlikely they'd be seen together by anyone from either of those institutions.

They entered the restaurant to the smell of homemade tortillas, peppers, and spices. Cerrabone ordered carnitas and chorizo tacos and a pink lemonade. Tracy got veggie and chicken mole and also a pink lemonade. A table in one of the window cubbies at the front of the restaurant provided a view of people passing on the sidewalk as Tracy and Cerrabone ate chips, salsa, and guacamole. Cerrabone, who never met a plate of Mexican food he couldn't make better with added spice, ordered a hot sauce that was simply labeled "Hot Hot Sauce." He dipped a chip in the dip, then added a drop of the sauce.

"Didn't your mother ever tell you that you'll burn your taste buds?"

"Actually, she told me the spice would kill tapeworms."

"Have you ever had tapeworms?"

"Not eating this hot sauce."

"Sounds like circular reasoning."

"Best kind of argument. I always win. Tell me, Tracy, are you treating me to one of my favorite lunches just because of all the favors I've done for you over the years, because I'm an extremely witty lunch date, or are you looking for some free legal advice?"

"I'm insulted," Tracy said.

"That's what I thought. Free legal advice."

"Why would I need free legal advice?"

"Because Chief Weber suspended you."

"It didn't take long for that news to get around the courthouse, did it?"

"Never does when a thrice-decorated detective tells the chief to stick it."

"Is that what they're saying?"

"Not that politely. So, it's true?"

Tracy filled Cerrabone in on the details, and as she did, their food and drinks arrived.

"So then, what is it you wanted to talk to me about?" Cerrabone asked in between bites of a taco.

"I need to ask you about some cold cases I'm working on."

"You're not supposed to be working on any cold cases."

"I'm an overachiever."

Cerrabone chuckled. "Tell me about it."

Tracy spent the next forty-five minutes eating and telling Cerrabone everything she had learned about the raid on the Diamond Marina, the two drowned men, harbormaster David Slocum's supposed suicide, and Lisa Childress's link to that crime site.

"You think she was investigating a possible story on crime within this drug task force . . . What did you call it?"

"The Last Line. And yes, I think that's exactly what she was doing."

"Do you know what happened or if she really does have amnesia?"

"Her amnesia is legitimate, according to an expert at the University of Washington. What happened to her that night, I don't yet know. What I can tell you is she definitely had a head injury. She had a can of bear spray, and she discharged that can."

"Presumably in the face of her attacker, which is why she didn't die that night."

"Presumably. I don't really know."

"You said this boat captain, Jack . . ."

"Flynt."

"Jack Flynt . . . told you there was some type of agreement in place?"

"He and his lawyer confirmed an agreement after his arrest in 2002. His sentence was reduced from twelve to five years."

"And you believe he received a reduced sentence because he told the authorities about this raid on his boat in 1995. But as far as you have been able to determine, no charges were ever brought against the drug task force or any of its members."

"Or anyone else, for that matter."

Cerrabone gave this some thought as he sipped his pink lemonade. He set down the glass. "Let's take this one step at a time. Anything related to the confiscation of drugs from the fishing trawler *Egregious* would have been within the purview of the FBI or the DEA."

"That's what I'd suspect."

"I'll ask around, see if I can get a copy of the agreement. As to why no charges were brought, I would suspect it has to do with the statute of limitations. The federal limitation on the prosecution of most non-capital offenses, including all drug crimes, is five years from the date of the offense, in this case the theft of the cargo on board the *Egregious*."

"What about arguing it was a conspiracy among the members of this force and possibly others?"

"Then the statute of limitations begins to run on the date of the last act in furtherance of the conspiracy."

"What exactly is the last act in a case like this?"

"The easy answer is, if the crime is ongoing—meaning they kept the boat and used it or they continue to hide the money—then the statute doesn't come into play. But you're talking about more than twenty-five years, Tracy. How are you going to prove the crime is ongoing? I would suspect the money was divided up and spent."

Tracy thought of Moss Gunderson and Keith Ellis and their purchase of a golf membership. She thought of Rick Tombs living in a $2 million home on a golf course. Cerrabone was likely correct.

"That's for the theft of the drugs, and all the other things they may have been doing," Cerrabone said. "The murder of the harbormaster, however, doesn't have a statute of limitations, nor would a charge of negligent manslaughter, which is what I would likely bring for the deaths of the two crewmen who panicked and jumped overboard, but you said those who took that ship wore facial coverings, that their identities were concealed."

"True."

"You have no evidence they were part of this task force."

"What I was told is that David Slocum overheard one of the officers use the term 'sergeant.'"

"That's it?"

Tracy knew it was thin, at best. Especially since it was unlikely Jack Flynt would ever testify and risk violating the agreement he signed.

"The harbormaster can't testify, and the captain might be able to testify as to the two men who drowned, but you're not exactly talking about the most credible witness, and you still can't pinpoint this drug task force. Tell me what you do have," Cerrabone said.

"What if I could convince Jack Flynt, the captain of the *Egregious*, to testify that the crewmen jumped overboard during the raid because they thought they were going to be killed?"

"Which might put Flynt himself at risk since he was engaged in an illegal act, and therefore it could be argued he recklessly caused their deaths. If that indeed happened and if, which I doubt, he mentioned it when he made his deal. So again, he isn't credible. A good lawyer would carve him up and say he was making it up and looking to make another deal. It also doesn't get you any closer to the Last Line."

"Del could testify that David Slocum told him that he told Moss Gunderson that there was a raid on the *Egregious* two nights before the two men floated up to the marina."

"A lot of 'he told' layers. It's hearsay, but with Slocum dead, it probably comes in, but again why didn't Del bring this up earlier, and again, it doesn't put the Last Line officers on the boat. Not enough, Tracy. What else?"

She fought against growing frustration. "What if I could get Moss to testify he told Rick Tombs about Slocum knowing about the raid, and Tombs cut him in on the take?"

"Why would Moss do that?"

"We could offer him some type of immunity."

"Only if there's a threat he's going to jail. There isn't. If he cut a deal and took the money, the statute bars those claims. You're asking him to impugn his reputation. There's no reason for him to do so. You have no leverage."

"Anita Childress can testify as to her mother's notes about her meeting with the harbormaster."

"Do the notes say she was meeting with the harbormaster?"

"No, but we have the record indicating Lisa Childress received a phone call from the Shell gas station earlier that night, which is right up the street from the marina."

"Again, it's thin. It doesn't mean the call was from the harbormaster."

"Yes, but Slocum died, and Childress went missing on the same night, and I can put the can of bear spray at that site, and Larry Childress can testify he gave his wife bear spray before she left the house that night to meet with a source for one of her stories. Which puts Childress at the site when or shortly after Slocum was killed. Why would she go unless it was Slocum who called her from the gas station? Dennis Hopper will testify Slocum used the pay phone at the station because he was paranoid he'd get busted for his grow operation."

"That's not bad, but the defense will argue you can't prove it's *the* can of bear spray, but a can of bear spray . . . Did you check it for fingerprints?"

"There was a cloth sleeve over the can, so it was never checked for fingerprints back when it was found, and it's no longer available."

"So you can't prove it's *the* can. And Larry Childress, from what I saw on television, isn't exactly a friendly witness. But for the sake of argument, let's say you can put Childress at that site. What have you proven?"

"That Slocum was killed because he was going to provide an investigative reporter with evidence that the *Egregious* was raided two nights before the crewmen washed ashore."

"But you can't prove the killer. Not to beat this poor horse, but you're no closer to the Last Line. I'm sorry, Tracy, but unless you can get something solid to testify as to who killed Slocum, then you're going to have a problem. In theory, if you could prove the murder, you might be able to charge Moss with being an accessory after the fact. You could argue Slocum witnessed the raid and was killed to prevent him from telling Childress about the raid and everything else, and that Moss helped to cover up the murder by calling it a suicide, but that's several big ifs. Not to mention defense attorneys would be screaming prejudice about these charges being brought decades after the alleged crimes, the loss of witnesses, faded memories, blah, blah, blah. My suspicion? My suspicion is that this came up in 2002 when Jack Flynt first raised it, the federal prosecutors kicked the tires the way we're kicking them, and they ultimately came to the conclusion that most of the cases were barred by the statute of limitations and there just wasn't enough solid evidence to get a conviction on Slocum's murder, and they decided it best to shut it down and move forward."

Tracy knew Cerrabone was just stating the truth, but her frustration built as each avenue she pursued reached a roadblock. "What about a conspiracy charge?"

"RICO?" The Racketeer Influenced and Corrupt Organizations Act provided law enforcement with a powerful tool against the leaders of a group formed to engage in organized crime and illegal acts, like the mafia. Leaders could be tried for crimes they ordered others to commit.

"It's an interesting argument. But the defense will argue the Last Line was not created to engage in illegal acts, though it certainly appears illegal acts were perpetrated. Whether the argument might win would most likely depend on the judge hearing the matter. If you get a judge pissed off enough about what happened, he or she just might agree. It would at least be a bargaining chip that might give you some leverage. The question is, are there any Last Line members still alive who might be willing to talk, and what exactly did they know? Rick Tombs is dead, and he appears to have been the primary conspirator, the guy you really want for those crimes. Those remaining haven't spoken in twenty-five years and might believe there's no reason to start talking now. They'll lawyer up, and the lawyers will know you have statute of limitations problems."

"I'm thinking more about the murder of David Slocum and the two crewmen."

"I know you are, but you haven't told me anything solid that ties the Last Line to the two crewmen, or to Slocum's death. Do you have admissible evidence to do that?"

At the moment, Tracy didn't. She had hoped she could convince Cerrabone, or the feds, to at least threaten to bring RICO charges. If she could, it was possible that one of the Last Line members might talk. The problem, however, as Cerrabone counseled, was no one had yet come forward. And no prosecutor was going to bring a charge just so a detective could flush the rats out of the sewer.

"Three men died, Rick. Slocum was murdered in cold blood."

"Didn't you tell me the ME's report was inconclusive?"

Tracy had. "How could anyone look at this situation and think justice was served?"

"It's not about whether justice was served, Tracy. It's about whether guilt can be proven. I just don't see it. Not now. Not after all this time. The statute of limitations exists for this very reason, to protect against stale claims and the loss of evidence and the loss of witnesses and their recollection. I wish I was wrong. I hope you can prove me wrong. If you can, I'll go after the people. You know I will. But now? Now you don't have nearly enough."

CHAPTER 33

Tracy met Del and Faz late afternoon in the back room at Fazzio's. She told them the outcome of her conversation with Rick Cerrabone. "The statute of limitations likely protects all of them against any drug or theft charges. As for the deaths of the two drowned men, and the murder of David Slocum, without something else more substantial, Cerrabone doesn't see a way to bring a case. He said there just isn't enough solid evidence for it to ever hold up."

"We need someone to tell us what happened," Del said.

"And if no one has spoken in all this time, it's unlikely they're going to start now," Faz said. "Especially since Tombs is dead. We don't know how many on this task force were even dirty and if any are still alive."

"I'm going to talk to Moss. Maybe I can bluff him, tell him I'm going to come clean, that I'm going to spill what happened," Del said.

"He's retired, Del, and the statute protects him from criminal prosecution. What good is that going to do?" Faz said.

"Maybe we can pressure him," Tracy said. "Maybe we tell him he's looking at an accessory after-the-fact charge in the death of David Slocum, but that we'd recommend that the prosecutor cut him a deal if he provides state's evidence and tells us what happened. Or if that doesn't work, we tell him we'll keep his name out of the newspaper to protect his reputation. He won't be a rat and he'll still be the big man at his golf club. That has to be worth something."

"I guess it can't hurt," Faz said. "Maybe there's a spark of decency hidden beneath all that camouflage."

"There isn't," Del said.

"That's a problem, Del," Tracy said. "We can't very well take the fight to Moss if we can't even put on the boxing gloves."

"I'll go with you, Tracy; I'm just saying don't get your hopes up."

She wasn't. Moss wasn't stupid, and she suspected he'd thought this through, maybe even went to a lawyer for advice.

———

Moss lived in Northeast Bellevue in a house just above Lake Sammamish. Tracy and Del parked in the circular drive. Daylight rapidly faded and dusk had set in. The home, dark-green wood clapboard with black trim, sat nestled within trees and shrubbery. Above the front door was a three-sided window made of stained glass.

Moss pulled the door open and stared at Tracy, about to say something until his gaze shifted to Del.

"Moss," Del said.

Moss smiled. He wore golf clothes as similarly outlandish as the clothes he wore the morning Tracy first spoke to him. His pants were red, his shirt black with red checks. A white belt. "Well, I guess it was just a matter of time before you two showed up. I heard you were friendly. Worked on the same team for a decade. Am I right?"

"Want to talk to you, Moss," Del said.

"Really. What about?" Moss grinned.

"You know what it's about," Del said.

Moss pulled the door open and took a step back. "Not a problem. Come on in to our humble abode."

"Who is it?" a woman yelled from another room as Tracy and Del stepped into a marbled entryway beneath a glass chandelier.

"An old friend," Moss said, keeping his gaze on Del. "One of my protégés."

The entry had a step down to a living room with comfortable brown leather couches facing plate-glass windows offering a view of the lake and across it to the homes on the other side. In the corner of the room, a telescope on a tripod faced the view.

The woman who entered the hallway had shoulder-length blonde hair beneath a light-blue visor and looked to be midforties, roughly thirty years younger than Moss. "You've never met my wife, Frieda, have you, Del?"

Del looked to the petite woman in stretch golf pants and a black turtleneck beneath a golf jacket that matched the color of the visor. "I don't believe so," Del said. "It's nice to meet you, Frieda."

"Del was a rookie who I trained a long time ago," Moss said. "Taught him everything he knows. Isn't that right, Del?"

Del looked to Frieda. "Everything but how to dress."

"Well, thank God for that." Frieda smiled. "I don't think the world could stand a second Moss."

Moss redirected his finger at Tracy. "And this is the renowned Tracy Crosswhite," Moss said. "She's famous for solving cold cases, honey. Won the Medal of Valor three times, I believe."

"Congratulations," Frieda said. "It's nice to meet you both."

"We just got back from golf and dinner at the club," Moss said. "You've never come out with me, Del. Do you golf?"

"Badly," Del said.

"We all golf badly, Del. It's just different degrees of terrible." Tracy feared Del might reach out and slap the smile off Moss's smug face.

"Honey, these two nice detectives would like to talk to me about one of my old cases. Even in retirement, duty calls. I'll be in the den."

"Will you be long?"

He looked again to Del. "No. I don't believe this will take much time at all."

Moss led them into a room of dark-wood paneling with an antique partners desk and a computer monitor on an inlaid leather desk pad. The monitor wasn't connected to a computer.

"Before we get started, would you mind opening your coats?"

Del did and Moss patted him down. "You wouldn't be wearing a wire, would you, partner?"

Del didn't answer.

Moss turned to Tracy. "Do not put your hands on me," she said.

Moss chuckled. "I heard you were a hard-ass. Heard you and Johnny Nolasco weren't exactly on speaking terms."

"We're not on any terms," Tracy said.

Moss moved the computer monitor to one side of the desk so he could see both of them. Before sitting in a leather chair, he asked, "Can I get either of you a Scotch or Irish whiskey?" Del and Tracy declined. Moss sat and put his slippered feet on the desk edge. "So, what would you like to talk to me about."

"A woman's life," Tracy said.

"You'll need to be more specific."

"Lisa Childress," Tracy said.

"The gal on the television? She's getting a lot of airtime. So is the husband."

"He's saying you did a shitty job," Del said.

"That's the beauty of retirement, Del. The stink no longer sticks to me." He looked to Tracy. "They're saying the wife has amnesia. Is it true?"

"Nobody knows," Tracy said, hoping the ambiguity might scare Moss into talking. It was a risk, but she could provide Childress with some protection. Moss's smile faltered slightly. "She isn't really talking to the media . . . yet. I know about the raid at the Diamond Marina, Moss. I want to know what happened. I want to know why you didn't report it."

"You mean the raid that the harbormaster told Del about? The one in my report that I still have? Why didn't you report that raid, Del?" Del looked like he was chewing glass. Moss smiled. Then he looked to Tracy. "Suppose I did know about this raid. Suppose I knew about it, and I went to Rick Tombs and told him I knew about it. Suppose I even told Tombs that unless he cut me in on the action, I would investigate that raid, and what would I find? I'd find a boat with an estimated fifteen million dollars in cocaine that was taken but never impounded. I'd check the evidence room and note that no evidence had been entered. I'd find no hard evidence that boat was ever raided or impounded. So what possibly could have happened to all that cocaine? And what happened to all the money that cocaine generated? Suppose I decided I was tired of taking it in the shorts, that I was going to get what was due to me, that I was going to join a country club myself, drive a nice car, and buy me a house on the water. Suppose I did that, and got a hot, young wife to boot, Detective? The statute of limitations would have long since expired, and there wouldn't be anything you or anybody else could do about it."

"No statute of limitations exists for the murder of the two crewmen, Moss, or the harbormaster," Del said.

Moss looked Del in the eyes. "You have some evidence I was involved in that?"

"What we're hoping to do is put together a case against the people who were involved," Tracy said.

"You worked homicide, Moss. You know what that does to a person's family," Del said. "Tracy's just trying to bring some justice to those families."

"Justice? Shit, Del, you weren't paying attention when class was in session, were you? If you had been, you would have known justice is what we make it." Moss shook his head. "We go to work every day and get beat up in the press for trying to keep people safe. And what do we get for it? A shitty salary. A shitty pension our ex-wives take half of. Look around, Del. This is justice."

"We're looking to make a deal, Moss," Tracy said. "We can keep your name out of it and protect your reputation."

"I ain't no rat," Moss said. He looked across the desk at Del. "So unless you have something more . . . something that could conceivably imperil my luxurious lifestyle here in my castle on the lake, I got nothing to say."

"When I do get that information, Moss, and if you know anything about me, you know I will, we won't come back offering a deal," Tracy said. "This is it. This is your chance to do the right thing. Once I walk out that door, the deal walks with me. You want to roll those dice?"

Moss grinned. "You're bluffing, Detective. You just rolled a three and crapped out. Game over."

"You're wrong about something, Moss," Del said.

"Yeah? What's that?"

"You can't buy happiness. You're still the same bitter, petty piece of shit who couldn't get past the fact that his wife chose a young, rich guy who could buy her all the things you couldn't. Yeah, you're living here in your castle, but you ain't happy, Moss. That's why you wear all those goofy clothes. What was that song? 'Tears of a Clown'? You're just a clown, Moss."

Tracy couldn't have said it any better. She followed Del to the door.

"Detective Crosswhite," Moss said. Tracy turned back. "Just one more thing. How is it that a suspended detective is here making a police call?" He looked to Del. "And what are you doing aiding her?" Moss smiled. "Now this is what you call leverage. You all have a good night."

CHAPTER 34

B ack in the car, Del seethed. Tracy didn't blame him. She would have liked nothing better than to have had something to slap the smile from Moss's smug face, but she didn't see any ability to do that.

"How the hell did he know you were suspended?" Del said.

"I don't know," Tracy said. "But Cerrabone knew it also."

"Cerrabone lives at the courthouse, Tracy. Hell, that place is a cesspool of gossip and rumors, and word travels fast. How did Moss hear about it way out here?"

"I hope you don't get hurt by this, Del. If anything happens, you just blame me. Tell them I didn't tell you I'd been suspended. They can't suspend me twice."

"I'm a big boy, Tracy. I'm here because I didn't do the right thing the first time. I'm not about to throw you under the bus to save my ass. If they want to come after me, let 'em. I've been doing this job long enough. My point is, there's a leak, and that leak is feeding Moss information. We need to be careful going forward about who we tell and what we say."

"You're not going forward any further, Del. This was the end of the line."

"Didn't you learn anything from hanging around with Faz? Italians are experts at queue jumping. We don't know what the end of the line is."

—

Tracy pulled into the Overlake Park and Ride on the east side of Lake Washington where Del had left his car. Tracy knew it had hurt Del's pride to go back to Moss with his hat in hand and leave without anything to show for the effort. Moss had used Del, taken advantage of his raw earnestness. When Del persisted, Moss had set him up. Tracy couldn't imagine what that must have been like for a young detective new to the job in a new city. Del and Faz had each told Tracy they'd had other professional choices, but detective had been their passions. They each had been driven by a sense of justice, of right and wrong, and a desire to do good. She knew that over the years Del must have conjured up a number of different scenarios on how he would get even with Moss, none of which had ever come to fruition.

This might have been his last, best chance, and he knew it.

"I really screwed this up when I didn't come forward all those years ago, didn't I?" He turned from the windshield and glanced at Tracy. Yeah, he'd screwed up, but none of them was perfect. The fact that Del cared showed he was still one of the good guys.

"What happened was not your fault, Del. Don't start taking the blame for what those people did. You had less evidence than we have now. You could have ended up fired or in a grave."

"Maybe. But maybe if I told someone in a position of authority what I had learned about the raid, that Moss hadn't reported it, maybe Slocum would still be alive and Childress wouldn't be in the situation she's in. Maybe we'd have some leverage."

"And maybe 'if ifs and buts were candy and nuts, we'd all have a merry Christmas,'" Tracy said.

Del looked at her and allowed himself a faint smile. He'd told Tracy that numerous times over the years.

"Faz once told me I have to learn to accept the things I can't change," Tracy said.

"Leave it to Faz to pass off the serenity prayer as his own," Del said with a sad smile. "That guy is one in a million." Del checked his wristwatch. "Best I get going. Celia will be waiting, and you got a little girl to get home and hug."

"I'm sorry, Del."

"What are you sorry about?"

"I know you've been carrying a heavy burden. I would have liked to have lifted it from your shoulders."

"Don't do that to me, okay? I'm a big boy and I got big shoulders. I'm responsible for the weight I'm bearing. But I don't think I could carry that weight if I thought I let you down too. I'll see you in the—no, I guess I won't see you; will I?"

"Not at the police department. Not for a while," Tracy said.

"Anything comes up, you let me and Faz know, right?"

"Absolutely," Tracy said.

She drove home. Silence greeted her. Most of the lights had been turned off. She softly placed her keys in the glass bowl so as not to set off the dog alarm, then saw Rex and Sherlock outside the window in the backyard. That meant Dan locked them out so they wouldn't wake Daniella, which likely meant their daughter had been fussy but was not asleep.

Tracy went outside and greeted Rex and Sherlock, then led them quietly upstairs. She pointed to the two large dog beds. "Basket," she whispered, and they dutifully went to their beds, twirled in circles, and lay down. Dan was not in their bedroom. Tracy went down the hall to Daniella's bedroom. The night-light illuminated the yellow walls and the wallpaper trim she and Dan had installed along the ceiling. Carousel horses pranced up and down, little boys and girls laughing on the horses' backs. Dan rocked in the rocking chair, his eyes closed, Daniella asleep against his chest. An open children's book lay on the floor beside the chair.

Tracy crept in. Dan opened his eyes. He gave her a tired smile. She reached for Daniella and hugged her before laying her in her crib. The little girl stirred but did not wake. Tracy covered her with a blanket, and Daniella turned her head to the side, her lips moving as if nursing.

Dan put his arm around Tracy's shoulders, and they watched Daniella for a moment before retreating from the room, leaving the door partially open so they could hear her in the night, though Tracy also slept with a baby monitor on her nightstand.

"She was fussy?" Tracy asked.

Dan shook his head. "Not too bad."

"I'm sorry I'm late."

"How did it go?"

She shook her head. "Not well. Moss knew we were coming."

"How?"

"A leak. I'm worried about Del. I'm afraid he's going to get suspended for going out there with me."

"You and a team of wild horses weren't going to stop him, Tracy."

"I know. Moss doesn't feel any guilt about what happened . . . At least not enough to do the right thing. It might not matter."

"What do you mean?"

"I took Cerrabone to lunch today and asked his advice, as you suggested. He doesn't think we have a case on any of the drug charges."

"Statute of limitations?"

She nodded and told him of her conversation with Cerrabone.

"What about the death of Slocum?"

"Bottom line is we don't have enough evidence to get very far, and Moss knows it."

"Tell me what you do have."

Tracy methodically went through what evidence she had, if she could get everyone to testify, and that was a big if.

Dan sighed. "I agree with Cerrabone. It's going to be difficult to get a prosecutor to bite off on a prosecution with what you have. What you're missing is a through line."

"A what?"

"A through line, that thing that holds a story together and makes it easily understood."

"Such as?"

"*The Wizard of Oz*. What's the thing that holds that story together? Dorothy trying to get home. She thinks Aunt Em is dying because Professor Marvel told her Em collapsed when she learned Dorothy had run away. So Dorothy will move mountains and cross oceans to get back home and save Em. Simple. Easy for a jury to follow and to understand."

"But Em isn't dying."

"It doesn't matter whether she is or not. What matters is what Dorothy believes. Or in my case, what the jury believes."

And suddenly it was clear. A through line. What Tracy needed was a good story, one that people would believe was true. And she knew exactly where to get it.

"You have that look," Dan said. "That look Faz says you get when you get struck by lightning."

"Dan O'Leary, have I told you that you're brilliant?"

"Not nearly often enough," Dan said.

"Then let me show you." She stepped forward and kissed him.

"Now we're talking," Dan said. "Wish I knew what I said that made me—"

"Dan," she whispered.

"Hmm?"

"Stop being brilliant."

CHAPTER 35

Del called Tracy the following morning; he'd been summoned into Captain Johnny Nolasco's office. Nolasco, the snake, wouldn't reveal who had told him, but he knew Del and Tracy had driven out to Lake Sammamish to talk to Moss. He also knew Chief Weber had specifically told Tracy to back off her investigation, Tracy had refused, and Weber had suspended her, pending a hearing.

"He wanted to know what you're doing," Del said. "I told him to ask you. When he persisted, I told him to pound sand. He told me I could speak to him or speak to a sergeant during an investigation. I opted for the sergeant."

"Shit, Del, I told you not to do that."

"Too late," Del said. "So I got some free time on my hands."

Tracy shook her head. Faz and Del were like her Rex and Sherlock. Two big galoots who were loyal to a fault. "Can you meet at the *Seattle Times*?"

"Yeah, what you got cooking?"

"I'm working on a through line."

"A what?"

"I'm going to give you the chance to do what you wanted to do twenty-five years ago."

"Which was what?"

"Tell an investigative reporter what happened; get the story out into the public domain and provide both of us with a little insulation."

"You're a little late."

"Just meet me there."

An hour later, Tracy and Del entered the conference room on the third floor where Bill Jorgensen, Anita Childress, and Melissa Childs awaited them. After introductions, they sat at the conference room table. Jorgensen smiled, like he held a big secret no one else knew.

"Thanks for coming," Tracy said.

"We didn't get the chance to thank you," Anita said, looking to her mother. "For making this happen."

"I'm sorry about the media at your grandmother's house. I wasn't the source of the information leak."

"My father told us," Anita said. "I wasn't happy about what he did or how he handled it, but I guess I can understand, given what he went through."

"How are you doing?" Tracy asked Melissa, who had remained quiet.

"I'm okay," she said, looking troubled. She smiled but it waned. "It's a bit overwhelming, you know, to wake up one day and find out you've had this whole other life." She reached over and grabbed her daughter's hand. "But we're working our way through it."

"It's a hell of a story," Jorgensen said, looking eager.

"It is," Tracy said. "But there's a lot more to the story than you know. A much bigger story that I think you all need to hear."

"Bigger than this?" Jorgensen said. "I'm all ears."

"I was going to tell you, but I think it's best that Del tell you. He lived it. He's been living it for the past twenty-five years."

Anita's eyes narrowed with curiosity.

"I'm afraid what happened to you might be partially my fault," Del said to Childs, sounding like a penitent.

"Your fault?" Childs said.

Del told her about his investigation of the two drowned men, and about the raid on the Diamond Marina, how Moss had covered it up, how Del had uncovered it but had been threatened with a falsified police report if he pursued it. "You were the only reporter digging deeper than the headlines, and I thought maybe you could, with some help, piece together what I had pieced together."

"Did I?"

Tracy told Childs what she believed happened that February night, the call from the gas station to her home phone, how Larry Childress had placed a can of bear spray in her bag before she left to meet the confidential source, how she had stopped to take out money and at a gas station convenience store to purchase a liter of Coke before she met Slocum in the Industrial District. She watched Childs for any sign of recognition. Childs looked intrigued but also concerned. A tear rolled down her cheek. "Are you all right?" Tracy asked.

Childs took a deep breath. More tears flowed.

"Melissa?"

"I thought I had killed him," she said.

Tracy's breath caught in her chest. "You remember?"

"Like the child in my dreams."

"Tell me what you recall."

"I awoke on the ground. I didn't know who I was or where I was. I didn't remember anything or anyone. I remember a black car. The passenger door was open. I remember looking inside and seeing a man slumped over, dead, and a gun on the floor. And blood. So much blood. I remember blood on my hands, his blood, I thought. I thought I had killed him. I saw another car. I had keys, but I couldn't remember if it was my car. I panicked. I got in the car and I left, but I didn't know where to go. I drove to a parking garage, and I have a vague recollection of a bathroom, of cleaning blood off my hands and the back of my head. My next recollection is being in a mall." She looked to Tracy. "I've waited every day for someone to come for me. To arrest me for killing that man. I thought you were that person."

"Why then did you agree to meet with me?"

"I was told you might know who I was, and I was tired of not knowing. I was tired of being afraid. I wanted to know who I was. I wanted to know the little girl in my dreams, and I wanted to know the woman who woke up to that horror. I wanted to know if I killed him. It was time I found out." Childs closed her eyes and inhaled a deep breath. When she opened her eyes she said, "I'm sorry I didn't tell you before."

Tracy worked to keep her emotions in check. Perhaps Childs recalled even more. She fought against getting too optimistic. "Do you remember anything else about that night?" Tracy asked, keeping her voice soft. "Do you remember seeing anyone else?"

"I didn't. Not at first. But later on, I had these images. As I said, it was like the images of Anita as a little girl."

"Images of what?"

"I recall a man. He wore a mask. He was tearing at it, groaning in agony. I remember him ripping it off."

Again, Tracy's heart skipped. "Do you remember his face?"

"He had short hair. I recall that. Pointed ears."

"Like a Doberman?" Del said.

"Like a Doberman," Childs said. "Yes."

"What about his build? Stocky. Muscular," Del said.

"I don't recall," Childs said.

"Could you pick him out of a lineup?" Tracy asked the ultimate question.

"I would be guessing," Childs said.

Tracy felt herself deflate.

"I've tried, over the years, to remember more, but I can't see the details of his face," Childs said. "And I wouldn't want to guess and be wrong."

WHAT SHE FOUND   303

Anita Childress leaned forward, speaking to Tracy. "You believe the harbormaster was killed because he knew about the raid on this ship, the *Egregious,* and was about to tell my mother, who could possibly expose this task force. But you don't know who killed him."

Tracy looked to Del. "I think we both know who killed him," she said.

"Rick Tombs," Del said.

To Melissa Childs, Tracy explained all the problems with the evidence, how much of it couldn't be substantiated and other pieces that wouldn't be admissible under the court rules. "I've spoken with an experienced attorney, and he doesn't think I have enough to prosecute anyone. Beyond all that, I think, based on what you just told us, that the person who killed David Slocum died in Arizona from cancer some years ago."

"Is there anyone alive who can testify about what this David Slocum knew . . . that it was the likely reason he was killed?" Anita asked.

"I can," Del said. "I spoke to him."

"What about the captain in prison in Surrey, British Columbia?" Jorgensen asked. "And the owner of the houseboat who found the bodies?"

"The houseboat owner died of AIDS a few years after the raid. Jack Flynt is a drug runner with multiple arrests who already made a deal once. Even if I could convince him to testify on the record, which he said he would not do, they'll say he's not credible, that he's lying to make another deal, and Del"—Tracy looked at her former partner on the A Team—"they'll question why he didn't come forward sooner and say he isn't credible either, and even if he is, it doesn't prove who killed Slocum, assuming he didn't commit suicide."

"In other words, it won't stand up in a court of law," Jorgensen said.

Tracy shook her head. "That's what the prosecutor told me."

"But it will in the court of public opinion," Jorgensen said, doing a poor job of hiding an emerging grin.

"A through line," Tracy said to Del. "You tell a story fairly and accurately and let everyone who reads or hears it decide for themselves. One other thing," she said to Melissa. "Getting the story out in the newspaper would also give you some insulation, in case there's anyone still out there who seeks to harm you for what you might know. We tell not only what happened, but we also tell about your amnesia."

"If I didn't know better, Detective, I'd say you're using the newspaper," Jorgensen said.

"Like you said, it's a hell of a story."

"Are they credible?" Jorgensen asked. "Your witnesses. Did *you* speak to them and find them credible?"

"You bet your ass they're credible," Del said.

"And you'll talk," Jorgensen said, redirecting his attention to Del. "You'll tell what happened?"

"I'll tell it all."

Jorgensen pinched his bottom lip with two fingers. You could almost see his mind at work, the headlines that would run in the newspaper. After several seconds, he looked to Melissa Childs. "What is it you want to do, Lisa?"

"What do I want?"

"It's a hell of a story," Jorgensen said again. "But it's your story, and it's going to draw a lot of attention to you and your family."

"I don't know what to do," Childs said.

"Can we have a moment? Me and my mother," Anita said.

"Absolutely," Tracy said. She, Del, and Jorgensen stepped outside the room and went down the hall to a lunchroom to grab coffee.

"Can I ask you a question?" Jorgensen asked Del. "You haven't spoken for twenty-five years. Why talk now? Why not earlier?"

"My former partner has a fabricated police report that says I knew about the raid and didn't say anything."

"Then this could hurt your career. You could get fired, couldn't you, for not saying something earlier?"

"I could get fired, but at least I won't have any more regret. I've lived for years with regret; I can live with getting fired."

"I don't see this as one article. I see it as multiple articles, a series with sidebars. I'd likely get the entire investigative team working on this."

"Are you really going to let this be her decision?" Tracy said.

"I'm a news reporter, Detective, but that doesn't mean I'm a Tin Man. I have a heart. I also have a daughter, and I once had a mother. I know what Lisa and Anita have been through and I'm not looking to pile on."

Tracy smiled at Jorgensen's reference to *The Wizard of Oz*. From down the hall, Anita Childress stepped from the conference room and came toward them. "We've made a decision," she said.

They walked back into the conference room. Childs's gaze remained on the table. Tracy couldn't read the meaning of her placid expression. Anita took her mother's hand. "My mother was one of the best investigative reporters in the Pacific Northwest. I became a reporter to be like her, to have some connection to a woman I knew of, but didn't know. We can never recover the years that were taken from us. But we can go forward with a clear conscience. My mother started this story." Anita paused and looked at each of them. "It's high time I finished it."

CHAPTER 36

O ver the course of the next week, Tracy and Del spent their days working with lawyers appointed by the Seattle Police Officers Guild. The guild had a duty to defend them, but also had an obligation to all their members. They were fighting hard to stop the city council from defunding the police department, and Chief Weber was putting together a strong case. Tracy knew the story that was about to explode across the front page of the *Seattle Times* could undermine Weber's efforts, if the department did not properly spin it.

When they weren't meeting with their lawyers, Tracy and Del met with Anita Childress and the investigative reporters at the *Seattle Times*. Tracy called Tyner Gillies at the Royal Canadian Mounted Police in Surrey, BC, and Gillies agreed to arrange for Anita and Tracy to again meet with Captain Jack Flynt, but Flynt, just months away from freedom, declined to talk on the record.

Tracy drove Anita to meet Dennis Hopper aboard his houseboat. Hopper, ever the character, greeted them from atop his deck.

"Hey, Detective. Did you change your mind about an older man?"

"Sorry to disappoint," Tracy said. "Still happily married."

"Too bad." He looked to Anita. "She's young enough to be my daughter, and that's too young even for me. Come on up. Front door's open."

"What was that about?" Anita asked as they stepped inside the houseboat.

"Nothing, but if he asks, tell him you're happily married with five or six kids."

Hopper told Anita about David Slocum working as the harbormaster and supplementing that income with a marijuana-growing operation on his houseboat. He also told her Slocum accepted cash when the *Egregious* moored at the marina. "Which is why he didn't tell anyone at the marina about the raid two nights before the two men floated to shore. He was cooking the books. That, and I think he feared if they found his plants he'd maybe end up in jail," Hopper said.

"Did he tell anyone about the raid?" Anita asked.

"He told me."

"Did he tell you one of the detectives came back to talk to him? Big Italian guy?" Tracy asked.

"He might have, but I don't recall it."

"Did he ever tell you a newspaper reporter came by, a woman?"

"I don't know for certain," Hopper said.

"Anything else you can think of?"

Hopper pondered this for a moment. "Did I tell you he got a little paranoid?"

"What do you mean?" Tracy asked.

"He asked me if he could move his grow operation onto my boat until things died down. We moved it in the middle of the night. Then he stopped using his phone. Said it could be bugged or something."

"How did he make his calls?" Anita asked.

"He'd go up the street to the Shell station. Back then it had a pay phone; you remember a pay phone? You stepped inside a booth and shut the door? Nah, you're probably too young." Hopper winked at Tracy.

They didn't get a lot of new information, but Hopper's statement that Slocum used the pay phone at the Shell station was certainly critical. It indicated he had likely been the person who called Lisa Childress the evening before his death and her disappearance.

Upon leaving Hopper's boat, Tracy drove Anita to the University of Washington to speak to Dr. Kavya Laghari. Melissa Childs had agreed to allow Laghari to examine her and perform a series of tests. Tracy had done some Internet research of her own, just enough to be dangerous, after Childs told them her vague recollection of the night in question and concluded there was enough uncertainty in the literature to make people believe Childs might remember enough to make the rats flee the sewer and look to make a deal. If Anita wrote the article just right.

"This is a most fascinating case," Laghari said in her slight Indian accent. "Based upon the information Detective Crosswhite provided to me, I classified your mother as having retrograde amnesia. After reviewing her file, speaking with her at some length, and performing my own series of tests, I am more convinced your mother has what we call dissociative or psychogenic amnesia."

"Which is what?" Childress asked.

"Dissociative amnesia is a rare type of retrograde amnesia resulting from an emotional shock. It's not caused by physical damage to the brain, like other types of retrograde amnesia." Laghari moved from her chair to her computer monitor, turning it so that Tracy and Anita could see the screen. "The MRI I performed on your mother's brain does not show evidence of a past injury."

"Would it, after twenty-five years?" Tracy asked.

"An MRI will show brain atrophy long after the injury. It will show injured or dead brain tissue reabsorbed after a traumatic brain injury. So, if, for instance, your mother had a stroke, we would see a white spot where the brain was impacted, and that spot would likely remain many years. But it is possible your mother suffered an injury that has healed; she certainly presented at the shopping mall and at the hospital as someone who had a head injury. We don't have any brain images from back then, so I can't say with certainty. Dissociative amnesia is a psychological response to trauma that can result from a violent crime. From what your mother told me—her dreams of a dead man shot in the head and not knowing if she killed him would meet that standard."

"Are the symptoms the same as the symptoms from a traumatic brain injury?" Tracy asked.

"Very similar. Being unable to remember things that happened before a traumatic event, being unable to recall autobiographical information, which is often referred to as a dissociative fugue state. Dissociative disorders usually develop as a reaction to trauma and help keep difficult memories at bay. In rare cases, the person may forget most, or all, of her personal information, including her name, personal history, friends, and family. The person may sometimes even travel to a different location and adopt a completely new identity, as was the case here. In all cases of dissociative amnesia, the person has a much greater memory loss than would be expected in the course of normal forgetting."

"But my mother has a memory of the traumatic information. She told us about it."

"She has only vague images that she cannot place in context. It must have been terrifying for her."

"Will she ever recover the memory she lost?" Childress asked.

"For most people with dissociative amnesia, memory will eventually return, usually slowly, though sometimes suddenly. In some cases, however, the person is never able to fully recover his or her lost memories. After so many years, I would say it is unlikely. I'm very sorry."

"Would treatment help?"

Laghari looked sympathetic. "At this point, I would say no. However, many people learn new ways of coping and lead healthy, productive lives. That seems to be the case with your mother."

"Is there anything I can do?" Childress asked.

"Your mother recalled you. She didn't know who you were, or how you related to her life, but she felt a connection to you. That is something to build on. If you have photographs of the two of you, or her life before she had you, put them in a scrapbook and give them to her. Not right away. She has enough going on at present. Do it in time. Go slowly so she is not overwhelmed."

When they left Laghari's office, Childress looked stricken.

"You doing okay?" Tracy asked.

"I keep waiting for someone to say they have a magic pill my mother can take that will make her remember everything, and each time I'm told that isn't going to happen, the disappointment is numbing."

"I'm not going to tell you that I know what you're going through or how you feel," Tracy said. "But I lost my sister when I was twenty-two. I lost my father to suicide after that, and I lost my mother before I had my daughter."

"I'm sorry," Childress said.

"My daughter will never know them. I don't envy the position you're in. But I wish I had another twenty-five years with them to create memories for my daughter."

CHAPTER 37

Two weeks after they met in Bill Jorgensen's office, a Saturday that dawned a dark gray overcast with the threat of rain, the first in a series of news articles exploded across the front page of the *Seattle Times*, and the story pulled no punches. "Rogue Drug Task Force Terrorized Seattle."

The story, touted as the first in a five-part investigative series, was accompanied by a sidebar on Lisa Childress's disappearance and sudden return. The two stories took up nearly all of the front page and continued on inside pages. The interior pages included another sidebar, which Tracy had urged Anita Childress to push to have published that first day. It recounted Anita's interview with Dr. Laghari about amnesia in general and specifically as it could have related to Melissa Childs. Anita had written the facts, but as with any good reporter, the story had a bent to it, and that bent insinuated Lisa Childress could remember some details of the attack in Seattle's Industrial District. What Anita had left out of the article was that the possibility was unlikely, if not highly improbable.

Tracy and Del were both quoted in the front-page article, Del for what happened in 1995, and Tracy with respect to her hunt to find and locate the reporter's lost mother. "It's one of those one-in-a-million cases," Tracy said in the article. "You start out thinking you're never going to find the person, and certainly not alive, then when you do, you think there's going to be a happy reunion among the family members, until you realize the person you're talking to doesn't remember her family or even who she once was. She just has these snippets of memories. And that is the cruelest fate of all, for the family. I hope Ms. Childress recovers her memory in full. What happened to her cost her, her parents, and her daughter twenty-four years. I hope they can find justice, in some form, for what has happened."

The article discussed how the statute of limitations on the drug and other related charges had expired, and how the people who raided the *Egregious* walked away with upwards of $15 million. The article added, however, that no such statute existed with respect to the deaths of David Slocum or the two crewmen.

As anticipated, the outrage within Seattle and Puget Sound was palpable, and it would certainly get worse as the series of stories continued. The *Times* had issued a FOIA request for the names of the members of the Last Line, and the newspaper's lawyers were already doing battle in court to obtain that information. The *Times* argued the members of the Last Line were no longer in any danger of being bribed or targeted for their work, and said that when their legal case successfully concluded, the newspaper would report those names. In opposition, lawyers argued that drug rings could still target the officers who served on that task force, especially if the task force was ripping them off, as insinuated if not specifically stated. The paper did not yet have a credible source that the drug money had infiltrated high levels of SPD or the Seattle government, but, again, the insinuation was unmistakable.

While the article identified Del, and said he eventually learned of the raid that his partner had concealed, the story did not yet mention

Moss Gunderson by name. It correctly stated that Del had not received any money, and that he came forward when news broke that Lisa Childress was alive and could recall snippets of what had happened. It quoted Del as saying he was relieved to get twenty-five years of regret off his chest.

"I should have said something the moment it happened," he had told the reporter. "It was wrong not to. I can't blame my reluctance on my youth or my lack of experience, but I looked up to my partner and to others in the department. I trusted them. They breached that trust and the public trust they swore to uphold. I did also, and for that I will accept any punishment that comes my way."

The article reported that Del had been suspended for pursuing information related to the story, and that he was speaking freely and honestly, though doing so could impact his career. "Sometimes the court of public opinion can be worse than the court of law," Del was quoted as saying. "I believe that will be true in this case. When people can no longer trust you, when they no longer see you as honorable, what are you left with? Not a lot. Sometimes, in those circumstances, it's harder to live with yourself than it is to live with what you did."

As the battle raged, the mayor promised an internal investigation into what had happened. The United States Department of Justice Civil Rights Division had further promised an outside investigation. Tracy waited for one of the members of the Last Line to jump ship, and figured if it was going to happen, it would be when the *Times* revealed names, and everyone had lawyered up. The *Times* did name the task force sergeant, Rick Tombs, and noted he was deceased.

Erring on the side of prudence, Tracy had urged Faz to push to have a patrol officer and police car park in front of Beverly Siegler's home.

"Are you kidding?" Faz said. "Have you watched the news? There must be a hundred reporters camped down the street, and a police helicopter has been keeping the skies over the house clear."

Tracy and Dan, Del and Celia, Faz and Vera, Anita Childress, Beverly Siegler, Melissa Childs, and Bill Jorgensen met in the back room of Fazzio's the Saturday night the story broke. They hadn't come to the restaurant to celebrate as much as to decompress.

When they had all taken their seats and the waiter had filled their glasses with an Italian Merlot, Tracy lifted her glass. "Here's to the court of public opinion," she said.

Antonio had prepared a feast. Plates of antipasto and calamari, carbonara, fettuccine Alfredo, ravioli, scampi, sea bass, veal cutlets, and chicken saltimbocca. Dan had quietly paid the entire bill. Antonio protested, but Dan had insisted.

They ate family style, sharing the dishes and enjoying their time together, as well as the temporary respite from the rest of the world in that curtained back room. Jorgensen told them the contents of the second article to run Sunday, including Anita's interview with Dennis Hopper that would confirm what Del had stated in the morning article and name Moss Gunderson as his partner and the person Slocum had spoken with. The article also stated that the *Egregious* captain, Jack Flynt, had declined to talk, citing a confidentiality agreement he had signed in 2002. Jorgensen said that the *Times*'s lawyers, moving with an expedited motion, had prevailed at a preliminary hearing on Friday entitling them to the names of those officers who served on the Last Line. They had learned the task force was composed of seven men, including Tombs, each handpicked by the sergeant. Of the seven, three had passed away. Leaving four alive.

"Lawyers for the task force members said they intend to appeal the trial court's ruling," Jorgensen said. "But without some danger to the task force members, the appellate court probably won't choose to hear argument. Our lawyers are telling us that we could have the names as early as next week."

"That should rattle a few trees," Faz said. He lifted his glass. "Hey, I just want to raise a toast to my partner, Del Castigliano."

"Don't do that, Faz," Del said, shaking his head.

"No. No. You've beaten yourself up long enough about this. You did the right thing. It's like confession. You tell the priest your sins, and he forgives them, and from this day forward you walk with a guilt-free conscience. *Salute.*"

They toasted Del, who looked embarrassed by the attention.

Del raised a hand. "Faz is now absolving sins. Am I lucky to be his partner or what?" They all laughed. Del stood. "I also want to say to you, Ms. Childs, and to you, Anita—" He paused and fought his emotions. Celia stood and placed a hand on his back. Seeing the big man this vulnerable made Tracy's eyes water. "I just want to say that I'm truly sorry that I didn't come forward sooner. That I put you in this situation and that I caused so much pain."

For a moment, no one spoke. Then Anita rose from her chair. "What happened was not the fault of anything you did or didn't do, but what they did to us. It took a lot of courage to do the right thing. We're both grateful. We're grateful to all of you."

Del stepped down the length of the table to hug Anita. When they separated, Melissa slowly stood. She paused, not for dramatic effect.

"Anyone who knows me . . ." She laughed and, after a beat, everyone in the room got the unintended joke and laughed with her, a release of emotions. When they finished wiping away tears, she tried again. "Let me start over. I'm not much for public speaking, but I can say this now, after spending time with my mother and my daughter. The person who disappeared doesn't sound like she spent a lot of quality time with either of you. She sounds like somebody who put her job ahead of her family. Sometimes, people say, it takes a tragedy to make us realize what we have, to make us realize how blessed we really are and what we could lose. Sometimes we have to know loss to appreciate what we find. The three of us might have lost years of memories, but let's not all delude ourselves by thinking those were all going to be happy memories." She paused for a moment, and Anita reached out and took her mother's hand. "I'm not a religious person," Childs said. "At least I don't think I am." The comment brought additional laughter. "I can't say God had a hand in this. But I will say I appreciate meeting and getting to know my daughter and my mother. How many of us can say such a thing at this stage of our lives? What I've learned is that life isn't about memories. It isn't about the past. It's about living in the present and looking to the future, and what that future holds for each of us." She looked at her mother and her daughter. "We can't make up lost time, but we can make the most of what time we have left."

As the evening came to an end, the plates clean and glasses empty, and the leftovers placed in take-home packaging, Tracy and Dan said their good-byes, then followed Anita, Melissa, and Beverly back to Laurelhurst before backtracking to the 520 bridge and heading home. The lights of the newly built bridge, as well as in the windows of the homes along Lake Washington's shores, reflected off the calm surface. Dan turned down the radio.

"Penny for your thoughts," Dan said.

"Boy, have you become cheap in your old age."

"Ouch."

Tracy smiled. "It was a good evening; wasn't it?"

"It was," he said. "So, what's bothering you?"

"Nothing's bothering me," she said.

"Boy, have you become a poor liar in your old age."

Tracy laughed. She kept her gaze out the windshield. "I was just thinking that it doesn't seem right, does it, not being able to get the people responsible."

"Seems you have," Dan said. "Isn't that what tonight was all about?"

"They got their money, and they won't spend a day in jail."

"Where Rick Tombs has gone is a lot worse."

"I suppose," she said.

"It's like Lisa Childress said, you can't worry about the past. You have to focus on the future."

Tracy sighed. "Tougher when your job is in the past."

"Thought you didn't care," Dan said, but he was smiling. Dan knew her too well. "You'll win your hearing on your suspension," he said.

"Probably. I hope Del wins also."

"That's a tougher call," Dan said. "He shouldn't be punished if the people responsible aren't, but life isn't always fair."

"No, it isn't," Tracy agreed.

"How would you feel about going back to work? Are you worried about blowback?"

She gave his question some thought. "There will be some from the brass, no doubt. I don't think there will be much from the rank and file. What happened was well before their time. We didn't rat out good cops. We ratted out bad cops, and bad cops make us all look bad. They taint our image. Coming forward was a step in the right direction. A step to hopefully prevent it from ever happening again. But I guess Del and I will both find out soon enough. One thing's for certain. Neither of us is going to run and hide."

They drove in silence to the end of the bridge. Tracy reached for her cell phone. "I haven't checked my messages; have you checked yours? I hope Therese wasn't trying to get ahold of us."

"I'm sure everything is fine. I didn't receive any text messages."

Tracy had missed a call, but it wasn't from Therese. It was from a 206 area code, which was Seattle. The caller had left a voice mail. She hit "Play" and the voice came through the SUV's speaker.

"Detective Crosswhite." A man's voice. "You're good to your word. I'm impressed. But you won't get them all, you'll miss one. Give me a call when you get a chance. This is Henderson Jones, by the way."

"What was that all about?" Dan said.

"I don't know." Tracy checked her watch. It was only eight thirty. She didn't want to wait to find out what Henderson Jones had meant. She pressed the number and returned the call.

A man's voice answered, but he sounded younger than the voice on the message. "Hello?"

"May I speak to Mr. Jones?"

"Can I tell him what this is about?"

"This is Detective Tracy Crosswhite. I'm returning his call."

"This is his phone. He went to the kitchen for a minute. This is his son, Deiondre. We met at the house. You kept your word, Detective. My father and I were just talking about it. He's impressed. So am I."

"He indicated he has some information for me."

"Hang on a minute." Deiondre called to his father. A moment later Henderson Jones greeted her.

"You kept your word," he said.

"Not sure how far that will get us."

"The walls are starting to come down, Detective. They'll crumble. They always do. Someone will panic, start to talk."

She didn't want to tell him they didn't have a lot of leverage to make that happen. A member of the task force might step forward to relieve a guilty conscience, though that hadn't happened in twenty-five years, so maybe she was dreaming. "You said something about my missing one. What did you mean?"

"Come by the house tomorrow. My son is going to be smoking ribs, and my other kids and grandchildren and some friends will be here also. I'd like you to meet them."

"I don't want to intrude on your family time."

"You will want to. I promise. Are you married?"

"I am."

"Kids?"

"A little girl."

"I don't want to intrude on your family time either, so bring them. Four o'clock. And bring an appetite. Deiondre's ribs are the best in Seattle."

"We'll see you then." Tracy disconnected.

Dan looked over at her. "Sounds like you have an ally."

"Yeah, but what did he mean, I'm going to miss one?"

"Who cares? The best smoked ribs in Seattle? Count me in."

"Seriously, what has he got going on?"

"Sounds like you're in the circle of trust," Dan said, stealing a Robert De Niro line from the movie *Meet the Fockers*.

Tracy rolled her eyes. "Let's hope the information he has is worth me packing on a few pounds."

"Hell, for the best ribs in Seattle, it will be worth it."

CHAPTER 38

S unday, Dan and Tracy arrived at Henderson Jones's home. On a beautiful afternoon, people walked dogs, pushed children in baby strollers, and played on the grass and asphalt courts of Martin Luther King, Jr. Elementary. The same men Tracy encountered on her first visit lounged in chairs on the lawn of the house adjacent to Jones's home. Tracy got out of the passenger seat, opened the back door, and retrieved a bowl of coleslaw, handing it to Dan. The coleslaw was her mother's recipe. No sugar and two teaspoons of Dijon mustard to add spice. Nobody made coleslaw like her mother, who told Tracy to never show up to a dinner invitation empty-handed. Dan had also brought a bottle of red wine, one of his better Barolos.

As Tracy removed a sleeping Daniella from her car seat, the men approached from across the lawn. "You're that policewoman who came to talk to Mr. Jones," one of the men said.

"That's right," Tracy said.

"He invited you for Deiondre's ribs?" The man smiled. "He must like you. He doesn't pass out invitations to just anyone for Deiondre's ribs."

"I heard they're the best in Seattle," Tracy said.

"Best anywhere," the man said.

"Will you be eating with us?" Tracy asked.

"Damn straight."

They made introductions and the men led them around to the back of the house, offering to carry the coleslaw. Three picnic tables had been set with red-and-white checked table coverings on a concrete patio. One table contained enough food to feed a small army. Overhead, ornamental lights were strung, though not yet illuminated. Beneath the lights, perhaps fifteen people had gathered—talking and drinking beer, soft drinks, and wine.

"Detective," Henderson Jones said. He wheeled over to her. "I'm glad you made it. Glad you brought your family."

"For the best ribs in Seattle, I wasn't staying home," Dan said, introducing himself.

Jones introduced Tracy to his daughter, Lachelle, her husband, and their two daughters, who were visiting from Southern California, as well as to his son Marshawn, his wife, and their three children. Lachelle's two girls, their hair in braids, touched Daniella's shoes and put out their fingers for her to grip.

"And who is this beautiful thing?" Lachelle asked, holding out her hands to Daniella.

Tracy had dressed Daniella in a striped, long-sleeve shirt, dark-blue pants, and booties. She also wore a sweater and a cape. "This is Daniella."

"Ooh, she is adorable. She looks just like you." Lachelle looked to Dan. "No offense. You're good looking too."

"None taken," Dan said. "I also think my wife is good looking."

Lachelle looked to Tracy. "You got him trained well." Tracy laughed. Lachelle took Daniella, who went without a fuss. Lachelle's two little girls looked like someone had given them a doll to play with.

Henderson Jones considered the coleslaw and wine they were carrying and thanked them. "But I told you the only thing you needed to bring was your appetite."

"Don't worry about that," Dan said.

"Deiondre said the ribs will be off in ten minutes. You can put the coleslaw on the food table, and feel free to have whatever you like to drink. Make yourself at home."

Tracy and Dan spoke to Jones's children, and she could tell they were proud of and loved their father. His oldest, Marshawn, reiterated what Deiondre told her—they lost their mother to a heart attack, and their father had raised them by himself, working two jobs to make ends meet. "We had to grow up fast," Marshawn said. "My father wouldn't accept anything but excellence from any of us. And he told us if we were hanging around the drug dealers, he would hear about it, and he'd tan our hides."

"He seems like a good father," Tracy said.

"He is. He didn't do it alone though. He used to say it takes a village, and our village included our grandparents, teachers, and coaches. My dad went to school at the start of every year and told our teachers that if our grades slipped he wanted to know immediately. He told our coaches if we didn't do the work in the classroom, they were to bench us until we got our grades up. Never raised a hand to any of us, but he got his point across," Marshawn said. "I want him to sell this place and come live with us. The market is hot right now. He can make a lot of money, and my kids would love having their grandpa around."

"He doesn't want to do it?" Tracy asked.

"This is his neighborhood. He grew up in this house and inherited it from my grandmother and grandfather. He'll die here. He says when he dies, the sale of the home will be his final gift to each of his kids. We don't want the money. He gave the three of us the ability to make money. We just want our dad."

Deiondre announced the ribs were done, and you would have thought he'd just read off the lottery numbers and everyone in the yard had won. Their enthusiasm was understandable. Tracy took one bite, looked at Dan, and nearly fainted. The meat was so tender it slid from the bone, and it had an apple-and-oak flavor.

"That's the wood," Deiondre said. "Slow cooked so the meat absorbs the flavoring."

Tracy and Dan ate until Tracy couldn't touch another thing. The two little girls took turns feeding Daniella and made sure she was well taken care of. As darkness descended, someone turned on the overhead lights and Deiondre turned on music. People danced to Marvin Gaye, Smokey Robinson, Diana Ross, and other rhythm and blues and soul artists. "This is music," Henderson Jones said. "I didn't let my kids listen to all that crap. They're just singing about drugs and other things kids don't need to be thinking about."

"You raised three great kids. You should be proud."

"Oh, I am. I truly am. So . . ." He wiped his mouth and set a paper napkin on an empty paper plate. "I imagine your curiosity has gotten the better of you, and your daughter's bedtime is fast approaching."

"I'd be lying if I said your comment last night about not getting all of the members of the Last Line wasn't at the forefront of my mind."

Dan stood from the bench. "I'll go dance with our daughter while you two talk." He walked over and picked up Daniella. The two girls also followed him onto the dance floor.

"You said I was going to miss one."

"That's right. One wasn't on the task force but was really the most important person."

"Why?"

"If you're going to be rolling drug dealers coming out of bars you need a good contact, someone who can provide you information on which bars, who the dealers are, where they're going to be and when."

"And you know who that person was."

"Yep."

"How?"

"Because we grew up together in this neighborhood. Our fathers knew each other."

"And this person supplied the task force information and in exchange received what? Money?"

"A big cut of the take," Jones said.

"Why would the Last Line trust this person?"

"Because she grew up just around the corner. She knew all of us."

"Was she a drug dealer?" Tracy asked.

"Oh, hell no. Her daddy would have never allowed that. He was a police officer."

A cloud lifted. Tracy's thoughts fell into place like the last pieces of a puzzle and she could suddenly see the picture. "Chief Weber."

Henderson Jones nodded. "Around here she's just Marcella."

"Why?" Tracy asked, hearing the incredulousness in her tone. "Why would she do it?"

"To answer that question, you have to do some research. Her father was a Seattle police officer. There aren't a lot of black officers now; there were fewer then. You think there's institutional racism? You should have been there in the seventies and eighties."

"He was discriminated against?"

"More than that. They set him up."

"How?"

"He and his white partner responded to a homicide at one of the apartment complexes over on Holden Street. They inventoried the crime scene and found close to twenty thousand dollars in shoeboxes in one of the closets. Weber's partner thought it was found money. The resident was dead. He stuffed close to ten thousand dollars in his pocket and told Weber the rest was his. Weber didn't take the bait. He told his partner to put the money back or he'd report him. They got into an argument, but the partner put the money back. Weber thought that was the end of it."

"Clearly it wasn't."

Jones shook his head. "A week later, Weber's captain calls. They want him to come in. He thinks they're going to ask him about the money. Instead, they tell him his partner and another officer, another white officer, claimed Weber stole twenty thousand dollars. Apparently, the victim had a roommate, and the roommate said there wasn't twenty thousand dollars in cash, there was forty thousand dollars, and that he saw Weber stuffing his jacket."

"They took the money and blamed him."

"Uh-huh. Now it's two white officers and a black resident testifying against a black officer at a crime scene. How do you think that went?"

"What happened?"

"Weber's father was dismissed from the force, but the prosecutor declined to bring charges when the two officers refused to testify against one of their own."

"That was big of them," Tracy said, her anger building.

"Weber worked nights as a security guard at a building around here. On the drive home one night, he walked into a gas station convenience store robbery, intervened, and caught a bullet. It lodged against his spine and put him in a wheelchair for the rest of his life. Marcella took care of him. He convinced her to make a difference, fight for change, eliminate racism and bias."

"Her platform."

Jones nodded. "She was a rising star; a competent, black, female police officer. The department couldn't promote her fast enough."

"How'd she get involved with the Last Line?"

"Back in the late eighties and early nineties, they were setting up task forces all over the state, a couple dozen of them. I knew about them because that was my business then. Marcella did a stint in narcotics as

329 WHAT SHE FOUND

they groomed her. She had a good sense about what was going on and ways officers could skim busts. They set up a force in Seattle."

"The Last Line."

"Marcella and Rick Tombs were close. They'd worked together in narcotics. He knew her background and she knew his. Marcella had a public persona, but she had never lost that chip on her shoulder about what happened to her father. This was the opportunity to get what she believed her father was owed."

"She tipped the task force to the dealers and the bars."

"No one on the street could figure out how this task force had so much information. How they knew all the dealers and all the bars where they were dealing."

"But you knew."

"I suspected it was Marcella. Had to be someone on the inside. Pretty soon we all suspected."

"Did you hear what happened at the Diamond Marina?"

"Not in any detail. Not like what was printed in the paper yesterday and today."

Tracy gave what Jones told her some thought. "How do I prove this, Henderson? How do I prove what you're telling me?"

"There's still some people around here who remember Marcella who might talk. A few. I can arrange it. Too bad Tombs is dead. You could have threatened him with some prison time. I suspect he would have sung like a canary. I can still get people together for you to talk to, but they won't have specifics."

Tracy gave this just as much thought. It would all be hearsay—what they had heard and suspected. Drug dealers and former drug dealers. There was no hard evidence. They would not be considered credible.

After a beat she asked, "Why are you doing this? Why now, Henderson?"

He gave a small shrug. "Because you cared."

"I'm sorry?"

"Because you cared enough to do what you did. Most of these officers, I told you, they come out here and ask a lot of questions, but they never do anything. You did. You earned this information."

Tracy looked at Dan on the dance floor. He had Daniella in one arm and spun and twirled the other two little girls. She knew Cerrabone would tell her that the word of aging drug dealers would not be enough. She didn't doubt a word Henderson Jones had told her, but in a court of law, the rules of evidence would likely preclude much of his testimony as speculation and hearsay. She was, again, back to the court of public opinion.

Maybe that was for the best. Tombs was dead, perhaps a form of justice, as Dan had suggested.

She looked back to Henderson Jones and smiled. She didn't want to tell him her thoughts, didn't want to dampen his spirits this night. "Would you be willing to talk to a reporter, get others to talk to her as well?"

"Absolutely."

Tracy thanked him for inviting them. "This has been a special night."

"A lot of good people lived here and still do. You do right by them, and they'll do right by you." He looked to the concrete patio as a Smokey Robinson song filtered across the yard. "What I wouldn't do to dance one more dance with my wife," he said.

Tracy smiled. It might have been Jones's best advice of the evening. She stood. "I'm going to go dance with my husband, then get my daughter home to bed."

CHAPTER 39

Tuesday morning, Tracy drove to Police Headquarters and parked in the secure parking garage on Sixth Avenue. Since her suspension, she no longer had a pass to get through the turnstiles in the lobby to the elevators. She called Faz ahead of time, and he arranged for a pass at the front desk. Tracy rode the elevator to the eighth floor. The office was in full swing, no doubt in part because of the *Seattle Times* articles continuing to run. Before arriving downtown, Tracy had called Bill Jorgensen, who told her he spoke to the *Times*'s attorneys that morning. There had been a delay in the court proceeding to get the Last Line task force names because certain members had confessed to ripping off drug dealers in order for their attorneys to argue that the possibility existed drug dealers might seek retribution. "The names might be confidential, but not the corroboration of what you were told," Jorgensen said.

Still, it seemed a hollow victory. They would not get the remaining members, and they would not get Moss Gunderson.

Tracy knocked on the outer door to Chief Weber's office, which was open. Inside, staff members talked with Weber. She held the morning newspaper in hand and glared at Tracy.

"You should not be in the building. I suspended you."

"Like a minute of your time, Chief."

Weber didn't immediately throw Tracy out of the office. Was it curiosity? Did Weber want to know how much Tracy knew? Or was it just hubris, excessive pride, and confidence that she remained above the law? In Tracy's experience, politicians—and Weber was a politician, despite professing to be and dressing as an everyday police officer—always liked to know what they were up against.

Whatever her reasons, Weber dismissed her staff. "Hold my calls unless it's city hall." She walked toward her interior office, waiting at the door. Tracy stepped in and moved to a leather chair at a round conference table but did not sit. Weber closed the door and also did not sit.

Weber gave Tracy an almost imperceptible shoulder shrug.

"You've read the articles in the *Times*," Tracy said.

"More than once," Weber said. "It's disconcerting to know what happened, but it didn't happen on my watch. I've contacted the union and legal counsel. If what you and Castigliano are saying is true, there will be an investigation by the Justice Department. But again, that was twenty-five years ago. Water under the bridge."

She was waiting for Tracy to play her cards.

"I spoke to the *Times* this morning," Tracy said. "The members of the Last Line still alive admitted to what the *Times* printed about rolling drug dealers and taking their money and their drugs."

"We're in damage control, as you might imagine. City hall wants to spin this. They want transparency so they can say that was twenty-five years ago. This is now. We aren't that police agency any longer. The prosecutors will have to decide if they can bring any legal action against any of the remaining members of the task force, those still alive. I'm not an attorney, but I'm told the statute of limitations prevents it."

"For the drug charges certainly. Not for murder. Not for manslaughter."

"Maybe not," Weber agreed. "If those charges can be proven." It sounded like a challenge.

"If I can put them on the boat, I can get the manslaughter charge."

"But not the murder charge," Weber said.

"I don't have to know who pulled the trigger," Tracy said. "All I have to prove is the group engaged in two acts of racketeering activity and I can get them all on the murder charge."

"RICO," Weber said. "Interesting—*if* you can get a prosecutor to buy it. That's a big if. The Last Line wasn't formed to commit illegal acts. Look it up. They performed a number of busts and took drugs and drug dealers off the street." Weber sounded like she'd already consulted an attorney.

"Yet here we stand," Tracy said.

"Here we stand."

"The Justice Department is going to be under a lot of pressure to get the people responsible," Tracy said. "The story is in the court of public opinion. No rules of evidence required there or in the Justice Department's investigation."

"So then what can I help you with, Detective? Did you come to ask for your job back?"

Tracy shook her head. "That will come in time."

"Probably. You might be ostracized though."

"For being a rat?" Tracy said. "I'll take that chance. But can you even make that offer?"

"Why couldn't I?"

"Because you might not be here," Tracy said.

Weber didn't immediately comment.

"What I want to know," Tracy said, "is how those members of the Last Line had such an intimate knowledge of the drug dealers and the bars they did business at to make their busts?"

"Narcotics always has reliable informants."

"No doubt," Tracy said. "Someone living in the neighborhood or from the neighborhood who can feed them information. Maybe someone who grew up in that neighborhood and knew the drug dealers. Someone with an ax to grind against the department, with bills to pay."

Weber's face remained placid.

"No response, Chief?"

"You got something to say, say it plain and clear."

"I know you were involved," Tracy said. "I know you were the source. I know you believed the department owed it to your father."

"That's a strong accusation, Detective," Weber said. "You have any hard evidence to back that up, or just speculation?"

Weber wasn't going to roll over. Not easily. "People talk, Chief. They always do. You press the right buttons, and everybody looks out for himself. That's just human nature."

"I wouldn't get your hopes too high."

"I'm giving you a chance," Tracy said.

"A chance?"

"To do the right thing."

"The right thing? Now what is that?"

"Once the Justice Department gets involved, the pieces of the jigsaw puzzle are going to slide into place."

Weber stared at her. "And what picture will those pieces create?"

"People lost their lives. Innocent people got hurt."

Weber looked at the newspaper. "Like Lisa Childress?"

"You didn't want me to pursue the Lisa Childress case, Chief. Why not? Afraid one of those skeletons would fall out of the closet? Like they fell out when Henderson Jones refused to take a plea deal?"

"A drug dealer," Weber said with a low chuckle. "Anyone credible who can corroborate *anything* you're telling me?"

Weber, like Moss Gunderson, knew Rick Tombs's death had led Tracy down a dead end. For now.

"You might be surprised." Tracy walked to the door.

"Do you know how I made it to this office, Detective?"

Tracy turned back.

"I'm a survivor. I scratched and clawed for everything I've obtained, my whole life. And I have succeeded."

Tracy pulled open the door. "Even a cat only has nine lives, Chief. Sounds like you don't have many left."

CHAPTER 40

Tracy departed Police Headquarters, called Del and Faz, and Faz suggested they meet at Fazzio's for an early lunch and to debrief.

"We keep meeting here and I'm going to be as big as the two of you," Tracy said when they had all arrived in the back room.

She told Del and Faz what had transpired that morning with Chief Weber, and that it was likely the chief had spoken only with Rick Tombs.

"She's too smart to have spoken with anyone else," Faz said.

"I got a call from an FBI agent," Del said. "She wants to meet. I'd love to get Moss."

"We have the least on him," Tracy said. "He can't be held on any charge involving the two crewmen, because if he struck a deal with Tombs, it was after their deaths. And we can't reel him in on the death of David Slocum if we can't prove Tombs killed Slocum. And right now, we can't."

"What about going after the files Moss said he kept at home, including the file he kept about the raid on the *Egregious*?" Del said.

"Maybe those could be used to prove he kept them for leverage, or blackmail."

"He'll argue those files represent the truth, which would implicate you. I'm not willing to sacrifice you to get Moss. Besides, Moss is too smart. I'm sure he has that file hidden somewhere other than his home."

"You tell Anita and Jorgensen yet about Chief Weber's involvement with the Last Line?" Del asked.

Tracy shook her head. "I'm heading over to Laurelhurst this afternoon to talk to Anita. Childs is heading back to Escondido."

"She's not staying?" Del asked.

"She's going to go back to let things settle for a bit, then she'll decide. She can't live a normal life here with the news vans and reporters parked outside the Laurelhurst home. Anita hired someone to handle her mother's press inquiries, and they're contemplating doing one interview and then shutting it down. She doesn't want the fame or any money."

They finished their lunch and went outside to bright sunshine. Faz departed for the office, leaving Tracy and Del on the sidewalk fishing for sunglasses.

"I talked to my attorney this morning," Del said. "He said my suspension was retaliatory and thinks I'll be reinstated before the end of the month. You as well."

"Weber said to expect blowback," Tracy said.

"Not based on the calls I've received. The people who might have been implicated are long gone. Those there now, who know me, think I did the right thing."

"You have a stellar reputation, Del."

"Just not three Medals of Valor."

"Bite me." Tracy smiled. "We might get a few cold shoulders for talking," she said. "But I can at least close my office door."

"Bite me," Del said.

Tracy left Fazzio's and drove to Laurelhurst. With the *Seattle Times* stories getting picked up by the AP and UPI, Melissa Childs was now national news, and the uniqueness of what had transpired, and the prior *Times* articles, caused the crowd of news cameras and reporters to seemingly grow larger than in previous days. Tracy parked in the driveway and ignored questions shouted from reporters as she walked to the front door. Beverly Siegler greeted her and welcomed her into her home.

Anita and Melissa drank coffee in the living room.

"I wanted to say good-bye before you took off," Tracy said. "And wish you luck. You're liable to have crowds at home for a while."

"I know," Childs said. "But I have to get back to my business, and the sooner I do, the sooner things can get back to normal. Hopefully."

Tracy asked to speak to Anita outside. They stepped out the sliding glass door onto a deck that overlooked Lake Washington and the 520 bridge spanning east to west.

"Don't forget to have the newspaper request the file for the internal investigation of Chief Weber's father," Tracy said.

"Those wheels are already in motion," Anita said. "Do you think anyone will talk?"

"I don't know. And I have my doubts about how much they might know."

Childress smiled. "The only thing I ever wanted was to know what happened to my mother. I want you to know how grateful I am, even if this goes no further."

"What's your plan?" Tracy asked. "Are you staying here?"

"For now. But if my mom decides to stay in Escondido, I might move there and also start a new life. It's ironic, isn't it? I never knew her and yet my life is emulating hers." She offered a pensive smile. "I feel like a burden has been lifted from my shoulders, like my life is just beginning."

Tracy knew all about starting over, and it had worked out well for her.

"Start with family," she said. "That's the most important thing."

EPILOGUE

T wo weeks after the final article in the series ran in the *Times*, Tracy pushed Daniella in a stroller through the Woodland Park Zoo. She'd given Therese the rest of the month off, and Therese had gone home to Ireland to visit her family. Dan had returned to work, though the emotional impact of Ted Simmons's death still lingered and likely would for some time.

Tracy had stayed in contact with Bill Jorgensen. He advised that the *Times* had obtained the names of the Last Line officers but had decided to not publish them, pending the outcome of the United States Justice Department's investigation. Though some had admitted to stealing drugs and money, charges for which were barred by the statute of limitations, they claimed, through legal counsel, no knowledge of the death of the two *Egregious* crew members or David Slocum, as published in the *Times*'s articles.

"They'll blame Tombs, and maybe the other two deceased officers," Tracy had said. She knew the Justice Department's investigation would be a long slog, with no resolution for months, if at all. She could get upset, but what good would that do? Bitterness was never a good recipe for happiness. Jorgensen said the *Times* had also obtained the files pertaining to Chief Weber's father, and that an investigative reporter had written an article in the series about her growing up in the same neighborhood as the drug dealers busted by the Last Line, though the newspaper did not call out Weber as being complicit with Tombs or the task force. Henderson Jones's statements could not be corroborated, and Weber had declined to comment. The insinuation might have implicated Weber in the court of public opinion, but Weber marched onward, unfazed. Tough, strong willed, and resilient.

That cat, it appeared, had a few more lives.

Tracy and Del were, to an extent, bulletproof by going to the *Times* and making the story public. Any discipline would be considered retaliatory and reflect badly on Chief Weber. Tracy wasn't worried about physical harm for the same reason.

Tracy focused instead on spending quality time with Daniella, taking her to places like the zoo, the Pacific Science Center, parks, and generally trying to accept the things she could not change. Faz, the big goombah, was right again.

It must have killed Del to admit it.

As she pushed Daniella toward the grizzly bear exhibit, the two bears lumbered around in their environment. Her cell phone rang. Anita Childress.

After greetings, Childress said, "I just wanted you to know that my last day is next Friday. I'm moving to Escondido to be near my mother. I'm taking your advice and putting family first."

Tracy smiled. "Do you know what you'll do?"

"Nothing for a while. I'm going to try my hand at writing a memoir."

"Well, you certainly have the material. How does your mother feel about you publishing the story?" Melissa Childs had declined all offers and invitations to talk about what happened to her.

"As long as I'm the only one asking her questions, she's fine with it."

"I'm happy for you."

"I decided I needed a fresh start, get away and go someplace completely new. I guess I'm still emulating my mother. And maybe you."

"Me?" Tracy said.

"I'm hoping to find myself and, maybe, someone to share my life with. Like you did. Maybe have children. I feel like I've been running in place for years."

Again, Tracy knew the feeling. She looked to Daniella, who was sitting up, watching the grizzlies. "And I'll tell you it's a lot more fun moving forward with people you love and who love you."

"Have you heard whether you're going to get your job back?"

"End of the month, I'll be going back to Cold Cases," Tracy said. She'd spoken to the union attorneys, who indicated the department would back down rather than risk news stories that one of their most decorated detectives was fired for solving a twenty-four-year-old case.

"Is that what you want?"

Tracy thought of Johnny Nolasco, and of Chief Weber, who would remain her chief and could make her life difficult, but she also thought of Del and Faz and Kins, who had returned to Police Headquarters after sitting through a long trial. Each had called Tracy several times to check in and tell her they hoped she came back. Daniella did not have any blood relatives on Tracy's side of the family, but she'd have three of the best uncles a girl could ever wish for.

Tracy also knew she couldn't turn her back on all those victims who had gone missing, or their families who'd gone years without closure. Most she would not find alive, not like Melissa Childs. Childs was the extraordinary case. Most would be dead, likely for many years, but again, Tracy could not control that. She could only do her job. Would it ever be enough?

Probably not.

But she could pray for serenity while she changed the things she could.

Solving cold cases was her calling, her way of accepting Sarah's death. And that was okay. If not for what had happened to Sarah, there would have been no closure for the families of the fourteen women buried in North Seattle and Curry Canyon; as well as for Kavita Mukherjee, the Indian college student killed in a park; for Kimi Kanasket, a Native American high school student run down in a clearing in Klickitat County; or Devin Chambers, who would still be the anonymous girl in the crab pot. Anita Childress would still be searching for her mother, her life on hold, and Stephanie Cole, the runner abducted from a park trail, might still be imprisoned instead of back home with her family.

Tracy wasn't meant to be teaching chemistry in Cedar Grove.

She was meant to be the voice for those who no longer had one. She was meant to find justice, in whatever form she could, for the families left behind.

"It is," Tracy said, answering Anita's question. "I'm not done yet. I feel like I'm just hitting my stride."

ACKNOWLEDGMENTS

I'm not quite sure of the genesis for this story. It could have been a conversation with my editor, Gracie Doyle. The issue of amnesia is both frightening and fascinating. Frightening because on February 12, 2016, I suffered a stroke due to a blood clot. The thought of losing memories terrified me, but as with most things in life, perspective eased my concern. The stroke was a stroke of luck. It revealed a valve that didn't close at birth, which I've had remedied. It has made me appreciate the present moments I have with my wife and our children.

COVID-19 continues to be an issue, and I continue to omit it from my novels, for the most part. Readers have expressed to me that the subject is everywhere, and books have become their escape. I respect this. I know many who have been touched by COVID and the havoc it can cause. My daughter had the virus, and though asymptomatic, she appears to have some long-haul issues I hope can soon be resolved. I hope you are all as well as can be, and this pandemic has not been too painful for you or those you love. I hope that life will continue to return to normal.

Each novel I give myself a challenge. In the novel *In Her Tracks*, I wanted to create empathetic antagonists, three brothers who are living the pain of their father's sickness. They were far from innocent, but I wanted the reader to have some empathy for them and the things they could not control. For this novel, I wanted to write the story from Tracy's perspective. This was a challenge, but I succeeded. It also allowed me to tell the backstory of Del's original investigation through an Amazon short story, "The Last Line." This was a lot of fun, as well as challenging. I had to be sure the backstory in *What She Found* comported with the story "The Last Line."

Luckily, I had a team to help me out.

As with all the novels in the Tracy Crosswhite series, I simply could not write this one without the help of Jennifer Southworth, Seattle Police Department, Violent Crimes Section. Jennifer has been invaluable, helping me to formulate interesting ideas and to learn daily police routine, as well as the specific tasks undertaken in the pursuit of a perpetrator of a crime. She recently retired, well deserved. I hope she is spending her time golfing, reading, and relaxing.

I also want to thank Alan Hardwick. Alan is a Renaissance man. A talented musician, he is a member of the band One Love Bridge, whom I've seen play several times, as well as a writer. He was a Boise, Idaho, police detective and founded that department's Criminal Intelligence Unit. In Edmonds, Washington, he served as a sergeant and acting assistant chief of police with the Edmonds Police Department. He was a member of the FBI Joint Terrorism Task Forces and the Washington Homicide Investigators Association. He now runs the Hardwick Consulting Group. I'm grateful for his assistance, and suggestion to . . . uh, write a better conclusion to the story, which I did!

I was saddened to learn of the passing of Dr. Kathy Taylor, forensic anthropologist for King County and the State of Washington. Kathy was always willing to help me with forensic issues and was the inspiration for forensic anthropologist Kelly Rosa. May she rest in peace.

I want to thank Kevin Lohman, a friend, fellow golfer, and marine enthusiast. Kevin helped with all things nautical in the novel. I had a scene in which he was the lockmaster for the Hiram M. Chittenden (Ballard) Locks, but alas, most of the scene was cut, though I was able to sneak in his name.

To the extent there are any mistakes in the police aspects of this novel, or the nautical details, those mistakes are mine and mine alone. In the interests of telling a story, and keeping it entertaining, I have condensed certain timelines, such as the time it takes to have DNA analyzed.

Thanks to Meg Ruley, Rebecca Scherer, and the team at the Jane Rotrosen Agency. They are literary agents extraordinaire. They do just about everything to make my life easier, and for that I am eternally grateful.

Thank you to the team at Thomas & Mercer and Amazon Publishing. I'm losing count of the number of books I've written for them. People ask me how I'm putting out more than one novel a year. The simple answer is I work every day, at least eight hours, and due to COVID, there wasn't much else to do but what I love—to create stories. I also get a lot of support from my writing team at the literary agency and at the publishing house. This is the ninth Tracy Crosswhite novel and my twelfth novel with Thomas & Mercer, as well as three short stories. Each time the team has made my novel better with their edits and suggestions. They have sold and promoted me and my novels all over the world, and I have had the pleasure of meeting the Amazon Publishing teams from the UK, Ireland, France, Germany, Italy, and Spain. These are hardworking people who somehow make hard work a lot of fun. What they do best is promote and sell my novels, and for that I am so very grateful. Most recently they took out a billboard in Times Square in New York City for *The Extraordinary Life of Sam Hell* and then for *The World Played Chess*. Maybe you saw the photographs on social media. I had to post them. What an absolute hoot for me, a wannabe actor in my younger days, to see my name on Broadway. I was both shocked and thrilled. I only wish my dad had been alive to see it in person. I'm sure he saw it from heaven.

Thanks to Sarah Shaw, author relations. Thanks to Rachel Kuck, head of production; Lauren Grange, production manager; and art directors Adrienne Krogh and Michael Jantze. It's getting redundant, I know, but I love the covers and the titles of each of my novels. Thanks to Dennelle Catlett, and congratulations on her promotion to head of publicity at Amazon Publishing. Dennelle is always there, always available when I call or send an email with a need or a request. She actively promotes me, helps me to give to worthwhile charitable organizations, and makes my travel easy. Thanks to the marketing team: Kyla Pigoni, Andrew George, Erica Moriarty, Lindsey Bragg, and Erin Calligan Mooney, for all their dedicated work and incredible new ideas to help me build my author platform. Their energy and creativity are astonishing. They make each new idea a great experience. Thanks to Mikyla Bruder, head of Amazon Publishing, and publisher Hai-Yen Mura for creating a team dedicated to their jobs and allowing me to be a part of it. I am sincerely grateful, and even more amazed with each additional million readers we reach.

I am especially appreciative of Thomas & Mercer's editorial director, Gracie Doyle. Gracie and I work closely together on my ideas from their initial formation to print. Beyond that, we have a lot of fun when we get together. Hopefully, again soon.

Thank you to Charlotte Herscher, developmental editor. All of my books with Amazon Publishing have been edited by Charlotte—from police procedurals to legal thrillers, espionage thrillers, and literary novels, and she never ceases to amaze me how quickly she picks up the story line and works to make it as good as it can possibly be. Thanks to Scott

Calamar, copyeditor, whom I desperately need. Grammar has never been my strength, so there is usually a lot to do.

Thanks to Tami Taylor, who runs my website, creates my newsletters, and creates some of my foreign-language book covers. Thanks to Pam Binder and the Pacific Northwest Writers Association for their support.

Thanks to all of you tireless readers for finding my novels and for your incredible support of my work all over the world. Hearing from readers is a blessing, and I enjoy each email.

Thanks to my mother and father for a wonderful childhood and for teaching me to reach for the stars, then to work my butt off to get them. I couldn't think of two better role models.

Thank you to my wife, Cristina, for all her love and support, and thanks to my two children, Joe and Catherine, who have started to read my novels, which makes me so very proud.

I couldn't do this without all of you, nor would I want to.

ABOUT THE AUTHOR

Robert Dugoni is the *New York Times*, *Wall Street Journal*, and Amazon Charts bestselling author of the Tracy Crosswhite series, which has sold more than seven million books worldwide; the David Sloane series; the Charles Jenkins series; the stand-alone novels *The 7th Canon*, *Damage Control*, *The World Played Chess*, and *The Extraordinary Life of Sam Hell*, for which he won an *AudioFile* Earphones Award for narration; and the nonfiction exposé *The Cyanide Canary*, a *Washington Post* best book of the year. He is the recipient of the Nancy Pearl Book Award for fiction and has twice won the Friends of Mystery Spotted Owl Award for best novel. He is a two-time finalist for the Thriller Awards and a finalist for the Harper Lee Prize for Legal Fiction, the Silver Falchion Award for mystery, and the Mystery Writers of America Edgar Awards. His books are sold in more than twenty-five countries and have been translated into more than two dozen languages. Visit his website at www.robertdugonibooks.com.